G⊕G

an end time mystery

Dan Richardson

GW00708312

www.gogbook.wordpress.com

Copy editing by Daniel Jacobs

Cover design by Ivan Listo

The book is published and digitally distributed by Avantoure UK Ltd
www.avantoure.com

Contacts
Contact author: gogbook@hotmail.com
Contact publisher: gog@avantoure.com
Contact designer: ivanlisto@hotmail.com

But thou, O Daniel, shut up the words and seal the book, even to the time of the end; many shall run to and fro, and knowledge shall be increased.

Book of Daniel 12:24

Something that's factual at this moment proves not to be factual in retrospect. That doesn't mean it wasn't factual at the time.

Donald Rumsfeld

PROLOGUE

A jaded crew, they'd seen it all. Mayan altars in rainforests, Nazi U-boat pens dug into mountains – and now a sun-baked island of mud houses and dusty palms, swarming with children, goats and flies. Across the river, a sinuous Corniche: sooty concrete and honking cars, the cacophony of Aswan. They'd staked their claim to the Temple of Khnum, but kids kept sneaking through the police cordon to ruin the shoot. The director's temper flared with each intrusion.

Rolling her eyes, the presenter rewound herself.

"You can see why they call this Elephantine Island. These rocks really look like a herd of elephants, bathing in the river. In Ancient Egypt this was a cult centre for the Nile gods. Each one had a temple on the island, whose ruins can be seen today. One temple was reconstructed more than thirty times over four thousand years. But the really extraordinary thing about this temple is its whirl hole. Come and see..."

Sashaying towards the shrine, she pretended to struggle with the lock they'd oiled earlier, opened the door wide and let the cameraman slip past to film her as she entered the chamber, squatting in the corner as she approached a gaping hole in the floor, edged with timeworn slabs. Warily, she crouched beside the rim.

"I'm at the top of the whirl hole. I can feel a draught from below. The shaft goes 19 metres down into the bedrock of the Nile. It was revered by the Ancient Egyptians as the Voice of the Nile. The sound emanating from its depths was the first sign that the river had begun to rise and the inundation was due." She paused to let the idea sink into the dimmest viewer's head. "This amazing phenomenon hasn't occurred since the Aswan High Dam ended the annual Nile flood that determined the lives of Egyptians for millennia."

She gestured meaningfully in the direction of the High Dam, upriver, beyond sight of Aswan. They'd dub her voice over some stock footage: the authorities didn't allow anyone to film their precious dam, for security's sake. Over drinks in their hotel, the crew had grudgingly conceded that perhaps the Egyptians had a point. No other country depended on a single dam for its harvests, nor could be washed into the Mediterranean by a dam-burst. Backing up behind it for 500 kilometres, Lake Nasser was the largest man-made reservoir in the world.

All went smoothly till the soundman signalled cut.

"Sound's fucked – some kinda sub-bass rumble."

"Can't you edit it out later?" the director protested.

"It's getting louder." Grimacing, ripping off his headphones.

The director swore. He'd planned to finish with the shrine before the helicopter took off. Once overhead, the noise would ruin any recording and he'd have to focus on the aerial shots. On cue, his VHF handset bleeped: the copter was awaiting clearance. "What's with the sound?" he demanded. "If we're going to shoot we need it now."

"Jeez, it's sub-bass with high-frequency overtone, unbelievable"

The VHF squawked again. "We've taken off. Be with you in a jiffy."

Looking up he saw his presenter and cameraman surging from the shrine, colliding with the soundman, sending him sprawling.

OOOHMMM...

They felt it in their guts, a sudden needle in their eardrums, at the roots of their jaws. Cold sweat slid down their spines. They staggered as the ground swayed...

With a thunderclap the shrine blew apart, a geyser erupting skywards, stones plunging in a torrent of water, crushing the film crew. Taller than a smokestack, greenish-black as motor-oil, it sent the stench of sulphur drifting over Aswan's bazaars. Cries of fear lost in a cloacal rumble as the helicopter hurtled overhead...

"I'm filming the geyser," the aerial cameraman radioed, anxious for his team-mates but determined to do his job. "Take us round again but lower," he told the pilot, bracing his knee against the Plexiglas, shooting boatmen transfixed on feluccas.

Gears snarled as the copter twisted upwards – away from the island. The cameraman's outrage stillborn as he turned to face the pilot and saw –

A gigantic wave pouring from the sky...

A seething avalanche of water three hundred feet high, falling on Aswan, pulverising the city, sucking the helicopter into a maelstrom surging down the Nile Valley. One hundred and sixty billion tonnes of water with the kinetic energy of thirty hydrogen bombs – unstoppable, inescapable without warning...

فَفَتَحْنَآ أَبْوَٰبَ ٱلسَّمَآءِ بِمَآءٍ مُّنْهَمِرٍ ۖ وَفَجَّرْنَا ٱلْأَرْضَ عُيُونًا فَٱلْتَقَى ٱلْمَآءُ عَلَىٰٓ أَمْرٍ قَدْ قُدِرَ

The instant the High Dam's turbines ruptured, phone and power grids crashed as far away as Luxor – one hundred miles downriver – the Flood racing towards it faster than a speeding car. For twenty million Egyptians, the sole alarm was a roaring wet wind that arrived seconds before their homes, schools and fields were obliterated. Only those whom fate had placed hundreds of feet above the valley floor survived.

إِنَّآ أَرْسَلْنَا عَلَيْهِمْ رِيحًا صَرْصَرًا فِى يَوْمِ نَحْسٍ مُّسْتَمِرٍّ تَنزِعُ ٱلنَّاسَ كَأَنَّهُمْ أَعْجَازُ نَخْلٍ مُّنقَعِرٍ

Seismographs across the Middle East registered shockwaves signifying an earthquake of seven or eight on the Richter scale, followed by a curious absence of aftershocks. Speculation among scientists was percolating through layers of bureaucracy when foreign intelligence agencies detected a sudden blizzard of messages between Aswan and Cairo, the Presidential Kubra Palace and Armed Forces GHQ in Abbasiya. Some were super-enciphered for the highest security, others scrambled or partly uncoded, as if the senders had been too panicked to encrypt them properly. One phrase occurred frequently.

BLACK DAY, BLACK DAY, it signified catastrophe in Arabic.

In the Negev Desert, an Israeli air force squadron prepared to launch its spy drones. At Fort Meade, Maryland, the US National Security Agency ordered an urgent 3° shift in the path of a low-orbital satellite tasked with monitoring Iranian nuclear sites, and appraised the CIA that Egypt should be prioritized.

BLACK DAY, BLACK DAY...

In Egypt, the wall of secrecy erected against the Flood was crumbling even before Al-Jazeera's broadcast. Mutinous Army signallers, dazed civilians on a hilltop where their mobile phones worked, local officials who couldn't keep silent – their terrified warnings seeped into society like serum through veins.

فَإِذَا جَاءَتِ ٱلصَّاخَّةُ يَوْمَ يَفِرُّ ٱلْمَرْءُ مِنْ أَخِيهِ وَأُمِّهِ وَأَبِيهِ وَصَاحِبَتِهِ وَبَنِيهِ لِكُلِّ ٱمْرِئٍ مِّنْهُمْ يَوْمَئِذٍ شَأْنٌ يُغْنِيهِ وُجُوهٌ يَوْمَئِذٍ مُّسْفِرَةٌ

Sohag, Assyut, Minya... the water engulfed the cities of Middle Egypt. Rushing north, spreading over ancient floodplains into deserts where none had flowed for ten thousand years. Cairo, Alexandria and the Nile Delta erupting in chaos as the tsunami advanced. Thousands dying in seconds, hundreds of thousands within minutes, millions every hour...

وَوُجُوهٌ يَوْمَئِذٍ عَلَيْهَا غَبَرَةٌ تَرْهَقُهَا قَتَرَةٌ

By nightfall, the age-old civilization of the Nile Valley had been erased from the face of the Earth.

1 OUTBOUND

"Smoke?" the pilot drawled, waving a carton of Marlboro at her as the yoke twitched, ignored, his Slavic face malevolently lit by the instrument panel. *He was winding her up* – it was obvious from the looks exchanged by the co-pilot and engineer, slumped in a cubby-hole with a porn rag on his lap. Carina *knew* that the plane was on autopilot.

"*Nyet*," she grunted, looking away.

This flight made Ryanair seem deluxe. Aside from the crew smoking, the aircraft was for carrying cargo, not people. As the only passenger she had a fold-down seat in its steely belly, ribs and cables vibrating with the engines' drone. It was chilly; they'd given her an old sleeping bag for a blanket. Noisy, cold and oily – she wiped her fingers on the underside of the seat and grimaced. Her cargo pants were creased and stained; a ketchup-sodden polystyrene tray lurking near her stiff new desert boots. She could smell herself over the ketchup, taste her rancid breath.

The toilet didn't bear thinking about.

Five hours down, one to go. They were over the Mediterranean, oil tankers reduced to pencils on a mottled tablecloth. The porthole glass was smeared but she refrained from cleaning it; her stock of Wipes was already depleted. She'd packed all her skincare essentials but hadn't foreseen the grimy aircraft. It seemed like a foretaste of Egypt, as Granddad's troopship had been met by bumboats before it even sailed into Port Said. She'd heard all his reminiscences as a child; he'd been as talkative as her father was taciturn.

A cold, manipulative bastard, actually...

Thirty years hadn't diminished her hatred. Only years of therapy and pleas by Nick had given her the self-control to endure dinners at Daddy's. Nick just didn't see him as she did, admiring Henry's donnish wit as his own father relished Nick's marriage into *real class*. Oxford scholars, riding to hounds, a world-famous ancestor – Carina's family had the lot. Everything except love, trust, honesty...

Poor Nick, trying to negotiate an emotional minefield, burdened with doubts. She'd seen his face tight with resignation as he fastened Buster's lead; counted the empties in the wine rack on Mondays. He'd been drowning in slow motion: redundancy, male menopause, mid-life crisis. Her therapist urged Carina to be supportive. As if she hadn't for the last fifteen years! Carina was so angry she skipped two sessions and paid for them on Nick's Visa card. He didn't even notice – or if he did, said nothing.

Some accountant he was...

The plane yawed, crates straining against their lashings.

She heard a crewman laugh and relaxed her grip on the armrest.

Egypt's ravaged landmass lay somewhere over the indigo horizon. The world's worst terrorist atrocity and humanitarian disaster was so last decade, somebody had quipped at a party. Cruel but true. Fresher crises had relegated Egypt to the sidebars of the news. It only became personal after Nick saw the ad in *Accountancy Age* and sent in his CV, not even telling her till he'd been offered the job. He chose their anniversary dinner to confess and was dumbfounded when she stormed out of El Molino.

Eventually they talked about it and she came around. Nick's salary would be far below UK rates, but he wasn't volunteering for the money. Working in Egypt would be exciting, worthwhile, a relief from stagnating in Tufnell Park. He'd wasted May and June – and five grand of redundancy money – on a 'first' novel that died in his hard drive, leaving only the memory of a fortnight in Tuscany to be cherished. It was time to get back to what he knew. Four months overseas as external auditor for an aid agency would spice up his CV, once he was back home and job hunting again.

She'd been swayed by his desire to go and the realisation that it would suit them both. Her workload was daunting, two exhibitions that autumn: catalogues, hangings, press releases and guest lists to finalize. She'd be working late at the Victoria and Albert Museum with little time or energy to nurture their relationship. With Carina out of the picture, Nick had nothing to keep him in London but a peevish neutered Labrador. Four months was more than enough for him to pine for their reunion, once the novelty of separation wore off...

The first month had vindicated her predictions. Nick had been enthused, sent her long emails and phoned every other night. Meanwhile, "Treasures of Gazprom" was proving to be a nightmare: artifacts denied export permits at the last moment, copy arriving late or unintelligible. Carina was so snowed under she hardly noticed that Nick's emails and calls were becoming terser and fewer as the second month passed.

Two weeks before the preview, a bombshell at five in the morning.

Hello, is that the Baring residence?

An American calling from abroad, an echo on the line...
Her mind leapt to her brother in LA, before his next words registered.

She nearly went mad over the next three weeks. The aid agency assured her that everything was being done, the Foreign Office that no stone would go unturned. At the V&A, her superiors sympathized through gritted teeth and that ambitious cow of an assistant Jenny calculated how to steal the limelight while Carina was away on compassionate leave.

She'd have flown out immediately had a visa been granted. Before the Flood, Egypt had welcomed tourists. Now visitors were few and vetted, an official confided during her third visit to the Egyptian consulate. He understood her position, but his hands were tied. Only the Foreign Ministry in Hurghada could authorise a visa.

It was Mr Baines who broke the impasse. While Whitehall officials urged patience, he personally phoned twice to assure her that the problem would soon be resolved. In Egypt Baines was virtually a UN proconsul, he asserted. A week later there was a sheepish call from the consulate and a holographic sticker in her passport. Then a spate of emails specifying or revising departures from obscure airports, finally settling on Kent International (surely an oxymoron).

She was almost thwarted at the last moment by malign bureaucracy. When the passenger manifest was faxed (faxed!) back by the Ministry, some sexist flunky had ignored the surname in her passport and substituted Nick's instead. Luckily the cargo company noticed the discrepancy and alerted her, but it took several frantic calls to Hurghada before a new manifest was issued. It confirmed her fear of Arab countries as chauvinistic and obstructive, if not openly hostile.

Besides, she was proud of being a Wilde, a descendant of the great Oscar. Though *bon mots* weren't her forte, she liked to believe she'd inherited her ancestor's aestheticism. Curating at the V&A might not be as scintillating a contribution to culture as *The Portrait of Dorian Gray*, but it required an eye for the essence of beauty, she'd tell guests at receptions if she'd had a G&T too many.

Anyway, names had resonance. Nick's surname, Baring, was perfect for an accountant, redolent of a posh private bank – though Nick objected that people (by which he meant accountants) associated it with bankruptcy and rogue trading. To her, it sounded utterly English and respectable, never mind that Nick's parents were of immigrant stock. His dad, Frank, answered to the nickname 'Load-Baring' on construction sites across the Thames Gateway, a self-made millionaire with more in common with Henry than you'd expect of a contractor and an Oxford Don. Both revered the aristocracy and belonged to the same Hunt. Hunting was, they agreed, a classless pursuit that was inherently classy, as Oscar might have said but didn't.

The hold was dark now, muted bulbs outlining crates and spars. She heard a litany of Russian and a voice confirming their entry into Egyptian air space in broken English. Through the porthole, only darkness below; then a wavering line of ivory that must be the coastline, followed by more darkness, seemingly endless.

Thirty minutes passed before she saw lights on the horizon, resolving into pulsars and corpuscles, towns and vehicles. Hydraulics engaged, turbines whined, her ears began aching and her stomach crept into her chest. She tightened the fraying seat-belt as the plane dipped towards the earth.

Somewhere down there, Nick had disappeared.

Somewhere she'd find him.

Somehow...

2 HURGHADA

The night was warm and smelled of jasmine and sewage. It was after ten, local time. She humped her case down the steps to the runway. No luggage handlers or shuttle bus so she dragged it to the terminal, swallowing to ease the pain in her ears. *Welcome to Egypt...*

An echoing sweatbox where posters curled behind glass, the hall was almost deserted. Her trolley squeaked as she wheeled it towards passport control, the immigration officer frowning as he stamped her passport. Customs scanned her suitcase and seemed disappointed by the lack of contraband. Photos of an Arab elder in ceremonial uniform stared from the walls. She barged open the swing doors.

MRS BARING caught her eye at once. There weren't many Egyptians waiting to meet passengers, and only three held signs. Not like the old days, when this was the Red Sea Riviera, advertised on buses in London. As the Egyptian holding her sign nodded dumbly a burly Westerner appeared, raising both hands as if to catch an easy pass.

"Carina! Welcome to Egypt. I'm Calvin Baines. Shame about the circumstances, but the Lord moves in strange ways – everything turns out right in the end. Let Sabr take your bag, you must be pooped. Those cargo flights are sure uncomfortable."

His voice was as mellow as Southern Comfort. Mid-sixties but attractive: tanned, with tin-grey hair, deep brown eyes, and a chin and shoulders that wouldn't put George Clooney to shame. His chinos were crisply laundered; her own looked and felt like dishrags.

As the Egyptian driver took her case, Baines outlined the arrangements. Carina would stay at the Residency, a compound for foreigners. After breakfast next morning, he'd brief her on the investigation at head office. Then they could drive around so she'd get a feel for the place and understand what Nick had been doing as one of the team.

Outside stood a white Land Cruiser emblazoned with four hearts forming a Saltier Cross in a circle ringed by the words *Salvation First – Saving Souls for Jesus*, all in crimson. *Oh my.* Still, if Nick had managed to work with them for nearly four months they couldn't be so bad. They were the lead agency for Egypt, in charge of the whole recovery programme; Baines was their CEO.

From the airport perimeter they followed a Toyota pickup full of soldiers along an unlit highway. Street-lighting was restricted to the city centre; hospitals and other essential services had priority, he explained. It was unwise to walk or drive alone at night. Most of the international staff had agreements to drive each other into town or share taxis when they wanted to eat out. Salvation First staff observed an 11pm curfew, unless duty required otherwise.

Carina wasn't surprised. The scene reminded her of a Kurusawa film. Bonfires cast sinister shadows on crenellated rooftops as goats and children dashed about. All that was missing was the clash of steel and screams of battle – instead she heard music and laughter. She wondered how it looked in daylight. She opened the window an inch and wrinkled her nose at the stink of burning rubber and manure.

"Better close it," Baines admonished. He hadn't flinched at the smell, didn't seem to notice it. Had Nick become oblivious too?

Something hit the windshield. The car lurched. A searchlight flicked over roadside shacks, an amplified voice barked as rifles bristled from the Toyota.

"Easy," Baines murmured. Carina realised she was clutching his hand. Seconds crawled by. Their driver slapped the wheel. "*Al-hamdillillah!*"

"Amen," said Baines. "Nobody hurt – just shook up," he acknowledged her fear delicately. "Some kid throwing a stone; could happen anywhere." She nodded, feeling nauseous; held onto the door handle until it passed.

Finally they reached the Residency, floodlit and enclosed by razor-wire. Baines gave her passport to a night porter and shepherded her to an enclosure of hacienda-style apartments. She smelt salt in the air, heard surf on a beach. The Red Sea Riviera, they called it, but she hadn't seen the sea yet in Hurghada.

"They've put you in a chalet. It's homier than a room, plenty of privacy. You'll want to sleep without noisy neighbours. Our own staff are usually in bed by midnight, but some of those Halliburton guys whoop it up."

The chalet was like a Portakabin designed by Liberace. Faux brass and marble gleamed in the strip-lighting; air-conditioning hummed and the TV flicked into life, filling the room with the roar of spectators. "Soccer", Baines grunted, silencing it. "Not what *I* call football". He inspected the bathroom. "Purdy. I've told reception to call you nine tomorrow; breakfast till ten, Sabr will meet you in the lobby at 10.30. I'll see you at 11 o'clock. God bless and sleep well."

Alone, she kicked off her desert boots. Her feet were swollen; she was rank with BO. Averting her eyes from Medusa in the mirror, she stripped off and tottered into the bathroom. The fittings were Italian; complimentary toiletries awaited her approval. She sluiced herself, applied shampoo and watched the foam vanish down the drain, kneading her scalp as her Reiki instructor had taught her. Now conditioner – it wasn't a brand she cared for, but never mind. A hangnail snagged in her hair, broken on that bloody airplane. She should cut and file it after showering, but she still had to unpack.

The key in the closet lock was stiff, it tore her hangnail. Cursing, wrenching the door open, she recoiled as three bulging parcels slid onto the carpet like a dismembered murder victim. She poked one; saw leather through a tear in the wrapping paper, ripped it open and found –

Nick's brogues and trainers...

Christ almighty!

She tore open another, found shirts they'd chosen together in John Lewis. A lump filled her throat as she fumbled with the third parcel. Felt towelling, pressed it to her nose and caught a trace of Nick's smell.

His bathrobe was damp with tears by the time she raised her head and saw the shoeboxes on the shelf. She nerved herself to examine them, like auguries.

One box held Nick's Shavemaster, skin cream and mouthwash. A toothbrush she didn't recognize – and a pack of condoms, unopened.

Jesus, what's this?

The second contained Nick's favourite CDs and a dozen Arab tape cassettes with smudgy garish covers. In the third were paperbacks and Nick's wallet, whorled with fingerprinting powder.

His cards, keys and a snapshot of them both with Buster were all there, as in London. Likewise business cards – though it was clear they belonged to Nick's time in Egypt. *Col. Avi, Dept. of Civil Affairs, Suez City. Harbourmaster Labib El-Masry, Port Safaga. GM Foster, Salvage Expert – No Task is Impossible.*

And a dog-eared card that read: EURO BAR Suez City. Girls, Live Show.

Suddenly she recalled the email that Nick had copied to their shared address by mistake. He'd made light of it at the time and she'd believed him, like a fool. *Wait for me at the Euro Saturday. Yasmina*, it had said.

Silently, Carina raged at his ghost, stifling her sobs with Nick's robe, cherishing his musk as if it was his final breath.

***

As a proud Saiyidi, or southern Egyptian, Sabr would always rather ride than walk – even on a donkey. He hadn't had a bicycle till he was eleven but was riding donkeys long before that, like most kids in his village on Elephantine Island. He'd been equally at home on the river, sailing a felucca with his father and brother between the islands of Aswan. Other Egyptians mocked Saiyidis – saying that the heat of Upper Egypt addled their brains – but no-one could deny they were natural masters of anything that moved – beasts, boats, cars or women.

Sabr's current job was proof enough of his skill as a driver. Of the million-odd Saiyidis who'd escaped the Flood and made it to the Red Sea coast, barely five thousand were employed as drivers by Salvation First, and only a handful got to chauffeur Baines, as he did. Besides a steady income, his job was prestigious by the standards of his camp, with perks his neighbours could only envy.

Like this, he thought, using his pass-key to steal into an empty flat in the Residency. His employee status didn't entitle him to one, but Magdy on reception would slip him a key if Sabr greased him with a fifty. Sabr couldn't stay there – the son-of –a-shoe made that plain – but using the bathroom was enough: the Residency had unlimited hot water every hour of God's year. To stand for half an hour under a cascade, scrubbing from scalp to toes, was bliss. He only regretted he couldn't bring a girl – but Magdy was adamant.

They both had jobs, paid in Egyptian pounds pegged to a wage in euros that never decreased. Not for them the shameful dependence on food hand-outs. Sabr knew he should (and often did) thank Allah for his good fortune, but a voice in his heart muttered that he (they) had all been cheated by whatever malevolent power had unleashed the Black Day.

He dried himself, dressed in the same clothes (Farida better have clean ones ready) and left the flat. Tossed the keys to Magdy (the fool nearly fell off his chair) and ambled to the car park. When Baines didn't need him, Sabr could drive the Land Cruiser as if it was his own, providing he kept the mileage within bounds and jiggled the mileometer for special occasions. He needn't wait at crossroads jumping at shadows, or ride a minibus down the darkened highway with a tenner folded ready for any bang-bang men.

The car had an alarm to call the Black Berets, but its real deterrent was the certainty of sanctions against the nearest *ezba*. The last stick-up had been five months ago: a Halliburton truck. After three days without water and hints of a shortfall in next week's rations, the camp elders acted. Kicked and beaten through the camp, the bandits were trussed and left on the highway for the internationals to arrest or drive over as they wished, on the understanding that supplies resumed as before.

Camps passed by his windows. Scores of former tourist villages – extending 50 kilometres down the coast from Hurghada – whose solidity had earned them the nickname *ezba*, as villages were known in the Nile Valley. Better to live in an *ezba* than in the shantyowns or tent-camps where misery festered, inflamed by lawlessness. In an *ezba*, gangs were part of the establishment, so Sabr could pay his dues in a civilized fashion, once a month, to the snakehead that ran it for some big dog at El-Gouna. So much for rent – the apartments' murky legal ownership was harshly enforced. Even if you pitched a tent on the beach they'd twist you for protection. However much Salvation First talked about ethical practices, corruption flourished under its nose.

By the time he reached Scheherazade, his *ezba* was settling down for the night. Many of the inhabitants were farmers from Qena who spent their days coaxing vegetables from the sand, yearning for the rich loam of the Nile Valley. At night they dreamt of being selected for resettlement. The poorest slept outdoors, within earshot of their plots. To steal so much as an onion would have invited a fatal blow from their mattocks.

So what – Sabr wasn't a farmer. His father had been a felucca captain, known on the river as the Aswan stallion. Sabr had trodden in his sandals; skippered his first group at fourteen, stuffed his first chicken a month later. She'd been Dutch or German, plump and blonde. She'd shown him where to put it with a sigh. At the end of the week she gave him a Walkman. By the time she returned next spring he'd slept with fifty others and forgotten her name.

All the men in his family got in on the act. With weekly windfalls, they built a two-storey house with tiled bathrooms and kitchens, beside the mud-brick *beit* that had been the family home forever. His brother Mohammed wed and moved in with his bride. Nine months after their pigeon night, a boy was displayed from the balcony. His mother kissed his eyes and swore that the next wedding would be Sabr's. His sister hugged herself; her own betrothal wouldn't be much longer…

He stamped on his memories as if they were a scorpion.

That was then, today is now.

"God is generous," called a drunk from beneath the stairs.

"Thanks God," Sabr replied, cursing under his breath, sidestepping sleepers on the steps. Being on the third floor was a mixed blessing. The water-pressure was lower during the two hours that the system functioned. Someone had to be there to baby-feed every jerry-can. But if the sewage backed up or looters raided the camp, the third floor was the last to suffer. On principle, he preferred that his shit fell on others rather than the opposite.

His flatmates were in the lounge, smoking hashish from a glass. Their next run across the Red Sea to a cove near Wejh wasn't until the night after tomorrow, God willing. They'd abstain the day before; their boss was strict as a sheikh about that.

"Fish are flying, Brother," they chorused, sliding the glass towards him.

Sabr raised its rim, sucked smoke. "Night of cream," he hissed.

The room was as messy as the inside of a stomach. That slattern Farida barely cleaned between cooking their meals and raising her own brat. All her family were dead; she had no origin. She lay with them each in turn, except on Fridays. Tonight she was Lutfi's. Sabr padded onto the balcony, feeling the clothes on the line as his eyes adjusted to the gloom. At least she'd washed his shirt and trousers. The seat of his jeans was almost worn through; he hoped they'd last till payday when he could afford another pair. Money ran through his fingers, he'd never learnt to save.

He bolted the door to his own tip and flopped on the mattress. Bed-springs squeaked through the wall. He thumped it and heard Lutfi curse, imaginatively. Sabr smiled wanly and groped for the Band Aid box. Extracted a Cleopatra cigarette smeared with opium. Masochistically delaying his pleasure, he set the alarm clock, which reminded him of that plastic bitch he'd be driving again tomorrow. *Alf zobra fi kussik*, he'd tell her with a friendly smile, if the Boss wasn't present – but no, imagine she repeated his words later. He contented himself with the thought, lit up and inhaled. Spun fantasies of women soft as candy-floss; willed himself to dream of anything but the Black Day…

∗∗∗

As Baines promised, the briefing began at eleven, in his office near the seafront. Its walls were lined with terminals and box-files labelled with cryptic acronyms or jargon: U5MR, CMR, Asset Management, Commodity Tracking. Only a Christian cross the size of a baseball bat and framed photos of Salvation First medics treating African babies belied the impression of an office at a Tesco warehouse.

Baines found her a padded chair and perched himself on the edge of a desk.

"We're not used to volunteers going missing. Of course it happens to professional frontline staff – it's a hazard of post-conflict zones. But this isn't Afghanistan. Hurghada is a secure posting and Nick spent most of his time right here at Head Office. When he visited camps or outstations it was always in daytime, with one of our drivers or another international.

"Nick isn't an aid worker – we know that. He's a decent guy from London who saw our ad and volunteered for the external audit team. He's here to check our books and confirm that nobody's fiddling the figures. His job description doesn't include negotiating hostile roadblocks or running supplies under fire. The worst risk for Head Office staff in Egypt is food poisoning at some restaurant." He paused to sip from a paper cup.

"That doesn't alter the fact of his disappearance, but it narrows the parameters. The police have ruled out any involvement with drugs or terrorism. So we're looking at something else – a mugging, maybe. Nick was last seen in town at about twenty-one hundred. His workmates were up for a night of it, but Nick wanted to return to the Residency. Perhaps he took a taxi on his own, staff do occasionally. It was two hours before curfew and Nick had been here long enough to stop feeling nervous."

"So you're suggesting he was mugged by a taxi driver – and then what? Surely Nick would have turned up by now? And how come I found his wallet in the chalet?"

"I apologise for that. I'd no idea the police returned Nick's things to the Residency, or a bellhop put them in the closet. It must've been a terrible shock. And it was only natural to assume that you'd been given his room. But that's not so."

"Never mind. What I want is my husband back. Or at least some answers while I'm waiting. Surely there aren't so many foreigners that one can vanish without a trace? And if Nick went to a restaurant and then took a taxi, where did he get the money to pay for them? His wallet was in his room, remember?"

And a card from a sex club, and condoms – but nobody was talking about that. She steeled herself to ask, couldn't imagine how.

Just do it! Now, don't wait...

A phone chirped shrilly. Baines snatched the handset. "I said no calls, Clarence...what, OK, thanks." He gazed at her sombrely. "They've found an agency car in the desert. It's at police headquarters. They want us there now."

"Nick, what about Nick?"

"They won't say till we get there."

The police station reeked of futility and rancid sweat. In their grubby robes, fake jeans or threadbare suits, Carina couldn't tell the detectives from the criminals pacing the cracked linoleum or arguing over dusty typewriters and case-files, unless they wore a holstered pistol. Baines introduced her to pouch-eyed Inspector who led them to an inner yard, where recruits were hosing down pickups. Spray drifted over a charred Land Cruiser. Carina gripped Baines's arm.

Jesus, no...

"It was found in a wadi, 190 kilometres away," wheezed the Inspector. "We're unsure if it was set alight or hit a mine – there are some left over from the 1960s. No body was found in the locality; we brought in search teams. There's no evidence your husband was in the car. He was last seen on foot, in town. We think the car was stolen after his disappearance. We remain hopeful, *insh'allah.*"

She thanked him mechanically, numb with relief. Baines declined the offer of tea and led her from the yard. "I'm mortified, Carina. How dare he scare you like that! I'll lodge a complaint with Hosni Basha."

"Who?"

"The Security Minister. He'll kick some butt, pardon the vulgarity. The Inspector's behaviour is typical of Egyptian officials. They make a gesture to show they're on the case, which often does more harm than good."

Carina felt euphoric. If Nick's body hadn't been found, if the torched car signified nothing, anything was possible. She'd find him alive; they'd laugh over her suspicions. *A bunch of us threw a party for a guy flying home. Yasmina and I discussed the bar-tab, that's all*, he'd say...

"Where now, back to the Residency?"

"Umm, I'd like to walk a bit, on my own." The streets throbbed with life; she wanted to share it. She saw two men embracing, children teasing a kitten, a pregnant woman shuffling by. Baines looked dubious but sensed her mood.

"Well, you have my number if you need me. Maybe you'll enjoy the bazaar. It's about two blocks in that direction. Follow the crowd."

The bazaar had gone down in the world. Jewellers' frontages festooned with cooking utensils; boutiques stacked with sacks of flour and drums of cooking oil, labelled *USAid: a gift from the American people. Not for Sale.* Shopkeepers ignored her and pedestrians gave way, but stares from loiterers made Carina uneasy. A ragged girl pawed her elbow, miming hunger. Damn, she could only find a wadded fiver in her pocket. She had some coins in her money-belt, but feared to open it on the street. As she wavered, the girl snatched the banknote and fled. Oh well, she'd not be so careless next time. The stench of rotting fruit and urine was nauseating. Flies swarmed around caged chickens and waxy carcases on butcher's hooks.

Turning to leave, Carina felt a stab of panic. Two streets forked, she couldn't remember which she'd taken. Had she passed that ironmongers or the other one? The flow of passers-by was unyielding, now she tried to go against it. A speeding moped and a peddler with a handcart forced her to leap aside, scraping her shin on the kerb. She might have fallen, but for two Arab women who dusted her down and walked away chuckling. Jostled from behind, surrounded by unwashed bodies, a gabble of Arabic.

I'm going to faint...

Suddenly the crush was gone and she stood alone, clutching a post-box, as people edged warily by at a distance. Blood trickled down her ankle. She staunched it with a Kleenex. Her palm left a smear of blood on the post-box's burnished chrome, incongruous amid the squalid bazaar. Everything was weird in Hurghada. Why on earth had Nick said he liked the place? But never mind – she'd noticed a half-familiar landmark and realized the highway wasn't far. Taxis waited there. It would be okay...

Five minutes later, she was flitting past squatted holiday villages. Baines had said that some housed eighty thousand refugees sleeping ten to a room. Tin hovels, canvas tents and browsing goats covered the wastelands between the walled compounds, each with a gargantuan Arabesque gate emblazoned with its name. *Arabian Nights, Sindbad's Paradise, Jasmin Village...* Occasionally, she glimpsed the sea between faded hoardings advertising hotel chains that had forsaken Egypt. As Nick had emailed, Hurghada was more like Gaza than Alicante, but it least it had the sea. In fact the local name for the swath of camps along the coast actually meant 'the sea' in Arabic: *El-Bahr*, they called it.

Now she was in Egypt, TV coverage of the Flood made more sense. Hurghada had been the main evacuation point for tourists, with footage of heartwarming renunions at Gatwick as the survivors jetted home. Meanwhile, the US Sixth Fleet was steaming down the Persian Gulf to assist, and Israel rushing humanitarian aid across Sinai, as the United Nations dithered. And then the Libyans got involved, up north, or something...

But that was two years ago. Now the emergency was over and the recovery was only one of many in a world battered by climate change.

"Ten dollar," demanded the driver, halting a prudent distance from the Residency's fence. Carina suspected she was being overcharged but lacked the will to argue. Her shin no longer hurt. The thought of returning to her chalet depressed her and a dip in the sea seemed absurdly frivolous – not that she'd packed a swimsuit. Yet she couldn't traipse around aimlessly.

Then she noticed a sign across the road, promising beer and burgers. If they'd ever been served those days were over, she realized as soon as she entered the café. Battered chairs and an all-male clientele more morose than any she'd ever seen, watching a mullah on television. She was about to leave when a boy hurried from the back.

"Welcome, welcome. We have tea, Nescafe, Sprite." His smile was angelic, maybe simple-minded. "No milk," he added. Carina shrugged. She wouldn't trust milk in a place like this, but a glass of sweet black tea from a kettle on the hob seemed safe, and might be refreshing. When it came she sipped and pulled a face. It was bitter – how odd.

An old man at the next table noticed her reaction. "Please excuse," he said. "Today we are all drinking unsweetened tea or coffee. It is forty days since the death of our friend. His own family died in the Flood; we were his only companions these last years."

Touched, Carina decided not to ask for sugar.

But it tasted foul, she couldn't finish it; the boy's eyes bulged at the size of her tip. *Why am I always apologizing*, she rebuked herself, anticipating the cool of the Residency as she crossed the melting tarmac road.

A chambermaid had tidied her chalet. On the bedside table was an envelope. Tearing it open, she found a message from Baines.

We're seeing the Minister tomorrow. Be in the lobby at 13.00.

3 HOSNI BASHA

Bronze eagles the size of elephants flanked the turn-off to the Presidential Enclave, far enough from Hurghada to maintain an air of splendid isolation. El-Gouna, it was called, Banies told Carina as guards checked their papers, cursorily searched the car and saluted. The Egyptian tricolour and Presidential standard flapped in the breeze from an unseen sea.

"We're early," he grunted. "I'll give you a tour". He jerked a thumb at the tawny glare outside. "The airport was built for tourists when El-Gouna was a resort. Now it delivers luxuries to keep His Excellency's people happy". His next words were drowned out as the car shuddered and a camouflaged helicopter landed in a haze of dust, booted feet dangling from its loading bay as if from the jaws of a preying mantis.

"- and patrolling the Enclave. Seventeen thousand square kilometres, mostly desert," Baines continued, as the runway receded behind them.

Ahead she saw an undulating golf course encircling a lake; freeways and residential zones. Tropical shrubs blazed on verges, giant portraits of the President spanned the avenues. Uniformed, robed or in casual dress, a rifle, Qur'an or child in his arms, for each honorific: *Defender of Justice, the Endower, Father of Egypt*. Gold and black Hummers with mirrored windows sped by. Carina recoiled as two teenagers veered their motorbike alongside to gesture lewdly.

"Regime brats," Baines scowled. "Nothing to do but waste money and make trouble – they'll probably crash the bike or kill someone. A housemaid got run down only last week". He touched her arm consolingly. "But the Almighty cares for each sparrow that falls."

She doubted it. "Aside from those jerks it all looks so *normal*. Not like Hurghada, I mean..." she faltered. "Nail bars, couples eating out. And then you think of how people live in those camps." She rapped the glass. "Look at that fountain – how many thousand people could wash in that, it's –."

"Obscene. Yes. But injustice is a consequence of original sin. We can only follow the right path, help people fallen by the wayside. Sinners who reject salvation can be left to the Almighty." Baines twisted his college ring and flexed his fingers.

"But you run an aid agency. Isn't all this skimmed off the budget?"

Baines wagged a finger. *Wait.* The car crested a bridge-ramp and Carina gasped, overwhelmed by the islands and lagoons basking beside a radiant sea.

"Some place! I wish I'd spent a holiday here." Immediately she felt foolish.

Baines politely ignored her gaucherie. "The Ministries are based in hotels: Security at the Golf, Armed Forces at the Paradiso, diplomats at the Mövenpick. You can tell the pecking order from their amenities."

They crossed another bridge into a zone of flats and offices. "Welfare," Baines confirmed, "the runt of the litter. It coordinates the aid effort – on paper. We ring-fenced all our programs long ago, so there's not much they can tap us for."

Yet the people on the streets looked well fed, Carina thought. No beggars; no shacks. They drove past a cinema, showing a rom-com she'd seen in London last year. What else do we have in common, she wondered, brand names?

The lagoons reappeared, azure fingers clasping an archipelago of palatial enclaves linked by tubular bridges. At checkpoints manned by sentries in black fatigues and berets, Baines flashed a laminated pass and was waved through. A powerboat surged from behind the headland and raced beneath the bridge, wet-suited figures bending over nets on deck.

Carina barely noticed the last checkpoint, distracted by peacocks on the lawn and gilded domes overhead. Arabesque lattices hung like curtains on white facades behind the palms. A fountain splashed in a glade.

"The Miramar Palace, it used to be a six-star hotel," said Baines tartly. "Where else to house His Excellency? To be charitable, the heated pool's said to help whatever ails him". He tapped the driver's shoulder. "Pull up beside the steps."

"He's sick?"

Baines nodded at two liveried Nubians approaching. "Later, you'll see for yourself". He helped her out of the car with old-fashioned courtesy. After the sun's caress the onyx foyer was chilling. Carina shivered while Baines argued with a supercilious majordomo. *I should have dressed better, he might have warned me.*

Another minion led them down a corridor lined with showcases of Islamic glassware, a dove-grey carpet silky underfoot. With a servile flourish, he opened a lacquered door and ushered them towards a pearly glow. Carina blinked at the pungent scents in the air. "What's going on?"

They stood on a balcony overlooking a hall suffused with light from chandeliers reflected by gilded mirrors and oyster-silk curtains. People milled about, exchanging kisses and handshakes, Western women in cocktail dresses on the arms of Arab men in silk *galabiyyas* or dark-suited executives. She caught snatches of English, German and French, as a waiter proffered a tray of champagne flutes and tumblers of orange juice.

"The *diwan*" – Baines swirled ice in his tumbler – "A revival of the court ritual of Arab monarchies, that Egypt waved goodbye to when they deposed King Farouk. Sheikhs and landlords, bankers and merchants – paying their respects, bidding for favours: an import monopoly or water rights for a bloc of camps."

Below them, three Arabs bickered over a cadaverous blonde till a drum-roll silenced the crowd, whose heads turned in unison. Two jackbooted adjutants strutted in, saluted and about-faced to meet a pair of bearded clerics, followed by a phalanx of Nubians with chromed Kalashnikovs. As tension mounted, six barefoot servants carried an enormous dais into view. Draped in crimson velvet, it bore a throne in the form of an eagle, its beak poised above the head of the enthroned ruler.

Shrunken inside a braided white uniform, face slack, skin like oatmeal, eyes hidden by sunglasses, gloved hands resting on a golden flywhisk in his lap and an embroidered cloth covering his legs. As the bearers set him down, the President's face tightened and his body sagged. The imam began a throaty declamation.

Adjutants moved through the crowd buttonholing people till a dozen were mustered near the dais, where a tall saturnine Egyptian in a dark suit whispered in the President's ear. Carina saw the President's mouth writhe, before the acolyte stepped back with a satisfied air and began hectoring the audience in Arabic.

Exclamations of alarm and anger from the Arabs, as the foreigners strained to comprehend or fidgeted in perplexity. With a gesture the acolyte silenced the clamour and spoke in a gentler tone, coaxing affirmations from the Arabs. Realisation was spreading among the expats as some translated for others, who looked bemused or shocked.

She turned to Baines for an explanation but he simply mouthed *Look*. The dark man was addressing the supplicants – or culprits. One shuffled forward, salaamed to the throne and began to plead. The acolyte cut him short, inclining his head towards the President. A twitch of the flywhisk, and he pronounced a verdict that brought a gold-toothed grin to the face of the accused. So he got off, Carina thought. The others seemed more cheerful too.

One by one they made their case and the acolyte delivered judgement. Carina watched for further signs of the President's intentions, but neither his face nor flywhisk moved. While the first four defendants withdrew with effusions of gratitude, the fifth slunk away, leaving the remaining men chastened. It seemed like a trial, but maybe something else had taken place. The mood in the hall was more relaxed, as if the drama was over – yet there was still an undercurrent of anticipation.

Baines touched her elbow. "The *diwan* will end soon. I'll fill you in then". Minutes later, a drum roll and a benediction heralded the departure of the President, borne backwards on the dais, followed by the Nubian guards, reforming into a phalanx as gracefully as a Venus flytrap enfolds its prey. The audience atomised into individuals, seizing drinks and cigarettes. Carina heard the blonde braying, "That's *so* cool!"

Baines drew her through an archway onto a terrace. Palm trees rustled and a waterfall cast cooling spume into the air. They settled into wicker chairs beneath a parasol rising from a table. Carina felt displaced, as if on holiday alone, unsure how to amuse herself.

Where are you, Nick?

"So tell me, you promised".

"As you saw, President Zaghloul is incapacitated. Rarely moves in public – never walks. But his mind is still sharp, it's said. His...wisdom...is divined by Hosni Basha. That's the tall guy. In any regular banana republic he'd have seized the presidency for himself. But he prefers ruling through a figurehead. He has the Security portfolio – those were his guys that checked us coming in. Armed Forces are busy with the Nubians down south, and the generals are poodles anyway".

He leant forward and pressed a crystal stud on the table. "The other Ministries don't do much but line their pockets. The *diwan* is about distributing concessions. Those folks saying their bit were 'proposing' deals, negotiated earlier in private. At the *diwan*, Hosni can ratify what they'd agreed, or set different terms – and they'll have to swallow them without a peep."

"So what was the uproar about?" A waiter materialised with a tray. Baines watched benignly as he set their drinks on the table without meeting their eyes.

"Hmm, that was different..." He trailed off, rubbing his bald spot. "Well you know that Muslims have strict dietary laws, like Jews. So when Hosni announced that the last batch of MRE was made with lard, they freaked."

"Emaree?"

"Meals-ready-to-eat – we use the military acronym. Took the product from the army and adapted it to refugee needs. Anyhow, if the meals *had* been distributed and, God forbid, eaten, there'd be rioting in the camps. But then Hosni played his ace: the batch was seized at the last moment and burned. The importer is under arrest. His competitors have been warned against selling tainted products. Praise Allah and the vigilance of State Security."

Carina thought a while. "So was it true, or just to impress people?"

"That's between Hosni and the guy on the rack. Maybe we'll learn the truth six months from now. It's easier to speculate *who's* meant to be impressed. Half the people in that hall are crooks. Perhaps it's an indirect warning about some other racket. That makes sense. It sure put the wind up those folks by the podium. They didn't know if Hosni had one of them fingered till just before they had to plead their case."

"So who was the importer? What's happened to him?"

"His identity is under wraps, but the verdict has been announced. Guilty of *fitna* and *shirk* – sedition and blasphemy – the sentence to follow by nightfall." Baines wet his lips. "The man's name is being withheld till his family can be taken to safety. And the criminal is punished before the camps even get to hear of it. Now *that's* law and order."

Carina felt cold, her bladder tight. She stood up. "Excuse me. Do you know where I can..." Baines pointed round the corner of the terrace. "I'll be back soon".

Finding the washroom took longer than she'd expected; its door resisted her impatient push before swinging inwards to crash against the wall.

"Jeez, you scared me." It was the cadaverous blonde, wiping her nose over a basin. Carina mouthed sorry, slipping into a cubicle, air freshener tickling her nostrils. She heard the woman sniffing. When Carina emerged she was closing a vanity bag.

"I saw you on the terrace with that Christian relief guy."

"Yes, I'm new here. I haven't a clue what's going on."

The blonde chuckled knowingly. "You will. Everyone learns fast. I came here six months ago. The first week I thought I'd died and gone to heaven. The second week it seemed like hell. Now it's normal. Stuff, I mean."

"I don't understand."

"Y'know – parties, executions; it keeps 'em focused." She glossed h

Carina's jaw dropped; the blonde laughed. "I'm Danni, from Perth, PA to Hassan Ali. You won't know him, and I wouldn't bother except for *this*." Danni waggled her vanity bag. "Generous isn't the word. Don't get me wrong, Hassan's not so bad. At least he doesn't skip from one daggy resort to another till his cards go ping. We've got a suite at the Paradiso with a Jacuzzi, maid, everything. He's not even married – he swears."

"You're not sure?"

"Y'know. Most of these Egyptians have a wife somewhere, in a villa past the golf club, or in Hurghada if they're stingy. Then again, not all of 'em bothered to save their wives when the Flood came. Hassan tried to reach his parents, but Cairo was gridlocked; he left with the last convoy and never saw them again. That was when he started using coke."

"How awful."

"Shit, that kind of story's normal here. Hassan counts himself lucky he's living at the Paradiso." Danni smiled archly. "Gotta run. See you later in the garden."

Carina returned to Baines. The sky was lambent as the sun sank into the desert haze. Lamps came on in the grounds; guests strolled towards a buffet by the shore. "Let's go down," he said, "I'll introduce you to some people."

"What about our meeting with the Minister?"

"Nothing happens quickly in Egypt. Be patient."

Stifling her frustration, Carina followed Baines from one encounter to another. It was like a tea party at Buckingham Palace – lots of different people, all distinguished, or simply self-important. In such surroundings, grandeur came naturally.

A French Egyptologist lamented the loss of the monuments in the Nile Valley. Only Abu Simbel and the Nubian temples remained. And the pyramids of Giza – had not Napoleon said they were immortal! How *triste* to recover a colossus from Luxor Temple. "Imagine, we found it 45 kilometres downriver. Now it will be safe – in the Louvre. Such vestiges must be saved for all humanity."

Nancy Somebody from Kansas called herself a retro-conservationist and dreamt of re-wilding Egypt with its ancient flora and fauna. "It's really exciting. Crocodiles have moved downriver from Sudan. This year we found breeding colonies in the Delta. Now we're setting up a hippo reserve in the Fayoum

Swamps. But my real dream-species is the Blue Lotus. The ancients used it for sex-magic – well, the priesthood and nobility did. We're modifying different lotuses from Ethiopia to recreate the original strain."

"And the Smithsonian is funding *that*?" interrupted Baines.

"Only the hippo reserve," replied Nancy. "A hovercraft is expensive to run, but I can't get around the swamps otherwise".

Carina was intrigued but Baines cut the conversation short, dragging her away to meet some moneymen. As Baines plunged into a discussion on derivatives, she found herself backed against a table by a red-faced banker from Surrey, who rattled on about investments.

"Splendid collateral: oil and gas in the Red Sea and Western Desert. Most of the rigs and pipelines weren't damaged at all by the Flood; only the refineries at Suez and Alex. The Gyppos need us to get them going, to pay for relief and reconstruction, and the Israelis are just the chaps to reopen the Canal. Funny how their Mandate was handed to them on a plate by Baby Gaddafi seizing Egypt's north coast... A bit of a chancer, like his father: did you know he made action films before stepping into the Colonel's boots?"

Only one person seemed aggrieved. Paul Craven, Agro-Coordinator, didn't hide his despondency as he slurped vodka. Monsanto's entire programme in the Valley had been set back by sabotage at their pilot scheme. Pumping and filtration plants bombed, seed depots burned, contractors murdered.

"I'm fucking disappointed by the Egyptians. With so much at stake – our investments and their country's future – you'd think the government could stop those frigging Nubians raiding us. Who cares if they zapped them *afterwards*? And with the Nile dropping, we're expecting more trouble soon."

Carina recalled that Nick had mentioned some Nubian insurgency in the far south, but he'd assured her it posed no threat to El-Bahr. As Nick explained it, the Nubians wanted their own share of the Valley where they'd lived since time immemorial, till the High Dam submerged Nubia beneath Lake Nasser. Now, she learnt from Craven, Nubian insurgents had ranged hundreds of miles north to strike within a few hours' drive of Hurghada.

"It's not good enough," whined Craven. "A gunship should've got there in thirty minutes."

***

With a spy-cam, Hosni watched the old man sink into Zizi's arms to snuggle between her melons as Lamees prepared an injection. Then Lamees would join them in the scented water, her red hair lapping his pigeon-chest as they pleasured him together. Hosni imagined them quenching his own piston. But no, let Zaghloul enjoy his whores, Hosni had already robbed him of everything else.

They first met nearly a decade ago, at a reception to celebrate Egypt's victory in the African Cup of Nations. Having scored in extra time after spending most of the match in reserve, Hosni was feted by everyone from President Mousa downwards. Industrialists and film stars listened to him like awestruck boys. Zaghloul had been a non-entity even then, despite his title of Deputy Vice President. *A Party hack*, Hosni thought as he shook the man's limp hand. *Abdel Sa'ad Zaghloul* – risibly named after a hero of Egypt's struggle for independence.

Hosni was fascinated by history and made full use of the libraries and courses open to a member of the national team and the General Intelligence Service. His strength and reflexes were matched by his mental agility. When Hosni accepted Zaghloul's patronage, he understood that this mediocrity would nurture his career long after other more charismatic patrons had found fresh protégées. As a childless widower, Zaghloul would cherish a surrogate son.

Within a year Hosni had leapt two ranks, into the Presidential Guard, evading rivals' intrigues as he'd sidestepped tackles on the pitch. Were it not for the Flood he'd have been content with his last job under the old regime, serving the top dogs. Security chief of the Presidential Flight: six Sea King helicopters and a Gulfstream jet, based at Cairo West military airport.

Normally, this was easy. Mechanics were responsible for their air-worthiness, pilots for flying them. He simply countersigned logs and flight plans, and ensured that his squad was deployed with its Fahd troop carrier. Sadat's assassination on the parade ground at Medinet Nasr, back in 1981, was the worst contingency they'd trained for. A nuclear strike by Israel rated five pages in the National Emergency Plan, but the Black Day was not anticipated. Six months afterwards, he met a Canadian expert who said that in many countries where such a threat existed, the endangered areas were a state secret, denied even to emergency planners.

So far as anything was certain that day, he knew he could rely on his squad. They'd all been through the same bruising with the GIS; scraped their hands raw on assault courses, learned to fire AK-74s, AR-18s, Skorpions, Uzis and Tavors.

Like every survivor of the Black Day, his memories of it were indelible. But where others recalled only fear and chaos, his were haloed with triumph, for he not only met the challenge but emerged all-powerful, through sheer audacity.

At the outset, he'd been like the other donkeys. News was seeping through the dike between the dogs and the herd. He knew from the faces of the Black Berets on the route from the Government Quarter that it was only a matter of time before they overcame their fear of their NCOs and officers – or *their* obedience snapped. Before it went off the air, state television admitted that an 'unscheduled release' of water from the High Dam was 'slightly affecting' Upper Egypt. Power outages trapped thousands on the metro or apartment-block elevators, as Cairo began sliding into chaos. And then Al-Jazeera broadcast the jihadi video and everyone knew the truth...

Cairo West was snarling with dogs and gorillas – the whole band of thieves and their bodyguards. President Mousa boarded his jet with the Cabinet and Chief of Staff. Six F-16s were already aloft, waiting to escort them to Sharm el-Sheikh – the helicopters to follow once the President was in Sharm and issued the final evacuation order. Hosni soon realised that the evacuation list bore little relation to the dogs there, never mind their bitches or pups. After conferring with Zaghloul – on whom seniority had devolved – he was authorised to promise a Hercules to carry the excess. That was how the goat-shit began – but the real manure came later.

At 14.34, the escort commander broke radio silence over the Gulf of Suez to report the launch of surface-to-air missiles – just before their flight vanished from radar screens. Frantic calls to Air Force HQ established that Israeli spy-drones had penetrated Egyptian airspace an hour ago. Air defence units had been on red alert since morning; nerves fraying and communications lapsing due to chaos at GHQ and jamming by the Zionists. A battery commander near Suez fired twelve SAMs at what he took to be retreating intruders. The President's jet and its escort were blasted from the sky.

The dogs panicked.

Many changed their minds about flying, summoned their cars and left. Much later, Hosni learnt that those who drove into the Western Desert survived, while those who tried to cross the Nile died when the bridges were swept away. At Cairo West, the fact that six helicopters weren't enough for everyone began to outweigh any hope of a Hercules, and scuffles started. Zaghloul's claim was better than most – he had priority-2 status – but he clearly lacked the nerve to fight for it.

It was then that Hosni seized destiny by the throat. How his squad gawked as he told them that their masters were now their prey! But that was nothing to the dogs' reaction when the Fahd's gun turret swivelled to cover them, as Hosni snarled through a bullhorn: "On the ground *now* – or we fire!" Three gorillas tried to resist and were shot dead; the rest crawled on the oily tarmac begging for their lives.

Zaghloul scurried into the Sea King that Hosni had chosen for himself, enviously observed by the other dogs. Even before Hosni announced that other seats were up for sale, they were groping for their wallets. He took only dollars, euros, gold or gems. Credit cards were trodden underfoot as the rotors stirred a blizzard of Egyptian banknotes that had already become worthless. As the doors slid shut, his troops shot into the mob surging forwards.

Two of them sat in each copter, pistols aimed at the crew and passengers. Hosni ordered a course for Hurghada, flying as low as the pilots dared. He'd done air-evasion drills before and prepared by pissing through the floor-hatch before strapping down. Soon they were hurtling up valleys over splintered peaks, drenched in sweat, puking, imploring God's mercy. Hosni had the satisfaction of seeing a wet stain on Zaghloul's crotch that the old fool didn't notice. His mouth twitched but only grunts emerged.

The pilots expected thermals and updrafts, but not sudden air turbulence of such ferocity. Warnings crackled over the radio as the air grew colder and moister; the floodwaters were propelling a high-pressure front northward.

"Look, look, over there!" The helicopter lurched as they craned to peer at the black, foaming torrent erasing the emerald valley behind them. Everyone babbled the names of mothers, brothers, cousins, cities, villages – pulverised, drowned.

Only their own peril distracted them from the horror on the horizon. Dense fog obscured the earth and skies; the pilots clawed for height but a chill wind swatted them down. An explosion tore the mist away to reveal a burning helicopter impaled on a ridge. Another pilot uttered a prayer as he spiralled into a ravine. In Hosni's copter, his Corporal began sobbing. He came from Edfu, which had ceased to exist hours ago.

Hosni slapped his face. "Where's your manhood?"

Zaghloul fainted at the sight. Cringing, the Corporal saluted Hosni.

Suddenly they burst into into sunlight with the coastline ahead and three Sea Kings behind them. Turbulence abated, the crew wiped their faces and passengers praised God. Hosni checked that Zaghloul was breathing and his lads were okay. If anyone had shared the Corporal's weakness, they'd recover now the danger was past and crave orders. Knowing what to do – and having the guns and skills to do it – was what distinguished soldiers from civilians.

So Hosni told them what to do once the helicopters landed …

The party was in full swing. Some Egyptian men were throwing women into a pool as a belly dancer gyrated under disco lights in a marquee beneath the palms. Platters of sea bass, lobster and lamb emerged from the kitchens. Carina and Baines were among those listening to a crocodile story told by a burly salvage engineer from Essex – the GM Somebody whose card had been in Nick's wallet, Carina realized.

"Three hundred tonnes of gold in the vaults of the National Bank – a bastard to pump out. Gas worked fine with the rats but didn't bother the crocs, so we had to electrocute 'em. We cut the juice before the team went in. God knows how, but a croc got in *after* we fried the others and ate a ganger. Ever since then, a guy with an M-16 has gone down with each shift, but they've never caught that croc. He might still be down there, chewing on Abdul …"

"Really, GM," a lady protested, "How can you? Think of the poor man's family."

"He didn't have one," retorted GM cheerfully. "I use gangers without dependents. More focused on cash – not hard to replace, either; lots of guys with the right skills lost their families. Most learn fast on the job. Tough shit if they don't."

Further revelations were forestalled by a fanfare from hidden speakers. A brief speech in Arabic with a postscript in English: *Please proceed at once to the north lagoon. Justice will be served in ten minutes. Thank you.*

"Sounds worth a bet," laughed GM. "Who'll give me odds he'll get halfway?" He began moving towards the lagoons; others drifted in the same direction.

"What did he mean? What's going to happen?" asked Carina.

"You don't want to know, much less see it," Baines replied.

"Tell me."

"This is Hosni's punishment for the illegal importer. His body must be defiled and his soul denied any hope of paradise."

"Meaning what?"

"Meaning they'll throw him into the lagoon. If he gets to the far shore, Allah is merciful. But the sharks make that unlikely – and they'll slash his hamstrings before they tip him off the boat."

4 HITTING THE G-SPOT

Carina fidgeted in bed, queasy from a surfeit of champagne, ashamed of not voicing, her outrage when the chance arose at El-Gouna. They'd been waiting outside the Miramar for their car when a flunky called them back into the lobby, where the majordomo swooped on Baines and led them through a cordon of bodyguards to be presented to Hosni Basha.

His grip was firm, his nails buffed. His face reminded her of a Scythian warrior's tent, skin taut over knobbly bones, eyes like jewels, mouth ablaze with gold.

"Your husband's return is our dearest wish," he purred. "My investigators have found no evidence that he left El-Bahr and the Israelis say he never entered Suez. If any clue is discovered, you'll be told immediately. Till then, O lady…"

He squeezed her hand and bowed as a flunkey took her elbow. She tried to recall the questions she harboured but could only stammer her thanks. *Idiot*, she berated herself, trailing behind Baines to the Land Cruiser.

"A good sign," he said, sensing her mood. "Hosni doesn't make idle promises."

"But there's still no news of Nick, and I felt sick shaking hands with a murderer."

He tuned the radio to a Gospel choir from Montana.

"I understand your feelings. Nick experienced them too. Most aid workers feel guilty about their affluence and frustrated by corrupt institutions. Some go off their food – sympathetic starvation, we call it. Nick seemed that way inclined till I helped him see beyond his own pain and the suffering of others, to the redemption people are finding in Jesus, the miracle that's happening in Egypt."

"I can't see things that way."

"You've only been here two days. You've seen some camps and the Enclave. That's not a balanced picture. But I can *show* you the miracle, like I showed Nick. Why not come with me on a pilgrimage to Saint Anthony's tomorrow and you'll see."

If Nick had sought something, it might shed light on his disappearance. What had she to lose by accepting Baines's invitation? "OK, I'll come," she said, feeling absurdly embarrassed, as though she'd agreed to visit a fetish club.

✳✳✳

The convoy left in a joyous mood. Beaten-up buses and Baines's Land Cruiser, its insignia freshly polished. Carina shared the back seat with a boyish evangelist who introduced himself as Luke Morrison, before asking if she was 'saved'. As she hesitated, the pilgrims began singing. "You wouldn't guess those hymns are from Dayton, Ohio," said Morrison proudly. "We've rendered Baptist hymns into Arabic; Coptic ones don't always hit the G-spot."

"Sorry?"

"The God-spot – no other reaction can beat it. Salvation through Jesus Christ our Lord offers satisfaction beyond any snare of the Devil."

Inwardly Carina scoffed, but her disgust at El-Gouna's decadence required a dose of morality as a dyspeptic needs liver salts.

"Baptism is glorious. The damned cleansed of sins and errors, reborn in the love of Christ," said Morrison fervently.

"What sins do you mean?"

"Their sins are like ours. The problem is their errors – believing in a false prophet and false doctrines. That's what'll condemn them to hell if we can't save them. That's what our mission is." His face clouded. "Saving the Mohammedans is uphill work. They recognise Jesus, but not His divinity. They might as well eat a Big Mac and spit out the burger! Where's the holiness in that?"

"Patience, Luke," soothed Baines. "Rome wasn't built in a day. Our work's going well, conversions on target. Worry about the Lord's work, yes – but don't be despondent. As Jesus trod the Hills of Galilee and felt his feet grow weary, so we, His followers, sometimes feel burdened – but His example inspires us to carry on!"

"Hallelujah, Sir. I don't *doubt*, I just get impatient, that's all."

"Soldier on, Luke. Leave the doubts to Jesus."

Carina stifled her nausea as they passed El-Gouna, dozing off as the evangelists picked over the Book of Revelation. Gog and Magog, ten-horned beasts and red heifers – no wonder people like her preferred Reiki.

When she awoke, they were in a gorge the colour of raw salmon. "Wadi Arraba," intoned Baines. "Arabic for the Valley of Carts, after the pharaoh's chariots that chased the Israelites towards the Red Sea. Exodus: Chapter 14."

"It's humbling to drive in Moses' footsteps," added Morrison. "Generations of Christians never had the chance. Millions of Mohammedans ignored the opportunity, wasting time on the *Haj* – tragic, really."

They turned onto a road that switch-backed towards a massif, rugged ramparts and cupolas. The pilgrims burst into song again. Had Carina known the words she might have joined in; she longed to be uplifted.

Saint Anthony's walls were twelve metres high, said Baines. Looted in the Dark Ages, it still had treasures to safeguard. Nobody was allowed inside during the Lenten Fast; supplies were winched over the wall. But now was the pilgrimage season, the postern-gate wide open. Dormitories, workshops and churches congregated like an extended family. As Morrison led the pilgrims away they were joined by a grizzled monk in a black cowl embroidered with stars, who introduced himself as Brother Makkarius.

"Our monastery was founded by disciples of Saint Anthony, who lived to be 105, his last twenty-five years in a cave, beasts and birds his only companions. Disciples buried him beneath the church that bears his name." Muffled singing came from a squat Byzantine edifice. "The *catechumens* are preparing for their baptism, so we can't enter now. Let's see some other buildings," Makkarius urged.

They visited a bakery where bubbling loaves emerged from beehive ovens, a library of manuscripts being scanned for propagation on Saint Anthony's website, and an ancient watchtower surveying the palm groves. As Makkarius explained, a fissure in the cliff yielded enough water for all the monks' needs, but supplies for pilgrims had to be trucked in. The spring was where Miriam, sister of Moses, bathed during the Exodus.

Bells clanged as pilgrims streamed by holding palm fronds. Makkarius beamed. "Now let us visit the holy shrines. Please remove your shoes at the door." He added something in Arabic to the driver, who shrugged and stalked away.

The Church of Saint Anthony smelt of candle-wax, ambergris and unwashed bodies, candlelight dancing on an ebony iconostasis. Makkarius genuflected before a wild-eyed figure wearing animal skins, flanked by placid lions and attentive ravens.

"Saint Anthony the Blessed. If a child is sick, a woman infertile, or something has been stolen, he will help if the person is righteous. Let us pray to him."

Carina barely hesitated. If there was the faintest chance of finding Nick she wouldn't spurn it for a vague agnosticism denying any hope of miracles. She lit a candle before the icon and knelt with Baines and Makkarius.

"God willing, he'll answer your prayer. To be sure, you should pray again in his cave on Jebel Qalah. Everyone does, even cripples who must be carried. And now let us visit the Church of Saint Luke, and then the Church of the Four Creatures."

Eventually the churches had been seen and it was time for the gardens. Monks weeded, robes hitched knee-high, chanting psalms. Something bright blue flashed among the trees, the sound of voices and splashing intensifying as they advanced. Makkarius halted. "Soon Mr Baines and I will visit the men's *anben*, and you, sister, the women's."

His meaning became clear as they entered a clearing with two enclosures of UN-blue polythene sheeting. Directed towards one, Carina turned a corner, found a gap and peered inside. Scores of women and girls knelt round a fibreglass tank that might have been designed for dipping sheep. Most had been baptised, but a dozen still awaited immersion at the hands of a blindfolded monk assisted by a nun in a wimple. The ritual took just over a minute, leaving the converts dazed or ecstatic. She slipped away after the sixth baptism.

Baines and Makkarius rejoined her, full of bonhomie. The monk twisted a palm frond into a crucifix. "Let this remind you of our endeavours. Don't forget to visit the cave. Saint Anthony never fails to help the righteous."

With such an endorsement, it was impossible to express any reservations when Baines asked her opinion of the baptisms. "Oh, yes, so well organised and meaningful."

"I'm glad. Nick thought the same when he was here. You know, a few more visits and I swear he'd have asked to be reborn. Let's pray he's able to, real soon."

Mutely, Sabr cursed the apostates. *Abandoning their faith for an extra sack of flour and a hovel in the Valley – God make them sterile!* He fantasised lighting a cigarette in violation of the rules – he wouldn't dream of it in a mosque, but the urge to defile this place was strong. *Each day they are corrupting us!* But that foreskin-priest was watching, so the Cleos stayed in his pocket. Instead, he studied the hen. *Carina*, it could be an Arab name, but she'd never be taken for an Arab woman. Tall, her bulk draped in men's clothing, hair silver at the roots; no make up or jewellery except a wedding ring. Other than that, she might've been one of the older chickens on his felucca. But those days were over, that sweet life gone.

Baines was calling, the monk relishing his humiliation. *I am Sabr al-Adawi, a Muslim – I won't yield to their infamy, even if I must accompany them to the cave of the Nazarene. My heart won't falter,* he vowed.

Soon, the path became perilous. Baines was limping but undaunted, the driver lagging; Makkarius had excused himself at the foot of the cliff. After ten minutes they reached a timber stairway with an iron handrail, snaking up a vertical rock-face. Carina would've turned back, but her prayer could only take wings two hundred steps above. Baines spurred her on with miraculous tales of Saint Anthony's life, as sparrows flitted across their path and ravines plunged to the horizon. They wiped their faces, quaffing water.

At last they reached the cave. Niches hewn from soot-cured rock were the only evidence of the saint's stay, together with pilgrims' petitions wedged into every cranny. They fumbled in their pockets until the driver obliged with a folded sheet of paper. As both men withdrew to let her compose her prayer, she unfolded it and read:

FIVE STEPS towards establishing JESUS in YOUR Life

The way to SALVATION isn't easy. GOD is merciful, and understands you may find it difficult. Just follow these FIVE STEPS and JESUS CHRIST will meet you halfway.

* Don't take the LORD'S NAME in vain. There is no GOD but GOD (Allah), as revealed by JESUS CHRIST, His only Son, and the Apostles. Mohammed was not a prophet, but he revered the message of JESUS.
* PRAY three times daily – at sunrise, noon and sunset. If you can't do this in a CHURCH every day, be sure to attend worship on SUNDAY. Praying at a mosque does not count. GOD will not hear your prayers.
* MAKE A PILGRIMAGE to a HOLY PLACE. The Monasteries of St Anthony and St Paul are easily reached (your Camp Director can help). The Haj is impossible now. Do not waste your time and money trying to visit Mecca. There is sickness there, and Egyptians aren't welcome.
* WORSHIP GOD'S MESSIAH fittingly. Icons and other representations of JESUS CHRIST and His Saints are holy. Geometric forms are diabolical.

- LIVE as GOD wishes. Fasting during Ramadan is not required. Wearing the *higab* demeans women.

Take these FIVE STEPS towards JESUS and He will welcome you with open arms! Then SALVATION WILL BE YOURS!!!

Translation of leaflet 2:1 from Arabic, for Stage 3 Clients.

"Not done yet?" Baines chided.

She reverse-folded it and wrote firmly: *Dear God, please save Nick.* How could she have let anything distract her from her prayer? She thrust it into a fissure and crossed herself, feeling hopeless. It had all been in vain, a delusion.

The descent was hellish. Searing gusts plucked her clothes like imps, stoking a perverse urge to leap to her doom. Nature this stark was morbid. Saint Anthony loathed women, loved desolation, foretold eternal torment for all but a few, basking in heaven. Christianity was apocalyptic and cruel long before Islam cornered the franchise.

Midway down the steps she drew breath at a turning where the driver glared at the horizon. He hadn't tarried this time, keeping well ahead. He was a moody sod – the sort that beat their wives. Why did Baines employ him? *Budge over and let me pass!* Her telepathic command struck home. He recoiled as if she was a tub of lard.

The step cracked like a gunshot as he stepped back.

Pitched him into the handrail – towards the abyss...

Instinctively she seized his wrist and swung him like a satchel towards safety, toppling them both into a thicket of scrub. Tasting blood as they lay entangled, panting like dogs, her heart thumping against his ribs.

Baines helped her sit and staunch her nosebleed. Numb with shock, she didn't register his words. It was some time before she could look at the fractured step, or nerve herself to continue. The whole structure was wormy and brittle.

Back at the monastery, monks salved their cuts, plying Carina with sweet tea laced with raw spirit, as Baines and Makkarius conferred.

"Best you return now," he said eventually. "I'll ride back later."

Silence hung between them in the car. Sabr wondered how to explain the Arab way of gratitude, the obligations it entailed, and how it irked him that she didn't recall his name. Finally he ventured: "Now we are blood relatives. I am Sabr al-Adawi."

She burst into tears. "I'm sorry, it's post-trauma. I'm glad I saved you," she sobbed. "It's just too much, losing Nick, being in a strange country, not knowing what'll happen next. And then those steps, just to pray for Nick...I'm that desperate, it's pathetic."

"No, you were right to pray to the saint, if you're Christian," he assured her. "I'd do the same with a sheikh if I had to. What else are they for? But truly, if you want to find your husband, I'll help. *W'Allah azim!*"

She was silent, calculating. Sabr wondered what she'd require. They could spend weeks searching the camps and the desert had more wadis than a nomad could explore in a lifetime. He regretted his generosity already...

"Do you ever go to Suez?"

"Sure." He hadn't expected that. "I'm going tomorrow. Why?"

"Take me with you."

5 YASMINA

Dust swept the highway as they cleared the last camps beyond Hurghada, tarmac crumbling as El-Gouna fell behind them. Flatbed trucks laden with girders, cement and machinery trundled past hoardings as long as a beach.

SUEZ CITY – CITY OF HOPE
HQ of the Canal Recovery Zone & Israeli Mandate
300km

Carina noticed Sabr's lip curl. He was waiting for her to pass comment. Should she acknowledge his wounded pride or ignore it? Either would be patronizing. Egypt needed help – the Israelis were willing and able. Having been the first on the scene with assistance – erecting tent cities in Sinai – their response had looked all the more altruistic beside Libya's, whose annexation of Egypt's oilfields had split the Arab world, clearing the way for a UN Mandate that recognised facts on the ground. But she couldn't say that to Sabr...

SUEZ CITY – INVESTORS' PARADISE. Only 285km.
The Israelites parted the Red Sea – Israel will reopen the Suez Canal!

Okay, so that deserved a snort of scorn for Sabr's benefit, yet it would seem gauche after her indifference. Damn his complexes for enmeshing her! She tried to ignore the billboard. A faint smile played on his lips, as if he'd won by manoeuvring her into a corner. Guilt – he was using it like that Gypsy who dangled her baby over their table at El Parco when Nick was still at Reckett, Blythely & Scarpa.
A new sign confronting traffic, edged in red.

SLOW DOWN
Have your ID and Licence ready
Vehicles exceeding the speed limit may be fired on

Sabr spat through the window. He drove with it down and air-con full on, heedless of global warming. Without asking, he took a cassette from the handful she'd taken from Nick's belongings. By now, she'd realized that tapes were the format best suited to Egypt's dust-laden air; technology here was as crude as life, and who could afford an iPod? Nick's own collection of Arab pop cassettes avowed their utility and catchiness.

Violins swelled, drums thudded and a sultry male crooned for his lost love. *Is that how you felt, Nick, why didn't you say?*

As the song faded, Sabr spoke.

"Before the Flood our blood was light. Life was hard but we were happy. Then the Black Day took everything – everything but our memories. These songs hold all the feelings we had. My school friends, the girls on the Corniche; picnics, feasts and weddings..." He turned to face her. "You see?"

A cement truck ahead...

"Watch the road!"

Eyes front, he continued speaking as if nothing had happened.

"Some singers were heroes on the Black Day. Mohammed Tharwat could've escaped – he had money, bodyguards – but he stayed to evacuate his orphanage in Tanta. And Sha'ban told us the truth. 'The thieves are leaving you to die!' he shouted on Nile TV. They interrupted the show and shot him."

She imagined officials mouthing assurances, eyes flicking to their watches. The panic of millions who discovered what was bearing down on them, hours – or minutes – before it obliterated their homes. Traffic stalled, mobs fighting for high ground.

Sabr changed gear and tapes simultaneously. "This is Saiyidi music from Upper Egypt". Staccato drumming and joyous cries filled the car. Steering one-handed, he thumbed a photo from his wallet. "This was my felucca. I took English, Japanese, all nationalities. That's my minibus, in the background."

She'd heard of such trips from Lucy at the V&A, who told all her friends in explicit detail after swearing each to silence. The Sabr in the snapshot looked the kind of stud Lucy had described. Carina glanced at the man beside her. His eyes were soulful as before, but bitter; his polo shirt frayed, its jaunty colours faded.

Sabr replaced the picture and tapped his wallet. "Suez is under the Israelis," he pronounced it *Is-ra-eelis*. "There's a checkpoint outside the city, but I have a pass. Then you'll see what I do for Mr Baines." He rummaged in the glove compartment and showed her a sheaf of documents. "It'll take a few hours."

Whatever. Just get me to Suez and let me find her.

Yasmina wiped glasses and feigned concern for a maudlin drunk. *He'll pass out soon, perhaps I'll have time for tea before the early crowd arrives.* She looked hopefully around the club for a bouncer. *Where are you?* *Licking candy in the backroom?* She hadn't been long at the Euro before she realised that Madam Hoda encouraged the staff to develop habits that put them under her heel. Sexual gratification might be enough for men, but drugs were the way to enslave women. They'd never been taught *that* in Pharmacology. How innocent they'd been!

Poor Aisha, after all they'd been through, to die in this house of shame. She prayed Aisha's weakness would be forgiven and her virtues rewarded in paradise. Surely God would see past her sins to the pure, kindly girl she'd been at Giza. She always wore a *higab* and long skirts, believed tight dresses and jeans were unseemly. She wanted to help people, to work in a hospital. Her parents agreed marriage could wait till she'd established her career. She liked going to films and cafes with her classmates, wrote poetry, sighed over pop stars. She didn't deserve what happened – nobody did. That the Flood was God's will was a terrifying idea. And if it was, surely the survivors had been punished enough? How many years must they suffer?

The drunk laid his face on the bar. *I'd like to tip an ashtray over your head.* Yasmina despised the Euro's clientele, but had to be agreeable. One day her fury would shatter her self-control. But at least she'd resisted the temptation to numb herself with drugs – unlike Aisha. It had grown insidiously. At first Aisha took barbiturates and Valium, to quell the nightmares and panic attacks that had worsened since they moved to Suez. In the camp at El-Arish, you struggled for bare survival. Suez was rough, but there was money to be made – you weren't just rotting in a tent. Yet Aisha's vulnerabilities fed off this margin of optimism, requiring stronger palliatives. She began visiting the backroom, emerging dazed yet serene.

Soon Yasmina noticed that when Aisha got her wages, Hoda consulted her red notebook, the one listing debts. Yasmina's fears were confirmed when she used the staff toilet shortly after Aisha. On the cistern lay a wad of bloodstained tissue and a phial of diamorphine hydrochloride – heroin. That night, Yasmina confronted her in their room. Aisha begged for understanding, vowed that she was already cutting down, would stop soon.

But she didn't. Her debts grew as her flesh shrunk. She abrogated the agreement that Yasmina had struck with Madam Hoda: that they would fish for drinks but not sleep with the apes. Yasmina could endure their infantile jokes and foul breath, their oafish compliments and paws, knowing there was a limit. But Aisha capitulated, let herself be taken upstairs by anyone who had money. "My periods have stopped, Yasi. I won't get pregnant. I can't," she said, as if that was a justification.

A harsh voice interrupted Yasmina's reverie.

"Your make-up is smeared. You're a disgrace." Madam Hoda had crept up to the bar, manoeuvring her bulk on pearly mules. She settled on a barstool, her cigarette case winking.

"Customers expect my girls to look fresh, even if they can't pluck the flowers," she said tartly. "You're not even trying. Only God knows why I hired you. At least your friend would rub herself against the clients."

Her complaints were cut short by an influx of customers: oilmen, aid workers, Israeli officers. Hoda rose with elephantine grace, patting her coiffure.

"Colonel Avi," she cooed, "Mr Brooke, Herr Gunter". Samira and Leila glided towards a banquette as Mustafa began to twirl his cocktail shakers.

"Sit with them. That German ape is loaded," hissed Hoda. So Yasmina fixed her mascara and prepared to laugh at his jokes. *What do you call an Egyptian with a lifebelt? Lucky. How many Egyptians can stand on the Great Pyramid? A million – till they start getting hungry. Or the Nile crocodile that said, "Gimme a break, I'm on a diet."*

An hour later the club was filling fast. Gunter had ordered champagne and whisky at Yasmina's urging and took this as licence to stroke her thighs. Colonel Avi and Leila had already slipped upstairs. She got ready to trot out her excuse. *I'm sorry, I'd love to go with you. But it's the wrong time of the month.* She found it worked well with Protestants and Jews, but Catholics didn't seem bothered. *If I didn't hate them so much it would be easy to succumb to their money,* she thought.

Then the epitome of all she hated swaggered in, greeting Hoda jovially.

"So where's that gorgeous slut Crystal? I've got to hit the road at eight."

Thank God. Sometimes GM stayed till dawn, gambling and using the girls. Crystal was his latest favourite; fragile and addicted as Aisha had been. Yasmina disliked her, but was haunted by the fear that Crystal would die as Aisha had. Yet logically, Crystal only risked an accidental overdose of

Hoda's pharmaceuticals. Aisha's overdose hadn't been an accident. Her killer wouldn't repeat the folly that made Aisha's death imperative. Crystal would be safe because she didn't *know*.

But *Yasmina knew* from what Aisha had said. At the time she'd focused on her injuries, sick with rage and powerlessness. Next day Aisha was dead. Hoda wept crocodile tears and pledged a decent funeral. But Yasmina had seen what Aisha had written before she sank into a coma, and understood her own peril as swiftly as she'd solved formulae at university.

"You're so mysterious," burbled Gunter, "You Eastern women," he burped. "I've tried Turkish before, but never Egyptian. Are you tastier?"

He pawed her breasts. Longing to claw his face, she squirmed free, invoking a call of nature. Gunter was disappointed but felt a genuine urge himself.

"*Ja*, me too," he slurred, weaving towards the men's toilets.

For form's sake and a respite, she went to the ladies'. Hagar was fixing her make-up. "Are you ill? You look awful."

Yasmina grimaced. Wished she could take something that would diminish her disgust and make Gunter vanish. Then she heard shouts and screams from the club. A fight, wait a bit. She rinsed her face, redid her eyes and lips.

It was nearly six before Carina began her search for the Euro Bar. It had taken ages for Sabr to admit that his errands precluded chaperoning her at police headquarters, and agreed to collect her two hours later. Really, she had no intention of wasting any time with the police; if they'd anything to tell her it would have already been reported to Hosni Basha. She had her own lead to pursue, however painful it might prove.

Between depots, she'd noticed a tawdry downtown that had to be her hunting ground. Elsewhere it was hard to tell residential areas from industrial zones, with people squatting factories that had withstood the Flood. According to Sabr, the streets were underwater for a week. Salvage and reconstruction efforts had focused on the docks and power plants, then on the refineries and Canal. The Israelis and foreign contractors had all this in hand, but residents' needs weren't a priority.

She'd seen in Hurghada how foreign workers sustained a micro-economy of bars and restaurants, but Suez was sleazier. Sabr had barely left her outside police HQ when she saw a poster of a woman's silhouette. *Paradise Club – We have what You Want*. Idlers clogged the sidewalks: morose labourers in *galabiyyas*, young men with sports jackets and gelled hair; women in sequinned jeans. The air was thick with grit and mosquitoes. Tacking from one neon archipelago to another across a sullen sea of Egyptians, her quest took her towards the sinking sun, choked by smog.

Her resolve was faltering when she saw the sign. *EURO BAR >>>200m*. Neon arrows guided her round the corner to another sign reading >>>*75m*, subtitled in what she guessed was Hebrew. And there was the bar, a windowless apricot façade above a winking euro symbol. Two guards sharing a waterpipe waved her in without scanning her. The *No Guns* logo was evidently for other people.

The lobby gleamed with fairy lights and dimpled brass, bouncers lounging near a kiosk itemising *Fixed Prices* in euros, shekels and dollars. Carina paid the entry fee but declined vouchers for a deluxe massage, private show, or non-alcoholic intoxicants.

"Feel at home," said the cashier, "First drink on the house". Pulsing music grew louder as she climbed the stairs and pushed open a padded door.

Shards of light careered over faces as a mirror-ball spun above the dance floor, teeth and cigarettes glowing mauve in the ultraviolet. Sidling past banquettes she heard lewd invitations and laughter. Like a fisherman sighting harbour in a storm, she made for the bar, where a few middle-aged foreign men in chinos and utility-vests sat talking.

An Egyptian barman smiled enquiringly. *Could you trust the drinks in a place like this? Women got drugged in clubs, even in London. Calm down*, she told herself, *that man's drinking Sprite from the bottle. I'll have a Sprite. No problem*. She ordered one.

"You're English, right?" said a drinker. "I like guessing from people's accents." He laughed. "I'd say you're from London"

"Spot on." He had a kippered face and wore a Rolex – an engineer or an oilman. The wall behind the bar was covered with stickers for drilling and engineering firms. Then she noticed a crest from a US warship and a shield with a Star of David, and wondered if he might be something military.

"Steve Redman, from Bechtel," he offered. "Rebuilding the refinery for when the Israelis re-open the canal. And you, with an NGO?"

"Umm, no, I'm not an aid worker, I'm an art historian. My name's Carina" – she paused, unsure which surname to give. Redman perked up a notch.

"Let me buy you a proper drink. No problem, they're not spiked – leastways not behind the bar. Sometimes a new face tries their luck in the crowd, but Hoda makes sure they never come back. Local grifters stick to other bars – it's safer for them."

"Who's Hoda?"

"The owner, over there." Carina craned to see a stout Arab woman with lacquered hair, tapping a desk-calculator and smoking. She glanced up and snapped at a barmaid. Carina looked away.

"So what's an art historian doing in Suez?" Redman asked. "Not the kind of place I'd associate with art, 'less you're talking antiquities."

"Personal reasons, actually. My husband went missing last month. He was working for an agency, as an auditor. He hasn't been found yet; I came out to see what was being done. The agency has been very kind and I've met Hosni Basha" – she paused to let the name register – "But still no sign of Nick."

"Right, I get it. I remember hearing about your husband. Everyone was concerned – still are," Redman added lamely. "I'm sure the cops are working on it. Hell, there was a guy from Schlumberger that went AWOL for weeks – shacked up somewhere." He faltered. "The point I'm making is..."

His words were lost in a commotion at the bar. Hoda was standing to confront a foreigner. His shirt hung loose, his face was flushed. He looked familiar.

"Fuck this!" he roared. "I paid for pussy. Not for her to nod off on me!"

It was that Neanderthal from the party at El-Gouna, GM. He thrust his shirt into his belt and pushed through the crowd. Someone must have complained, for suddenly GM was pummelling a man to the floor. "Cunt, you won't be fucking no-one either. Not that you'd a hope with that frigid bitch Yasmina." He stomped away.

His victim rose painfully, helped by a friend. "My rib...is broken", he gasped, "Get me to the Israeli hospital." The helper paused to speak to an Egyptian girl and threw banknotes on the table. The girl laughed as they left, a scornful Nefertiti in Lycra.

"Excuse me," Carina told Redman, "I think I see someone I know."

Returning to the table Yasmina found Samira and the apes gone and a foreign woman sitting there. "Wait, stay," she blurted as Yasmina turned away. "We need to talk."

Why? Some Westerners were feminists who desired their own sex. Was this plump, ill-dressed lady one of them, or merely a wife who hadn't yet learned that trusting a man is trusting water in a sieve? "I can't talk with customers unless they buy me a drink," Yasmina said coolly. "I'm with friends."

The woman rolled her eyes. "They've left. I spoke to your friend – I thought she was you at first – she said you were in the toilet. So I sat down to wait for you."

"What do you want?"

"My husband disappeared a month ago," she said flatly. "One of the last emails he got was from a Yasmina, wanting to meet him at the Euro. And I found a card for the bar in his wallet. It wasn't hard to put them together – or find you." She slid a photo from her shirt pocket. "That's Nick...do you know him?"

As Yasmina's mind flinched in shock, a distracted cortex compared Nick's image with her own memories of him. In the photo he looked flabby and complacent, whereas she'd known him as thin and nervous, even before he got scared. And now, right where it all began, his wife was ready to pelt Yasmina with questions....

"You *do*. So tell me – "

Yasmina cut her short.

"We can't talk here. My shift finishes at eight. Come to my room – it's not far. Wait by the kebab stall on the corner and wear a headscarf – do you have one?"

Nick's wife nodded sternly – a formidable lady to have tracked him to a brothel in Suez, but still naïve. Yasmina considered not showing up at the stall and hiding indoors until Nick's wife went home. But she couldn't deny her a spoonful of truth.

Not after she'd led Nick on.

Her Saint George, he joked, before it turned sour

Disappeared meant dead, the Flood had taught her.

Yasmina's room was smaller than their bathroom in London, filled by a sagging queen-size bed and cluttered vanity table, posters of fluffy cats tacked to the walls. *A real tart's bedroom*, Carina sneered as the girl delved under the mattress. *Did you bring Nick here, did you fuck him on that bed?*

In mute reproof, Yasmina produced a primus stove, kettle, spoons and glasses. As tea brewed, she smiled wanly. "I know what you're thinking, but it wasn't like that." She stroked the bedspread. "My friend Aisha used to share it. We never brought men here. She...worked upstairs at the Euro, and I don't." Her chin lifted. "I just talk with customers, make them buy drinks. That's all."

"And Nick?"

"He was different."

"Different?"

"Like the English gentlemen I read about in school."

"Oh." *A lame response, she couldn't help it.*

"He held my hand once, but only after we'd got to know each other. He cared."

I bet he did.

But maybe Nick hadn't taken the plunge. He was a wuss with women, after all. And Carina couldn't help being impressed by Yasmina's aura of sincerity, until it occurred to her that prosititutes were artful liars.

"When did you last see him? You arranged to meet on Saturday, did he turn up?"

"No, but I knew where he'd been. I'd told him about Aisha and the idol."

"Come again?"

"The Anubis she saw before she was killed."

"Killed? Jesus..."

"It's complicated -"

Carina's SMS bleeped.

Wr ru?

Shit! Sabr wanted to drag her back to Hurghada just when she was getting somewhere. She couldn't think how to explain it, so she simply messaged: *Cu l8r in hrghda.* He'd take her word for it.

Meanwhile, Yasmina had changed into a housedress and was plucking black robes from a hanger.

"Can't the housework wait? I want to hear about Nick."

"I'm not cleaning. We're leaving. I'll show you where I took him. Others know more than me, you should ask them. Put this on." She handed Carina a robe and showed her how to wear it by draping herself in the other. It covered her from head to foot, leaving her face bare, but with plenty of fabric to draw across it if necessary.

Carina hesitated. This sounded risky, yet it was real progress. She didn't fancy wandering around in a burqa, but if journalists had done it so could she. Almost immediately she found that its floor-length hem was like a pesky cat underfoot. She would have fallen on the stairs if Yasmina hadn't held her.

They emerged by a backdoor into a rancid alley. Dogs barked.

Yasmina gripped her wrist. "We have to reach the *mogaf* before curfew."

"*Curfew? Mogaf?*"

"*Ssshh...*"

Mogaf meant a bus and taxi depot. Curfew was self-explanatory. Israeli troops searching vehicles at sandbagged checkpoints. She sat squashed beside Yasmina and three older women in burqas on the backseat of a minibus. If they could get outside the city before curfew the Israelis wouldn't stop them, Yasmina confided.

They made it with ten minutes to spare.

The minibus assumed the sanctity of an ark; passengers opening packets of crisps or settling down to sleep. As the anonymous women snored, Carina strained to hear Yasmina's words, her breath caressing Carina's ear.

"You know how I first met Nick? It was the day my friend died of an overdose. She went upstairs and didn't return. So I went to the room she used and found her. I shut the door, went downstairs and was sick in the toilet. When I got back Hoda was angry, said I wasn't working hard enough. The club was nearly empty and the other girls were with a group. Nick was sitting alone. 'Make him buy liquor,' she told me.

"Maybe you can guess how I felt. Trying to smile, pretending I was interested in his job, his life. And he didn't even order fancy drinks – just a cocktail for me and coffee himself. Hoda was glaring at me from the bar, and Aisha lay upstairs..."

"I don't believe this."

"What do wives know about men?" Yasmina hissed.

6 LOSING THE PLOT

In adapting to Hurghada, Nick became a stranger to himself. No pinstriped suits or polished brogues – most of Salvation First's staff wore chinos and Timberlands. With an agency laptop slung from his shoulder ('durable in extreme conditions' its manual said), Nick fancied he looked like a real aid worker. He'd sent Carina a photo of him hoping for a flattering reply but she only whinged about her Gazprom exhibition at the V&A.

So much for his feelings...

Each day he steeled himself for the piss-stench of the camps; the feral children demanding baksheesh. Eventually he stopped giving any, felt guilty but consoled himself that few aid workers did. It was demeaning, fostered dependency and rarely benefited the neediest, their credo had it. A sober assessment of a bottomless pit...

While it was easy to rationalise baksheesh away, food was another matter. He'd never shared Carina's weight obsession or guilt about eating well – yet here he grew nauseated by the Residency's buffet. Fried eggs, hash browns and blueberry muffins for breakfast; beefsteaks and burgers for dinner. Lo-calorie salads swam in Hawaian dressings ladled from tubs. His colleagues went back for seconds and left them half eaten. He assumed the remains were consumed by the kitchen staff or sold on the black market.

Beyond the Residency, Egyptians ate donated wheat, rice and beans – or stale MREs if their camp was at the end of a long supply chain. He'd visited a camp where people rioted after months of eating 'Cat food'. Fortunately their fury had been assuaged by proper rations before he arrived. Even so, Black Berets watched from the rooftops, cradling Kalashnikovs. Usually the police kept out of the camps, which locals called *ezba*, or villages. He wasn't sure if it was ironic or expressed a genuine yearning for their old homes. There was so much he didn't understand about aid work, his fellow 'internationals' and, least of all, Egyptians.

International law defined those in Salvation First's care as Internally Displaced Persons rather than refugees, but staff were encouraged to say 'beneficiaries' or 'clients' and internal memos full of imperatives such as 'client-focused performance' and 'beneficiary enpowerment'. From distributing food and medicine to erecting water tanks, every action required a carousel of invoices between contractors, Salvation First and UN enities (the list of acronyms ran to three pages). To audit a warehouse involved inspecting accounts, receipts, sacks or machinery, to complete an interactive form with 162 checkboxes.

What Egyptians made of it, he couldn't say. SF had 35,000 'nationals' on its payroll: drivers, warehousemen, mechanics and labourers. Their calloused hands were always ready to help if Nick needed a stepladder to inspect crates in a warehouse. When his Land Cruiser had a flat tyre the driver refused Nick's assistance – pointing at his laptop and miming an oily-fingered mess. No hint of reproach, even when Nick trampled a prayer rug with his shoes by mistake.

He knew that they couldn't afford to offend their employers, yet some risked clumsy thefts that an audit was sure to uncover. In his second week on the job, three loaders bolted in their lunch break when Nick began checking. Calling Head Office to report the scam, he'd been told to move on to the next depot and never learnt SF's response – but when he appeared at the grain silos in Safaga next day, foremen quaked. Try as he might to avoid behaving like a potentate, he was treated as one.

Even with the best intentions it was easy to put your foot in it – or *on* it, like that prayer rug. Aid workers had been lynched for less in Afghanistan. But here there was no such fanaticism; if you believed SF's evangelists, Islam's appeal in Egypt was waning. Nearly every mosque in the Valley had been destroyed by the Flood; those in the camps were makeshift, overcrowded.

Yet three of Egypt's holiest monasteries had survived unscathed – Saint Anthony's and Saint Paul's in the Red Sea Hills and a convent overlooking the Valley. The 'Miracle of Dirunka' was cited as proof of God's intent. On the morning of the Flood, local Coptic Christians had flocked to the Convent of the Virgin outside the city of Assyut for the inauguration of their new bishop, thus escaping the fate of their Muslim neighbours, drowned as the Saved watched in terror from their hilltop Ark. Surely it demonstrated which faith offered salvation and which was falsehood? Had not Egypt been Christian, long before Islam? Floods were God's way of punishing sinful humanity, of sparing some to make amends. God was merciful.

It was restful in Saint Anthony's refectory, with lunch cleared away and monks in the orchards. Nick closed his laptop, drummed its lid and sighed.

Figures were figures. Three 4m x 6m silage tanks of heavy-duty polyurethane dyed UN-blue to order, @$15,625. Over $50,000 for tankering water; $85,600 of bladder tanks, pumps and hoses. And that was before factoring in the pilgrim convoys: buses, drivers, petrol. Baines mightn't like it, but he felt duty-bound to raise the issue.

It was awkward, he admired Baines. Nobody could doubt his success in industry before he entered aid work at a senior level, nor fault his personal habits. Softly-spoken yet peppery, he neither smoked nor drank nor seemed to have a sex life. His work and faith were so all-consuming there was no room for anything else but a nostalgic devotion to the North Carolina Tar Heels. He'd been a line-backer at college, so Nick had heard from a logistician who hailed from Baines's home state.

A sportsman turned engineering tycoon, turned humanitarian saviour: a remarkable man. Yet Nick sensed a dark star on the verge of implosion. Baines had no outlet for the pressures of his work; a nervous breakdown would be a personal tragedy with dire consequences for the refugees in his care. Nick was in no position to query Baines's mental health, but an auditor was entitled to doubts about cost-effectiveness...

"Hey! How're those figures? Nobody been stealing spoons I hope." Baines's voice echoed off the flagstones.

"No, but a few line items *do* concern me," Nick ventured. "Baptisms and pilgrim convoys cost almost $500,000 last year. *Some* members of the public might reckon that disproportionate, beside $800,000 for upgrading antenatal clinics or $2.5 million for schools. Mightn't some donors be unhappy?"

Baines scowled. "I'm sad you're hung up over a misconception, Nick. Baptisms and pilgrimages are *definitely* within our remit – a core objective, in fact. I realise some folk – let's call them *secularists* – might object to that, but none of us at Salvation First finds any reason to doubt our priorities – nor do our donors. Schoolbooks and clinics are important, and we're aiming to spend plenty more on both. But right now we have to establish a moral-spiritual base, or *nothing* will turn out right. There's no long term without a short term."

"I don't understand."

"I'm talking about Egypt's recovery, a new society. Muslim culture is stagnant – in Egypt or any other country you can name. Oh, I know they were civilized when Europe was in the Dark Ages, how the Arabs preserved the classical legacy that inspired the Renaissance – but they've stalled ever since. Can you think of anything good they've done in the last 500 years? No

– but we all know the bad stuff. War, terrorism, tyranny, oppressing women, squandering wealth on palaces and weapons of mass destruction…"

"Isn't that over-simplifying? What gives us the right to decide Egypt's future?"

"Nature hates a vacuum. The Wahhabis or Shi'a would be pushing their poison if we weren't here. The Flood was a catastrophe, but it provided a unique opportunity to start afresh. Christian values will hard-wire this society for progress and democracy, prevent it from relapsing into the mess that prevailed before. You're sceptical, but I'm not into wishful thinking. Our theology is rooted in reality."

"I still don't get how converting Muslims to Christianity will do all that."

"The Chinese say that a journey of a thousand miles begins with a single step. Baptism is the first; the rest follow naturally. The practicalities are complex but the essence isn't. Take land reclamation in the Valley. The world's leading agri-businesses are investing millions of dollars and the kind of know-how Egypt could never match, to create farming communities with decent housing and sanitation, schools and clinics. Settlers will be taught best practices and given seeds and equipment. All we ask is they worship the true faith, work hard and live cleanly. What's wrong with that?"

Nick was stumped. If baptisms were in SF's mission statement, no impropriety had occurred. Accountancy was an exacting profession with a rigorous code of ethics, but human rights and faith were beyond its remit.

Besides spoiling his appetite the camps nixed Nick's libido. In London he'd regularly woken with a stiffy that detumesced over toast and the *Telegraph*. Here his penis was simply for pissing. It was, advised the *Red Cross Handbook for Emergency Workers*, a common reaction to stress – in Nick's case surely caused by disorientation, not danger. Moreover, Egypt had none of the sexual stimuli that bombarded him in England. No celeb boobs or bare tums in the aisles of Waitrose. Egyptian women wore baggy black or grubby pastel wraps, younger ones swollen by pregnancy, the middle-aged toothless. Only adolescent girls were beautiful and his imagination shied away from them.

In theory, he might have fancied some of the female international staff – outnumbered ten to one by guys – but they were married, pledged to celibacy till Mr Right proposed, or so utterly wholesome that Nick gladly left them to unwed evangelists in the fug of hormones that hung over the Residency's disco (no alcohol permitted). How it found an outlet he didn't know – or cared.

But he did find a new vice – smoking *sheesha* waterpipes.

In England he'd once smoked but gave up long before he met Carina, who hated tobacco. Here, he'd idly tried a waterpipe at a cafe near Mersa Allam and discovered that he enjoyed the soothing apple-flavoured smoke and being fussed over by an attendant with tongs and bits of charcoal. It wasn't like puffing away outside your office or a friend's flat. It was leisurely, sensual, ceremonial…

The Residency was non-smoking, like the cafes in Hurghada frequented by staffers. For a *sheesha* you had to go to an *ahwa* – a shabby tiled den serving black tea and coffee, backgammon and TV the only diversions for its Egyptian male clientele. Such places were at every junction on the highway; there was one across the street from the Residency. Its 'tea boy' was pushing seventy, a wiry Nubian whom Nick secretly nicknamed Mr Sheesha. He rarely said much even to locals, just took their orders and fixed their *sheeshas*. Deftly, unobtrusively, he had the bowl alight in seconds.

Once, Nick brought Morrison. The evangelist objected to the TV showing Al-Jazeera. *Propaganda, the only trustworthy channel is Fox, the rest are liberal or satanic.* Nick stifled his irritation and ordered a *sheesha*. When Morrison cited the destruction of the ancient Library of Alexandria as proof of Islam's hatred of learning, a long-forgotten nugget of Nick's schooling surfaced.

"It's a myth, Luke. Muslims never burned the Library; Christian mobs did. Muslims were blamed later, to help justify the Crusades."

If Mr Sheesha understood this he gave no sign, but with hindsight Nick saw this as the moment when the old man decided to reveal his fluent English. Thereafter, whenever Nick came alone, Mr Sheesha initiated conversations and controversy.

"The Israelis destroyed the High Dam, to enslave us."

"Come on!" Nick protested. "We've all seen that video of the jihadis with their bomb, saying that Egypt must be punished for betraying the Palestinians. Why should the Israelis blow up the Dam if Egypt had signed the Settlement? It doesn't make sense."

Each of Mr Sheesha's explanations was wilder than the last. It was to stop the Muslim Brotherhood from revoking the treaty, after the Jews failed to regime-change Iran and Syria. It was British Intelligence and the Royal

Family, getting away with murder as they'd killed Diana and Dodi Al-Fayed with a disco light. It was Bill Gates and the Rothschilds, ready to brand the neck of every Muslim as they'd barcoded Westerners. Always a plot of some kind – *mo'amera*, he called it.

Eventually Nick could take any non sequitur with equanimity.

"Mr Nick, are there mosques in London?"

"Sure, lots of Muslims."

"But do you *know* any? Do you know their imams?"

Some preachers sprang to mind, but they'd been expelled years ago. "Er, no, I don't know any imams, but there's the Regent's Park mosque."

"I trust your choice, Mr Nick. Please take a gift to this sheikh – a recording of our Sufi music." Mr Sheesha placed a cassette on the table, bearing a palm tree logo.

Drugs, Nick speculated. He could prise open the cassette before it went in his luggage. *A terrorist message?* He'd listen to the tape and if it didn't sound like Sufi music he'd bin it. But surely he was being paranoid? Mr Sheesha was just making the point that he wasn't a beggar – maybe he was a bit loopy?

That night he played it in his room. Not the usual dervish swirl of oboes and drums, just a man croaking over a droning viol. Nick liked Arab pop, but he could only endure a minute of this dirge. He put the cassette with his other tapes and forgot it.

✳✳✳

One morning he awoke with a boner, surprise forgotten as his hand quickened. In the afterglow he heard voices singing in the conference hall and smiled, stroking his thighs. Sound, touch, smell – his senses were invigorated.

The rip tide of his libido roiled all morning. Mesmerised by the hair of a redhead in the queue for lunch, by a pale throat swallowing at the next table, back in his room he wanked again. Next day he was captivated by Trudy in Finance, her elegant hands caressing paper. As his flipbin filled with Kleenex, he considered declaring his lust at Sunday service – not that he'd ever attended, but sinners were encouraged to participate. Yet SF's pastoral care was spurned by engineers who bragged of brothels once they'd sunk a few beers. No way would he blab for them to laugh about it...

Instead, Nick trawled for details. *Hurghada is out. You have to go to Suez for fun.* So he learnt at a restaurant near Head Office. *There are lots of clubs where you can find women*, his informant confided, lurching away. *But the Euro is best...*

✳✳✳

Nick was halfway through his favourite accountancy joke when he noticed her shoulders shaking. The dim lighting left room for doubt, but he couldn't convince himself she was convulsed with laughter. *She's crying, what did I say wrong? I haven't even touched her – not that I would.* Everything he'd heard of the Euro's reputation was confirmed by the girls on a nearby table. One was necking, another fondling her bloke's crotch.

But this Yasmina ...she wasn't like the others. For all the dusky cleavage and waxed legs on show, she'd been as remote as Venus till a moment ago.

"What's wrong? Did I say something? I'm sorry! Please don't cry. Here, take this..." Nick fumbled for a hankie. She wiped her cheeks. "Maybe I can help."

Yasmina tapped her glass. "You're not spending enough. Madam Hoda expects each client to spend $50 an hour. You've only spent $15.50."

Nick felt simultaneously cheated and protective, still cherishing the delusion that she was drawn to him. She was really upset – or was it an act? He looked at her heaving breasts (pear-sized) and decided to push the boat out.

"So what would keep Madam happy, champagne? I'll order and you tell me what's bothering you. Stop crying, she's watching."

Yasmina wept silently. "Tell me," he urged, "And *smile*, she's looking".

A waiter brought a magnum of Crüet de Haifa and Madam Hoda switched her attention to some new arrivals, summoning more bargirls from the shadows.

"Was it something today, or bad memories? I imagine you've been through a lot."

"You *can't* imagine," she retorted. "Having your whole world become a nightmare – losing your family, home and friends. Forgetting your hopes to queue for water, depending on enemies for charity and welcoming the chance to play a whore ..."

Mortified, he groped for words. "Right, you have to think of the future. Getting out, I mean. Maybe I could find you a job in Hurghada. How old are you?"

"Twenty-one" – it sounded like an accusation. "I was at Giza University when the Flood came. Our faculty heard the news in the afternoon. My own town was underwater by then; so was Aisha's. We fled together for the Giza Plateau, through the chaos on Pyramids Road. Twice I fell and she pulled me up."

"Amazing – and where's this Aisha now?"

Yasmina's eyes brimmed. With a fluttering gesture, she rose and swayed off to speak with Madam Hoda. Hoda watched incredulously as Yasmina returned to him.

"Come upstairs." She touched his arm, her face a soft mask. "I want to show you something." The bargirls at the next table sniggered. Nick itched to proclaim his innocence – to suavely decline her proposal – but his tongue felt like a sock in his mouth. *Go with the flow*, he rationalized, feeling proud of his prize – or was he hers?

The stair-carpet was sticky underfoot as he followed her buttocks like a hound. . "Have fun," someone called. Nick flushed. What am I doing?

But he trailed her along a corridor to a padlocked chipboard door.

Unlocking it, she drew him in, her hand soft in the dark, scent mingling with a mousy odour. He was poised to caress her when she snapped on the light in a windowless garret. On a soiled mattress lay a teenager, a syringe hanging from her arm, trailing over a bedside table smeared with lipstick and broken phials.

"See – look here." Yasmina indicated a livid pink scrawl.

His stomach heaved. A fly buzzed.

As he blundered outside to vomit, Yasmina began shrieking.

7 THE HEN WILL PAY US!

Carina felt sick with fury. She could imagine Nick flirting with some floozy at a tax seminar, but never this nightmare. He couldn't be so reckless, so unlucky, such a bastard. The bitch was lying. Yet this was the only lead she had to his disappearance. She had to think like a detective. "Why my husband, was it blackmail?" she hissed.

"No, no." Yasmina murmured. "He seemed honest; he was an auditor. I hoped he'd make a scandal. But I was scared. I had to make him understand what happened, what Aisha scrawled on the table. *O/D.* – it wouldn't mean anything to most people, but any pharmacologist would understand. If she'd meant to kill herself she'd have left a note. *O/D* was the best she could do to warn me that GM killed her."

"The engineer?"

"Him – he took her whenever he was at the club. Even when he was so drunk his carrot shrivelled up. Then he hit her and called her a whore. To prove he was a *man* he showed her a gold statue of Anubis, said he'd found treasures beyond dreams. Then he assaulted her with the idol."

"O God."

"Yes, God saw, as I saw Aisha afterwards. She told me what he'd done and how he warned her to be silent. Whatever lies were told afterwards, I know the truth. But every tree sways in the wind. If you hadn't found me tonight, I'd never have spoken again – telling Nick was mad enough. But you can listen to Hani, Nick did."

"Hani?"

"We're going to see him now. You can ask him everything."

Lurches and grinding gears sounded their ascent in the darkness as the lights of Suez receded. Their headlights flitted over boulders, goats and children, kerosene and shit on the wind. Eventually the minibus reached a plateau, halting amongst high-walled villas. Carina struggled out, stiff with cold. Yasmina led her to a steel door and muttered through a slit. Bolts retracted, a man peered out and beckoned them in.

Soon they were warming themselves over a brazier in a lounge hung with icons – valuable ones, Carina judged. It seemed to fit what Yasmina had told her about Hani. Before the Flood he'd been a master goldsmith, working for jewellers across Cairo. His knowledge of their strong rooms and caches was the basis of his present career, advising robbers where to look in flooded basements, valuing loot and brokering sales in Suez. He owed Yasmina a debt, for some unspecified reason to do with the Euro Bar.

Stooped, in a grey *galabiyya* and slippers, Hani greeted Yasmina like a favourite niece, smiling as they conversed in Arabic. "Welcome, my house is yours," he told Carina, waving them towards a sofa as a sleepy-eyed boy brought tea.

"Mm, yes, Mr Nick was here some weeks ago," Hani confided between slurps. "We talked for hours. Not just business, but matters between man and God." He nodded at a pearl-encrusted Virgin. "He wanted evildoers punished, murderers brought to justice. He said Mari Girgis was England's saint, too."

"Sorry?"

He indicated another icon, of a sloe-eyed knight spearing a dragon from a white horse. Saint George – minus the Crusader cross.

"But what did Nick mean?" She couldn't imagine him using such imagery, let alone confronting evil with a lance.

"You've met GM, yes? For over a year he was my best customer. He bought gems and antiquities to sell abroad. The *antikas* were stolen from museums on the Black Day. The government saved Tutankhamun's gold, but left thousands of artefacts behind. Many were taken by staff or looters; others were found in the mud, long afterwards.

"One of my finders was Abu Karim. He'd always been a thief – he'd steal the kohl from your eyes – him and his brothers. Nine months ago, they started bringing me wonderful *antikas* – gold statues, jewellery, ivory chests. GM bought many..." He stopped, embarrassed.

"Go on, please."

"GM pushed me to let him meet Abu Karim. They didn't share any language so I thought I could control things. But GM outsmarted me" – Hani laughed mirthlessly – "He slipped Abu Karim a note in Arabic, suggesting they meet in secret. The rat took the bait, and from then on I never saw another of those *antikas*."

"So GM started dealing with him directly. That's what you told Nick? And I suppose Nick planned to expose him...but hang on, didn't you also say murder?"

"Yes, there's more. Abu Karim stopped bringing me *antikas*, but I'm sure he kept finding them – in one place, not different locations. But finders keep their spots secret. And that secret died with him." Hani cleared his throat. "One night they went back to the site, taking their cousin along. Only the cousin returned, screaming about devils. Two days later a boatman found Abu Karim and his brothers near the Nile. They'd been gutted like sheep, tied to poles with their own innards. May God have mercy on them".

"Didn't anyone investigate?"

"Not the police, but his family. Uncles and cousins took their guns and went to look. But they were shot at; four were killed, six hurt. After that nobody wanted to risk their lives – not against devils." He saw Carina's expression. "You might not believe it, but people in the Citadel do. They've seen the lights on the plateau and heard the djinn fighting among themselves when the wind carries the sound across the Nile. I don't blame them for being frightened. I wouldn't go near the place."

"Djinn?" she said. "You don't mean genies? Come on, be serious." They stared at her po-faced, daring her to laugh at their superstitions. There was no point in antagonising them; she had to focus on essentials. "Nick didn't say he was going there? Surely you talked him out of it!"

Hani replied: "Calm yourself. Perhaps he considered it, but he couldn't have done anything without Abu Karim's cousin, and that's unlikely."

"How can I be sure? Can I speak to this cousin?"

"Tonight is impossible; tomorrow, God willing. I'll send a message to the Citadel, but it may take time to find Tariq. It's after one now. We must sleep. I have a room for guests. Please come this way."

Carina awoke at ten, disoriented. It was reassuring to see Yasmina with rolls and cheese for breakfast. Hani's household had been up for hours; the message had been sent. Any reply would be passed on. Meanwhile, perhaps she'd like to see the Muqattam by day? She wouldn't attract attention wearing a headscarf and *melaya*, Yasmina assured her. Carina made a mental note not to call the robe a burqa in the future. It only covered your face if you wanted it to.

The Muqattam turned out to be a dusty plateau, eerily colonized in imitation of Tuscon, Arizona, before being abandoned to the Third World. Beauty parlours and KFC outlets gaped emptily at wheel-less cars as people rode past on donkey-carts and bicycles. The inhabitants were clearly of a different class than the original residents, squatting on kerbs spitting peanut husks, wiping their noses on the sleeves of their *galabiyyas*.

Yasmina explained how the rich had fled for Sinai in their Volvos as the poor discovered their peril and fought to reach high ground. For those in Bab al-Wazir or El-Khalifa, salvation was nearby: the Citadel loomed above their neighbourhoods, its mighty ramparts only surpassed by the natural fortress of the Muqattam Hills, behind. Mobs burst into the Citadel and swarmed up Muqattam Road to loot the villas. Many drifted away after the floodwaters subsided, but others ventured down to pick through the wreckage, clashing with the Bedouin that had fed their goats on Cairo's rubbish dumps, till each acknowledged the other's tenacity and agreed: *We are cousins – against the world*.

"Now you'll see the city," Yasmina warned, leading Carina through a derelict pizzeria, to a terrace with a crumbling balustrade. "There."

Far below was the Citadel, a sandcastle spared by an oil slick, minarets like lances above the head and shoulders of a mosque, dwarfing enclosures where people milled round bonfires. If you looked no further it might have been an engraving by a romantic artist, captivated by the Orient. But the reality she saw when she lifted her eyes was Armageddon...

It was if a septic tank had exploded, effluent thickened by rubble, covering the entire land except the hill beneath them and a faraway plateau. Through the oozing khaki slurry flowed a stream of piss that was the Nile. Dazed by the scale of the devastation, Carina groped for minutiae: twisted trains and bridges, trees and cars poking from the mud. Everywhere, each detail, vile desecration...

She might have wept but Yasmina dragged her away.

Walking back to the villa Yasmina was relentlessly positive, describing the stratagems that enabled people to live on the plateau. The Citadel had a well dug in olden times, but the Muqattam had always relied on piped water. Now people used donkeys or camels to carry water from the Nile, built cisterns to catch showers in winter, and hung tarpaulins over pits in the sand to harvest moisture overnight. A single pit might collect twenty litres a day. A park on a spur of the Muqattam supplied fruit and vegetables, given irrigation.

Back at the villa, there was news: the cousin, Tariq, had arrived.

An eleven-year-old urchin whose filthy fingers darted over the sofa (earning him a rebuke from Hani) and Carina's mobile (she smiled weakly) to the cigarettes on the table. He lit up hungrily. "Who's the hen? Is she looking for a fuck-boy?" he snapped in gutter Arabic.

Son of dirt – Yasmina couldn't believe his insolence. Hani slapped the table. "You came here for money – keep your tongue clean or you'll go back to the Citadel with nothing but blisters," he warned.

Hastily Yasmina poured water on burning rice. "Never mind ...This lady has come all the way from England to hear your adventures. She doesn't want to ficky-ficky." As Tariq digested that, Yasmina promised Carina she'd translate his words in a moment. Everyone waited for him to speak.

"I'll tell you coz my cousins are dead and the loot's gone." He swiped a finger across his brow, the gesture meaning *Maktoub*, our fate is written on our foreheads. "They kept the secret for ages before Abu Karim told me how he looked down to check his footing in the mud, and saw gold. An inch of luck beats an acre of cleverness! So he got digging and found more treasures from the Siq"

"I don't understand."

Tariq shrugged. "Abu Karim worked in Jordan once. He saw an ancient city at the end of a wadi no wider than a donkey. The Siq, he called it, I dunno why."

Yasmina half-understood: *Petra. The boy meant Petra.* "So?"

"He said the entrance was like that but narrower and full of mud. They bust their guts digging it out, but they couldn't squeeze up the shaft. So they needed me".

"You went up a shaft? Alone?"

"Nah, I never got there. We meant to arrive when the sun was in the eyes of folks in Tura, but the devils rose from the grass ahead of us. They caught my cousins and made them kneel. I ran and hid in a canebrake. When dawn came they'd gone, praise God."

Yasmina shuddered. "God be praised." She stroked his arm consolingly; he hugged her clumsily. *Ugh*, he stank. She shook him off.

He seized Carina's mobile.

"Show me games."

While he thumbed, Yasmina related his tale in English.

Carina's face fell. "What did he mean by devils?"

"Must I ask?"

"It could be important."

For the first time, the boy's voice quavered. "Like men, but with skull faces and hairy backs. My cousins were shouting, I didn't see what happened next..."

Yasmina guessed he knew how their bodies were found. She ended her translation, "Enough?"

"Not yet. Ask him if Nick wanted to go there?"

Tariq replied volubly, miming a driver.

"He says Nick talked of trying, but not with a boat. He feared crossing the mud that way, said he'd use the air rider instead". Yasmina frowned. "I don't know the English word. It's like a car that sits on a fat rubber cushion. A salvage team used one last summer, clearing out the steelworks at Helwan".

"A hovercraft, you mean?"

"I guess."

"Jesus – he took a *hovercraft*?"

"Tariq can't say. He hasn't seen any since the Nile began to drop. Maybe Nick found one, maybe not. Tariq doesn't know; they only *talked* about it."

"So he *could* have gone looking for this Sick?"

"Only God knows."

"I'm not taking that for an answer," Carina snorted. "I want to go there, see if there's any sign of him. If there isn't, but that bastard GM is tomb-robbing, someone can arrest him and make him talk." She looked triumphantly at Yasmina.

"You don't know the danger."

"That's not stopping me. I want Tariq to guide me and you to come too." Yasmina gaped. "I'm serious, I'll pay you. Tariq's been there, he knows the river. You're both survivors, you need money. I'm set on finding Nick whatever it costs. I haven't been through a flood but I can handle swamps – I've walked in the Peak District."

Tariq butted in, demanding a translation. Yasmina had hardly begun when he slapped his thighs and crowed. "*W'allah*, the hen will pay us! In blues or greens, mind – no *Yahudis*." He used the Suez argot for euros and dollars, but spurned the shekels that were the Recovery Zone's third currency.

"What's his answer?"

Maktoub, Yasmina accepted her fate. She'd plunged Nick into a cesspit, she owed his wife recompense. They were both looking at her expectantly.

"He said, 'Visa or MasterCard?'"

Eventually they settled on two thousand greens split fifty-fifty, half upfront. Tariq swore he'd take them as far as the spot where his cousins had fallen and describe the site as they'd told him. Beyond that, their fate was in God's hands.

8 TARIQ'S RIFLE

They descended from the Muqattam on donkeys, Tariq in the lead. The hen clung to her beast, gawping at the precipices and potholed tarmac. *Trust women to worry when things were looking up!* As the minarets of the Citadel drew closer, a file of donkeys laden with copper pipes came up the road. Tariq confided to Yasmina that he scorned their loot. 'White is gold above black' was his watchword. Players, TVs and fridges were ruined by water; smart finders ransacked the upper floors of blocks that had withstood the Flood. The only risks were a run-in with other finders or if the building collapsed – *maktoub.*

Yasmina wasn't impressed – the snooty whore. She should remember whose territory they were entering. The Citadel was *his* world. One word from him to the guys and she'd be spreadeagled in an alley. At a fanged gate where buses once turned around, Tariq bade them dismount and entrusted the animals to an older kid with the condescension of a Porsche owner to a car-hop.

Ignoring prying bystanders, he chivvied the women towards a toppled minaret that spanned an oily pond. Awnings flapped in the fetid wind sweeping across a plain of sludge. Acres of tenements had simply dissolved, leaving hardly a brick, mocked by skeletal towers in the distance, beacons for looters.

Tariq let them wilt in the sun while he prowled the souk. Having scavenged with anyone that would take him, he knew what was needed but had always lacked the cash. Now, with some greens in his fist (and the rest in his drawers), he satisfied his desire for a flashlight, an axe, a crowbar, boots and gloves, and a real weapon. Ever since the Black Day he'd dreamt of a gun that would earn him respect. His rusty flick-knife was a joke. A toothpick, the guys called it.

But today, when he was flush, there wasn't much to buy – a battered carbine that might've washed down from Aswan; a police officer's slam with a dodgy slide, which the seller offered to fix for thirty extra. Others only sold bullets. He'd almost reached the last stall when he saw it... a wondrous rifle tall as he, fit for a king.

He imagined the guys' faces, twisted with envy.

The seller wanted a hundred but Tariq beat him down to sixty. "Your manliness exceeds your generosity," the man swore as Tariq savoured his treasure, its weight in his hands. Suddenly, he felt two metres tall.

Carina hid her amusement behind her burqa. Tariq's rifle belonged in a museum – and had surely come from one. A Mamluke arquebus, heavy as a bazooka, its stock inlaid with mother of pearl, its barrel engraved with turbaned riders hunting gazelles. She doubted it had ever been used in battle, or could fire even with the right ammunition (musket balls, anybody?), but if it kept Tariq happy, fine. Toys for boys…

Women were in tune with reality. Yasmina scrutinized the provisions that Tariq had assembled: two cartons of feta cheese, three cans of tuna, a fat plastic bag of Egyptian loaves and a six bottles of cloudy water. And some nasty eau-du-cologne – why? The boy was too young to shave. Carina didn't get a word of Yasmina's speech, but his petulant responses reminded her of Nick after his solo shopping trips to Waitrose, curtailed in the interests of marital harmony.

It was almost noon.

Only now did she dig out her mobile and find it switched off, laden with messages, its battery nearly flat. She hadn't recharged in Suez, Tariq had been playing games for hours, but there might be power for one message…

✳✳✳

Sabr spat furiously on the tarmac of Suez – his soul was about to burst from his nose. Yesterday, a gust of wind had snatched his exit permit from his clipboard on the Corniche. Then the hen missed their rendezvous, texting that she'd find her own way back to Hurghada. *How*? Alarmed, he'd visited all the hotels where she might stay in Suez, glumly checking into the last, where an Alexandrian pimp rubbed his ID as if it was the belly of the virgin whom he offered a heartbeat later. Sabr had declined but consoled himself with a bottle of rotgut brandy.

This morning he'd overslept, slurped tea for breakfast and still got no reply from her mobile. Calling Hurghada, his fears were confirmed. The hen hadn't returned to the Residency, she'd vanished as abruptly as her husband had. Baines chewed Sabr's face, ordered him to get down to Civil Affairs, report her missing and *find her*…

By God's will, he'd loitered outside the Governorate building that now flew the Star of David before submitting to the indignities of the Jews. His mobile bleeped, an SMS from the hen, his prayers had been answered.

Off 2 geezer platter 2 look 4 nick. More l8r.

Raving mad, he thought, as he deciphered the predictive text. First she vanishes in Suez, now she appears somewhere near the Giza Plateau, over 100 kilometres from Suez. He texted back furiously but there was no reply, no connection even.

A minute later, a suet-faced sentry had confiscated his mobile – joining others in a lead-lined box – and exchanged Sabr's ID card for a plastic tag. Another guard led him upstairs to a stale office where an Israeli basha with nostrils like a shotgun muzzle interrogated him in crude Palestinian Arabic. *I know how you've learned it, oppressing our cousins*, Sabr seethed silently.

The Israeli could withhold an exit permit indefinitely, but they both knew he wouldn't. Israel and Salvation First jealously guarded their mandates but were obliged to cooperate, so such jousting was as normal as salt on the table. But a missing Englishwoman was off the menu, the Israeli said dourly. Any action by the Border Police must adhere to the Mandatory Protocols. It was a matter for his superior officer.

The door shut behind him like a bank vault.

Colonel Avi thought rapidly. It was one of the qualities that had earned him the rank of *Tet-Alef* in the IDF and secondment to the Border Police as Head of Civil Affairs for the Mandate, administered from Suez. His orders to restore the city's infrastructure and public services were far from bogus, but not the whole story. The re-opening of the Canal was a geopolitical milestone. That it should happen under Israeli auspices – and stay under Israeli control – would determine the region's future for generations. His remit went far beyond sewage plants and warehouses.

He needn't open the encrypted file to refresh his memory of his last report to Jerusalem. An analysis of two months' communications intercepts from the Giza Plateau; humint from goatherds and salvage workers (wild rumours, mostly); and his own appreciation of events, based on the above and satellite photos from Jerusalem.

It cannot be ruled out that Libya is establishing a strategic foothold far beyond the territory of its self-declared 'Protectorate' on Egypt's northwest coast. The oil and gas in its desert hinterland is valuable but its strategic significance is marginal – unless

Libya extends its reach to the Suez Canal. By emplacing missiles on the Giza Plateau, Libya could choke-off Israel's new strategic waterway, thus gaining undue leverage in peacetime and a decisive advantage in war.

The Giza Plateau is far outside our Mandate, and attempts to infiltrate Bedouin trackers led to their deaths and poor morale among the others (who cannot be relied on for future missions there). Since GHQ prohibits the use of drones or the infiltration of an IDF reconn team, we are limited to Ofeq imagery.

I fear a serious threat is developing. We must be alert for any opportunity to penetrate the plateau.

Now one had presented itself.

"*Beseder*, Viktor," he told his second in command, "Here's what you do…"

9 KEEP BUGGERING ON

Carina spewed weakly. Nothing left but bile yet her guts kept heaving. The air seethed with flies and contagion. Hastily she rewrapped her head like a Tuareg. Now Tariq's eau-du-cologne had evaporated, nothing could mask the stench. Sewage and stagnant water; bovine carcasses embalmed in wagon-grease; rainbow pools of diesel. Dancing over an odour like the fox-scat Buster loved to roll in, but fouler.

The smell of rotting corpses, millions buried under rubble, mashed to slime or preserved like Irish bogmen to emerge from the mud. Since the dam's destruction, the inundation of the Nile had returned. For thousands of years it had sustained Egyptian civilization – farmers planting as it receded, reaping bumper crops after idle summers.

Now only putrid flesh was harvested by vultures, rats and flies.

Vultures bold as drug dealers, bickering over morsels as two stood guard against raiders. A flurry of claws and the defeated fled bloodied. The victors were unruffled by Carina; indifferent to live humans when they were surrounded by a feast of the dead.

Rats were different.

Twice they disturbed nests that reacted ferociously.

The first time a horde charged Carina froze, screaming.

Next thing she knew, Yasmina was slapping her, pain overcoming hysteria. *Stop it, stop, please!* Nobody had slapped her like that since Daddy.

Tariq gloated over the rats he'd ruptured with his boots. One still twitched; he crushed it with a grin.

Savages from a nightmare...

For ages they'd been traversing fallen flyovers. A car or a lamppost poking from the sludge could be a stepping-stone. Anything to avoid swamps that sucked you down or harboured crocodiles, Tariq said. Yasmina was glad Nick's wife didn't understand Arabic. *Now is the time to endure, as Aisha and I did on the ledges of the pyramid.*

Ever since then she'd shunned Cairo's ruins, forcing herself to gaze from the Muqattam in homage to the dead. Yet now, amid the wreckage of the city she'd loved, the topography wrought by the Flood had an awful fascination. Having idled on the Nile Corniche as a student, she now saw the river unbounded by embankments, raw and wild. The island of Gezira, with its sporting club and wealthy enclave of Zamalek, had totally disappeared. She recalled someone saying it had no bedrock, was merely silt that formed an island in the time of the Khedives.

"Giza Towers," Tariq pointed. "That belly-dancer had an apartment there, and Saudi princes. They told her to stop shaking her playthings, that she was dirtying the name of the place. Look at it now!"

Once the Towers had been luxury citadels where servants were tortured with impunity, their owners envied and hated by Cairenes. Now they were fallen bookstacks strewn across Bulaq. It was impossible to tell one district from another unless a landmark survived – the tip of Roda Island, with its forty-storey hotel, green with mould to the sixth floor, the rest charred.

By now they were near Old Cairo. Nothing remained of its ancient churches or synagogue, the Roman bastions or Mamluke aqueduct, but the flyovers of Qasr al-Aini had survived. Ahead, Tariq halted at the crest of a four-lane ramp, laid his rifle on the tarmac and eased the pack from his shoulders.

"Let the hen catch up," he said.

Tariq's heels were blistered, his treasures a burden. The rifle was awkward, but at least he could balance himself with it like the tightrope walker he'd once seen at a circus on the Prophet's birthday. And it was manly to bear arms; soon he'd perform heroic deeds with this weapon. Meantime, he could change into his sandals without loosing face. Yasmina scolded him but she was just a whore. And the hen was searching for a rich husband – or had he run away with a fresher chicken?

Never mind, she'd pay him in full. If he had to drag her across Cairo to rob her at the end, he'd get his greens. The whore was different, strong and determined enough to resist. The guys wouldn't hesitate to throw them both from a bridge after taking their pleasure. But Tariq was alone and didn't care about what was between women's legs. It was something men did that made them foolish, so women could earn money on their backs. He recalled his mother sponging herself before the rent-chaser arrived in the cuckold's hour. Each week another excuse as Tariq fumed on the roof or kicked a football on the streets. For a widow with a child to feed there was no dignity. Often she stifled tears of shame in their shared bed.

Tariq had vowed to survive, no matter what. God had spared him on the

Black Day so he might prosper. Every day he looked for a chance to claw some gain. His mother would be proud of him, he'd sworn on her deathbed

Reeds blurred the distinction between land and water, thickets taller than Yasmina's head. Tariq thrusting aside stalks like a water buffalo, she and Carina struggling behind. Suddenly she saw sunlight on open water, geese honking overhead. Tariq yelped joyfully, plunging waist deep to heave himself aboard a camouflaged felucca.

"My water-taxi is ready for a cruise," he bragged.

It was eerily relaxing, sailing past skyscrapers that had pan-caked down into the mud. Already she'd distanced herself from their tragedy, saw only twisted steel and fractured concrete. *Maktoub*, Yasmina could do nothing to rewind the spool of destiny that had ensnared millions, but Carina kept bleating about it. Like all Westerners she couldn't accept fate, her imagination restricted to the films she'd seen.

Yasmina's irritation festered. She'd already been in a disaster movie. This cosseted Englishwoman didn't know what happened when the cameras rolled indifferently, when *you* were suffering. She pointed at the escarpment.

"When the Flood came, I was on that side of the river. Everyone headed for the plateau. All of of Giza was moving. Cars stopped for no-one, people clinging to buses, families on motorbikes. We were lucky; some boys from the faculty stole a van, saw us walking and took us aboard. We were so embarrassed: we'd hardly touched men before, let alone sat on their laps!

"When we got there, crowds were milling round the Giza pyramids. Soon they began to climb – hundreds, thousands, struggling for the highest level. God blessed us. There was a blacksmith, his wife and daughters were on the other side of town. Aisha and I became the daughters he longed to save. He heaved us up; beat anyone who tried to stop us. Until we stood a few steps below the summit and looked back over Cairo.

"It was sunset – the sky turned crimson. The Flood came with the noise of a sugarcane crusher, a wave the height of a five-storey building that flattened them like cardboard boxes. Nobody knew how high the Flood would reach; water crashed on to the plateau. We clung tighter, fought to climb higher. Darkness fell....

"A million of us squatted on ledges as the floodwaters raged below. Few had brought food or water. Nobody had considered bodily needs, or the sick, or pregnant. There were some who helped, delivering babies or bringing water from the lake. But others became monsters, feeding off the dying. So it was for days.

"Then the Israelis came in their helicopters. Everyone raised their arms if they had any strength, clawing for the nets. Finally the water began to sink and it was possible to climb down. So Aisha and I were saved. They flew us to a camp near El-Arish."

Carina bowed her head contritely. Yasmina's anger still festered. Two years had not effaced the shameful memory of soldiers raising the Israeli flag over the Great Pyramid, as she and Aisha wept for joy at their deliverance

Sabr drove as fast as he dared. The road from Suez was a cutting extruding bones and cars. Reaching Cairo's ring road, he accelerated. The section traversing the Muqattam had never been engulfed; bulldozers had simply ploughed through gridlocked vehicles. Few skeletons; people had abandoned their cars to traipse into the desert. Once he passed some Bedouin grazing camels. They waved. Perhaps nobody had driven this way since the Helwan steelworks were cleared a year ago.

The Israeli's directions were simple. When you reach Ma'adi, look for the road of steel plates laid over a railway. Follow it past the quarries and steelworks, down to Tibin. The pontoon bridge across the Nile at Tibin had been rendered unsafe when the river rose for the first time since the Black Day, but Israeli intelligence reckoned it was still traversable. It was hateful that his fate depended on their expertise, but such was life.

They'd given him food and water, and even a windcheater in case it turned cold. He'd like to throw it away, but it was a sturdy garment that would be welcome in his wardrobe. If he unstitched the label nobody would know its origin. Anyhow, wearing an Israeli jacket didn't make you a traitor any more than putting on a *galabiyya* made you an Egyptian. That settled, he clicked in another tape and began to sing along with Amr Diab.

In Suez, Colonel Avi lowered the volume with a sigh of exasperation. The bugs that Viktor had planted in the Egyptian's car worked fine. They hadn't yielded any data yet, but the Colonel didn't expect anything until the asset reached the plateau. Intelligence was a waiting game. Meanwhile, he didn't have to suffer this warbling.

***

Back to Hell, thought Carina resentfully. Her back ached from the bench where she'd crashed out until Yasmina shook her awake. The river looked dreary as before. Turbid with silt and debris, its banks choked with rubble or reed-beds swarming with mosquitos. Hastily she rewrapped herself; the burka had its uses, whatever Yasmina called it. Tariq seemed oblivious to the swarm as he nosed the felucca into a mud
bank and lept ashore to tie its rope. Yasmina followed nimbly, leaving Carina to disembark unaided as the Egyptians conferred, gazing at the plateau. From the wheat sprouting all around, she guessed this had once been farmland. A mangy dog barked from a heap of rubble.

A shoelace had come undone, she bent to tie it.

Yasmina gasped.

Glancing up, Carina saw a crocodile. *Run*.

Its belly rasped across the mud, its jaws parted in anticipation. *You're mine*, its eyes said. She was paralysed with terror.

Tariq struggled to brace the gun and yanked its trigger.

—

Furiously, he flung it at the creature's eyes. The crocodile arched backwards, dived for the riverbank and disappeared with a splash. Tariq stood crying soundlessly; Yasmina embraced him. He wiped his eyes and smiled tremulously.

What about me? They didn't understand, she'd never faced death before, or crocodiles in the wild. Her courage had evaporated as they were nearing the point of no return. If an easy way of returning to Hurghada or Suez had existed, she'd take it, but re-crossing the ruins of Cairo was unthinkable. Yet she couldn't continue...

"If we don't arrive before dark, he can't show us the way," said Yasmina implacably. Mutely, Carina acquiesced. *The only thing to do is keep buggering on...*

Tariq led them through waist-high pampas grass, skirting walls of un-cut sugar-cane swaying overhead. By the time they turned west again, the sun was low over the plateau. In the indigo dusk, a giant centipede resolved into a mangled tourist coach. Had the tourists known what was coming – had they tried to escape?

Tariq patted it fondly and said something to Yasmina.

"He's finished; he wants his money – and another hundred for a new gun."

Carina nodded, delving into her money-belt. "Tell him he's the bravest boy that ever lived. But next time, buy one that shoots," she smiled, proffering the cash.

He snatched it, turned and bolted. Stupefied, she saw figures surging from bushes.

Bloody mouths set in a rictus of delight; bodies quivering with spines. One pounced like a cougar, dragging her down.

She felt paws on her thighs, rolling her over. Haunches straddled her chest as the burka was ripped from her head. A serrated blade flashed towards her throat...

10 THE SIQ

For six thousand years the Siq had slumbered undisturbed.

The builders of the pyramids knew nothing of its existence or their remote ancestors who created it. The origin of their own civilization remained an enigma to the Egyptians as it would to scholars in ages afterwards.

How did such complex hieroglyphs, such sophisticated architecture and bureaucracy, seemingly emerge from nowhere?

Egyptologists have speculated about a Zero Dynasty before the known ones of the Archaic Period, but found little evidence – let alone a royal tomb full of artefacts and scrolls, to answer all these questions and more.

It would be the Holy Grail of Egyptology, the kernel of Egyptian civilization.

Had the Siq been found by archaeologists, it would have upended notions of how Egyptian architecture began. Zoser's Step Pyramid at Saqqara had long been deemed the crucial leap from earthbound tombs to the soaring structures of the Pyramid Age.

But the Siq told a different story.

A chasm in the plateau, widening to a majestic bowl open to the sky. A cavity that inspired the ancestors to create a labyrinth by in-filling with boulders and shaped stones, starting at river level and completing the upper levels from the top of the plateau.

There they raised a four-stepped pyramid no higher than a palm tree, concealing an entrance to the labyrinth. Stuccoed and whitewashed, it was a shrine to the god-kings whose mummies lay underground while their souls roamed the cosmos. Generations of priests recorded celestial phenomena, equinoxes and eclipses.

Farmers knew only that the god-kings slept in the underworld. As word of the White Pyramid spread throughout the Valley, the priesthood grew more secretive about the labyrinth. On the plateau, it became a crime to speak of it; spies and torture stifled indiscretion. Myths and rumours might flourish in the Delta, up the Valley, but the truth remained secret – holy.

Only the high priests and reigning monarch might enter the Siq. Masked by ritual, the priests' task was to prevent rats from consuming the provisions for the god-king's afterlife, or moths his garments and regalia – a shameful necessity that might cast doubt on his divinity or the infallibility of the priesthood, should it be known.

The monarch visited it once – on the day of his accession – to inspect offerings and the stone plug that sealed off the lower levels, where his divine ancestors lay amongst their treasures for eternity.

He would never join them there.

Kings now built funerary enclosures on the desert fringes of Abydos, , far upriver, using techniques learnt in the labyrinth. Graded stones and mud compacted for stability; corbel-roofed chambers and passages faced with ashlars, intersected by inclined shafts for moving sarcophagi and funerary boats.

One day the pyramids would elevate the pharaohs towards the sun-god – but the first god-kings dwelt among the subterranean deities of earth and fire, time and reckoning.

In the Siq there is ample evidence of a custom abhorrent to later dynasties – human sacrifice.

Servants and concubines, farmers and soldiers; stupefied with poppy cordial and garrotted with ox-hide cords; bound in a foetal crouch to be desiccated by the hot sand, mummified without embalming. In their shrivelled hands, the tools of their profession: a kohl brush or ostrich fan, a hoe or javelin. On their chests, tablets inscribed with their names and the glyphs for 'duty' and 'eternity'.

Beside the three rooms of human corpses, a fourth packed with animals. Cats and dogs with jewelled collars, an eviscerated bull soaked in natron. Despite incense cones and sealed doors, the miasma of arrested putrefaction has seeped into store-rooms, garments and baskets of grain.

Hence purification rites in the Womb of Sekhmet, at the apex of the Shaft of the Creator. For centuries, priests chanted the Litany of Re, poured libations of milk and beer and filled the shaft with fragrant smoke. No mortal could open the door to the Holy Abode or see their newborn in the Hall of Offspring. The lustre of gold and bronze, amethyst and carnelian, was only perceptible to their eyes, in utter darkness, as the universe had begun.

The darkest secret was the shaft to the Nile, whence the Divine Afterbirth was expelled. To ensure it never compromised the inviolability of the Holy Abode, it funnelled upwards from the Nile, narrowing to the width of a child's head for a length that represented the twelve hours of night. For gods, its constriction was irrelevant; they moved through space and time as birds crossed land and water.

This felicity might have endured forever, had not their offspring warred in the heavens. Rain diminished to dew upon the Delta, grasslands turned to desert and a red mist arose in the west. Each year an ocean of sand fell from the skies and swept across the plateau.

They implored Sekhmet and the Creator to curb their children, in vain.

Eventually they lost hope, ceased sweeping a path to the pyramid and uttered the Rites of Closure for the last time. The Creator had shown His will, cursing the infernal serpent Apophis and his ally Sukkoth, and rewarding Re with esteem at Memphis. The taboo on the labyrinth was sealed by the silencing of the sweepers and the culling of the priesthood on the plateau. Within a few generations its location had been forgotten, every contour submerged by sand, the shaft to the Nile choked by silt.

Pyramids rose, dynasties came and went and foreigners mingled their blood with the flow of the Nile. As silt accumulated, the river receded from the plateau.

Nothing disturbed the Siq – existing outside time, beyond knowledge.

Until the Flood –

Its stupendous force sucked the shaft as if it was a drinking straw, dragging small artefacts from the burial chamber to lie embedded in the mud when the water subsided. And so Abu Karim found a golden idol at his feet and the Siq's existence was revealed.

But not to anyone who cared for the knowledge it embodied.

GM gazed raptly at the calf strapped on a pallet. Eighteen tonnes of gold, he'd got the fucker up the shaft without a dent. What a story that would make! He'd be a name to remember for all time. Howard Carter and all those guys hardly anyone remembered now. They'd seem like pygmies beside him. Pygmies!

For GM, that wasn't a figure of speech. He'd met the shifty little runts while he was in Burundi, so he knew what he was on about. Anyway, they didn't have fuck-all to do with what he'd been hauling up the shaft. Gold-plated beds and stools, gilded sarcophagi and mummy cases, jewelled masks and chests and statuettes...

He scrawled on the clipboard proffered by Mahmoud or Mustafa. Rag-heads, they all shared a few names and swore blind on their mother's honour. Screw 'em, he'd soon be out of here. He dealt with the boss – they were nobodies.

Without him, none of this would be happening.

It was GM who realized the tomb existed, even before he'd found Abu Karim. It took skill to bluff him into revealing the locality – the plateau had hundreds of ravines. But he convinced Abu Karim he'd be an ideal partner: a salvage engineer who could deal with buyers abroad as AK never could.

Ducking under a flap of the camouflaged hanger that masked the dig-zone, he felt the humidity. His job involved as much sweat as a navvy's but the dosh was in another league. And what other internationals were carrying off the biggest heist of all time?

Automatically he checked the pumps and air-hoses that regulated the Siq's atmosphere. Dust saturating the air, or pockets of methane or carbon-monoxide, could be fatal without a respirator. But it was easier to work unencumbered, a trade-off between speed and safety.

Early on they'd worked above ground, pinpointing the spot with seismic imaging and bulldozing waves of sand to clear the pyramid, before breaking in and climbing down the well. His granddad had been a mason in both senses, and would have been proud to see handholds carved sixty centuries ago, bearing his own flesh and blood in pursuit of the Secrets of the Lost Pharaoh.

At the bottom, an echoing chamber shaped like the belly of a whale, where hieroglyphs danced in their torch-beams. Someone whooped and GM told them to shut it and only talk in whispers – the roof might collapse.

But he'd been wrong about that – and as dismayed as the rag-heads by what happened next. The first exit they found was a short horizontal corridor ending in a wall stamped with seals. Surely *something* lay behind it – or had the tomb been plundered long ago? He'd ordered them to fan out, search for other corridors.

Everyone froze at a shriek in the gloom, followed by a meaty thud.

Sweeping the floor with their torch beams they'd found the spot where it became a void. GM could tell the Gyppos thought the same as he did when they saw the edge – bevelled to cause intruders to stumble in the dark.

They were all spooked by the aperture. GM heard the Arabic for *cunt* muttered as they gestured to ward off the evil eye. He wasn't superstitious, but imagined an adversary dead for thousands of years, a female phantom of the labyrinth. He was half-minded to call it quits for the day, till a Gyppo volunteered to abseil down and recover the body.

No surprise its skull was pulped – pitched ten metres down, headfirst. The surprise was the basalt at the bottom. None was indicated in the geology; anyhow the Gyppo reported a smooth, manmade slab.

A plug-block, sealing off the lower levels…

GM called time and consulted his database of pyramid surveys. Plug-blocks were more often assumed than proven – some Egyptologists doubted their existence altogether. Ancient looters left no accounts; latter-day treasure hunters dug around obstacles rather than trying to raise them.

Next day he went down to examine the slab. The size of a Ford Focus, over ten tonnes he guessed, its surface incised with sun symbols, snakes and scorpions. In movies, tomb raiders always had a map or clues to help them with stuff like this. He prodded the pictograms, willing one to trigger something, but nothing happened.

Ground-penetrating radar confirmed that the slab fitted grooves in the walls tight as an Ulsterman's arsehole. They tried drilling, but the vibration threatened to bring the shaft down and the drill-bits only pitted the slab. Explosives he rejected: shaped-charges would split the block, but the shock waves could collapse the shaft and probably the treasure chambers below.

Meanwhile, Team B had broken through the false wall in the corridor. The first chamber was no larger than a beach-hut, its stone shelves piled with garments embroidered with silver thread, which turned to dust when touched.

Three more sealed chambers full of rags or baskets of grain. As they cracked the fifth seal, the stench of rancid bacon swept into the shaft. *Mummies* they'd cheered – and mummies there were, but not as they'd expected. Excitement as they'd stripped the turquoise and silver from the necks of the cats, fading as they exposed one room after another of human cadavers, scrolls and clay tablets – but no jewellery.

The schedule was slipping.

On GM's orders, earthmovers tore away the upper layer, gouging a crater to expose the shaft. The air in the shaft still reeked of the mummies they'd pulverised.

His only regret was for the ancient boat. Lashed together from tarred papyrus, it had a raked prow and stern bracketing a teak pavilion amidships. The JCB driver swore he hadn't known it was there – the ground just collapsed beneath his treads. GM kept a piece of the pavilion, inlaid with turquoise, but the boat was beyond salvaging.

Their luck changed two days later, when they exposed the rear of the plug. Sunk into the basalt was a lug bound with rawhide and palm-fibre cables, hanging in the darkness. They pulled them in and found the ends charred; directed arc lights to reveal a massive counterweight at the bottom of a well.

GM was chuffed by the simplicity of the mechanism. An oil lamp lit beneath the cable which restrained the counterweight, allowing the last priest time to climb the shaft before the slab descended. They hacked away the ancient ropes replaced them by steel cables, raised the slab and pinioned it with pit-props in the shaft.

From then on, it was wonderland.

The shaft descended past a hall upheld by columns in the form of gods, that so impressed GM he took the trouble to identify them. Anubis, the jackal-headed god of embalming, flanked by Qeb-hwt – a giant ostrich that washed the entrails of the dead – and the falcon-headed god of darkness, Sokar. At the apex stood Ptah, the Creator, wrapped in bandages. His wife Sekhmet had the face of a lioness and wore a sun disc symbolizing the destructive power of her father, Re, who assumed a ram's head in the underworld. The last column portrayed the writhing serpent that lived in the waters of chaos and tried to prevent Re from crossing the sky.

The columns could only be removed with major underpinning, and his crew was far too busy with loot that could be hauled up the shaft. Caskets and weapons inlaid with ivory and ebony; turquoise, carnelian and lapis lazuli jewellery; bronze or granite idols. Rummaging through brittle scrolls and sealed jars of gummy residue, they'd found and lost treasures in the litter underfoot.

But those paled beside the stuff in the burial chamber. Jewelled furniture packed round a gilded tomb as large as an elephant, flanked by a solid gold falcon and calf. The tomb consisted of boxes nested one inside another. In the third one, a king and queen shared a sarcophagus with a lid of beaten gold, replicating the contours of their bodies. They lay full length, her carnelian fingers clasping his ivory dick in a gesture of ownership, her lip curled smugly.

Nothing like them had ever been found.

GM resolved to lift the sarcophagus intact – way harder, but the mummies would fetch ten times more as a pair, untouched. And what he said went ...

Now debris crunched beneath his boots in the empty chamber. The only evidence of how the tomb once looked was some digital footage made when everyone was masked. If Egyptologists ever found out what he'd done, they'd curse him as a looter, so it was better he never appeared on the Discovery Channel.

It was funny how it all began – at the Euro.

Eavesdropping on barroom conversations was GM's habit. This *parlez-vous* had involved a French Egyptologist and a Kraut whose words slurred as they sank whisky. The Frog seemed happy to hold the floor, banging on about smuggled antiquities. Reputable museums had their hands tied by international conventions and watch-lists, while dealers and collectors traded in secret. It was bad enough when artefacts from Egyptian state collections vanished into private hands, far worse when un-catalogued treasures were lost to scholarship.

GM had already smuggled a few items packaged as tissue-samples or isotopes, so he listened intently as the Frenchman talked of 'artefacts of unknown provenance'. At a private viewing in Manhatten, the Frog had seen a stele whose hieroglyphs were peculiar. A colleague in Italy had puzzled over the authenticity of a model boat with odd cartouches, for an undisclosed fee. And so on...

While the Frog hadn't drawn the obvious conclusion, GM saw it at once: an unknown tomb or cache, exposed by the Flood.

He knew from experience in Bangladesh that floods could uncover as well as bury – and the Aswan dam-burst had been the worst flood in history. He recalled the pieces he'd bought from various dealers: some of Hani's were too fragile to have survived the Flood had they been dredged from the cellars of Cairo's Antiquities Museum.

So he'd focused on Hani, and winkled out Abu Karim.

The sucker never dreamt what GM had in mind. As soon as he'd heard what the Siq was like, GM realized it would need the full Monty: pumps, compressors, drills and bulldozers. No way to avoid being noticed by the scavengers from the Citadel – they'd overrun the site like rats.

He understood that some *force* was needed to secure it, to terrify trespassers. And he knew only person in Egypt who could deliver that, for a share of the loot.

Approaching him was nerve-wracking, but it all went sweetly. An agreement sealed in whisky, which resolved logistics and security. Helicopter re-supply, and a welcome for intruders out of Nightmare on Elm Street.

It had all gone perfectly except for that slut Aisha.

How he loved making her do everything he could imagine when he felt as randy as a coach-load of builders at a lap-dancing club. Especially when she begged him not to! Except that one time when he'd drunk too much. She shouldn't have laughed, that was way out of order. He could've done it if she'd helped, instead of taking the piss.

So he'd showed her what kind of man he was, using the idol as a dildo.

Next day he realised he had to shut her up – first with a beating, then to be certain. It meant a thousand bucks to that witch Hoda, but it was nothing, really.

11 A LOST DONKEY CHASE

God protect me from evil, Sabr intoned. This place was cursed. Hundreds of buildings choked by grit and slime, overgrown with creepers; vultures nesting the heights, jackals roaming the canyons. Once this had once been Ma'adi, a snobby suburb of high-rise condos that he'd seen as the guest of a doctor who'd enjoyed his safari. He'd tried to maintain his poise despite the apartment's size and opulence but lost it when the guy's sister joined them. Effortlessly sexy and superior, she reduced him to a Saiyidi donkey with a few words and flicks of her eyebrows.

Was she long dead, or had she escaped and was now waxing her legs in Dubai? The rich were aliens, colonising and abandoning territory with no more care for its inhabitants than flies. Yet even rich people had perished; loath to abandon their property till it was too late, without bodyguards to force their way through the traffic. She might be dead – those perfect legs, that smirk, crushed by tonnes of water and rubble. *Maktoub...*

Sabr knew that Ancient Egyptians believed that the souls of the dead travelled west to meet Osiris, facing judgement in the caverns of the underworld traversed each night by the sun-god. *Superstition*, Islam decreed, yet Sabr couldn't help feeling that by travelling through these ruins in the path of the sun, he was offering his soul to Satan. Jackals and vultures were the creatures of the underworld. He whispered a prayer to the blessed Saiyida Zeinab, protectress of Cairenes, whose shrine had miraculously survived the Flood and now stood on an island in the Nile that only the righteous could see, it was said. May her *baraka* protect him from what lay ahead...

How many prayers were uttered on the Black Day? Sabr had been returning to Aswan from Abu Simbel when he heard the news from a taxi driver, tearing his *galabiyya* in grief. "Everything's gone!" he'd screamed, beating the windscreen till his fists bled.

When Sabr grasped what he meant, he turned away from his bewildered tour group and prayed for the safety of his family on Elephantine Island – but in the pit of his stomach he already knew they were dead.

Had he always lacked faith in God, or did it die that day?

Ever since, he'd prayed with a false heart. Hashish and sex couldn't dispel the nightmares that drove him to opium. He longed for certainty and righteousness, as he doubted they existed. He was damned, even before he began working for the Christians.

Now he was paying for it.

Beyond the ruins of Ma'adi was the pontoon bridge. As the Israeli had warned, hawsers had snapped; with the river falling, it could pull apart any day. But there were planks and rolls of steel mesh, left behind by Bechtel engineers. *You'll have to improvise*, the Israeli had said with the confidence of sixty years of victories behind him. Sabr had only Hezbollah to inspire him, and that had been years ago – but they'd surprised the Zionists then, taught them that Arabs couldn't be taken for granted. If God was with him, he'd show them, too. He began dragging a plank towards the first chasm as the bridge swayed beneath him

Colonel Avi smiled grimly. The car had been stuck on the east bank for over two hours – but not stationary. Changes in its GPS coordinates suggested it was being used to drag things. He could hear the Egyptian's curses fading as he moved away from the vehicle. If he didn't succeed by nightfall, the whole mission would likely fail. He wouldn't have the guts to try again next day, even if the bridge didn't break meantime. The next few hours would show whether the Egyptian succeeded; the tracker would mark any progress.

With a sigh of pleasure, he turned to re-read the last draft of his article for the Jaffa Defence Centre's *Strategic & Historical Review*. He wasn't sure if the title – *Post-Flood Egypt: a New Intermediate Period* – was punchy enough, but the article read well. A pity Viktor was such a philistine, or he might show it to him now.

While the great Flood that destroyed much of Egypt two years ago was a catastrophe of unprecedented magnitude, the emerging strategic landscape is in many respects similar to certain eras in Egypt's ancient history.

I refer to the Intermediate Periods separating the Old, Middle and New Kingdoms and the Late Period. During these intermediate epochs, state power fragmented and the union of the Two Lands (the Nile Valley and its Delta) collapsed, while external powers seized territory and intervened in the affairs of local dynasties, eventually seeding their own, of extraneous ethnicity.

So what are the features of this New Intermediate Period?

Today, there is no longer any human civilization as such in the Nile Valley and Delta, but elsewhere, rival polities claim sovereignty over nominal national territory, large parts of which are now under the de facto or de jure control of neighbouring states. Polities must contend with these external actors and vice versa – and resources are a crucial determinant of their inter-relations.

What the United Nations recognises as the sovereign successor to the Republic of Egypt that existed before the Flood, Egyptians know as El-Bahr (the Sea in Arabic), after its location on the Red Sea littoral. This terrain is almost totally devoid of fresh water and fertile land, with infrastructure geared to a tourist industry that no longer exists. Its five million refugees are entirely dependent on external suppliers for water, food, and other essentials. All that makes it viable are oil and gas reserves within its territorial waters, which are being mortgaged to pay for the relief and reconstruction effort. This 'state' claims authority over the entire land of Egypt, but effectively controls only the Red Sea coast and the middle reaches of the devastated Nile Valley.

By contrast, the so-called Rightly Guided Emirate in the oases of the Western Desert has fertile land and water to sustain its population of four million at a basic level, but no energy sources beyond raiding the oil and gas fields in the hinterland of a Libyan 'Protectorate' on Egypt's northwest coast. Neither is recognised by the United Nations or acknowledges the other's legitimacy, and there are sporadic clashes along the ill-defined border (or wasteland) between them.

To complicate matters, the ancient land of Nubia that was submerged by Lake Nasser in the 1960s has re-emerged, and the surviving Nubians are moving down from Wadi Halfa in Sudan to reclaim the land of their ancestors. Although most are simply founding villages, militant factions have wrested areas from the nominal authority of El-Bahr and recently shown their ability to strike far down the Valley, at foreign development projects.

Finally, there is the Israeli Mandate over Sinai and the Canal Zone – where our ancestors once toiled under the Pharaoh's whip in the Biblical Land of Goshen. Today we have returned in a different spirit, to aid refugees, rebuild cities and restore the Suez Canal for the benefit of all humanity. Naturally, there are those who would thwart these aims or impute ignoble motives to the Mandate's efforts, but anyone who values peace and progress in the region must recognise that it has been the *sine qua non* of stability since the Flood.

And so, as the Ancient Egyptians believed that Creation emerged from a watery chaos at the dawn of time, a new Egypt is emerging whose contours are still in flux...

Sabr spat on his blistered palms: God willing, the worst was past. He'd nursed the car across the makeshift bridge-spans and was now on the west bank.

Mosquitoes swarmed beneath date-palms festooned with rotting mattresses. Upstream, shoals of rubble split the river into channels, merging into murk. Recalling the millions of lights that once glowed there, he shuddered. Coming from Aswan, fifteen hours by train, he'd been overwhelmed by Cairo on childhood visits. His father had worn his best *galabiyya* and held Sabr's hand lest the crowds sweep him away. Years later, doing military service, he'd got fed up being teased by Cairenes about Saiyidis. He finally decked someone in Ramses Station and had to flee, hiding in a carriage under the seat of some fellow Saiyidis, who kissed his beret when Sabr told them how he'd upheld the honour of Upper Egypt.

Now such loyalties were fading and honour was dead. Sabr shook his head and turned to face the plateau. The ground climbed unevenly, no road visible. He smoked a Cleo to delay the next step – whatever that was. The Zionists had briefed him this far but no further – only warned him to be careful. *Careful of what?* he'd asked, but the Israeli only shrugged. Sabr should've refused the mission, sold the car and gone to ground, but the prospect of losing both his job and his *ezba* was unnerving. Already he missed the comforts of Scheherazade, where Farida would be his tomorrow. He wouldn't even have a spliff tonight.

Cursing, he started the Land Cruiser. A chorus of shrieks, a stripy blur across the glade. He ducked behind the steering wheel as the shrieks turned to laughter. When nothing worse happened he swept the trees on high-beam and saw monkeys. Lowering the beam, he got another glimpse of the creature dashing for cover – a zebra. He remembered the zoological gardens that once existed in Giza. How the animals escaped the Flood and settled upstream, only God knew.

What else had survived – lions? Was that what the Israeli had meant?

Beyond the trees the earth was glutinous as rice. Rubble gave some purchase in first gear and he was lucky to find a spur of harder mud. A rising moon cast the terrain into crisp relief. Sabr saw – felt – the mud slope change into a flag-stoned causeway, ascending towards a misshapen mass silhouetted against the sky.

His heart sank as he reached the top and saw the pyramid, stripped of its shell, its core exposed. Beyond loomed another, sharp-edged yet oddly shaped, as if the architect had changed his mind towards the end. Sabr couldn't recall which of the sites had a pyramid like that; there were so many pyramid complexes spread over a huge area.

He cut the engine and listened.

Wind hissed across the plateau, thick with dust. Green lights wavered distantly. As the gusts ebbed he heard a wail like a child's voice from the bottom of a well, and a mechanical throbbing. The wind rose again, grit scouring his arms and cheeks. Clouds were massing as the temperature plunged. He shrugged on the windcheater and zipped it to the collar. At least he'd be warm – but what next? The plateau was vast, the lights could mean anything – he could spend all night driving from one to another on a lost donkey chase.

She might be anywhere.

He examined the lights with binoculars. Some were roiling fluorescent smoke, others spluttered like a welder's rod. They didn't look like campfires; maybe the warning referred to them. But if he was to find Carina, how could he not investigate the only signs of life on the plateau? *Be careful...* There was just enough light to drive without headlamps and the terrain offered plenty of cover. Make for the nearest and take it from there, he decided.

He was about to start the car when a tract of desert lit up like a bathroom window as the blinds are dropped. It was over so fast he only saw it because he was facing that way – but the image was burned onto his retinas.

Forklifts and machinery in a prefabricated Rubb Hall like the ones used by Salvation First as rapidly-erectable warehouses.

The agency had no projects here that Sabr knew of, but armies used such halls too. If it was a secret military base, then whose? El-Bahr was far away, the Libyans and the Emirate nearer, the Israelis closer still. But the Israelis wouldn't send him to spy on their own base, El-Bahr had its hands full, and the Emirate was so short of fuel they went to war on camels. That left Baby Gaddafi's lot in the Protectorate – which would explain why the Zionists were interested.

Now he understood.

12 RUBBISH PEOPLE

She awoke in darkness. A heartbeat between joy and terror as she realized she wasn't blind but captive – blindfolded.

Hostage...

Her mind churned, a murky kaleidoscope of victims grovelling before hooded killers, reciting their rhetoric. Anything to delay the swipe of the butcher's knife, the severed head held proudly to the camera in the name of God.

She heard herself panting, hyperventilating...

Breathe deeply –

She rolled over, gasping as the circulation returned to her arms, bound at the wrist. Memories flooded back. The man who'd torn her burqa had said something that spared their lives. They weren't demons. There'd been nothing spectral about the knee in her spine, the hands that tied her or the rancid heat of his body. She'd been dumped on the ground; blacked out.

She squirmed across the slimy floor till she reached a wall. The exertion left her breathless, the air was stale. She guessed that she was in a hut somewhere on the plateau. From the smell, it had once been a goat-pen or a toilet. *The last straw, to die in a shithouse* – an echo of her grandfather's mordant humour that was oddly soothing.

He'd known this part of the world as a soldier. Seen Italian captives herded like sheep at Tobruk, before tasting defeat himself a year later: Panzers rolling over the wire, Rommel triumphant. Thirty-three months in a POW camp near Salzburg, hunger gnawing as rations dwindled. But he outlasted the war to marry Gran. His motto was: keep buggering on – KBO – Churchill's, naturally.

She heard a mechanical drone overlaid with the stamp of boots. Hinges squealed, and heavy footfalls separated. She cringed as they closed in.

Hands fumbled at her ears and wrists. Agonizing brightness as the blindfold fell away; prowling silhouettes that resolved into soldiers in battledress – and Hosni Basha bending over her, face shadowed by a naked bulb swaying overhead.

"Mrs Baring! Praise God you're unharmed!"

"I ..." she gagged.

He handed her a canteen. She gulped convulsively. The water surged through her veins. Nothing had ever tasted so wonderful.

"Not too much at once, it's bad for your kidneys."

"I hurt like hell." She massaged her ribs.

"My soldiers have orders to seize anyone approaching the plateau. *Your* arrival was not expected. We've been watching for weeks and planned to arrest them all tonight. Instead we find you with two Egyptians, in a matter of national security. Can you explain *that*, Mrs Baring?"

Her head whirled. The police were here, GM's arrest was imminent. "Nick – we came to look for Nick. Have you found him?"

"Not yet, we're searching – so much ground to cover. If we arrest the criminals we may learn something. Tell me, please, how you learnt of this activity? And why you think your husband is here?"

"Yasmina told me about him; then Tariq explained about the Siq and how Nick planned to use a hovercraft to get there. It's a long story..."

He waved at a pair of camp-chairs behind him. "I'll order tea and you can explain from the beginning."

"Where are the others? Are they safe?"

"In custody while their position is investigated. We are protecting national security, we must know *everything*. The sooner you answer my questions, the sooner you'll go free."

They sat silently till tea arrived. Syrupy-sweet, it acted on her metabolism like amphetamine. She mustered her thoughts and began to relate all that had happened since Suez. The Security Minister listened, hardly saying a word till she had finished.

He tented his fingers beneath his chin. "I hope the others confirm your story. Meanwhile, you are all guests of State Security until the operation is over. If you're guilty, we can't allow the criminals any warning; if you're innocent, we can't have you hurt in the crossfire. I'm sure you understand."

He barked at the guard by the door, who snapped to attention. As soon as Hosni Basha left the room, he began picking his nose.

Hosni moved among his troops, cuffing them fondly. They were the camel's hump, toiling in this dustbowl for months, under a *khawaga* who didn't hide his contempt for Egyptians. Surely the pig would pay for his insolence once the Siq had been cleared and his expertise was redundant – soon, very soon.

Over sixty crates sat in the dispersal zone – draped in desert scrim until the helicopter arrived – with thirty more still to be moved from the Rubb Hall. It amused him to imagine Zaghloul's pride and the foreigners' shock when he announced the completion of manoeuvres on the Giza Plateau. They would be so mesmerized by El-Bahr's assertion of sovereignty none would realize it served other ends.

It was a deception worthy of Mohammed Ali – an outsider who'd seized Egypt by the neck and dragged it into the modern age after six hundred years of misrule by the Mamlukes. Hosni's own ancestors would vouchsafe this, for they had been Albanians, given land and wives in the Delta for disposing of Mohammed Ali's enemies. In Egypt, the Basha's slaughter of the Mamluke emirs as they left a banquet in the Citadel was admired as essence of perfidy, for its elegance and gallows humour.

Hosni flattered himself that his own seizure of power was even defter than his hero's, against immeasurably greater odds.

Egypt under the Mamlukes had been misruled but rich, whereas he'd recreated authority in a wilderness. Foreigners had sunk their fangs into Egypt – Jews, Libyans and Christian spiders. Whatever grudges Hosni bore against those fools in the Emirate at least they were Egyptians, Muslims.

His seizure of the treasure would clear the way to power and gratification that the Basha would have envied. Hosni could retire to Dubai in utter luxury, or enjoy absolute power in El-Bahr, with a fortune to shape it into a new Egypt. He'd be Hosni the Great in the history books – on par with Seti I or Ramses II.

Not bad for a ragamuffin from the slums of Tanta!

In a year or two he'd depose Zaghloul and assume the Presidency. But why shackle himself to that feeble title? If he was ruler, with a pharaoh's treasure, surely he should proclaim himself thus?

What a poke in the eye for the monkeys of the Emirate! Ever since the Flood, he'd been vexed Tutankhamun's gold ended up there, cursing whoever routed it into the Western Desert, cheating him of a treasury. But now he was on the verge of gaining another. He'd select the finest regalia and wear it with pride. The monkeys of the oases could hardly do the same with theirs...

It would be just reward for all his efforts.

Reconciling logistics and security had been the greatest challenge. With the Israelis controlling the only land approach, they'd come from the south over the same mountains that he'd flown on the Black Day. This time there was no panic; they spent weeks establishing a supply dump at an abandoned air base in the radar-shadow of the highlands, before landing on the plateau.

First, a holding force to lay-up and secure the perimeter – stealthily, by terror, as Psy-Ops manuals recommended. The first sheep to the abattoir had been Abu Karim and his brothers – left as a warning for all. Their cousins decimated by snipers and the stalking of nocturnal intruders, till none dared venture there.

Phase two, *maskirovka*. The Russian term for deception tactics was apt, since the donkey of the supply operation was a Mi-6 heavy-transport helicopter that first flew when the Soviets were building the High Dam. Flights could be timed to evade satellites, but not sustained excavations. For that they practiced diversion, igniting pot-lights or smoke-flares at other locations. Broadcast eerie cries and screams to mask the noise of drilling. How easily the looters from the Citadel were convinced that the plateau was haunted by djinn!

The final phase was *closure*. He savoured the American term which anesthetised the wounds of covert action. Eliminate witnesses, leaving only a blast-site for interpretation – the truth would stay under a blanket.

The Englishwoman's disappearance would mean more tedious correspondence between her embassy and his Foreign Ministry, only floors apart in the Mövenpick. But her fate would weigh far less than the oil and gas being extracted from El-Bahr's waters, arms sales, or services rendered.

As for the Egyptians, they were merely vermin whose extinction would go unnoticed. A whore from Suez and a thieving brat, as Hosni had been a lifetime ago. Rubbish people, to be swept away to clear the table for a banquet. The Baring woman had sealed their fates with her naïve confession. It was only right she should realize her folly, when Hosni rubbed GM's face in his own vomit. *Before they all perished in the Siq...*

Tariq was asleep when they came, yet Yasmina saw his body twitch before they even entered the cell. It was the same two as before, the stocky Saiyidi and the bearded one who'd pawed her earlier; without their demonic masks and costumes, simply brutish men.

"Up, the Basha wants you."

Tariq lay still as a toad, spying from under his eyelids.

"And you, kid, on your feet!"

Yasmina steeled herself for what was coming. Since Hosni Basha entered their cell she'd imagined every agony, yet he'd hardly bothered to interrogate her and barely glanced at Tariq. Only sneered and said:

"*W'Allah*, you're stupider than a Danish cartoonist. What did you think you were doing, sticking your nose into my business? You should've stayed in Suez, sucking Jews. The Englishwoman would still be in Hurghada if it wasn't for you."

He was right. Confronting power was futile, faith in justice, lunacy – certainly in Egypt, if not the world over. Every year of history was another load of evil on humanity's back. But now defiance flared within her again. She met her abuser's eyes and saw a cur obliged to yield a juicy morsel to its pack leader. He spat on the floor.

"Move – the Basha's waiting."

Outside the cell, moonlight illuminated crates under netting by a landing strip. More guards fell in beside them with another prisoner. Carina looked dazed.

You betrayed us as easily as a child, she thought, reaching for Carina's hand.

GM had just finished wiring the last charge when he heard noises from the shaft. It was that Gyppo Special Forces twat, coming to bug him again. *Asshole.* He'd already wired the charges into the genny supply when the guy demanded he use stand-alone sources. Fucking backseat driver... He'd complained to Hosni, who backed GM's decision – but it seemed the twat hadn't learnt his lesson...

He cocked his head, listening. Working with Gyppos, he'd grown used to their agile tread on the steps. This was different. He touched the remote detonator in his pocket, locked on *Safe*. No way would GM surrender it to anyone till he was out of the tomb and off the plateau – then Hosni could do as he liked...

Turning away from the sacks of RDX packed around the detonation charge, he faced the ladder bridging the ten-foot gap between the floor of the chamber and the mouth of the shaft in the ceiling.

First Hosni and a Gyppo boy descended; then two women he'd never have expected: Yasmina from the Euro and the wife of that wanker Baring. A guard trained his rifle on them from the shaft.

"You got drunk and blabbed to a whore," chided Hosni. "Now your words have brought these hens to us. What now, *siddiqi*?"

If there was one thing GM hated worse than being called 'my friend' by a rag-head, it was being shown up by a rag-head and a bint. Hosni was a cunt, but the real snake in the grass was Yasmina. She'd learned something from Aisha and waited to take her revenge, the devious bitch. And now Hosni was flourishing a pistol, throwing hand-ties on the floor and motioning GM to act.

"OK." He tied the boy first. "So a fucking art historian got nosy."

GM bound her too, with a kick for good measure. "But the real problem is this slut Yasmina. Just leave us alone, we can sort it out together."

"Have fun, *siddiqi*. I'll see you at the landing zone," Hosni answered.

Sabr lay in the sand, straining to catch voices on the wind. Men's for certain, but he'd swear a woman screamed for an instant. Moments later the wind shifted and he clearly overhead a man with the sibilant accent of Egypt's Mediterranean coast, where Libya had established its Protectorate under Baby Gaddafi.

"The *Inglizi* has stayed below to enjoy the cows alone. Perhaps he'll let us milk them afterwards! Me first with the fat white cow..."

"Libyan dog-jism, I'll milk *you*, God willing," Sabr vowed silently. An Englishman, women – it could only mean that the hen and her husband were here. He'd found them both! But the Libyan's words boded ill – if they were prisoners, how could he free them? The honey of hope turned to gall in his throat.

Despite the cold he was sweating like a Dane. He shook off the windcheater, craving a cigarette, tortured by the smell of tobacco from the enemy camp. They were confident that intruders would never reach its perimeter, guarding the approaches from the river and the north, but not the deep desert – who would come from there?

He glanced back at the outcrop that hid the jeep from view. He'd crept up a gully and crawled to a dip in sand for cover. So close, the Rubb Hall obscured the stars, leaking light through its skin. He heard the throbbing of compressors, and generators droning in another direction. His ears led his eyes to them, surrounded by sandbags to muffle the sound and minimize the risk of fire. He couldn't see anyone on guard and the sandbags cast ample shadow. Darkness was his ally – suddenly he knew what to do.

He began crawling, praying that the guards remained distracted by the prospect of enjoying themselves once the Englishman had finished.

13 COLONEL AVI'S APOTHEOSIS

GM winked at the wife in the corner. He'd stuffed a rag in her gob and tied her to the lad so they wouldn't vex him, but he hadn't blindfolded her. He *wanted* her to watch what happened next. His nuts tingled as he turned to the slut on the plinth of the sarcophagus. Blood trickled from her nostrils and a tit peeped through her blouse where he'd grabbed it as he slapped her. He'd left her hands untied, knew he could beat her into submission, would enjoy a little resistance...

This would be payback for all the times she'd stiffed him at the Euro, for the shit she'd meant to dump on him because of Aisha. Advancing, he unzipped his fly.

Get this...

As he lunged, Yasmina hurled a fistful of grit at his eyes.

Planted her foot in his eggs, felt them rupture. *That's for Aisha!*

He squealed like a ram being gelded, reeled back and hit the floor. She sprung forward ready to stamp on his throat – but GM was doubled up groaning, as Carina turned puce behind him. She raced over, extracted the rag and supported Carina's weight as the boy cursed them both. The knots and plastic hand-ties resisted her trembling fingers.

"His knife, on the floor ..."

Yasmina saw a silvery device fallen from GM's clothing, the kind that aid workers brandished in the Euro, a fanfare of tools they called a Leatherman.

She thumbed open a blade and slashed at the rope, imagining it was GM's throat.

He was still twitching and moaning. *Kill him – for Aisha.*

She couldn't. Carina was staring at her.

She cut their ties and threw the knife aside. Tariq darted to the ladder, turning to look at her as he grasped the rungs. She seized Carina's arm. "Hurry!"

The ladder disappeared through an aperture in the ceiling. As her head cleared the hole, Yasmina quailed at the sight of the shaft rising like a monstrous oesophagus, its sides melding into narrow rock-hewn steps divided by a steel ramp, steep as the Great Pyramid. In the muted glow of amber lamps she spotted the boy, forging ahead.

Tariq's sandals slid on the greasy steps, dust swirling in the updraft of pumps echoing in halls looted under the eyes of the old gods. So much for their magic, it had less effect than a fart. If only Allah had granted him the chance to plunder this treasure house. But he'd risked his life for a handful of greens – and only kept those because he'd hidden them where the Basha's soldiers wouldn't fancy looking.

Something glinted in a niche on the far side of the shaft. Craning his neck, he saw a bronze statuette somehow overlooked by the devils, which might fetch a good price in Suez. At least he'd come out of this with something. Cautiously, he began traversing the ramp. Wide as a tram, it must've been installed by the devils to help them move stuff – a steel cable ran overhead, shiny with lubricant.

Just in reach, he reckoned – and then his foot slipped on a smear of oil.

Yasmina heard him scream down the shaft. Saw him scrabbling for a hold, sliding down the ramp towards her. She had seconds to react, to save his life – to risk her own.

She could've stepped back and watched him hurtle by, but she hunched her shoulders, tensed and threw herself into his path. A stunning blow, pain exploding like fireworks, her flesh skinned raw. She tasted blood and dust. Choking, coughing, her body trembling against rock, Tariq gripping her wrist, her shoulder on fire.

Tariq spat grit and wiped his face. His cheek was bleeding but he grinned at her. He'd nearly wrenched her arm from its socket pulling her off the ramp, a second after she'd shoved him to safety on the far steps. His reactions were swift as a cat's. They clasped each other as they drew breath, fervently thanking God.

They were about to resume climbing when Yasmina heard a wail, far below.

They'd left her behind to die in the shaft. Cobwebbs clutched at Carina's hair; her legs trembled. Grasping a ledge, she dislodged a skull that shattered at her feet. She could only endure like Granddad in the POW camp. As a child she'd thought it sounded jolly – brewing hooch and building secret radios – but later realized otherwise. Shortly before Granddad died he'd taken her to lunch in Saffron Walden, confessed to bayoneting an Italian who'd surrendered, and watching cattle trucks full of Jews pass by his camp one winter. "One is capable of anything," he said sadly.

Now she understood it viscerally. If a chance had arisen in the burial chamber, she would have kicked GM in the balls herself. Freed of the gag she'd felt a murderous rage and might have stabbed him if Yasmina hadn't dragged her away.

But the important thing was to *escape*. Granddad tried twice, getting halfway to Switzerland the second time. *Keep moving* was the escaper's credo. To fortify herself with the distance she'd come she glanced back down the shaft.

GM was lurching up the steps behind her...

Morphine sang in his veins.

He'd dosed himself with syrettes from the first-aid box he kept at hand on jobs. Morphine first – enough to quell the pain but not so much he nodded off – then methamphetamine for energy. Say what you like about Hoda, her pharmaceuticals were ace. They'd seen to Aisha, now he'd deal with the others while he was whizzed...

He climbed robotically, the Leatherman rigid as his family jewels were mush. If he couldn't fuck her, he'd cut Yasmina's throat once he'd dealt with the others. He'd settled with Aisha – now he'd do *her*...

He could see the Islington cow's fat arse above him.

Not far and I'm gaining, he gloated. *It doesn't matter which one's first!*

She shrieked for help – he heard Yasmina respond. His fingers itched for her throat. Baring's wife was faltering, looking back in terror. *Almost there!*

And then he heard hammering, echoing down the shaft...

Looting derelict buildings had taught Tariq to read cracks and sense weight. Some gangs broke through party walls or ceilings to reach apartments where the stairs had buckled. So when the shaft narrowed and he saw the steel props flanking grooves in the walls, he grasped their meaning at once. This was no precaution against rock-falls, but a tomb-robber's version of forcing a lock. There was even a sledgehammer, invitingly at hand.

It was longer than his arm but swung readily. The steel prop flinched from his blows. "Hurry," he called down the shaft to Yasmina. Panting, she took the last dozen steps towards the opposite prop. "Hit it," he urged.

Yasmina found a rock and swung it clumsily with both hands. At first she didn't have the right swing – the steel column hardly quivered – but soon both props were shaking in tandem from their blows. He glanced down the shaft.

Fifty steps below the hen was doubled over, the man shambling up behind like a zombie. Tariq yelled at her to get upstairs so they could drop the slab, but she didn't understand till Yasmina told her in American. She was as thick as semolina.

Suddenly the prop bent, jumping sideways with a screech.

Sand poured on his head; the shaft rumbled like Satan's bowels.

"Back, back!" he screamed. The lights flickered...

Yasmina reeled away from her own prop as it bent like liquorice.

"Move!" he cried, racing up the steps. Glancing back he saw the slab falling as slowly as a theatre curtain, Yasmina safely clear but no longer following. She was waiting for the hen, to grab an arm once she'd passed the slab. Drooling with fury, the zombie was only a few steps behind...

The lights were fading, the updraft expiring.

God raised Tariq's eyes to a weapon in an alcove. As his hand closed on its hilt, he heard a triumphant cry, turned and saw the zombie lunging for the hen's ankle.

Hissing curses, Yasmina slid down the ramp to kick the zombie's face, sending him somersaulting down the shaft, his legs sliding beneath the slab, his torso following...

The slab settled on his belly like a busdriver on a cushion.

Blood frothed from his mouth.

Groaning, the zombie fumbled a box from his vest, twisting a dial.

As he did, everything went black.

"*Kuss ummak*, get those generators on!"

Not without the ignition keys you won't, Sabr smirked as he circled the perimeter. *And I threw them away!* Soldiers were blundering towards the generators leaving the Rubb Hall unguarded. Now all he had to do was find the English and escape. Easier said than done, but he sensed that Saiyida Zeinab and all the sheikhs were blessing him tonight. Now, if he slipped behind those crates there...

Moments later he was inside the Rubb Hall behind a row of compressors. Casings still hot, the acrid smell of lubricant; he pinched his nostrils to avert a sneeze. As his eyes adjusted to the gloom – some moonlight penetrated the hall – he saw a gaping pit, sides riddled with cavities, hoses plunging into total darkness.

What were the Libyans doing here? Building a secret bunker?
And that smell – like the mummified cat he'd found as a boy.
He froze.
Someone was coming from the pit...
A dwarf with a sword – he didn't believe it!
Was this really a set for Baby Gaddafi's latest movie?

Tariq sensed him before he smelled his aftershave. Coolly, he waited for the women to catch up, loud as turkeys. As they came in sight of his enemy, Tariq ducked behind a crate. Darting to another, crawling through a ditch, he worked his way round to his enemy's back clutching the sword. Closing like a fox on geese, ready to chop like a butcher, it wasn't what he'd imagined but it had to be done...

Tariq examined him from behind, unarmed, not even in uniform. This would be easier than he'd feared – a stab in the back rather than face to face.

And then the hen interfered.

Clucking as she fell into a hole, drawing the man out before Tariq could get close. He heard Yasmina jump in and raced forward himself, but when he rounded the corner they were embracing like contenders on Who Prays to be a Millionaire, gabbling in American. He caught the word *jeep*.

His intended victim glared at Tariq's sword. "Put it away, kid."

So this guy was really their ally – he didn't get it.

There was a burst of shooting outside.

"*Yallah*," Yasmina ordered, "Lead us to the car."

Now was the denouement – Colonel Avi could tell. The bug in the Land Cruiser hadn't transmitted a peep recently, but the one sewn into the Egyptian's windcheater was supplying realtime intelligence. Besides oaths used by NCOs the world over, his Arabic was fluent enough to identify such phrases as "That circuit", "Ready soon" and "Leave no survivors."

His hand stole to the button that would send the night shift to the bomb-shelter. Should he call Taba airbase and demand an immediate strike on the plateau? What was happening there? It was ominously quiet. He turned the volume to max.

Someone fired up a generator.

The charges exploded, tearing the Siq apart, igniting fuel and crates on the surface. Cedar palanquins turned to ash and golden masks liquefied in the inferno. A fireball churned in the sky, its incandescence visible over the horizon from Suez. As its radiance faded there were screams of agony.

Colonel Avi reeled back, deafened. On the CCTV monitors he saw Arabs pointing at the sky, but no sign that Suez had been hit. He caught his breath, righted his chair and sat down to send an urgent message to Jerusalem.

Events have moved swiftly since my last report. Seizing a chance to send a native asset to investigate the Giza Plateau, I determined that there was indeed a Libyan missile battery on the verge of becoming operational. Mindful of the threat to Suez, I exercised my discretionary powers, ordering my asset to neutralise the battery. From the explosions registered by our Commint, it seems he has complied. I urgently request satellite or drone verification of the damage caused to the installations.

He cracked his knuckles, imagining the consternation it would cause and the plaudits for his initiative that would follow.

14 HUNTING WITH COBRAS

Sabr knew that the Blessed Zeinab had cast her protection over him. How else could he have saved them from the fiery pit, or realised that only the desert offered safety? And now she was guiding his limbs as he raced the jeep without lights past boulders and ravines. Sabr exulted in his daring and this sign from God that the *baraka* of Saiyida Zeinab hadn't died with the Flood, even if the tombs of the sheikhs no longer existed. He would've sung their praises, but the women began bickering.

Squashed between them, Tariq stoked their quarrel with digs that Yasmina translated whenever her own bile flagged. All debts had been settled. She'd aided Carina at terrible risk to herself. She'd avenged Aisha's death and her own dishonour. Now she wanted out, back to Suez. And she was furious with Carina for exposing her so readily. Were Englishwomen so useless they couldn't even *lie* properly?

The hen wasn't having any of it! Yasmina had agreed to take her money; a deal was a deal, like in Europe or America. What happened on the plateau wasn't Carina's fault. How was she to know that Hosni and GM were in it together? And even if she'd realized, fabricating a story *wasn't her*. If Yasmina and Tariq were so good at lying, it was because they were Egyptians. And why was Sabr driving into the desert, away from the Valley?

A ripple of firecrackers in the darkness ended the argument.

Sabr slapped the steering wheel; he'd been right to shun the bridge! His compatriots shifted nervously as they understood, but the hen seemed unsure, despite the drone and lights above the Valley.

"The Basha has called a helicopter gunship to destroy the bridge," he announced as breezily as he'd told tourists that their felucca would be becalmed until the wind changed. "They'll be looking for us soon. We must hide in the desert – and sleep. Aren't you tired?"

Still he drove for another hour across the undulating terrain, slower now the helicopter was a firefly in the night. Eventually they reached a cluster of *yardangs* like giant brioches left in an oven for eternity, whose overhangs would mask the car if the gunship flew this way. But Sabr's chief concern was sleep. He was so exhausted, even the proximity of two women didn't excite him. Besides, tonight he would sleep in the arms of Saiyida Zeinab, serenely as a child.

Kuss ummak, swore Hosni, salving a burn on his cheek. If GM was alive, he'd flay him an inch at a time for letting the scum escape. He wasn't sure if GM had detonated the charges or the fugitives were responsible – but half his treasure had been vaporised, his troops decimated and secrecy gone to shit. He'd only survived by God's will; the landing zone was over a kilometre from the tomb. And yet, it seemed he'd be denied revenge...

Hunting with helicopters at night, avionics were everything.

Apaches had sensors that could detect a fox at two kilometres or make a car show up like a cowpat on a tablecloth. How Hosni longed for a Heli-Brigade to swarm over the desert... But only a single squadron of Apaches had survived the Flood, and *they* were far upriver in Nubia. All he had were Cobras – older gunships on a derelict airbase in range of the plateau. As it proved, only one was on standby and its sensor was jinxed, making it as much use as a foreskin to a Jew.

He ordered it to stand down and mechanics to work through the night on the other Cobras. The search would resume at dawn, but the odds of finding them were slimmer than a goatherd on Jebel Attrash.

They awoke at dawn, chilled. Sabr found a rusty can, filled it with sand and soused it with petrol; using the improvised stove to heat a mess-tin of water for tea to accompany their 'Bedouin breakfast' of stale bread, which the Egyptians dunked to Carina's disgust until she realised that anything was preferable to eating woodchip. She even felt better afterwards though she'd never dream of such a diet in England, even in detox.

As the man among them, Sabr opened the parley, self-importantly. In his opinion it would be fatal to swing back towards the Valley so long as helicopters were searching for them. Yet they had no more food, only one jerry-can of water and fifty litres of fuel, which wouldn't last for more than a day or so... *No comfort there, then.*

Yasmina drew in the sand to explain her plan: circling north and crossing the Delta to reach Suez, where the Israelis might protect them in return for information. Sabr hooted derisively. The Delta would be waterlogged for weeks, and anyway, why should a bargirl be of any interest to an Israeli unless she was sitting on his lap?

As Yasmina replied furiously in Arabic, Carina's patience snapped.

"Don't I get a say? Why don't we call Mr Baines? He'll rescue us; protect us from Hosni; fly us out of Egypt on an agency plane."

"When the Sphinx speaks," Sabr scoffed.

"*You*, not us," explained Yasmina. "We haven't got passports or any foreign country to welcome us. Even Muslim states don't want Egyptian refugees. The only places we could run to are the Israeli Mandate or Libya's Protectorate. Sabr can think what he likes, but I'd rather live under the Israelis than the Libyans – *especially* if I have to sit on their laps."

"*Mitnaka*," spat Sabr, "You'd rather fuck a Jew than an Arab."

"No, I don't want sex with anyone – and I won't if I can avoid it. But that's easier in Suez than in the Protectorate. You wouldn't understand that, being a *man*."

"You're crazy. A good fucking might clear those ideas from your head."

"I don't have to listen to this, you're not my brother!"

"Stop it," Carina yelled. "I made a perfectly reasonable suggestion and you're at it like cats and dogs. I don't care what you think of each other. Just call Baines – or I will." She dug in her pockets and then hurried to the car to search the dashboard. *Christ* – she'd lost her mobile on the plateau, the guards had taken it...

Smirking, Sabr produced his own with an ironic bow.

She stabbed the keys before registering a flashing icon. *No signal available*. "Shit, shit..." She felt like throwing it on the ground.

"*Mish mumkin!*"

Sabr was glaring at her – no, at Tariq. He'd been rummaging in the car and found some binoculars – Sabr's.Tariq danced away, sprinting up a hillock to pose on the summit, surveying the desert. Sabr pursued him, cursing. When he was halfway uphill Tariq ran down to meet him, jabbering. Sabr grabbed the binoculars and scurried to the summit. When he returned his face was set.

"Helicopters, fifty kilometres away."

Her heart sank. Should they stay put among the rocks or flee over open terrain? The white Land Cruiser was as conspicuous as a flag. She was starting to think like Granddad in the tank battles of the Western Desert.

Sabr began cuffing Tariq towards the jeep. She didn't understand what he was barking but Yasmina looked horrified. Do *something*, she thought. *Intervene*.

Brutally, Sabr flung Tariq across the bonnet, slapping his face. The boy squirmed free, struggled upright and drew his penis from his trousers. Face clenched as if his teeth were being drilled, he began to urinate, jerking the spray like Jackson Pollock.

"Throw sand," urged Sabr, "Before it dries."

Suddenly it made sense.

Camouflage.

Outside Suez, Colonel Avi waited at the airport to greet General Debka, anticipating the Ofeq satellite that would soon pass over the plateau, transmitting realtime imagery to its earth station in the Negev. He could hardly wait for confirmation of the damage caused by his agent, an inspired choice who'd surpassed his own expectations if the truth be admitted – not that he'd be so naive. The only flaw in this scenario was that clouds might obscure the plateau. Radar and infrared imaging were powerful but interpreting data was like trying to make sense of Kabbalah. Even if the analysts agreed that a blob or dash was metal, not rock, they might as easily be coaches as missile launchers. And his Commint had all but dried up: the windcheater bug hadn't worked since the explosion, and talk in the Egyptians' car was often drowned out by music. Only the tracker faithfully recorded their snail's crawl into the Fayoum Swamps, one of the vast depressions left waterlogged by the Flood.

Sabr cursed, hammering the steering wheel. Stuck in this *zift* for the sixth or seventh time! He admitted to himself that his dead reckoning had gone 180°. Even if he had a compass, he wasn't certain how to plot a course. And only God knew how the terrain had altered since the Flood. The Fayoum was once the Garden of Egypt, famous for its fruit and poultry. Now congealed mud and oozing quagmires, devoid of any landmark but the windswept lake they'd been circling for the past two hours. With hindsight, Sabr should've stayed on high ground rather than leaving the plateau; now they were trapped in these marshy lowlands, axle-deep in *zift*.

The others piled out to unfasten the traction-mats, knelt in the mud to free the wheels and force the mats into place.

"Now I know what it's like on an adventure safari," moaned the hen. "Give me a holiday with lots of pampering any time."

"I'd be happy with a shower," said Yasmina, her shirt dark with sweat along her spine. "Even a shift at the Euro would be better than this."

"*Khara alaik!*" cursed Tariq. "Stop blabbing in American and put your backs into pushing. This place is driving me crazy. No people, no animals. Nothing to eat but a pack of dates – and you're lucky I found them."

"And scoffed half before we noticed," Yasmina retorted. "So generous…"

"I'm still growing; I can't diet like a rich lady. Look at the hen – she could live for a week on the fat on her hips!"

Sabr smiled; Tariq spoke truly. Carina was blithely unaware of his insult. "*Yallah*," he called, revving the engine.

Mud flew into their faces as they pushed. The car heaved free and bounded away; they scrambled in before it stalled. Sabr groaned when he saw the fuel gauge: the mud was drinking their diesel like a farmer at a wedding. At this rate, they'd get bogged down forever in an hour or two. And Tariq kept making a big show of watching for helicopters with the binoculars, which weren't even Sabr's but belonged to the agency.

"Break them and I'll ream your ass," he warned.

"Don't worry, it's already wider than your *zobra*," Tariq riposted.

Son of dirt! The kid's mouth was filthier than Sabr's felt at that moment…

Yet over the next hour, it seemed Zeinab's *baraka* had returned. The mud firmed and they passed onto a smooth saline crust beside the shore. Sabr accelerated and put on Amr Diab to raise their spirits higher. *Yallah*, *habibi*, he sang. Tariq and Yasmina joined in and the hen hummed along. For a while it felt as carefree as a safari, and Tariq forgot about watching for helicopters.

The sky was clear – ideal for reconnaissance. Colonel Avi peered at the screen over General Debka's shoulder, his breath misting its coveted insignia. Soon he'd wear four stars himself; the satellite would confirm everything. "A Mi-6 transport helicopter, like the Libyans use," Debka growled. "And those are pallets and forklifts. But where are the launchers? The blast pattern shows a single detonation, but a battery would be dispersed. If they weren't destroyed, where are they? They can't have been loaded onto the copter in the time it's been there."

Colonel Avi coughed awkwardly. "Perhaps they're hidden in wadis, camouflaged – the Libyans are good at that." He saw Debka glower. "No, I've got it: the battery never dispersed from its set-up configuration. All six launchers were in a huddle when my agent blew them up together. The fireball was visible from Suez." That sounded better. "They're trying to cover up what happened, as usual."

"If you're right, I'd be the first to say you've earned a fourth star. But doesn't El-Bahr's air force have a Mi-6 too? How can we be certain it's Libyan? I can't see any insignia. The image is degrading as the angle gets acuter. It'll be gone in a minute."

Colonel Avi prayed silently. Just as the image was occluding they saw the helicopter lifting off, but its direction was unfathomable.

"I wouldn't count on that star yet," said Debka cruelly.

Sabr's back ached from straining over the tyre-iron. Two blow-outs in an hour – praise God for the extra spare on the roof. The saline crust had grown teeth that tore the rubber like chicken-skin. He glared at the fossils protruding from the salt. Trust women to drivel on about the dawn of creation while he and Tariq bust their guts. He had to drive slowly, nervously, like a woman.

The lake turned red as chilli sauce in the sinking sun, every ripple of terrain accentuated by shadow. Sabr rummaged among the cassettes the hen had brought. Nothing took his fancy. The car balked. He felt a jolt, heard something tear loose from the chassis. The others began bleating.

"I don't need wailing. Get out and help."

Ten minutes later it was clear the damage would take hours to fix, even if they had proper tools and spares. He could change a tyre but repairing an axle was beyond him, and the women were as much use as a shoe in a mosque. At least Tariq didn't mind oil on his hands. God help them if the hen broke another fingernail!

"It'll take a long time," he said, superfluously. "Better next morning. Start collecting wood – I'll make a fire and you prepare tea."

"I don't believe this," snapped the hen. "You strand us in the middle of nowhere and tell us to make tea. Sod off, I'm not your slave."

Tariq seized his arm before Sabr could reply. *"Usqut!"*

The Egyptians tensed, straining to hear above the cries of waterfowl and the rustling of reeds. Even the hen fell silent. Distantly, they heard the beat of rotors and saw a helicopter racing over the mud they had struggled through hours before.

Dusk faded in a blur of activity; nightfall brought rest and tenuous security. They had camouflaged the jeep with reeds, now they could only squint through the foliage and wish their pursuers gone. The helicopter followed a zig-zag search pattern, its searchlight probing like a burglar in a darkened flat. Coming nearer...

15 NANCY'S ARK

Nancy smiled, her cheeks like winter apples. "You're darn lucky I decided to visit this side of the lake ahead of schedule. Otherwise you'd have died there. There's water to drink but nothing to eat unless you can hunt crocs or hippos. Don't suppose you can, right?"

Carina shook her head weakly. She still hadn't got over the shock of Nancy's appearance. They'd been cowering in the jeep as the helicopter drew closer when there was a roar from the lake and the hovercraft swept into view. For a moment she cherished a wild hope it was Nick, arriving to save them. She'd sweated over his fate as the helicopter hovered overhead, training its searchlight on the craft.

"You don't want to mess with the Smithsonian, I told them," Nancy boasted afterwards. "I said, I'm American, I work for the Smithsonian, I have a permit to be in the Fayoum Swamps from Hosni Basha, so if you've any other questions, ask him!" Apparently deterred the helicopter had buzzed off, as Nancy nosed her hovercraft ashore. With two turbo-fans mounted at the stern and a boxy cabin amidships, it bore as little resemblance to the Channel hovercrafts of Carina's youth as a go-kart to a Mercedes.

While Carina still hoped that Nick would emerge, the Egyptians nerved themselves for an assault. Instead, an unarmed woman climbed ashore, singing to herself. Carina knew she'd heard that voice before, associated it with laughter. It wasn't Nick, but it was someone who'd help them. And her intuition had been proved right.

Nancy Milgram might be dotty about re-wilding Egypt – as Carina recalled from the garden party at El-Gouna – but she handled the hovercraft as easily as a golf-buggy at a country club. It was, in fact, a Swamp-Master from the Florida Everglades, where she'd done her post-grad fieldwork. "I fell in love with the Everglades," she confided to Carina. "You can't imagine what it meant to me, all that primeval fertility. I couldn't wait to leave the prairie behind.

"The Fayoum is magical, a primeval lake coming back to life. Forty-five million years ago this whole area was beneath the Tethys Sea that covered the Sahara. As the sea shrank, all kinds of proto-whales got stranded and became fossilised. We can't bring them back to life without viable DNA and there isn't a hope of that – but hippos are easy. We flew a dozen cows and three bulls in last year, as soon as it became clear the lake wasn't saline. With luck, they'll have had one litter since then and be ready to calve a second anytime now."

Nancy steered the hovercraft into a limpid stretch of water and dulled the engines till they weren't any louder than Tariq's snores. She turned on a monitor and swivelled the camera towards the shore.

"Yay," she crowed. "There's an Indian file coming up the arroyo to graze. Lemme count them. Right, twenty-five... almost what I expected. I bet most of the cows are due to drop any moment – yeah, there are a few calves already, riding on their mothers' backs."

Carina peered over her shoulder. Despite the eerie X-ray view of their internal organs, the hippos were clearly visible, cows swatting each other's rumps with swatches of reeds as the bulls watched tetchily. They lived in groups of up to thirty, under a dominant bull and other males, who fought for supremacy with their teeth. Yet hippos were vegetarian, which made them kind of cute.

"They're such *social* mammals," enthused Nancy. "Wallowing and sleeping all day, then heading off for chow together. Of course, for farmers, it's no fun having a herd uprooting their crops. The Egyptians organised hippo hunts as early as the Pre-Dynastic era. Cultivation gradually reduced their habitats to a few swamps. The last hippo in Egypt was shot in the Delta in 1815 – and that was it, till now."

She glanced to see if the Egyptians were listening. "I know the Flood was a disaster," she whispered, "But it was a blessing from the hippos' standpoint. Now most of the Valley and Delta are an ideal habitat, with no human predators. Sure Egyptians will reclaim them eventually, but meantime colonies can be established. Since it became a freshwater lake and the reeds grew back, the Fayoum is perfect. We're lobbying for it to become a hippo sanctuary, in perpetuity... Gee, I'm sorry – I could talk hippos all night, when you're falling asleep. Let me fetch the airbeds."

Having slept well under mosquito netting, Sabr awoke to discover that the strange craft ran to hot showers and Continental breakfast. Wearing clean clothes, a croissant in one hand and a mango juice in the other, he could tolerate being lectured by this woman whose dungarees and oily hands made her look like a mechanic. Surely she was a lesbian – would a normal woman go roaming swamps without a man?

The lesbian explained that her visits to the lake coincided with the hippos' mating and calving. At mating time, the chief bull would try to cover every cow in the herd despite constant challenges from rivals. Mature bulls were covered with scars from such combats. Her job was to monitor the herd and locate other sites for herds as yet unborn.

While the hen listened intently, Sabr saw no reason to get excited except the fact that one bull would fuck all the cows after fighting the other bulls. It sounded like a good life for a man. He'd bet his own *zobra* the bull basha was hung like an elephant. Surely that was why the lesbo came here so often, to watch these creatures enjoying what she feared to do with a man. Such deviancy explained her dual nature: she behaved like a man, yet hung flowerboxes on her craft. Perhaps Allah had created her simply for this moment, so they might be rescued and enjoy a cruise. God's ways were wondrous.

Eventually, the lesbo told them to clear away while she hauled up the anchor. When he stayed seated she snapped, "You too, buddy. There's no freeloading on my hovercraft." Face burning, he complied. God protect him from her evil eye. Tariq, too, leapt into action, glad of a chance to poke around.

Yasmina's head ached from the American's chatter. She couldn't resist lecturing a captive audience. As if Yasmina cared about the mating habits of animals! Yet Carina was fascinated, focusing binoculars on every bulge in the water, every herd on the mudbanks. The creatures seemed oblivious to the hovercraft's approach; perhaps they were used to its presence. Its engines sank to a murmur as the craft idled offshore.

A fat wrinkled sow burst from the water. Beneath it, Yasmina glimpsed a submerged leviathan. An infant, riding on its mother's back.

"That's so cute," cooed Carina. "Have a look."

Yasmina took the binoculars reluctantly. She'd last seen a hippopotamus in the Zoological Gardens at Giza, not long before the Flood. And now these playful, ugly creatures were flourishing where millions of Egyptians had perished, with the American and her hovercraft as Nuah and his ark.

Bitter fruit of the Black Day...

Sabr used his own binoculars to espy a different union. He'd found the bull basha, a giant scarred as a butcher's block, which had just seen off an interloper on the shore. Now the basha was about to assert his rights over a cow. Sabr strained to see its truncheon, thick as a fire hose. He envied the bull's freedom to satisfy its urges, unburdened by marriage or children. Pawing and snorting, it lumbered forward to mount the cow.

"Look at this," he commanded the women.

Carina gave him the cold shoulder, but Yasmina took the binoculars. She focused, laughed, and slapped them into his palm.

"Look yourself, you'll learn something."

By God she was right! The cow had moved on to fresh grazing leaving the bull bewildered, its pizzle trailing in the mud, until it slunk into the lake to conceal its shame.

Disgusted, Sabr turned away, to see Tariq clutching a bulbous pistol. The boy winked conspiratorially.

"You're crazy," Sabr hissed. "Put it down before the lesbo sees you."

"Let her pop!" Tariq snickered, aiming the muzzle at the bull in the water. Sabr could have wrenched the gun away but hesitated till it was too late. He wanted to punish the basha for his own humiliation.

With a bang and a whistle, a flare arched over its head. Roaring, the bull lunged towards the hovercraft. Jaws like an earthmover's scoop vanished underwater, as the deck rocked and the engines roared above their screams.

"Hang on!" cried the lesbo.

Sabr reeled against the cabin, saw Tariq go headlong across the deck, heard women shrieking as the craft spun around, rising from the lake. Stunned, he watched the foaming water as Tariq jeered at the receding bull basha.

Stacking plates in the dishwasher, they smiled at Tariq wriggling beneath the Land Cruiser as Nancy berated Sabr with a monkey-wrench from her tool-locker. It was just comeupench for masculine arrogance, and all the sweeter that they had to acknowledge a woman's technological superiority. The homely chugging of the dishwasher somehow diminished the disparity between Yasmina's life and her own, Carina felt. Sharing the cosy galley, talking about men's foolishness, there wasn't a gulf between them.

Seen objectively, she wasn't responsible for Yasmina's past or their present predicament. The Egyptians had chosen to follow her for their own reasons – it was hardly Carina's fault they'd survived so far. Anyway, they were Muslims. According to their religion, Allah decided all. If the Flood destroyed Egypt, if the planet was cooking, that was God's will too. *Everything is inevitable – if it wasn't, it wouldn't happen*, a poster in a squat in Cambridge had assured her on her nineteenth birthday.

Her reverie was interrupted by Nancy thumping the window pane. It was time for the guys to get a nod of appreciation after slaving under the jeep. Dutifully she rose, catching Yasmina's eye, sharing a grin as they climbed from the galley to the deck.

"Maybe you're not so clueless," Nancy conceded, after crawling beneath the chassis herself. "If you shaped up some more, I'd consider hiring you as grease-monkeys. Now go shower before lunch; you smell like hippo poop."

Whether or not this was meant to remind them of their misdeeds, Tariq and Sabr both opted for a shower rather than a dip in the lake. Over lunch, Nancy stated her intentions and invited them to consider their own. She was heading for her supply dump on the far side of the lake. They could stock up on gas and water; she'd charge a fair price. Afterwards she could let them off there, or bring them back to the eastern shore next day, depending on whether they aimed to reach the oases or return to the Valley. Tactfully, Nancy neither asked if they were fleeing, or why helicopters were pursuing them. However, she pointed out, under the Smithsonian's concession, her satphone and email were routed through Hurghada, and she was bound to respect El-Bahr's laws. Without saying so, she made it plain that fugitives would be unwise to send any messages, and should vanish into the Western Desert without associating themselves with the Smithsonian.

"Talk it over outside, I've got to work on my laptop," she concluded.

They sat on the stern deck, re-hashing the near miss with the helicopter and Nancy's warnings. "I can drive us to the oases," insisted Sabr. "We'll follow the sun till we reach the Bahariya. They say the Emirate is poor but faithful; a sanctuary for Muslims."

"What about me? I'm not a Muslim," Carina protested.

"No problem. Just say the *Shahadah*."

"Pardon?"

"The profession of faith," explained Yasmina. "What every Muslim says at prayer. If you recite it three times, Allah would welcome you into the *umma*. It would make us happy, too."

"Er, thanks, I'll think about it…Meantime, aren't there any phones in the oases? I'd rather call the consulate in Hurghada or someone in London than depend on charity."

"With God's permission," muttered Sabr sullenly.

"If only I had my own satellite link," mused Carina, "I could call from here."

"This isn't a safari," he snapped. "The agency doesn't give satphones to drivers. Even your husband only had a laptop – and that's missing too."

Yasmina hissed something in Arabic at him, but Carina interrupted.

"Hang on, what did you say about Nick's laptop?"

"It disappeared at the same time as him."

"But I've seen Nick's possessions and Baines said nothing was missing."

"Whatever; it wasn't on the list they gave to the police." He shrugged and glared at them. "Well, they treat me like dust, so of course I read their messages."

16 SALVATION FIRST

Most nights Nick surfed in his room at the Residency, watching Test Match highlights or delving into the apocalyptic world of Christian evangelism embraced by his employer. It seemed both laughable and chilling with its whores of Babylon and the tribulations awaiting humanity once the faithful had been 'raptured'. There was even a Rapture Index – the Dow Jones of Armageddon.

Events in the Middle East (or 'Holy Land') were the fulfilment of a divine plan that would culminate in the conversion of the Jews to Christianity. Egypt's destruction was foretold in Ezekiel 29: 9-12.

> And the land of Egypt shall be desolate and waste; and they shall know that I am the LORD:
> because he hath said, "The river is mine, and I hath made it".
> Behold, therefore I am against thee, and against thy rivers, and I will make the land of Egypt utterly waste and desolate, from the tower of Syene even unto the border with Ethiopia.
> No foot of man shall pass through it, nor foot of beast shall pass through it, neither shall it be inhabited forty years.
> And I will make the land of Egypt desolate in the midst of the countries that are desolate, and her cities among the cities that are laid waste shall be desolate forty years; and I will scatter the Egyptians among the nations, and disperse them through the countries.

Two thousand years on, its apocalyptic resonance was confirmation enough for believers. Millions who might have otherwise been sceptical were swayed by Ezekiel's mention of Syene – the ancient name for Aswan, the source of the Flood. Only cynics drew attention to inconvenient details that didn't fit the reality. For example that Egypt had been devastated from Aswan to the Mediterranean, and not 'unto the border of Ethiopia' – or that survivors massed on the fringes instead of being scattered among neighbouring countries. And Salvation First aimed to resettle a million refugees a year in the Nile Valley, once the pilot projects were running smoothly. Maybe that was over-optimistic, but it was hard to imagine the Valley remaining uninhabited for forty years...

So the prophecy was both true and false – rather like accounts, really. If the Inland Revenue was as credulous as evangelicals, Nick would be living in a seaside villa with a pool rather than a two-up two-down in Tufnell Park. As if.

Naturally, hundreds of websites cited the prophecy as evidence of God's plan. The reference in Salvation First's 'faith statement' was less fulsome than he'd expected from an agency tasked with rebuilding Egypt. The only other mention was at the start of the 'About us' section, stating that the agency 'arose from an initiative by the Salvation Mission of St Ezekiel (Pastor N. Kreutzer)', merging two evangelical charities in the US with support groups in Europe and Australia.

Reading between the lines, it had merely held seminars ('capacity-building') until Baines became CEO. Within a year, however, its list of donors was as blue-chip as its investments portfolio – a double-barrelled testament to his reputation on Wall Street. SF first showed its mettle in Zimbabwe, in a complex emergency combining famine, flooding and anarchy after years of drought and civil war. While not the lead agency, SF was praised for feeding nine million Zimbabweans at the height of the crisis, though its recovery programme was criticised for introducing genetically-modified maize into the African biosphere.

With each disaster its reputation was enhanced or grew more dubious, depending on your standpoint. In Central Asia, SF's 'hot' engineering teams prevented nuclear waste from contaminating the Fergana Basin, but the agency's missionaries were blamed for riots in Tajikistan. In Bangladesh, it performed prodigies in the aftermath of the Great Cyclone, but was accused by the press of doing nothing to save Muslim shrines. ("If you're not being criticised you're not doing your job," Baines retorted). Or the earthquake that levelled Hama in Syria, where SF was first mandated as lead agency. Again its achievements were praised, but its field director was accused of trying to bribe the Mufti of Damascus to restore certain shrines to the Christians and later resigned from the agency.

Nevertheless, four months after the Flood, the United Nations mandated Salvation First to be the sole relief agency in Egypt, where scores of NGOs and UN agencies had added muddle to chaos. Critics carped that SF only got its unique mandate because the US government threatened to slash its contribution unless the UN complied; or because Baines donated $800 million of his own fortune to jumpstart the funding process.

Baines took personal control at field HQ, shrugging off jokes about its location in the Empire Hotel. Within six weeks the agency suppressed cholera and typhoid in the camps, which had killed over 460,000 refugees. Nutritional metrics improved and neighbouring states sighed with relief that millions of Egyptians wouldn't overwhelm their borders. Israel, Libya and Arabia might detest each other, but they had that much in common.

Diplomatically, it helped that SF's mandate was endorsed by the head of state of the legitimate residue of Egypt, namely President Zaghloul of El-Bahr. Conversely, the Emirate wasn't deemed a disaster zone and the few states that recognised its regime were far away and unable to help. Even the Wahhabis of Arabia turned a deaf ear to their pleas, yet seemed prepared to stomach Christian evangelism in El-Bahr, so long as Egyptians didn't swarm across the Red Sea to Jeddah.

Cynicism might be the essence of international relations, but some of the evangelistic sites predicted events that were utterly bizarre. At the last trump, sinners would be transmuted into animals and insects as a prelude to eternal damnation. Even the Chosen People wouldn't be spared unless they bowed down before Jesus; all but 144,000 would perish in the 'mother of holocausts' for refusing to do so, according to a site that claimed a worldwide audience of one hundred million. At least Salvation First helped the victims of disasters rather than ghoulishly anticipating them – however odd some of their donors might be.

Nick rubbed his eyes. Enough surfing; it was time for tea and a spot of backgammon over a waterpipe prepared by Mr Sheesha. The old man seldom failed to remind Nick about the cassette he'd promised to give to the imam of the Regent's Park mosque once he was back in London. Stepping outside the Residency, he was surprised to see the teashop dark and shuttered. He crossed the road, wondering if he should knock on the door. Three men in dark clothing were lounging by the wall, and a navy blue pickup with the orange licence-plate that signified police idled nearby. He veered away, trying to pretend he'd mistaken something, but it was too late.

"Passport." The cop smelt of beer and had a simian physique.

He thumbed the pages, squinting at stamps; showed it to a colleague, who muttered and shrugged. "OK, go, go." As Nick turned away, a fourth man emerged from behind the teashop and slung a laundry bag into the pickup.

When the teashop reopened a week later, Mr Sheesha had gone. In hospital after an accident they said, but nobody seemed to want to talk about it.

17 HITLER'S BRAINS

I'm scared, Nick admitted to himself. When Yasmina had told him about Aisha's murder, he'd become fired up about discovering what GM was doing without realising where it might lead. He had been thinking like an auditor, seeking evidence to present to Baines. But after abandoning his mad idea of bribing the hovercraft crew to take him across the Nile, he began to understand that GM could only have been operating under somebody's protection. After three months in El-Bahr, Nick knew that little escaped Hosni Basha's notice. How could GM have another patron when the Security Minister was so omniscient? Which meant Nick was setting himself against a despot who could order a man's death as casually as a cup of tea.

He might be British, but *habeas corpus* held no sway in El-Bahr – and accidents could always be arranged, as with poor Mr Sheesha.

The tape was still an enigma even after Nick had played it to the end and heard Mr Sheesha's epilogue in English, relating his friend's demise and anticipating his own fate. It hinted at some revalation about the Flood, but whatever secret the tape held was contained in the mournful ballad – and that was in Arabic. Besides some invocations to Allah, Nick couldn't fathom a word. But it was clear that the café owner's friend had revealed his knowledge to the wrong person – the singer's fate and Mr Sheesha's 'accident' left no doubt of that.

It all led back to Hosni Basha. Who else could safeguard the plateau while GM looted it? Who else had a silver postbox in the bazaar, for anyone to leave a message? Who else invited Mr Sheesha's friend to El-Gouna before he was tortured to death? Who else could arrange a hit-and-run and send police to search the teahouse?

Nick longed to leave Egypt, but his contract still had three weeks to run and the audit wasn't written up yet. To quit early meant an explanation to Baines, which Nick was loath to give. Baines's signature was part of the paperwork required for an exit visa. If Baines took umbrage at Nick's exposure of GM's crimes it would only need a word to reach Hosni's ears and Nick would have signed his own death warrant. Even Baines couldn't prevent Hosni from committing another murder.

Anyway, was Baines trustworthy? Delving into Salvation First's donors, he'd been struck by their congruent interests. Companies specializing in infrastructure, resource extraction, agri-business and privatised public services flocked in SF's wake like gulls behind a trawler. According to Craven, the genetically modified crops that the agency had woven into its recovery programme in Zimbabwe were to be established in the Nile Valley. And the homes, roads and schools that would follow would all be built or owned or managed by the same corporations that had responded to SF's appeals.

Some were household names, others familiar from the business pages of the *Telegraph*. Most had websites which avowed their responsibilities to society and the environment, citing donations to charities including Salvation First. While self-interest was evident in some, it was difficult to discern any motive for the largesse of MacDonald's, Disney or Fox Media Group other than pure humanitarianism. As for SF's non-corporate donors, they were mostly religious organisations, interlinked by thousands of homepages and chat rooms with a godly slant.

Yet there was one name that yielded only sixteen results – and strange ones, too.

Google the TransHumane Society (with its odd elision) and you got links to institutes dedicated to the attainment of immortality and the creation of super-beings, some studiously scientific in tone, others featuring such postings as:

> Hitler had no brains but it is a fact that many Nazi-scientists moved to the US and many other Nazis fled to Argentina so one could possibly say that Hitler's brains are working somewhere else now. But what's the problem? The developments mentioned are meant to improve mankind, make man more resistant to certain plagues and increase his intelligence – a bit similar to improved crops. And after the supercrops, why not go on to create superhumans? Plastic bodies are according to these scientists an improvement since they would be better resistant to many chemical substances and also against other dangers human beings are confronted with in present society. And the children of those who oppose it will be angry, because they are doomed to be mediocre in a class full of highly intelligent children. Or they will be angry because they have a life expectancy of 80 years as opposed to the genetically modified humans who live 200 years.

What kind of weirdo would write that, with a name like Kreutzer to boot? How many nutters were out there in cyberspace? If you believed in the notion of Six Degrees of Separation, there must be a connection between them all.

18 THE SAVANNAH

Nancy's supply dump was as odd as her hovercraft. An ancient temple named Qaroun's Palace after a mythical pharaoh, actually built in homage to the crocodile-god Sobek, Nancy said. She'd chosen it because the exterior walls and roof were intact, and the steel entry gate easily locked. Corridors and chambers were stacked with drums of fuel, spares for the Swamp-Master, boxes of water, food, and assorted fossils found beside the lake.

Under Nancy's direction they beached the jeep, fed a fuel-line into the Swamp-Master's stern tanks and began gassing up. Then they filled the Land Cruiser's tank and jerry-cans and loaded food and water, Yasmina noting every packet of figs. From then on, they couldn't rely on anyone else until they reached Bahariya Oasis. By Nancy's map, just over 100 kilometres westwards by an old camel trail. She'd given them her spare compass to check their bearings. They'd reach the oasis in a day or two if nothing went wrong.

"Okay folks, chores done. Let's kick back," Nancy said, fixing a tray of drinks. Rather than relaxing aboard the hovercraft, she led them back into the temple, up a stairway furrowed by footsteps. "Every time I do this I think of priests taking libations to the shrine of Re – and me enjoying a Mint Julep." Two shaded loungers provided a soothing vantage point overlooking the shore. Flamingos waded past egrets and herons, wagtails and bitterns flitted among the reeds, and hawks circled overhead. Carina sprawled on a lounger, sighing with pleasure.

Shyly, Tariq curled up beside her. Showered, shampooed and wearing clean clothes (ridiculously large, but better than rags), he'd been transformed from a malodorous delinquent into an adorable boy, pointing at the birds and relating their Arabic names. Her attempts to repeat them made him laugh. Tariq was a sweetie, Carina's Mint Julep delicious. Even Sabr was on his best behaviour, telling stories of duck hunting with a sling-shot as a child. He made it seem as if he was confiding valuable ornithological data to Nancy, but his eyes kept flicking to Yasmina.

"I was never allowed out to play," she confided. "I grew up in Minya at the wrong time. Jihadis were killing policemen, tourists and innocent Muslims; the police arrested and tortured people; broke into houses, burned cane-fields. We wanted to live in peace with their neighbours but the jihadis tried to create hatred between us. They said they were fighting for Islam, but we knew many of them were from families that had been bad for generations. My parents kept me indoors, studying – that's how I got such good grades and they offered me a place at Giza University."

"It was the opposite for me," Carina confessed. "My parents were always packing me off to ballet classes or art lessons. They said it was to develop my talents, but they just wanted me out of the way so they could work longer hours or meet their lovers. When I faced up to the fact I was too tall for Sadler's Wells and couldn't paint, they complained I'd wasted all the tuition fees. I left home soon afterwards."

Secretly, Sabr agreed with the hen's parents. If he'd worked like a donkey to pay for a daughter's education and she ran off leaving his name dirty, he'd take his belt to her. As for her father's lovers, even a donkey deserved any hay on the path. Sabr's own father had enjoyed himself with chickens on his felucca until he was too old to handle either – and his mother had never breathed a word.

That night they slept aboard the hovercraft with the deck lights on. Sabr wondered if the lesbian meant to prevent him from ploughing Yasmina's field, until he heard gruff barks above the rustling the reeds and, once, the unmistakable howling of wolves.

Next day it became clear that predators were spoilt for choice. Salt-pans and wadis that once offered only rodents and the occasional gazelle were now a savannah, teeming with wild ruminants. Grasslands veined with cloven-hoof prints and trails of droppings; abloom with violets, oleanders and exotic orchids that Yasmina surmised had been washed down from the Ethiopian highlands.

"*Louk*," urged Tariq, clutching Carina's arm. In the distance, a dozen animated feather dusters were loping across the savannah, pursued by a tawny blur. One of the dusters swerved too late and the blur pounced; Sabr saw its pug face for an instant.

"A cheetah," he informed the hen. "I knew they'd been seen near Abu Simbel, but not this far north. They've followed the ostriches from Sudan."

"*Waddan*," shouted Tariq, pointing at a curly-horned sheep on a rock. The boy was itching to kill something with his stupid sword... thank God he didn't have a gun.

The hen ruffled Tariq's hair fondly. "He's such an animal lover."

They stopped for lunch on a pasture speckled with wildflowers, gazelles grazing unperturbed by their intrusion. This land was as innocent as the Garden of Eden, thought Yasmina. Only Man was sinful, and the only man here had sin on his mind. Sabr kept looking at her – no longer slyly as when the American was there, but shamelessly. So far she'd kept him at bay by talking to Carina, but when the Englishwoman disappeared 'for a tinkle' he seized his chance.

"*Ya gazala*, you're as shy as those beauties. Your eyes are velvet but flash with fire. Do you burn for me?"

"Your blood is a slap," she said icily.

"Let me please you".

"Then hide your tongue." He was such a buffalo; why should she yield to him when she'd spurned offers of hundreds of dollars – even marriage – at the Euro? Yet she couldn't deny her cheapened value in his eyes. Though she was still a virgin, any Egyptian would regard her as a whore. Better the shadow of a man than the shadow of a wall, people said. Perhaps she should plan a future instead of marking time, as if God would undo the Black Day. When what you want doesn't happen, learn to want what does…If she ever got back to Suez, she'd look for an older, half decent foreigner who'd overlook her past.

Having decided that, it didn't matter if she encouraged Sabr a bit. "Well, if you want to be nice, fetch me a drink." He was quite handsome, really, and not that bad if you ignored his obsession with his pigeon. She'd known a lot worse at the Euro.

In a trice he'd returned with a mug of water and a knowing smile.

19 DUNE WITH AN ENGINE

"Na'am, *Mustafa here. A maybe on Jebel Qatrani – what? Yes, Your Presence, between the lake and Bahariya. The spotter wasn't sure, he didn't report it till they were halfway back to base for refuelling – Aiwa, he deserves that, Sir.*"

He flicked channels to the crew's circuit. "*Listen! The boss ate my face because Mahmoud fucked up. We're taking over his search zone, and if we don't find the car we'll be shark bait too!*" They chorused their assent as the helicopter veered around.

Twenty minutes later they were flying over a fractured massif untouched by the Flood. And there, near the lip of an escarpment, was a white car. They'd found what the Basha was seeking where others had failed, he exulted. While Mahmoud took a swim he'd be enjoying the girls at El-Gouna. Tough luck on Mahmoud, but everyone knew what the score was working for the Father of Lies.

The car made no effort to flee as they circled lower. He could see an arm poking from a window and bodies slumped inside.

"*Take us down. Cover us as we close in.*" But he was being over-cautious.

The Land Cruiser fitted the description but he doubted that the bodies could have got into that state in a day or two. He wrenched open a door, gagging at the smell. The driver wore a galabiyya and sandals but the discolouration of the others made it hard to tell what race they belonged to, though from their hair, two had once been women, and one was surely a child.

He saw a notebook in a twisted hand and prised it free; its pages were brittle. He cursed when he saw the cover labelled in childish letters. MY DESERT SAFARI

Victims of the Black Day...

"*Yani*, we're somewhere here, between the trail and the highway," Sabr blustered.

"Big deal – that's hundreds of square kilometres!"

"So you figure it out, you went to university!"

"And you ran safaris, Mister 'Aswan Desert Lion'."

Trouble was, he'd never learnt to use a map and compass properly. Like most safari guides he'd driven with guys who knew the route until he'd memorized enough landmarks to find his own way – with GPS as a back-up.

But now it was down to real navigation he was floundering. Yasmina and the hen kept confusing him with different ways of aligning the compass; as for Tariq, a goat could sooner read the Holy Qur'an. If their situation weren't so grave it would be funny as a toupée on a judge.

They'd left the savannah for a desert of pale dust overlying ribs of stone that cracked beneath their wheels. Ahead, blistering scallops of sand built up to a golden wave on the horizon. The only landmark – as Sabr kept insisting.

"Ghard Abu Muharrik, the Dune with an Engine. Nothing can stop it. It swallows palm groves and roads, falls down cliffs and makes baby dunes to carry on its travels."

"Are you thinking we'll catch a ride? It looks a bastard to climb and it goes on forever. You haven't a clue where we are," said the hen cruelly.

"Never mind turning over old coals, we have to find a way across the dunes," interjected Yasmina, stating the obvious and confirming Sabr's point.

"God willing. But we shouldn't travel by day, we might be seen. Better at night, by the light of the moon – we can use the stars to navigate." They thought it over and bowed to his wisdom. "Good, so how about tea?" he suggested.

More copters had flown in to widen the search. By day there was some sense in trawling the desert, but at night they might as well have stayed in bed. Their IR sensor made a roomful of Syrians seem reliable, thought Sergeant Mustafa as a glow appeared on the screen, yet again.

At first he dismissed it as a wild sheep or a big cat, but as the ambient temperature sank its infrared spore was as plain as a Nubian's nose. They'd been disappointed before, but this time he scented success.

They'd get close to be sure of an ID, then rocket the car...

Straining with their backs to the jeep as Sabr revved the engine it felt as if the whole dune was shifting. The car stalled and began sliding; they leapt clear. This was crazy – they should never have listened to him. They'd crossed the ridge in bright moonlight to discover that it was a foothill of a Himalayan range which darkened as the moon fled behind clouds. Its face seemed almost vertical; disturbed, sand began flowing like molasses from the bottom upwards, a waterfall in reverse. Even in the dune's lee Carina heard the wind moaning. Up to her calves in sand, her hair thick with it, she cursed Egypt's desolation. The wheels were axle deep – she wanted to cry...

"*Dahrik!*" the boy yelled.

The Egyptians leapt to their feet. Tariq was pointing…

A light, speeding towards them…

Sabr wrestled a jerry can from the roof, Tariq grabbing food as Yasmina swept a torch over the seats, its beam catching Celine Dion's face. Impulsively, Carina seized three of Nick's tapes and stuffed them into her pocket. It was all she had of him; the last link between the normality of the Residency and the wreckage of their hopes.

Yasmina grabbed her arm. "Run, run…"

They lurched up the dune sobbing for breath. Stumbled over the crest and slid down the far side, as the helicopter pinned the car in its searchlight. A second later, the crest was silhouetted against a mauve glow; then a fireball and a wave of air that skimmed the crest like a spatula, showering them with sand. The sky thundered.

"Your father's eyes," crowed Sergeant Mustapha. "Take us round again to make sure they're not hiding."

"Aiwa, but look at the horizon – a storm's coming."

Stars were fading as an impenetrable mist advanced. He couldn't hear it above the engine, but felt the copter yawing as the wind gathered power. Aboudi was right; the mother of sandstorms was heading their way. It was time to go.

He looked down on the flames. Even if they hadn't been incinerated they would surely perish – without water in the desert, with a storm rising. Khalas. He'd report that they were dead and the whole crew would get wasted at El-Gouna.

20 EXEGESIS

"So let me get this straight, Baring..."

Baring. Nick shifted nervously. Baines had heard him out in silence, now his voice was dry as the Sahara.

"You're saying that our *lead* salvage contractor – GM Foster – is *looting* a tomb on the Giza Plateau. That he *killed* a bargirl and arranged for some other Egyptians to be gutted? That *maybe* he's in cahoots with Hosni Basha, to pull off the heist, right?"

Nick nodded dumbly.

"So let's look at the evidence." Baines circled the desk to perch on a corner. "The testimony of a Suez bargirl, a fence and a juvenile – that's it?"

"And mine – they told me things," Nick insisted.

"Any sworn affidavits? No, I thought not. Just your word for it – hearsay." Baines shrugged. "Any physical evidence? None I can see. No gold, no incriminating documents or recordings. And you didn't even *reach* the plateau, never mind see any tomb-robbing.

"Nothing to stand up in court – you wouldn't find a DA in the States who'd touch it with a stick. Salvation First is registered in Arkansas and mandated by the UN, so any defence counsel would argue US jurisdiction. Even in Egypt charges like that wouldn't stick unless the police got hold of your witnesses. Who just happen to be in Israeli Mandate territory, which raises the diplomatic ante.

"Now look it from *our* side, the agency's..." he paused for a gulp of water. "How does it look to our donors and public if an SF volunteer accuses a senior contractor of murder and grand larceny in collusion with the head honcho of the country we're trying to help? Talk about shafting us on every level...

"And now look at *your* conduct: a married man visiting red-light bars, mixing with hookers. Adultery is grounds for divorce in any country. How would your wife feel, ever thought about that?" Baines raised a finger in admonition. "Ok, so GM also went to the Euro – but he's not married and everyone knows his morals. The agency has to cut engineers some slack, has to be realistic – but our auditors must be squeaky clean."

"But –."

"Nick," – they were back to Nick again, like a cop to a suspect – "If we were playing soccer like you do in England, I'd say I was showing you the yellow card. Understand? One more mistake and off you go. You haven't only disappointed me personally, but you've betrayed yourself – and your wife."

Baines turned towards a flowchart.

"Dismissed."

The day passed in a blur of shame. Baines's words ran like a tape-loop in his head, inter-cut with savage self-reproaches. How could he have acted so stupidly, against his own interests? Swept away by Yasmina's emotions, a quixotic urge to right wrongs, to punish GM – he must've been mad! The truth was, he *had* fallen for her. That first night in the Euro he'd wanted her; if the evening hadn't lurched into tragedy, he'd have slept with her. Only later Nick realized that she'd used him to ensure that Aisha's death wouldn't go unmarked, that a trail of guilt would remain. But by then, he'd already returned to the Euro to see her again.

The first time he'd justified his action as concern, fearing Madam Hoda might punish her. But no, Hoda had even paid for Aisha's funeral, Yasmina told him, and Madam herself assured him he was an honoured guest later that that evening. After that, he joined other internationals on a joyride to Suez most weekends. Stayed at the least scuzzy hotel and went drinking and dancing – not only at the Euro, but nearly always if Yasmina was on duty.

At first he'd been shy to ask, twice visiting the club on her nights off, before the other bargirls took pity on him and divulged Yasmina's schedule. Soon he came to know all the girls; hard-faced foxes who enjoyed bitching about the regulars. GM was one – and far from a favourite. His sadism matched his callous persona.

"Nice one, son," GM guffawed when they eventually met there. "Had enough of the old five fingers, fancy some Arab pussy, eh." He patted Nick's gut and walked away laughing.

"I hate him," hissed Yasmina. "Aisha would still be alive if it wasn't for him." Her eyes misted. She laid her head on his chest. He hugged her tentatively, then tighter. "You're so nice," she breathed, disengaging.

He grew familiar with her perfume, the warmth of her hand, the feel of her spine as they danced. He never took liberties, never groped her as other foreigners did to the bargirls. She never asked him upstairs again. Aisha's death lay between them, as it had brought them together.

One night she asked him to walk her home from the club. It was raining, the first rain he'd seen in months. Drains flooded, streets emptied, stalls closed. His heart thudded as he walked beside her, not touching, anticipating what lay ahead, thrusting Carina from his mind.

The stairs were dark. She led him by the hand, as she had at the beginning. He had no excuses, only desire and trepidation. After weeks of celibacy, he might be too excited or nervous to perform in bed. And Yasmina confessed to being a virgin. It was a lot to handle, even without feeling guilty.

Her room was no seraglio. Nick stood awkwardly as she burrowed under the bed, sat like a prat on the edge as she brewed tea. Yasmina seated herself at the end, ignoring the bed-springs groaning, blew on her tea and sipped. It wasn't going as he'd imagined, he sensed romance slipping away. Should he make the first move?

"Nick" She put her glass aside. "There's something you must know, about Aisha's death and GM..."

When she'd finished, he felt almost as sick as when he'd seen the corpse. A tragedy had become murder, and Yasmina an avenger seeking a champion. Him!

As she said goodnight, she'd kissed him. Only for an instant, but the softness of her lips had stayed with him through the desolate streets, back to his hotel, and lingered in his mind for days afterwards.

By evening time, Nick was determined to get drunk. Officially the Residency was dry, but the receptionist would send a gofer into town to procure spirits if baksheeshed. An hour later, the guy was at his door with a bottle in brown paper. Unwrapping it, Nick cursed. A familiar figure in Regency attire strode across the label, but the lettering read *Johnnie Wadie Whiskey*. It was one of those Egyptian brands he'd been warned about. He thought of demanding a replacement but balked at waiting another hour. He needed a drink now.

It tasted crap, but after the second glass his tongue was numb. Bitterness, self-repproach and tangled feelings for Yasmina churned inside him as the room grew fuzzy. She'd relied on Nick and he'd failed her. She'd manipulated him, she was stringing him along; he was old enough to be her father...

He felt her kiss as his cheek hit the carpet and darkness closed over his head

Next morning he overslept and was cursing himself for missing the driver when he saw a note under the door. Vision blurred, he could hardly read it. *Safaga warehouse visit cancelled. Stay in, work on the audit. Baines.* He'd been grounded, no reason given: another slap in the face, just when he was feeling like shit.

His bowels twitched as he raced to the bathroom. Diarrhoea spattered the bowl as sweat burst from his pores and his skull imploded. *That fucking Johnnie Wadie, he'd finished the bottle, never again.* When the squits stopped he staggered over to retch into the basin, sluicing bile down the plughole as he doused his face. Quaffed from the tap; tore open the foil on two Paracetamols with shaking fingers.

He felt like curling up in bed and dying, but forced himself to dress and go for breakfast. A few muffins and curling Edam slices on the buffet table, the refectory was empty but for three SF staffers drinking coffee. When they saw Nick they rose and left without acknowledging him. He'd been sent to Coventry.

Back in his room, fury took over. He hefted his laptop and was about to hurl it to the floor when sanity prevailed. He kicked a cupboard so hard that louvers broke. *Fuck it, fuck them.* He hadn't felt so angry since he was a teenager. Though his Dad had gone spare when Nick was cautioned by the police, he'd been nostalgic for his own youthful vandalism. But it had to stop; a criminal conviction would bugger up Nick's aim to be an accountant, they agreed. So he reined himself in, stuck to the middle-class thuggery of money and law.

Accountancy: handmaiden of money, masseur of figures. He'd been through reams of printouts and audited a dozen warehouses – but the only grand malfeasance was GM's tomb-robbing, which was surely a private venture. He couldn't envisage Baines's complicity; it wasn't his style and he was already a billionaire. Whatever his agenda was, it was on another plane.

He looked at the printouts and his rumpled bed. His skull throbbed, his joints ached. *No contest...* he hadn't the strength to do any work.

It was nearly dusk when he woke. His mouth tasted foul but the pain had ebbed and his stomach was calmer. He padded to the bathroom. The name slipped into his mind as he was brushing his teeth, unannounced as an assassin.

Kreutzer.

It lay there like a cat wanting to be noticed, picked up and stroked. *Kreutzer*.

It meant something, something to do with –

He'd seen it before, sensed some connection with –

Fanaticism. A dystopian yearning...

He rinsed his mouth, booted up the laptop and Googled Kreutzer. Over 87,000 results – Tolstoy's *Kreutzer Sonata*, travel agencies, consultancies, hardware stores, fetish sites, provincial newspapers... How to narrow it down? And then, like a trap springing, Nick had it. Even before inputting + *Salvation First* and hitting search again, he somehow anticipated what he'd find.

Pastor in court over humanitarian agency

Little Rock, AR

Pastor Norman Kreutzer of the controversial Salvation Mission of St Ezekiel has denied being unfit to register a new tax-exempt foundation with the IRS. "Similar false charges were laughed out of court by the people of Alabama," said Pastor Kreutzer on the steps of City Hall. "I'm sure justice will prevail in Arkansas, and the Federal bureaucracy will be exposed for what it is – a lackey of ZOG" [the so-called 'Zionist Occupation Government' alleged to exist by Militia and Christian Identity groups]. Despite his reclusive lifestyle, Pastor Kreutzer claims a wide readership for his biblical and civic literature. "Millions of Americans have given their hard-earned bucks to see God's work done, and they won't be disappointed," he pledged. The humanitarian agency's name has yet to be finalised, but he favours Salvation First, "Because that's Christ's message to us all."

With that to start with, he'd been able to focus on Arkansas newspapers such as the *Jacksonville Patriot* and *Benton Courier,* which had their archives online. It didn't take long to uncover several articles about Kreutzer – one related to the first result he'd found on Google.

Pastor wins case, resigns from agency

Little Rock, AR

Pastor Norman Kreutzer claimed victory in the State Court yesterday, when Judge Marlene Tucker ruled in his favour against the IRS. The controversial pastor of the Salvation Mission of St Ezekiel called it "A great day for freedom and God's work", and vowed that the Mission's new humanitarian agency would "spread its wings over the afflicted." However, Pastor Kreutzer stated that his own role would be minimal. "I've done the spadework, but the agency should be managed by professional aid workers, not simple preachers," he said. His resignation from the board of trustees would take effect next month.

As his search progressed he made himself halt, put the notes on Kreutzer in his pocket and shambled to the refectory for a late supper. Chilli con carne, no thanks. He wolfed a limp salad for vitamins and rice pudding for comfort but barely tasted them. His mind was on Kreutzer, waiting in the bedroom.

By midnight he'd got into newspaper archives from Mississippi and Alabama, college yearbooks and voter registration rolls. The skeleton of Kreutzer's life was there, flesh was taking shape. Nick rose from the desk, faced the mirror. He was crushed by fatigue, vampire-eyed, unshaven. He looked at the empty bed, yearned for a woman's warmth beside him.

Carina, Yasmina...

He dreamt of his teeth rotting, of skulls emerging from mud.

Next morning he was woken by the cleaner, clattering his Hoover with sadistic vigour. Nick skipped a shower and went to the refectory. Ate like a rugby player: cereal, eggs, cheese, rolls and jam; juice and coffee to jump-start the system. Morrison was staring at him from the buffet like he'd farted in church. Sod him. He'd tried to do the right thing – for the wrong motives maybe – and now the pious bastards didn't want to know him.

Back in his room the cleaner had left. Printouts stacked beside the laptop in mute reproach. The audit – fuck. But then he relaxed. All they wanted was a sign-off to show the donors and put on their website. No cross-checking required, only compliance.

He locked the door, showered, put on fresh clothing and sat down at the desk. Ruffled the printouts like fur; touched the notes in his shirt pocket.

Kreuzter was still in the room, like a cat.

A vicious skulking old tom, tainting the air with his noxious spray...

Nick pushed printouts aside, fired up the laptop and spread out his notes. Rafts of scrawl linked by arrows and circles. It took a while to realize what some of the entries referred to. Eventually he had it straight and to began to type into a document-file.

It was late afternoon when he pushed back the chair with a sigh. He'd gone as far as he could with what he'd found on the internet. Made some guesses, knew he'd missed some inferences. But it was written.

Norman Kreutzer

Born 1945, Montgomery, Alabama. Father a Celestial Wizard of the Ku Klux Klan. Both father & son involved in anti-Civil Rights violence in Selma 1965, but no charges brought against them. Graduated top in microbiology at Arkansas State University in 1967 & went on to work at Fort Detrick, Maryland, on classified govt. research. Resigned in 1988, supposedly for health reasons; a later whistleblower's report suggests that two employees faced child porn charges & dismissal without pension if they didn't go quietly – during the same period that Kreutzer quit.

Founded Salvation Mission of St Ezekiel in 1989, registered for tax-free status. Investigated by the IRS in 1990, its status confirmed after court hearings. Moved to Arkansas 1992; active in impeach Clinton campaigns. Summons for non-payment of speeding fines & litigation in state courts over property taxes on his cabin at Bull Shoals in the Ozark Mountains.

Known business interests: registered director of Goshen Realty, shareholder in Arkansas Overview Press.

Author of: *The Prophet Ezekiel – His Message for Our Times; How Events in the Middle East are Foretold in the Bible; The Evangelist's Primer for Action Now; Rapture vs. Martyrdom; Why Turning the Other Cheek is Not a Christian Option; and Rollback - God's Way Forward in the New Millennium* (all Arkansas Overview Press).

Strangely, K. doesn't seem to have a website of his own (though his books are advertised on evangelical, survivalist and white supremacist sites) or an email contact address. Nor is he in the Arkansas State phone directory or any local ones [check more?? how??].

The final part was cut-and-pasted from a paedo porn site with literary pretensions, featuring 'true tales' of teenage nymphets and rugged survivalists, besides the kind of images you'd expect of *Arkansas Beaver Magazine* once you'd got over a small linguistic misconception, not uncommon between cousins across the Pond.

It was impossible to date the interview with any accuracy, but it must have been after Kreuzter disappeared from public life. It took place at his cabin in Bull Shoals and featured a photo of Kreuzter with the journalist, a Sonny Bono look-alike who called himself Beaver Hunter. Barrel-bellied, spade-bearded, a backwoodsman, Kreutzer looked capable of strangling a puppy just to show a child how it was done.

Beaver Hunter: Thanks for inviting me to your place. We've heard a lot about you.
Kreutzer: I'm just a regular guy, standing up for what I believe in.

Beaver Hunter: But a guy who's seen off the Feds, BATF and the IRS. That takes some doing!

Kreutzer: Guess so.

Beaver Hunter: So what's your secret, Norm?

Kreuzter: Knowing the law so they can't cheat you in court, and bearing arms so they can't take you alive. The Constitution and Sam Colt made this country great. It's as simple as that.

Beaver Hunter: Hallelujah. So can I see your guns?

Kreutzer: Sure, come this way.

Beaver Hunter: Hey! A Steyr AUG, an AN-94, a SIG 550 and an Israeli Tavor – you sure love assault rifles!

Kreutzer: Ain't all. My house is full of traps. See this bottle of bourbon on the table? A junkie housebreaker finds that, takes a swig and *gugghh*, dead as a coot in five seconds. Cyanide, mister, just what the doctor ordered. Better than a burglar alarm.

Beaver Hunter: Right. Cool. So tell us about the beavers.

Kreutzer: Those underage charges were a frame-up by ZOG. They were thrown out of court. If a man wants to invite some beaver to hang out at his cabin – and they're overage, mind – then there's no harm in that. And if the Feds bust in without a proper warrant, then it's only right to sue their asses – especially if they leak the video to KATV...

Beaver Hunter: I see why you're pissed and our readers think you did the right thing – that's why they voted you Beaver Man of the Month!

Kreutzer: I'm surely honoured.

Beaver Hunter: And when you're not skinning beavers, what keeps you busy?

Kreutzer: I lobby for the National Rifle Association and fundraise for the Trans Humane Society, to do God's work.

Beaver Hunter: Amen to that.

21 YO, NICK

Someone thumped on the door.

"Yo, Nick, where you been hiding?"

It was Lester, the earthiest of SF's evangelists, a New Orleans Baptist who ascribed Hurricane Katrina to God's judgement. He loved evangelising Egyptians; his only gripe was the absence of pork, the basis of his favourite Cajun dishes.

While Morrison looked askance at alcohol-free beer, Lester sometimes drank three bourbons in an evening. He laughed often and loudly without it grating, was genuinely solicitous of colleagues and the refugees, and didn't tolerate racism. Several times, Nick heard him deliver stinging rebukes to what he called 'Cracker Christians'.

"Nick, come out, we know you're in there. We're hot to hit Hurghada, those lobsters are snapping, the Stellas defrosting..."

It wasn't the food and drink so much as being welcomed back into the fold, the camaraderie of Salvation First. Though Nick's doubts about its donors were growing with each hour he spent on the internet, he found it impossible to resist the allure of belonging, of sharing experiences with colleagues.

Anyway, a night on the town was the only antidote to his depression. They didn't know the details but everyone understood that he was in the shit for *something*. He'd suffered days of ostracism, now he was being offered kindness, if not absolution.

"Ok, Lester, give me a minute," he shouted.

He took the laptop, fearing to leave it. Guessed that Lester and the others would think he was trying to score brownie points by bringing it along. *Nick sure works hard – poor guy*. His humiliation throbbed like a burn but he was content to be among them. Laughter, high-fives, promises of a joyride to Suez with the guys from Water & Sanitation.

He could see Yasmina. He'd emailed her twice, finally eliciting a laconic *Wait for me at the Euro Saturday,* strangely sent to the mailbox he shared with Carina rather than his SF account. No *XXX*, thank God, just *Yasmina* at the end. He prayed Carina wouldn't think much of it, if she noticed it at all...

He was thinking like an adulterer before he'd even slept with Yasmina. He hadn't emailed or phoned Carina in nearly a week. When he did, words stuck in his craw, every sentence a minefield. *The weather's fine, missing you* seemed simplest. Her emails spoke of "Treasures of Gazprom" as if it were wilful and demanding deity rather than a museum exhibition. She hardly had a word for him...

They'd drifted apart – further than the distance between them.

"Lawd knows what women want," intoned Lester. "Surely more than guys can figure." The others laughed. They were on the highway past the airport, six inside a spacious old Peugeot taxi. Nick saw the Esso station on the edge of town flash by.

They went to Sinbad's, busy as always on Friday night, rooftop tables cocooned in candlelight. Nick sipped beer. His stomach stirred in protest, a burp sneaked by his epiglottis. Lester winked across the table. Platters of *mezze* arrived, garish as flowerbeds. One of the evangelists said grace.

Nick dabbed at some hummus but couldn't work up an appetite. Took a swig of beer and regretted it – his guts flopped over like a seal. He half rose from the chair, dug in his pockets. Damn, he'd left his wallet behind...

"Hey guys, I'm not feeling well, something I ate yesterday. I'm going back to the Residency to lie down. Lester, I hate to ask, but could you lend me fifty – I forgot my wallet."

Jeers, not least from Lester, but of course he obliged. "No problem, get yourself home in a cab." He squeezed Nick's arm.

"Bye, brother," they chorused.

In the street he looked up to wave goodbye, but they weren't to be seen. A salty wind agitated plastic bags in the feeble glow of a few working streetlights. It was only two blocks to the highway where taxis waited. The laptop felt heavy.

Oddly, Nick felt safer walking through this town of refugees than he did on Holloway Road after dark. Morrison maintained that the internationals were inviolate; Egyptians couldn't afford to alienate their benefactors. Lester had scoffed at that. "Plenty of Welfare muggers in the States," he said. "Much as I hate to admit it, Egyptians are more *neighbourly* than us, less criminal; something to do with Islam perhaps – one of the few upsides to it."

A shrill whistle from across the street.

"*Ya* Mr Nick!"

An Egyptian, grinning from the window of an SF Land Cruiser.

Nick didn't know him, but he couldn't put a name or face to half the local staff. It wasn't that all Egyptians looked alike, only similar. And that was just the men: in Hurghada you seldom saw women unveiled. For that you had to go to Suez, where they'd gaze at you longingly with dark almond eyes.

"Come with us, we'll take you to the Residency. Save money."

The Siren calls of status and economy. Egyptians looked out for each other, extended their benediction to the internationals.

"*Shukran, habibi.*" Nick believed in mastering the basic courtesies. It showed respect for the host culture, a willingness to understand. Like sitting beside the driver, rather than lounging in the back like a colonialist.

He was seated before he sensed the man behind, turned and saw Hosni Basha, aiming a gun at his spine.

Salvation First's one-day seminar on personal security had stressed the importance of prior awareness (he'd blown that one) and relationship-building in hostile situations. Their instructor admitted at the outset that Egypt wasn't one of the badlands, but the same lessons applied.

Don't provoke them. The optimum time to escape is in the first hour – the time when hostage-takers are jumpiest and most vigilant. Now Nick's back was clammy, his crotch swampy, their advice didn't add up. The kidnap driver barely glanced at him now that he'd completed his small deception and relieved Nick of his mobile phone.

Hosni Basha dominated the car. Nick had seen him at El-Gouna, heard of his cruelty and duplicity. Father of Lies, the Egyptians called him when nobody was listening. No – that wasn't so; both ruler and ruled revelled in the fear that his name evoked. *His eyes are everywhere, his reach is long.* Often they avoided uttering his name, dragging fingers down their cheeks from the corner of their eyes, miming the Wadjet Eye that symbolized the divine vengeance of Ancient Egypt.

"Where are you taking me?" A lame response, but he hadn't the bravado for bluster. Why bother when he *knew* what he'd aroused by his intervention – a cobra on the back seats. His neck grew stiff from glancing over his shoulder.

"Later, later," Hosni Basha murmured.

They passed the Residency and the final checkpoint before a clear run to Port Safaga. Sentries stiffened at the sight of the ID flashed from the Land Cruiser's window. For Nick, who'd previously had *laissez passer* on his own terms, it was chilling to be ushered towards oblivion with smiles and salutes.

Do something...

Nick nerved himself for the next checkpoint, by Safaga's grain silos. Sentries moved like marionettes in the arc lights. "Help! I'm English," he croaked. Perplexed, they sought elucidation from Hosni Basha. A few words of rasping Arabic and they were dragging oil-drums from the road, beckoning the Land Cruiser onwards.

"Fool." The muzzle dug into his temple, Nick imagined the bullet penetrating his skull, the erupting exit-wound. "Shut up, we haven't finished with you yet."

They turned inland, headlights sweeping rocks and tumbleweeds as glowing eyes slunk away. Jackals, Nick thought, as he glimpsed a road sign with Arabic numerals. Was that 160 or 185 kilometres? They were on a road to the Nile Valley, he knew that much.

He dared a glance at Hosni Basha. Alert, relaxed, the gun in his lap: a killer automaton in sleep mode. Hosni stirred, cleared his throat.

"I've met many foreigners, Mr Baring: businessmen, aid workers, generals. Many were greedy or stupid. Only *you* surprised me. To be *so* stupid, without a hint of greed – that's rare. Like some species that should have died out long ago. I wanted to meet you, I was curious. Tell me, tell me *really*, why you stuck your neck into this? *Why?*"

For *Yasmina* – he couldn't say, wouldn't endanger her, even if they tried to force him ... His stomach fluttered, he feared he'd fart and shit himself. He clenched his sphincter, moistened his lips.

"For justice..."

"*Justice* – one of those words you foreigners love to sing while you're doing the opposite. *Justice* – it makes me laugh to hear it from an Englishman. You feel so superior to us Egyptians, so *righteous*. But your forefathers robbed a thousand tombs; your British Museum is stuffed with plunder. Surely a treasure made by our ancestors belongs to us. I am Egypt's ruler. Whose claim outweighs mine?"

"Five million refuge..." Nick bit his tongue. *Idiot!*

Hosni sniggered. "More hypocrisy – an accountant should know better. If your heart bleeds for our refugees, then ask the banks and corporations stealing Egypt's oil and gas to open *their* pockets. Our wealth is mortgaged to pay for food aid and projects to lock us into *their* economy. The Jews have stolen our Canal. So who is the bigger thief? My crimes are nothing beside theirs."

He fell silent, staring into the night.

The last checkpoint had been an hour ago – Nick surreptitiously checked his watch. They hadn't taken it, was that a good sign? Scrabbling for any crumb of hope...

The car was slowing down.

"*Hawid shimaal.*" Turn left, he understood.

The car bumped off the tarmac onto a dirt track. Rocks closed in, they were in a wadi strewn with thorny hummocks, heading – *south*, he reckoned. Ten minutes' later they bore right – *west* – into a side valley, then into another, snaking wadi. Nick lost his bearings, his last toehold on hope.

The driver said something, tapped a dial on the dashboard. Of Hosni's reply, Nick understood only *badi shwaya*, 'a little later' His guts were churning again...

The engine faltered, then recovered; soon after, another stall. The driver tapped the fuel gauge and Hosni leant forward, close to Nick's ear, and whispered:

"It will look like an accident – or suicide."

Nick felt his bowels loosening.

"*Hosh al-jeep.*"

The car stank, his legs were wet. The driver hopped out, followed by Hosni, fanning his nose ostentatiously. "If people could see you now – or smell you."

They frogmarched him over a rise into an amphitheatre of cliffs. He staggered, the sand cold where he fell. They dragged him up by the armpits, kicked him on. He heard himself mewing like an animal...

Barbed wire trailed across the sand. The Egyptians halted behind him.

"Step over the wire. Keep walking."

Hosni waved the pistol, the driver grinning.

"Move – keep walking or I'll shoot you."

He stepped over the wire, legs slimy to the ankles. Carina – he'd never hold her again. At least she'd never see him like this. Thank God they'd never had children. He'd die without leaving any trace, not a cell. A year from now she'd be moving on, placing ads in *Guardian Soulmates*.

"Lie down."

He fell on his knees, stars melting in his tears.

Hosni raised his voice across the distance. "In the 1960s, Israeli commandoes raided Egypt from across the Red Sea. Our generals had the coastline mined, and certain wadis inland. This was one of them. Later, when the Jews never returned, we marked them out with barbed wire to warn off the Bedouin. That was long ago, but landmines stay active forever. So keep very still."

Laughing, they withdrew into the gloom, back towards the Land Cruiser. They'd left him here – they hadn't shot him. In the starlight Nick saw his footprints receding to the wire. *Wait, you'll survive*, he promised himself.

Minutes passed, then a sound: not a car engine but something from above – a dark mass descending beyond the ridge. Soon it leapt into view again, a giant insect that swooped towards him, raising a haze of sand. A whirlwind tore at his clothes as he shielded his eyes. Gradually the dust settled and silence fell.

The helicopter was gone.

And so were his footprints, erased.

22 SHREK

Muesli and honey in his mouth, her voice from the hall. *Have you seen my bag?* On the kitchen table as usual. *Here, darling.* She pecked his cheek. *Must run...* Buster barked and licked his hand. The front door clicked shut.

Carina!

Home -

He jerked upright, blinking at the sun, reeking like a wino. *If people could see you – smell you.* Nick groaned.

London was a dream – reality a nightmare.

He'd slept in a foetal curl, some instinct ensuring he hadn't rolled onto a mine. Flexing his limbs like a crab, fearful of disturbing the sand, he understood that survival was measured in seconds and inches. Perhaps he'd only been given a choice of suicides. Dying of thirst would be slow. An explosion might kill him instantly or leave him maimed, to bleed to death.

His throat was raw. *Water*, if he didn't drink soon, he'd be too weak to do anything. *Water*, a sloshing jerry-can on the roof of the Land Cruiser. *Water*, it was waiting for him. Go get it, Buster...

He heard himself laugh like a hyena.

Don't lose it.

Staring at the sand, glittering with quartz, he imagined jumping – one, two, three, four, six, maybe *eight* steps to the wire. But mines could lurk anywhere, exposing an antenna or utterly invisible underground. Sweat ran down his spine. *Think!*

The agency's induction week devoted a day to security, including a lecture on mines by an army retread with a suitcase of 'samples'. *This one will shred your legs below the knees, Gents. This'll jump in the air to blow off your nuts. And with antitank mines, they'll bury you in a matchbox.* He'd explained mine avoidance and how to respond if your jeep detonated a mine, but when someone voiced what everyone in the class was wondering, he rolled his eyes. *That's for professionals, son,* the lecturer said, before relating a 'solution' which seemed improbably simple, childishly naïve.

Now Nick had a chance to test it himself.

Wristwatch stowed, sleeves rolled and a biro with its nib-cone removed.

He wiped his palms on his trousers for the umpteenth time. He no longer smelt or tasted anything – had only three senses. The biro in his right hand, sand ahead – don't think about the distance to the wire, just the angle of the pen, keep it shallow, about 30°.

He slipped it into the sand like a scalpel, felt tiny pebbles shift and something resisting – recoiled, but made himself return with fingertips, gently as he'd stroke a baby. After a minute, a rock appeared. He sat back, arched his spine and cursed. Looked back at the cleared space before him, selected a point three fingers to the right, bent forward and resumed probing, trying to establish a rhythm

After clearing a strip a foot wide, he rested, sucking a pebble, drawing saliva like the dregs of a waterhole. He extracted his watch and felt a thud of despair. It taken over an hour to drive a corridor less than arm's length towards the wire...

Now he knew how African slaves had felt: heat and thirst and backbreaking labour, always in fear. All that bondage in Babylon stuff rang truer than an audit by KPMG. When you feared for your life, money was as abstract as free will among ants.

His escape corridor was two metres long when he found a mine, just beneath the surface. *Step over it, move on*, his body urged – but he knew that if he leapfrogged it now he might trigger it with his heels later. He put the pen aside and began digging, painstakingly as an archaeologist – trying not to think of it exploding in his face.

It was big as a soup-plate, an antitank mine oxidized to an ebony sheen. After exposing it, he kept it in his peripheral vision like a sleeping cobra. He was running on adrenalin, probing and digging to the rhythm of songs in his head. Music and rhythm beat pain and fatigue, a Gospel choir sang. He bowed beside the mine, clearing the way ahead. *Hallelujah, Lord...*

He found the next one after his fourth rest break.

A malevolent nodule meant to sever a leg. An antipersonnel mine cost six bucks, their lecturer had said. Nick couldn't probe forever, his fingers felt arthritic, however often he switched the pen from hand to hand. He had to be bolder, faster.

He rose to his feet. Scanned the ground – *Go for it, before your nerve fails.*

Leapt, landed on one leg, wobbling like an inept stork, his safety zone instantly diminshed to his footprint.

He tottered. *Fuck*, tensed his calf.

Now! His gut was hollow...

Sand impacted under his feet, his knees coiled for another jump. *Yes!*

He landed badly, stumbled, hopped and came down with his ankles together. Two inches from his toecaps, a plastic doughnut surfaced, with a prong like a bee-sting.

He couldn't face straddling it to resume digging.

The wire was within spitting distance, had he any saliva to spit.

It's now or never. His heart thudded as he braced himself.

One, touchdown, *two* –

He was flying – *falling* – feeling barbs rip his skin.

He sobbed with pain and joy.

He'd made it across the wire...

Next thing he knew, he was nosing a mudguard. The jeep's flanks rose like a cliff, the roof-rack an eyrie. *Water* – it was up there. He hauled his weight over the bonnet and windscreen to claw at the rack. Two plastic jerry-cans roped with elasticised cords. He struggled with the hooks. A red can slid towards him, heavy with liquid. *Water!* He fumbled with the screw cap.

Black, viscous engine oil – he croaked in despair.

His heart jumped. The other jerry-can was *blue*: he hadn't been thinking – blue for water, red for fuel or lubricants. He repeated it like a mantra as he fumbled with the hooks. *Water...* Suddenly the can sprang free, and Nick felt its weight like an electric shock.

Empty –

He slid onto the bonnet and sobbed.

He was a child again; felt tadpoles slip through his fingers in cool green water. Fireworks on Bonfire night, school discos and acne; the trauma of moving to a posh school where he didn't know anyone. Meeting Carina, black-tie events, passion subsiding into tedium. His life on fast forward, rushing towards the end. It was true what they said about your final moments...

He didn't want to die.

He beat the bonnet feebly.

Sensed the engine, knew its fuel tank was empty. He'd seen the gauge the night before. Fuel, speed, revs, oil, temperature, water...

Water –

...in the radiator...

It was nearly full, tasted rusty, delicious as beer at sundown. He sunk a litre before he thought of anti-freeze, laughed weakly between sucks on the siphoning hose he found in the boot. *Not in Egypt, for sure.*

He slept in the car, wrapped in a dustsheet and oily newspapers. It was cold, but not as cold as in the sand. The desert was like a moon, burning hot in the sun, with a frozen dark side. He dreamt of London again, Carina laughing as Buster sprayed them with pond-water. He grabbed Buster by the collar, felt his soft jowls. *Don't go in the pond!* Nick scolded, but Carina didn't believe him about the shark.

A shark in Hampstead Pond, she smiled.

He knew it was in the depths – waiting to break the surface, to seize a dog or a child. Its teeth were white, it had Hosni Basha's smile. As it rose towards the surface, only Nick could hear it thinking: *If people could see you now.*

He woke with cramp in his legs, thrashing across the backseat till the spasms eased. He knew what it meant – dehydration and lack of salt. He'd survived another night, but each day was a new battle...

Soon after, his spirits rose. He found a packet of crisps and a can of Sprite in the driver's door: a real power-breakfast, salt, sugar, fat and fizz. In the boot, there was an Evian bottle half full of tap water, which he'd overlooked yesterday. He siphoned the radiator dry and filled it to the brim.

He found his laptop, too. The shit-stain on the casing reminded him of his filth. He couldn't waste water on washing himself – sand would have to do. Stripping off his trousers and boxers, he began scrubbing. His legs were sickly white – he'd never worn short trousers in Egypt, the agency discouraged it.

Half naked, he considered his situation.

He was lost in the Eastern Desert with 1.5 litres of water and a handful of crisp crumbs. All the technology to hand was useless: a jeep without fuel, and a laptop far from any wi-fi. It had some battery power, but nothing on the hard drive had any relevance to his predicament, though he played a few tunes just to hear some familiar voices in the wilderness. *Should I stay or should I go?* That was it in a nutshell...

In induction week they stressed that staff marooned in the desert should wait by their car to be rescued. But nobody at the agency had any idea of his location, nor would realise he was missing for another day at least. And if the alarm was raised, Hosni could misdirect the search teams to other areas. It would only take a day or two before Nick died of thirst and his body could be 'discovered'. Staying put would be suicidal.

He could only save himself by walking out of the desert.

The question was: *which way?* Was he nearer the Nile Valley or the coast? El-Bahr meant the agency, civilisation, the British Embassy – but also Hosni and GM. The Valley was *terra incognita*: aside from Craven's agri-projects, the rest was desolation. A place to hide, but not to summon rescuers...

But the real question was starker: where was the nearest water? A litre and a half wouldn't even replenish what he sweated doing nothing.

Walking consumed water, hastening the onset of dehydration. If he didn't walk out in the next 24 hours, he'd die anyway.

And if he walked, how far could he get – thirty, fifty kilometres?

Numbers – he'd dealt with numbers all his life. Now it hung on them.

In the end he rested till an hour before sunset and headed west – towards the Valley – trusting in a wadi that ran only slightly off true towards the setting sun. It seemed a good omen when he encountered wispy scrub after half an hour. But soon he was cursing the thorns that scratched his calves and tore his trousers. A rising moon barely touched the wadi until it widened into a junction awash with pale sand. Nick searched the stars for The Plough; scratched a compass in the sand, staring at the gullies, gauging their orientation.

This one, or that?

It was chilly. He drew the dustsheet tighter, stamping his feet, fretting with indecision. Don't wimp out now, *decide.*

That one...

He took a swig for luck, carefully resealed the bottle and hung it from the sling he'd improvised after stripping the car of anything useful. He'd even taken a wing-mirror for signalling. But why the laptop – it was useless deadweight. Ingrained respect for any valuable object, or perhaps as a talisman, he wasn't sure.

Firing the car had also been irrational. However hard he tried to think straight, part of him was going loopy. At the time, he'd justified it as an SOS – a pillar of smoke and fire in the desert – but that was nonsense, he'd started walking away as it burned. It was more like crossing the Rubicon. Or maybe he'd just wanted to hit back at the agency – he got a thrill from poking a rag into the petrol tank and igniting the dregs.

Warmed by the memory, he advanced into the wadi, thick with thorny plants linked by rodents' tracks. He wondered if he should try digging for water. *No – you'll waste your strength for nothing,* an inner voice warned in the tone of Carina's admonitions. *Don't leave the house with wet hair, wear a hat outside, finish your smoothie, it's organic.* She got angry if he teased her for being a hypochondriac – would have a fit if she could see him in rags, filthy and unshaven.

The thought drove him faster, deeper into the wadi. It grew darker as the rocks closed in; the ground was strewn with boulders. As doubts returned, he faltered. If he twisted an ankle, it was over. He couldn't afford any errors. Should he turn back and try the other wadi before it was too late? Would it prove a better route?

Decide, decide.

Cut your losses, write off a bad debt.

He turned back, cursing under his breath, mouth dry with anxiety.

Two in the morning: the moon overhead, the wadi starkly floodlit. His breath plumed in the air. Shooting stars crossed the sky as regularly as planes over London. He felt suspended between one reality and another. He could look down on his body trudging through the canyon and see himself on the sofa in Tufnell Park, both equally real yet intangible.

The Evian bottle was nearly empty, perhaps five swallows left. His stomach knotted with cramp. For the past three hours he'd been chewing his last treasure, a stick of chewing gum found in the car. His light-headedness was a blessing in disguise – it helped him distance himself from his body.

He'd found a new carrot to sustain him. Every hour when he rested for five minutes (*no longer,* Carina reminded him), he'd snap open the laptop and play a track or two. The music brought tears to his eyes, choked him up, filled his belly like prawn crackers. It was magic. Now he blessed his impulse to take the laptop, bore its weight happily, like a newborn baby or a holy relic.

He was starting to hallucinate.

Images flitted across the canyon, pulsating with life. Hieroglyphs, giant hawks and scarab beetles, spirals and whorls. He was entering the realm of gods, stepping back into prehistory. Long-horned cattle led by herdsmen in loin cloths and plumed headdresses, followed by gigantic boats bristling with oars and masts, jerking as if caught in a strobe light.

If he could beg a ride on a boat or even grab a cow's tail and be pulled along, he'd save himself. He tried to speak but only croaks emerged. He waved at them desperately, stumbling past herds and flotillas of craft – *I'm here, don't ignore me* – but he'd become invisible, a phantom in a netherworld.

He'd never emerge.

The images ebbed like water down a drain. He was shivering. He put down the laptop and fumbled for the Evian bottle. It was sickeningly light. He swallowed once, again, rolled the third mouthful round his mouth like vintage port. Funny how he'd acquired a taste for it from Henry.

The thought triggered a rush of memories: visits to Oxford where Nick was ushered in Henry's wake to the High Table or dinners ruined by Carina's simmering resentment of her parents – Henry especially. Nick found him amusing, despite suspecting his father-in-law of despising him. Both Henry's children were disappointments: Rupert, gay and living in Los Angeles – seldom spoken of – and Carina, who didn't become a ballerina or a painter or even *marry* an artist – merely an accountant.

"Mediocrity is the enemy of genius," Henry often remarked, a shade pointedly if you were looking to take offence. Nick never had – or at least betrayed his vexation – but that would change in the future. He mightn't be a genius but he wasn't a mediocrity either – not walking out of the desert, he wasn't.

Sometime afterwards, the stars began to whirl and suddenly Nick was down, down into darkness, awareness fading...

Mud, he was lying in mud, mushy as yesterday's cornflakes. How he'd crawled to the waterhole he couldn't remember. Skimming off the slime he quaffed till he gagged, wallowed in gluey liquid as the sun rose – euphoric. He'd survived the desert, he had water; food could wait. He'd heard of earthquake victims surviving a week on water alone, he could do it, he'd come this far...

He still had the laptop. Caked in mud, it came to life and demanded his password as blandly if he was in the Residency. He treated himself to the Arctic Monkeys, the music like a triumphal fanfare for a victorious army.

Sometime later it all went pear-shaped.

Stomach cramps, vomiting, fresh diarrhoea...

Like being churned in a washing machine, boiled and pummelled.

Exposed to the sky, a tortoise without its shell, as kites drifted lower...

One landed in front of him beating its wings, as another landed behind. Nick heard the slither of its claws in the sand but kept his eyes on the bird in front. He rolled sideways, grasping the dustsheet as it closed in. Flung the cloth over it, lunged for the laptop and slammed it down on the heaving fabric, hearing sinews crack as the other vulture took fright and fled. Nick collapsed, felt another spasm coming on...

✳✳✳

Next thing he knew: owl's eyes – tawny and bushy – as a hand spooned gruel into his mouth. An Arab face, etched by hardship, grizzled hair wrapped in a faded turban. The man's fingers were blunt and grimy. He smelt as Nick must stink to a stranger.

"*Inta minayn?*"

"I'm –" Nick lost what he was about to say, forgot what he'd understood. More incomprehensible Arabic, as a finger prodded his ribs.

"I'm English, *Inglizi.*" The owl snorted, thrust another spoonful at him.

Nick swallowed, groaned and fell back into oblivion.

When he came round, his wrists were tied together and his ankles tethered to a peg; legs naked and fouled again. He felt weak and listless, but the fever had abated and his body seemed plumper, swollen with water. He digested all this with detachment, it seemed inevitable, no cause for alarm.

A shadow fell from behind as the old man walked by. His *galabiyya* was cut off at his knees, his sandals fashioned from car tyres. He held a thick wooden staff in one hand and Nick's laptop in the other. For some reason, he made Nick think of Shrek – an uglier, older, hirsute version.

Shrek squatted, growled, mimed scrubbing and slapped his thighs. Nick got the message and blushed; sand-cleansing was becoming a habit he could do without. Sanding away, Nick appraised Shrek. He didn't seem hostile, only watchful. He turned the laptop over in his hands, sprung the catch and opened it like a book, wedged it into the sand.

Okay Shrek, if that's what you want...

With an ingratiating smile Nick crawled towards him, beckoning at the laptop. The tether was long enough for him to reach the keyboard. Shrek withdrew, but didn't stop him from booting up the screen. Nick was gratified by Shrek's reaction to the Alpine wallpaper; looked for something to drive home his psychological advantage.

"Get this." He double-clicked icons on his Favourites menu.

A monochrome etching on an Eau-de-Nile backdrop, overlaid by a serpent's nest of calligraphy, filled the screen. Shrek gasped and leant forward.

It was the only Muslim thing on the hard drive. The website of Al-Azhar Mosque, Egypt's Islamic authority, existing in cyberspace (and corporeally in Dubai) long after its Cairo namesake had been obliterated. When Nick got into evangelical websites, he'd viewed a few Islamic ones for comparison and found Al-Azhar quite user-friendly. It even issued fatwas online...

Shrek sat transfixed like a lottery winner whose final numbers are drawn. He slapped his knees as Nick switched at random between the Arabic pages, before remembering the battery and shutting down. Shrek stared at him reproachfully; thrust himself upright with his staff and stalked away to pray beyond Nick's reach.

Nick considered hurling the laptop but feared he'd miss. Better crawl back to the peg, try to work it free or abrade the rope on a rock. *There*, that one might do... he began sawing, keeping one eye on Shrek's prostrations as the strands frayed...

He glanced up – saw Shrek lunging with the staff.

Pain exploded in his kneecap.

Shrek poked his chest, pushed him down, snarling words that obviously meant: *Don't try it again*. He threw a strip of rag at Nick, gesturing at his eyes.

When Nick refused, Shrek's staff bored into his stomach.

Doubled up in pain, Nick yielded. What else could he do?

Later he received a bowl of mushy pulses sprinkled with salt, the crystals tart on his tongue. Eating blindfolded was awkward, but better than not eating at all. He licked olive oil from his fingers and wiped them in the sand.

He heard Shrek muttering, drawing nearer.

The stick prodded his stomach. Fingers threaded a rope across his chest, under his armpits; a weight dragging his back as Shrek removed the blindfold. Nick blinked; the sun was low on the horizon – another day nearly gone. Then he saw the load, and realised that Shrek had other ideas.

"*Yallah*." He motioned Nick to rise.

The hobble-rope allowed him to walk and his burden wasn't as heavy as he'd feared, but it took another jab at his ribs before Nick complied.

It was humiliating to be enslaved by an old man armed with only a stick, but Shrek was strong and tireless. He jabbered and chanted, often turning to Nick for approval, prompting him to respond in Arabic.

By the time they halted that night, he'd learnt that a pious *"W'Allahi"* might be rewarded with a slug of water from Shrek's goatskin.

Five or six days later – he'd lost count – the nature of their relationship was clearer. Shrek was mad, but lucid in his insanity. He saw Nick not as a slave but as a disciple. The blindfold and hobble were used without malice, as on an ox in a threshing mill. Food and water were inducements to obedience, rewards for achievement. To punish, Shrek could withhold either, or strike Nick. Soon, affirmations weren't enough; Nick had to learn prostrations and prayers, a mishmash of Muslim and Coptic ritual. The words wouldn't stick in his head; Nick stuttered over alien gutturals as Shrek frowned, between impassioned speeches when he gesticulated at the sky and stamped the earth.

They'd been skirting the fringes of the Valley, waterholes left by the receding Nile, slithering across floodplains, round hills of rubble and isolated palm groves where Shrek shinned up trees to hack off clumps of dates as Nick lay tethered below.

He bore the instruments of his own servitude: the ropes and tether-peg, food and water. A sooty cooking pot and two bowls, the dustsheet that served as a blanket and the laptop that Shrek treated like a gold ingot – all wrapped in the bundle on Nick's back.

The ropes chafed his armpits; he tore the flares of his trousers into rags to use as padding. Shrek had returned his trousers when Nick began to learn the prostrations. He'd bathed himself at the first large waterhole, his torso pale and bruised, his calves sunburnt and scarred. A grimy vest and shirt; trousers like a biker's beachwear - he looked the antithesis of an accountant.

But what really shocked him was his reflection in the wing-mirror. Flaking skin, rat's bristles and matted grey hair, haunted eyes with a tic in one cheek, teeth streaked brown and yellow. He looked like a tramp pushing sixty.

He knelt and wept; howled obscenities.

Shrek watched him indifferently, as if he was a donkey, braying.

It was day ten – thereabouts – when they met the Bedouin. Nick was trailing as usual, when suddenly they had company. Three riders on camels with a pair roped behind. Shrek halted and invoked God, honey and peace (the only words Nick could understand) as he raised his arms to the sky.

The Bedouin smiled among themselves.

Now! Go for it... Carina's voice.

Nick shrugged off the bundle, lurched forward and blurted:

"*Ana Inglizi*, help me, *minfudlak*, I'll pay you *fluss ketir.*"

He dug in his pockets and remembered using the banknotes as arse-wipes. "I'm English – call my embassy. *Fluss ketir*, they'll pay you anything that you want if you get me back home..."

The Bedouin looked bemused.

Shrek launched into a speech that wiped the doubt from their faces. He gestured at Nick's hair and trousers, then toed open the bundle, exposing the laptop, the wing-mirror and other junk.

"*Huwwa magnoon*," Shrek asserted. *He's crazy.*

The Bedouin laughed, dismounted and pumped Shrek's hand, eager for tea and conversation. Nick was ignored, an outsider, mad.

He looked at the wing-mirror and thought: *Maybe they're right.*

23 THE *ZAR*

"Tell him to be quiet, please," she begged Yasmina. They'd been cooped up together for days, Carina thought despairingly. Three of them, sharing a soiled mattress dragged as far from the squat-toilet as possible. Her hair and clothes were impregnated with the stench. She could feel lice creeping over her scalp. Her eyes were inflamed...

"*You* tell him," snapped Yasmina.

Tariq kept talking, fidgeting; stopping her from escaping into day-dreams. Boasting how he'd saved them, led them to a lone palm tree, a shadow in the sandstorm. A fluke of nature: a tree emerging from a fissure plunging to the water-table. A rope tied to the palm trunk, ending in a bucket that yielded brackish water each time it was raised. Okay, he'd stumbled on the rope, but did he have to brag about it incessantly?

At least Yasmina didn't prattle or caper round the cell. And it was a relief that they weren't sharing it with Sabr – their jailors seemed keen to separate him; a pity they hadn't taken Tariq too. If not for Yasmina, she'd be totally at sea. Nobody else spoke English and their jailors wouldn't talk to them, anyway.

It had been so ever since their arrest (or rescue). From the moment the riders appeared, it was as if only Sabr counted, stammering replies to their questions as Yasmina knelt self-effacingly and Tariq looked hangdog, dropping his sword in the sand. The riders were evidently suspicious of them, but beyond that, Carina hadn't a clue.

Yasmina didn't enlighten her till next day, when they were left alone to defecate. Embarrassed, gazing in opposite directions till it was over, before gathering to whisper until they were called back to camp to prepare supper.

They'd been captured (or rescued) by a camel patrol from the Rightly Guided Emirate. Four oases in the Western Desert, far beyond the Valley; unscathed by the Flood and ruled by Taliban-types – such was the Emirate. It was a thorn in the side of Libya but of little concern to faraway powers, raiding Libyan oil pipelines but otherwise shunning the outside world as *Kufr*, the Realm of Unbelief.

The patrol had been on alert since a raiding party sent word by courier pigeon of a pillar of fire on the horizon. The palm-well was a watering hole for patrols, so they'd been found by chance – or God's will. Three Egyptians with a foreigner! Were they spies, criminals, or rightfully fleeing *Kufr*? A man with two women and a boy, unrelated by blood or marriage! It was crazy, but they suspected Sabr of being a pimp with two prostitutes and a sidekick in tow...

She'd almost laughed when Yasmina explained. But it wasn't a joke.

And so they were handed from one bunch of Taliban types to another, from camels to Toyota pickups or over-burdened trucks until they reached Farafra Oasis. The smallest of the four oases in the Emirate: hardly more than a solitary village of mud-brick dwellings backing onto palm-groves – but not so primitive that it lacked a prison.

Their cell window faced an alley with an oblique view of a bazaar, which hushed when muezzins called the town to prayer, voices swooping like starlings. Yasmina and Tariq prayed three or four times daily, obliging Carina to cede the mattress, which she resented, though she knew it made sense to show the guards that they were pious Muslims, not a bargirl and a thief. So far they hadn't been harmed – merely stuck in a cell and fed rice-slop and dates. On the third day they were taken for a shower, able to wash their clothes and given burqas to wear while they dried. Their evening mush contained slivers of meat and vegetables. It seemed a hopeful sign.

Next day was Friday, it transpired. Loudspeakers came bronchially to life; from noon till four o'clock, oratory rolled over the town like thunder. Somehow Tariq nodded off halfway through, while Yasmina looked shell-shocked by the end.

"Taliban," she muttered, glancing at the spy-hole in the door.

"What were they saying?"

Yasmina's voice rose. "Emir Yussef explained to the faithful what is right and what is forbidden. Alcohol, immorality, not observing the fasts and the call to prayer – these are *aib*, against religion. He warned the *munafiqeen*, the hypocrites, not to pretend belief in Islam, warned of the punishments for paganism, for promoting *Jahilliyya*. May God help him in his task."

Carina's heart sank. *I thought you weren't like that – a fanatic.*

Tariq stirred, scratching himself, and hawked into the toilet.

You're disgusting, I'm sick of you both. She buried her head in her arms.

"You must eat, Carina."

Yasmina had seen it before, on the Great Pyramid, in the camps at El-Arish. People lost the will to live, stopped washing, rejected food. Listless, empty eyed, letting flies crawl over their faces.

"You must." She spooned gruel into Carina's mouth, wiped away a dribble.

"Why bother with her, I'll eat it."

She continued feeding Carina till the bowl was empty.

Tariq pouted. "She's just a stupid hen. Look at the shit she's landed us in."

He had a point. The Englishwoman had bribed and bullied them into leaving their homes (did Yasmina *really* think of Suez as home?). Now her money was gone and she was helpless as a child. At least Yasmina had left the first instalment of her wages in Hani's safekeeping, and she suspected Tariq had also secreted some cash. But Carina had spent her own last funds buying diesel from Nancy – and her credit card was worthless in the Emirate.

Yasmina wasn't sure if they even used money here. Emir Yussef's sermon had included a diatribe against it, and she'd heard rumours that the Emirate had reverted to a barter economy. It had resources for agriculture and handicrafts – palm groves, springs, fields and livestock – but not for any modern industry. Electricity was reserved for propagating the faith, as the Emir's amplified broadcast had demonstrated.

Carina tensed and blurted: "Nick, is that you?"

Allah, her mind was going – but then Yasmina heard voices too.

The door opened and Sabr entered, frowning. "Come quickly."

He turned on his heel, leaving the door ajar.

"And wear your burqas," he shouted from the corridor.

He was now their guardian, Sabr explained. Farafra's sheikhs had acknowledged him as a protector of the weak – as the Holy Qur'an enjoined men to be – and insisted he enforce modesty on his womenfolk. To venture outdoors uncovered was punishable by whipping. To speak to adult males outside one's family was only permissible to save life or uphold Islam. A woman's world was her family, to seek otherwise was *aib*. So Yasmina should forget that she'd studied chemistry, and Carina her airs and graces. They must show him respect and walk four paces behind him, as was seemly.

Tariq, as a boy, could walk two paces behind him.

Carina's eyes blazed behind her burqa. She had to grasp that this was deadly serious – they mustn't show even an ankle. They must both preserve their honour – his dignity. They didn't know how close they'd come to being branded harlots. Only his eloquence had persuaded the sheikhs of their innocence – they owed him their lives.

"Look over there, that's Chop-Chop Square. That's where they kill criminals or cut off their hands, the guards told me. If we'd arrived a week earlier we could've seen a whipping. Mind you, people are good Muslims here, there's not much need for punishments. The executioner is bored, they say."

Windowless houses spilt downhill to a highway lined with hovels. He was glad to see the women keeping their proper distance, though it must be hard to walk in those sacks. Carina trailed behind like a pregnant cow. She hadn't said a word since he freed her from capivity – she hadn't shown any gratitude for all he'd done. She'd wrenched his whole life askew with her stupidity...

His anger made what he had to do easier. Anyway, there wasn't an alternative. He wasn't going to lose one of his few possessions while the hen kept hers, which was a hundred times more valuable. Actually, why shouldn't he take hers and give his own to the driver? God, Farafra was a flea-hole. *Hamdillilah*, they'd been freed just in time for the weekly truck to Dakhla. Before the Flood, he'd heard that it was a nice oasis with people who knew how to enjoy themselves. That sounded more his style. Perhaps there might be hashish: there was nothing against it in the Holy Qur'an.

The truck was piled high with boxes and mattresses, two greybeards and four burqas sitting on top. Good, he needn't worry about pickpockets – not that he had much to steal. He waited for Carina to catch up. "We're travelling on this, it's the best I could manage," he apologized. "Give me your hand, I'll help you aboard."

In a trice he'd slipped the watch from her wrist and into his pocket. He'd expected protests – been ready to remind her of Chop-Chop Square – but she hardly twitched, clambering aboard without a murmur. The watch felt heavy in his pocket. It was Swiss and gold. Smiling, he unstrapped his Chinese Timex.

"*Ya raïs*," he hailed the driver, "See what I've got for you."

Four hours later they were in Dakhla Oasis. The driver had promised to take them to the only town in the oasis, but halted well short, at a nowhere village called Al-Qasr. Sabr raged and begged, but the son-of-a-shoe wouldn't budge. These people called themselves Muslims but behaved like Jews! Still, the oasis was an improvement on Farafra: lush fields and a rose-hued escarpment.

In Al-Qasr, modern houses climbed a gentle hill to a mud-brick settlement going back centuries. *There are empty houses*, people assured him. *Don't think of taking mine*, he read in their eyes. They hadn't got anything left to barter but the Swiss watch and the clothes on their backs. Tomorrow, he'd try to find work somewhere. He cursed at the thought of three mouths to feed. Men had to worry about *everything* – it wasn't fair!

"Hurry, women!" He felt better for saying it.

A labyrinth of ashen walls and shadowy passageways, houses barred and shuttered or over-spilling with residents. He lacked the nerve to force a window and was glad that he hadn't when he asked a local man why so many houses were sealed.

"Why, plague. It came in Sha'ban, when Allah determines man's fate for the year. God is merciful: they died quickly in their homes – not in hospital, with chicken fever."

Bird flu had afflicted Egypt for years, but the pandemic that everyone feared never occurred – instead, the Flood came. Now Sabr understood that chicken fever had swept through the oases last winter. The Emirate hadn't sought help from the outside world, but submitted to God's will, resulting in the deaths of hundreds until the plague was lifted by God's mercy.

At last he found an empty hovel with the makings of a fire: cobwebs, husks and dried dung. Duty discharged, Sabr sprawled on the *mastaba* and let the others work, encouraging Tariq with a kick. He'd screwed up trading for supplies in Farafra – the agency's binoculars would've fetched more here. Still, tea, sugar, flour, rice, oil and onions – they wouldn't starve tonight.

Water, he'd forgotten. Where could he find it? He couldn't just order the women out searching without an escort. He could send Tariq, but didn't trust him – the boy might sniff an opportunity and never return. Tariq had no origin, his parents were mud.

The jar was heavy in Yasmina's hands; Carina clumsily filling the other, her burqa sopping wet. If it hadn't been for the old woman sweeping an alleyway they'd be stuck. Umm Salah was a godsend – she'd not only led them to the well, but lent them two clay water jars and a cooking pot from her own home, with some pickles and salt as a gift. Just the thought of pickled carrots and turnips set Yasmina salivating.

Umm Salah drew her inside as Sabr fretted in the lane. She cast off her burqa, her face wrinkled as a raisin. "God sustain you, I know your burdens are heavy."

Yasmina felt a tear slide down her cheek.

"Daughter, tell me your fears." It could be her mother talking.

"My companion – she's lost hope. I have to feed her like a baby."
Umm Salah drew her close.

"For every sickness there's a medicine. Women's wisdom can cure women's woes. For women in need, there is always the *zar*..."

The ritual was held on Friday, when men were at the mosque. It was for *women*, Umm Salah stressed. Imams said it was sinful, but what did they know of women's suffering? It had healed their afflictions since the time of *Jahalliyya*; the existence of djinn was stated in the Holy Qur'an. Everyone knew that djinn possessed people, especially women – how could it be otherwise, when djinn were always male?

Yasmina had heard of *zar* rituals but never met an initiate, let alone a priestess. It ran in the family, Umm Salah said – her mother and grandmother had also been *kodia*. It was an honourable profession, only secretive due to men's suspicion. And even *they* turned a blind eye when their own wives were possessed. Only Emir Yussef and the Taliban were implacably hostile. If it weren't for their spies in Dakhla, nobody would bother her, Umm Salah asserted.

With the *zar* in three days, Yasmina must decide quickly. If Carina were in England she'd take antidepressants or see a psychiatrist. But in the Emirate, the *zar* was the only remedy available for her misery. More than that, Yasmina trusted Umm Salah, sensed power in her. Her professors at Giza would have mocked her intuition, but she recalled hearing one complain that a *kodia* had cured a patient after years of medication had failed. Umm Salah spoke truly: men disparaged the knowledge of women but secretly feared it. Yasmina couldn't think of any reason to reject her invitation.

Persuading Carina proved easy. Her depression made her suggestible, and the prospect of a hot bath was irresistible. The only obstacles were Sabr and money – or rather, recompense for Umm Salah's services and the expenses of the ritual. Transactions were awkward without money. As a day-labourer, Sabr was paid in rice at one farm, dates at another, or even woven mats. Their only valuable possession was the watch that he'd hidden behind a brick, which he'd never yield. Taking it wouldn't be a sin – the watch was rightfully Carina's. But first he had to be persuaded to escort them to the house in time to prepare for the ritual.

She hoped Carina's condition would be argument enough, but Sabr didn't seem to notice – or care, if he did. Perhaps he was too tired or dispirited at the end of the day – he wasn't used to agricultural work, he complained. Or perhaps he was just a selfish ape, without compassion for others.

Either way, though, he was a *man*.

That evening she spoke softly, moved fluidly, combing her hair languorously, one leg raised on the *mastaba*. Stretching her bare arms, she felt his eyes on her playthings. "Tomorrow" – she licked her lips – "I was hoping to go to the baths. Umm Salah has promised to soften my skin, and shave me." She lowered her eyes. "Take me and Carina in the morning, before you go to pray..."

And after prayers... hung unspoken between them...

Henna spider-webs on her hands and feet, kohl rimming her eyes, Carina looked a fright, but the Egyptians chorused approval. With only women around, she felt safer. Yasmina was her friend and Umm Salah the nearest thing to a Reiki instructor in this awful oasis. Carina's skin glowed after a hot bath and a massage with aromatic oils. The white *galabiyya* was crisp, her brass charms and bracelets tinkled. She was ready...

Doubts returned when she saw the room. Lime-washed and shuttered, cushions facing a stool supporting a brass tray covered with a white cloth, dried fruit and nuts, and burning candles. Umm Salah entered with a censer trailing cloying smoke, followed by two women holding tambourines and a wizened man with an hourglass-shaped drum. His eyes were clouded; they guided him like a toddler.

"Sit." Yasmina pulled her onto a cushion. Three more women entered, garbed as Carina was, and sat down beside her. Across the room, the musicians were warming their instruments over a brazier, as Umm Salah paced to and fro wafting incense.

"Relax. Watch what the others do. Don't worry."

The drummer tapped out a rhythm, the tambourines joined in.

"Allahu akhbar, Allahu akhbar." Umm Salah circled the altar, fanning smoke over the fruit and candles. The drumming intensified, filling the room.

A haggard young woman leapt upright, spread her arms and swayed, rolling her head. "Al-lah," she groaned, slapping her thighs and tossing her hennaed hair.

"Al-lah, Al-lah," voices chorused. A matron lurched towards the altar. Umm Salah stepped forward, intoning verses echoed by the others. Carina felt a cry growing in her stomach. She beat her thighs and shook her shoulders, panting like a steam train. "Al-lah!" the sound exploded from her lips.

The haggard girl and the matron circled the altar jerkily, heads thrown back, hair like waterfalls, groping the air or slapping their bellies every second beat.

Umm Salah moved beside the girl, chanting, fanning her with smoke, as the drummer changed rhythm, the tambourines their timbre.

"Umm Salah has identified the spirit plaguing her," whispered Yasmina. "It comes when she is fertile; it makes her husband's carrot wilt."

Preternaturally arched, calves straining, the girl swished her tresses like a horse's tail and hiccupped, then jack-knifed and belched explosively.

Umm Salah knelt beside her, coaxing. Bluish smoke shrouded their figures, the candles blazed up and the musicians beat a new tempo, faces shining with sweat.

"Al-lah, Al-lah..."

A third woman circled the altar and fell writhing on the floor, foaming at the mouth. Carina heard fabric rip. "Look at her stomach," Yasmina whispered.

Crimson worms were rising from the doughy flesh exposed by a rent in her robe. Her eyeballs had rolled into their sockets; her hair was flecked with spittle. Umm Salah swung the censer and sprinkled white dust over her till she subsided.

"The spirit's submitted. It's left her womb." Yasmina nudged her gently. "Dance, let your sorrow go."

Suddenly Carina was on her feet, swaying.

"I should've guessed, her djinn isn't Muslim. That makes it harder, he may want arak to drink. I have to discover his identity, his animal form," reported Umm Salah hoarsely. The kodia was tired but resolute. She'd never yet abandoned a woman once her djinn had been aroused, she assured Yasmina.

Carina shuffled round the altar to the pulse of a goatskin darabukka drum, head rolling, hips twitching. Her face ran with sweat, the galabiyya clung to her body – she'd lost weight since Suez. Eyes shut, mouth open, she'd been dancing for hours, it seemed. The slower the beat, the more intensely she twitched, the deeper she moaned.

The others sat reciting the Qur'an. They'd washed their hands and faces with rosewater and brushed their hair. They looked serene. Could the zar really change their lives, make one woman fertile and another's husband regain his manhood? Yasmina wondered.

At a signal from Umm Salah the *darabukka's* tempo slowed. She resumed chanting the Qur'an, wafted fresh smoke over the altar and un-corked a bottle, sprinkling droplets that made the candles flare blue. Yasmina smelt *arak* – raw alcohol.

The *kodia* took Carina's arm, made her halt and take a swig. She shuddered and choked, Umm Salah thumped her back till the coughing ceased and nudged her into motion again. As they circled past, the *kodia* hissed:

"Now I know him: it's Yehnr, who takes the shape of a crooked horse. He's cruel and clever, but cowardly."

Carina gyrated, unseeing, running her fingers through her hair with flicking motions. Candles guttered, smoke and shadows thickened. Abruptly the bass drum ceased and a *tabla* broke into a flurry of beats. Carina threw out her hands as if to deflect a blow; spun to face her demon as it circled her.

Racing shadows, the rhythm of hooves – Yasmina could *feel* it in the room, an icy wind as it passed. Loping, not galloping, a wolf masquerading as a horse.

Carina shrieked and spat, clawed the air, eyes blazing.

The *darabukka* boomed – she froze.

Again – she sagged to the floor.

Dousing her with rosewater, Umm Salah cried, "*Hat qattar!*"

Her son ran in with a brown cockerel. In a moment, he'd slit its throat and blood was pumping into a bowl that Umm Salah held beneath its twitching body.

Setting it on the altar, she added a pinch of spices, stirred it with her finger and turned back to Carina. Yasmina gasped but the *kodia* ignored her, turning Carina over and dabbing her face with blood. As her mouth opened, Umm Salah put the bowl to her lips.

24 *ALF MABRUK!*

The bus wasn't going anywhere. Windows thick with dust, tyres missing. Tariq looked inside; broken seats, litter, nothing worth taking. But seeing it took him back to Cairo long before the Black Day. Dad had been a bus conductor till the booze killed him. Rages, thrashings – they'd been better off without him. No salary, but their earnings weren't squandered on liquor, and stallholders were sympathetic to the widow, Umm Tariq. School – who could afford it? He'd been on the streets since he was six, hawking Kleenex, jasmine posies; learning how to flatter or stab at any weakness.

His idols were the *khirtiyya*, the hustlers who preyed on tourists and Egyptian hicks. Rewarded by hotels, shops and travel agencies, they grew their nails long to show they needn't dirty their hands. He'd made some friends, done little jobs and looked forward to joining them when he was older. But then his mother got the cunning disease, withering between one Eid and the next in their room in Bab al-Wazir. Truly, the Black Day had been a mercy – they'd no hope of finding money for her treatment. It took her quickly – better than a slow painful death.

It was sad he hadn't been there to comfort her, but Allah had decreed otherwise. He'd sensed the unease on the streets; drifted back towards the Citadel from habit. Truck-loads of Black Berets were mustering on the square below, shields and visors glinting in the sun. People chanting *Allahu akhbar*! Plumes of tear gas, a volley of shots as the crowd surged forward the Bab al-Azab. A truck rammed the gates and they rushed up to the heights of the Citadel, as a howling wind heralded the Flood's coming. He'd cowered below the terrace where the minarets of Mohammed Ali's mosque reared above the drowning city like arms raised in despair.

But he'd survived, like others from Bab al-Wazir. Street weasels and barbell-lifters without fear of the police anymore. Gangs formed quicker than you could say "Who's your cousin?" They took Tariq forraging when Abu Karim didn't want to know him, before the Siq was found. How *that* had changed Tariq's life, setting him on the path to this dismal place.

He was homesick for the Citadel, he hated the oases. No lights or music or television. No money to hustle and nothing to steal, unless you were willing to risk losing a hand for some carrots. Religion was fine, but not too much, not like *this*.

Worse, he had no friends – kids here spat on his hand or hit him with their sandals. The two women were no comfort either: always yakking in American, Yasmina only noticed him when they needed palm fronds or dung for the fire. And Sabr spent all day working like a buffalo, snapping at everyone in the evening.

That was *before* Sabr's watch went missing, and the women returned smelling of roses. The hen collapsed with a smile on her face, oblivious to Sabr's fury – he was so angry, he forgot how to speak American.

Give Yasmina respect, she was cool as a Coke can! Waving a bloody *galabiyya* in his face, screeching that the hen was *ma'zura*. Possessed – that put a chill on Tariq and left Sabr grinding his teeth. *Ma'zura* also meant 'excused', for nobody possessed by a djinn was responsible for their actions.

Then she ate Sabr's mind like candy. One minute he was growling, the next preening himself as she shoved her doorknobs at him, begging him to forgive them both, stupid women involved in women's nonsense...

"Walk with me in the dunes at sunset," she simpered.

Tariq pushed his plate aside and crept from the hovel.

Mohsen was four years his senior, with a moustache like a donkey's lip. The other boys were hardly older than Tariq but took Mohsen's lead, scorning him as usual until he said what he'd seen in the dunes. Suddenly they all wanted details.

"And his pigeon, he let it fly?"

"Sure, right into her dove-cote," Tariq replied.

"*W'Allahi*, she moaned?"

"*Aiwa*, like she was licking honey," he confirmed.

"*Ya wahled*, I bet your pigeon was stirring!"

Tariq wasn't sure why – he'd merely been curious – but he knew what would impress them. "Sure, I had to let him fly."

"You were in her dove-cote too?" Their eyes popped.

"Well, my pigeon flew that way, but her nest closed 'fore I got there."

"Closed?" Mohsen gasped.

"Yeah, closed – nests do. Don't you know anything about pigeons and doves?" The challenge was so brazen Mohsen was struck dumb.

"Anyway," Tariq continued, "My pigeon flew over her and dropped its dung. She was happy – she said my bird was quicker than Sabr's."

"A whore," breathed Mohsen. "One in our oasis at last..."

***

The Taliban came when they were eating, four of them. "*Salam aleikum*," they chorused, looking at the floor, seeing no reason to remove their sandals. Sabr rose to greet them.

He mustn't antagonize them, must protect the women. They'd huddled in the corner under their burqas – good. He remembered Yasmina in the dunes, sand trickling through her fingers, turning to him, eyes wet...

They went without resistance to a shabby villa, where it went as Sabr feared: a sharia trial by five beardies. The most hostile had a tangerine brush like a fox's tail: Sheikh Hamza. His fellow judges were raven-haired or silver-bearded. Sabr felt like a lamb among lions.

"*Zinah!*" roared Sheikh Hamza, "Fornication!"

"Patience, Brother," cautioned a greybeard, "A trial before a verdict."

"So put your hand in water and tell me it's wet. My eyes are their judge – look at their faces. Their shame betrays their guilt. *Zinah!*"

"Convene the court then. Let us hear witnesses."

Each purified his breath before swearing to uphold Allah's law on Earth. As judges, their dignity was inseparable from the righteousness of their verdicts. To sit rigidly upright on a dais while witnesses quaked at their feet was only fitting. The boy Mohsen testified first on the Holy Qur'an.

"We were hunting quail in the dunes. They walked past together as we were resting. The man spread a cloak, they lay down and he touched her hotplates."

Sheikh Walid let the vulgarity pass – there'd be time to rebuke him later. "And then?" he prompted.

"His pigeon flew into her dove-cote. They cooed together."

"Zinah!" Sheikh Hamza growled. "I told you."

"Call the next witness," ordered Sheikh Hikmet.

Another brat edged into the yard, lowering his eyes. Good, he showed proper respect. "Tell us what you saw, boy."

"It was as Mohsen said. They cooed together, many times. I had a stiff neck by the end." Boys – they fizzed with lust, all one could do was marry them young.

Sheikh Hamza laughed. "Ay, you saw enough."

The last boy was called and corroborated the others' testimony.

Nonetheless, it was a thorny judgement *— proof of fornication required four male witnesses, and here were only three – the fourth man accused, denying everything. Naturally, the woman also swore her virtue, but her testimony was worth only a quarter of a man's, in this case one twelfth of her accusers'. Justice hinged on the veracity of the alleged fornicator.*

Sheikh Hamza had no doubt. "Stone them both – a harlot and a pimp."

Sheikh Walid disagreed. "Without a fourth accuser, the charge is worthless. The word of three boys against a man's – this is folly."

"Nay, he lies. Examine the harlot, let's see the marks of lechery!"

"Peace, Brother," Sheikh Hikmet interjected. "Let us first consult the ahadith *and* fikh, *there's a commentary by the jurist Ibn Tamiyya you must consider."*

Eventually, as the dawn prayer approached, they reached a consensus.

"Marry *you* – no way!" Yasmina threw a brick across the room, narrowly missing him.

"*W'Allahi* it's marriage or death by stoning. They told me straight out. Prove you're good Muslims, or die as fornicators."

"But I only kissed you; you only squeezed me for a minute."

"Yeah, but those beardies say we opened the bonnet, that I plugged your tailpipe. I've denied it till I'm white as a Dane, but they won't listen."

"*Marry* you – that's impossible."

"Like the Black Day we never imagined, like a chemistry student in a whorehouse – impossible, sure."

"A *pharmacology* student – *not* a whore, I never was."

"No, so what've you been doing here? Baring your legs, lying in the dunes, letting me touch your playthings? If that isn't a whore, show me a virtuous woman!"

"You're such a hypocrite – you've wanted to fuck me all along!"

"*Fuck, fuck,* your slutty mouth proves you're a whore. The sheikhs were right, you're *aib*." He ducked as she threw another brick at him.

Having condemned them to wed, the sheikhs took a paternal interest in the ceremony. Sheikh Walid donated a sheep for the feast; Sheikh Hikmet sent watermelons and Sheikh Hamza offered to officiate. With Tariq deputised to escort them, the women spent hours at Umm Salah's, beautifying themselves and preparing Yasmina for her wedding night. Carina's blood was no longer heavy, she'd come to life, throwing herself into the event as if Yasmina was her own daughter. Even Tariq had been helpful lately, trying to make amends for his laziness, no doubt. *Al-hamdillilah*, blessings were raining on them.

Yet Sabr was nervous. He'd stuffed foreign chickens and Egyptians of no origin, but bedding a *wife* for the first time was different. He had a nagging fear that his pigeon wouldn't fly. Yasmina was a fireball, burning your nose one moment, licking it the next. He'd called her a whore but didn't want to believe it. The thought of her milking Jews was repugnant. She'd sworn by the Prophet's Companions she was a virgin, but she was an artful liar. Well – he'd discover the truth on their pigeon night.

It's true what they say, thought Yasmina, *bed is the poor man's opera.* She'd never worn so much kohl, not even at the Euro (how distant it seemed). Or had silver coins plaited in her hair, or worn a tomato-red gown with viridian embroidery. Even her veil was edged in silver thread. The bridal costume came from Umm Salah, whose eldest daughter had last worn it; the headdress had been in the family for generations.

Her own parents had often envisaged her wedding: their daughter in white satin, a honking cavalcade of cars to a restaurant by the Nile. A doctor at Minya's University Hospital was their ideal – though they wouldn't mind a consultant from Cairo if she met one. How they'd be horrified to see her now, dressed for a rustic wedding in a hovel, to an uneducated driver who boasted of seducing foreign women. Hardly a great accomplishment, when they used to flock to Egypt to find lovers.

Still, it bothered her. Everyone knew foreign women were shameless, did things only prostitutes in Egypt would do, so Sabr's expectations would also be shameless. She'd flirted, let him kiss her, touch her playthings once, but that was all for Carina's sake. To sleep with him was irrevocable; to surrender her virginity to a husband she hadn't chosen, after spurning rich foreigners, utterly perverse.

If marriage wasn't consummated, it became invalid in God's eyes – and under sharia law. But how to –

"Umm Salah," she called, "Umm Salah..."

✳✳✳

Sabr felt bloated with lamb and pigeon. He hadn't eaten so well since Hurghada. The only thing missing was alcohol or smoke, but he'd learnt not to expect them in the Emirate. Even music was *haram* here – ribbons of tape fluttered outside shuttered cassette shops. Musicians found other professions, or else: he'd heard of an *oud* player whose hands had been broken. Only muezzins and bards were sure of employment, reciting the call to prayer or Qur'anic verses at funerals and weddings.

As Sabr couldn't afford a *munshid*, Sheikh Hamza had volunteered his larynx. He seemed to have forgotten that he'd once urged their deaths, now acting like a kindly matchmaker who'd brought them together – which he had, in a way. His recitations were surprisingly melodious, but he'd come with a full iPod's worth. Guests were yawning surreptitiously.

Sabr looked at his bride, sitting stiffly on a borrowed chair in borrowed finery. She was a beauty, proud and fierce despite the dirt she'd swallowed. If her name was dirty, it was only because of the Flood. Otherwise, she'd have been a bride to boast of, a graduate from a devout family, long respected in Minya.

If the Flood turned the world upside down, why should he be ashamed of her?

He patted her wrist, the most he'd have of her till the guests had departed. She smiled at him mechanically. *You're scared, I'll be gentle with you tonight*, he vowed.

Sheikh Hamza pumped his hand.

"Marriage is half of religion, *alf mabruk!*" A thousand blessings!

That was the last Sabr remembered.

25 SHOW ME HOW TO CLICK

"Wake up, husband."

Yasmina shook him.

Her face was bare of make-up. A dingy housedress swathed her body. His mouth was parched, his brain scrambled. *Last night* – he couldn't remember anything. The last thing he recalled was a red-bearded sheikh saying...

"Hurry, they're waiting outside, they want us *now*," Yasmina insisted.

"Who..."

"Taliban," she hissed, "From Kharga, from Emir Yussef!"

Beyond the ragged blanket screening their *mastaba*, he saw Carina thrusting clothes into baskets as Tariq glared at a shadow blocking his escape route. Someone kicked the street door.

"In God's name..."

He tried to think straight – *last night*, now *this*.

Maybe *he'd* been possessed by a djinn?

The door crashed open; a Talib stalked in. "Your women are faster than you. Perhaps your hair is longer than a girl's." Every word an insult – but he held a pistol.

"He who has but one hair left on his head, let him honour it." That shut the bastard up, quoting the Prophet at him. Sabr turned away before the man regained his wits. "Wife, fetch my shoes." What *did* happen last night?

Djinn had eaten his memory.

Telephone poles buried to their necks in sand, dunes smothering a highway. In four hours they'd seen only a lorry, a Talib pickup and a madrassa bus – but suddenly there were donkey carts and bicycles by the dozen. A triumphal arch flush with calligraphy welcomed visitors to El-Kharga City, capital of the Rightly Guided Emirate.

It wasn't Carina's idea of an oasis town: boulevards lined with low-rise flats like rejects from Maidstone, some encased in dried mud like giant termite mounds. Sabr was also intrigued, judging by his gestures as he quizzed their escorts, who'd mellowed during the journey. The Taliban replied all at once, laughing or scowling.

Yasmina whispered a translation. "Those flats are either too hot or too cold, without fans or heating – since the Black Day there's been neither. People remembered how old mud houses stayed cool in summer and warm in winter, and got together to build them. It's a lot of work, not everyone agrees to share the labour."

"Shut up," grunted Sabr, half-turning.

He'd become a right bastard since assuming the role of patriarch, thought Carina. If they ever got back to civilization she'd make sure he suffered. Thank heaven for sisterhood: Yasmina had cared for her, Umm Salah had cured her, and they'd found a solution for Yasmina's dilemma. Veiled women bewitching men, djinn – it was the Arabian Nights come to life.

The *zar* had been life-changing. She'd cast off despair, found hope and audacity. She'd survived maniacs, gunships, sandstorms, prisons. She'd find Nick in this alien land, her love was powerful. She was more than an interface between the V&A and Gazprom or an unloved Daddy's Girl. None of that mattered now. The *zar* was incredible: a Vesuvius of women's energy. If she ever got home – if life returned to normal – she'd fly Umm Salah over to start *zar* workshops in London.

If, if… Stifled by her burka, heartened by Yasmina beside her, Carina could only wait to discover what Emir Yussef intended for them.

The Scorpion had branded him forever. His spine was twisted from a stinking womb where you could neither lie nor sit upright. His eyes had never been strong even as a schoolteacher, but years of darkness had left him unable to bear sunlight, and not even his wife saw the scars on his body. But the worst wounds were in his mind – the humiliations inflicted at Kharga Prison, the hellhole they called the Scorpion.

He remembered every assault. Dogs lunging for his genitals; croaking answers to a woman's name, crawling in a negligee as the sergeant with a broom-handle urged the others on. Only faith and brotherhood sustained him. Brothers shared Qur'anic verses like water and dates in a desert, fortifying each other. He'd entered the Scorpion a timid pamphleteer charged with terrorism – and emerged a warrior, afire with jihad.

Allah had chosen him to rid the oases of impiety. The Valley had been destroyed as a warning; El-Wahat spared to guide Egypt back to righteousness. In time, God willing, the Emirate would topple the regimes of pharaohs, Jews and Crusaders. Once Egypt was reunited and cleansed it would merge with the great a Caliphate spreading across the earth till all humanity was united beneath the banner of Islam.

Meanwhile, the Emirate was imperilled by unbelievers. To the north, heretics drained the oil and gas that were Allah's bounty. Beyond the Valley, hypocrites, Jews and Crusaders tried to subjugate the faithful and lure them back into Jahilliyya, the era of darkness before Islam. But he, Emir Yussef, Commander of the Faithful, would thwart their plots, God willing.

The Scorpion remained; he had learnt its lessons.

Some Brothers wished to demolish it, but his counsel prevailed. There was need for it till victory, to protect the Emirate and deliver justice, he argued. Even the dissenters approved the fate of their jailers. It was proof of the Emirate's mercy that they died quickly. He had their heads salted and set on spikes beside the highway to watch over the prison.

A bird alighted at his feet, scent ravished his nostrils. The serenity of the Palace of Roses was balm to his soul, its pristine chambers just reward for years of flea-infested cells. It had once been a hotel with every vice to tempt foreigners – a swimming pool, alcohol, unveiled women. Now the pool was a fish-pond, the bar a library; no-one doubted the virtue of the wives and daughters living in the compound.

Even now, his daughters were helping their mother cook supper. Their eldest son, Jihad, was away with the patrols, and young Islam playing football. Every day he thanked God for preserving his family through the years of the Scorpion, to reunite them in freedom and comfort. Others had not been so blessed; their families suffered for their faith or perished during the Flood. Surely they now enjoyed paradise, God willing.

Yet, shamefully, this wasn't enough. In prison they'd transcended their allegiances to the Brotherhood, Jihad Islami or Hizb ut-Tahrir – but the infamy of personal betrayal had festered, emerging when they were masters. Their torturers were dead, their persecutors humbled. But the maggot of mistrust burrowed among them, fattening on disunity – fitna, the second of the deadly threats faced by Islam.

As Commander of the Faithful, his exegeses had been doubted, his verdicts disputed. Not all on the Emirate council were Brothers; village sheikhs still had influence. Every meeting was like a marketplace, each man's self-interest dressed up like a bride, trumpeting her virtue as she swayed like a harlot. They sensed that he was withholding things; that others in the Abode of Peace *beyond their isolation thought differently.*

By God's will, the foreign woman held the keys to the proof, in the House of the Forbidden.

✳✳✳

It must have been a bank once. Granite facing scarred where signs had been torn away, bronzed doors and window-grilles still intact. Their guards lost their bravado, muttered invocations against evil. This was the Beit al-Harami, where all that was forbidden but could not be destroyed was quarantined.

Why not destroy it anyway? Sabr asked a Talib.

Scowling, they urged him on with a rifle butt. Tariq cringing in their wake, the hens stumbling over their burkas on the steps to the basement – was this how it ended? Had Allah spared him on the Black Day for *this*?

The vault door stood ajar, an electric kettle wedged underneath. A wispy-bearded hunchback limped towards them. *"Salam aliekum."*

Emir Yussef didn't introduce himself – who in the Emirate would fail to know him? Ten years in the Scorpion, his sufferings ignored by the people of Kharga. Then, suddenly, Brothers as mighty as their oppressors had been, lusting for vengeance on the hypocrites andtyrants, with Emir Yussef as Commander of the Faithful.

As if reading Sabr's thoughts, he declaimed:

"When the Black Day came, people found their televisions and phones mute and smashed them in fury. So began the cleansing: posters of harlots and cassettes of lustful music; barbers, purveyors of beer and *arak*. Even schoolbooks were burnt if they deviated from the word of God. To be able to read the Qur'an and count the days and months is sufficient for boys. If a few show a gift for scholarship, we have volumes of jurisprudence rescued from a storehouse of impiety. Imagine the wisdom of God beside pagan idols, in a so-called museum!"

He drew breath. "Soon, the Emirate will be entirely rid of *kufr* technology and any trace of *Jahalliyya*. But for now, we must act in the world that exists and deal with Satan's instruments. The internet – a sewer of desires – serves the righteous waging jihad. Our Emirate doesn't reject telecommunication, only restricts it to godly purposes. When a computer was found, radiant with the wisdom of Al-Azhar, we knew this was the herald of signs – and surely there followed a pillar of fire and smoke, seen by our scouts."

He beckoned. "Come – see why the unbeliever is needed."

In candlelight, the vault was aglow with gold: chests and statues stacked beneath thrones and divans, plastic buckets filled with jewellery. A familiar visage stared at them from atop a filing cabinet. Carina gasped.

"But that's –"

"Tutankhamun's treasure," finished the Emir, in English. "Also treasures from Tanis and other nests of idolatry. By God's will, the convoy was halted in Bahariya by the Flood. So the idols fell into the hands of the righteous, to be recast in the service of Islam. We've melted some down already."

Sabr was amazed. Acknowledging a *kafir* woman in a foreign tongue went against every Taliban custom.

"What was *haram* will become *halal* – a transformation pleasing to God. But I didn't bring you to Kharga to show you that, I brought you to unlock *this*."

He limped into the vault, returning with a grey plastic box. Turned it over – his fingers had no nails – to show red letters branded on the lid, above a handwritten label.

SALVATION FIRST PROPERTY
Nick Baring

Carina's heart pounded as she activated the laptop. The battery level was low; she didn't know how much operating time was left. They were all staring at her: she'd cast off her burqa – it was stifling – but the Emir said nothing. For the first time since she arrived in Egypt, Carina felt empowered. Her fingers stroked the keys that Nick had touched only weeks ago. His presence – his work, his soul – was bound into the silicon and plastic, the software, the files.

Her own image appeared on screen. The preview of Gaudi's Lustre-ware at the V&A – she'd worn a frock that displayed her boobs; Nick had been all over her afterwards. She sensed the Emir's disapproval; luckily the password box obscured her cleavage. Her fingers twitched on the keyboard.

She prayed that Nick had used the same password as on his home computer in London. He was hopeless at remembering different passwords. So let's try...

carina&buster

The preview photo vanished, replaced by an Alpine scene studded with icons.

Excel folders – spreadsheets and accounts, dozens of them. Short-cuts to Sky Sport and Classic Sitcoms, application icons like heraldic banners.

The Emir leant over, breathing peppermint. "Al-Azhar, look for Al-Azhar."

She couldn't see anything that fitted the bill, didn't have a clue what he was on about. There was a folder entitled *Weird*. She double-clicked, frowned at the file names and opened one at random: *Flood*

It was an article from the *Daily Telegraph*, dated two years earlier.

The Flood and 9/11
By our Security correspondent Brian Moody

As with 9/11, the terrorists and their victims perished together, so we shall never know exactly what happened. But we know that 129 tourists and 36 Egyptians were aboard the cruise boat *Nubian Heaven* when it was hijacked on Lake Nasser, somewhere between the famous rock-cut temples of Abu Simbel and the massive High Dam at Aswan, in the far south of Egypt.

At 10.05 local time (08.05 GMT), the boat approached the High Dam's passenger dock, an hour ahead of schedule. Instead of mooring there, it entered the inner harbour and sank right beside the dam in seconds – it's thought the terrorists blew a hole in the hull. As it touched the lake-bed, a second, atomic bomb exploded, sending a tidal wave over the dam's crest while the force of the detonation struck its base. The resulting whiplash stress was a contingency its designers had never anticipated.

As the dam collapsed, a 300-foot-high cascade of water swept down the Nile Valley, destroying everything in its path. Within an hour, millions of Egyptians were dead; by nightfall, the death toll exceeded fifty million, with millions more stranded on hilltops or islands.

Meanwhile, TV channels around the world were playing clips from the 'jihadi video' sent to Al-Jezeera, showing the terrorists ranting against Egypt's ratification of the Final Settlement of the Palestinian issue, and posing beside their bomb aboard the cruise boat.

Why old news? She skipped to the end, hoping for a clue.

Despite the chaos in Egypt, the CIA, Mossad and MI6 were able to establish that the dam was destroyed by a one-kiloton nuclear device, one of several "suitcase nukes" manufactured in the Soviet Union, which went missing in Belarus in 1998. How it came to end up in the hands of Islamist extremists has yet to be established, but such a threat has been intelligence agencies' worst nightmare since the end of the Cold War, especially after 9/11.

No enlightenment there. She opened another file, CB, and saw:

Calvin Wesley Baines

Born 1952 in Fayetteville, North Carolina. Father an engineer & Baptist pastor. Graduated *summa cum laude* in civil engineering from Duke University, North Carolina. Played for NC Tar Heels at the Rose Bowl & served in the Air National Guard. Joined Bechtel Corp 1978; managed infrastructure projects in Alaska, Philippines, Iran, Saudi Arabia, UAE, Thailand & China. Left Bechtel to found Sigma Solutions in 1994. Voted *Fortune* "Entrepreneur of the Year" in 1997.

A registered Republican & substantial contributor to congressional and presidential campaigns. Married Rosalyn De Witte 1979; one daughter, Shelley...

Emir Yussef struck the table. *"Khalas,* find me Al-Azhar!"

She opened the Favourites menu and found a column of webpages. Evangelical ones – Nick really had got into it, Baines hadn't been lying – and one that looked different. Yes – Al-Azhar Mosque and University, double-click.

Emir Yussef's eyes bulged as the homepage appeared. *"Allahu akhbar!"*

She glanced round. Yasmina kneeling in her burqa, Tariq transfixed by the gold and Sabr trying to ignore a pistol aimed at his head. *Oh God, what next...*

"Show me the Arabic pages. Show me how to click."

"I will but..." – *don't stop* – "I must know where this came from. It's my husband's; it's the first sign I've had since he vanished ..." Her voice broke.

He pondered. *"Mashi,* one revelation for another, let none say I'm unjust. Some Bedouin brought it to us; they knew the Emirate hungered for Al-Azhar's guidance. I rewarded them generously" – he waved at the treasures. "By God's will, none knew the password till you arrived – so I might decide if it is righteous. The wise should judge before fools have their say. So show me how to turn its pages, and go."

"Wait, how did the Bedouin find the computer – *where*?"

He sighed. "In the Valley; a wandering sheikh and his fool – they had the computer. The sheikh showed them Al-Azhar, let them see a few pages – then he traded it for a camel and they went on their way."

"The sheikh, this fool, what did they look like?"

"Magnoon: mad. Enough! Show me how to click or your guardian dies."

✳✳✳

The Emir was as capricious as the sheikhs had been. One minute Sabr was set for a bullet in the basement of the Beit al-Harami. An hour later, they were cooing over their rooms in the Palace of Roses. One day a hovel with three mouths to feed, next day an en-suite bathroom each. He heard Yasmina in the shower. She'd be sweet-smelling and shaven, her hair brushed out. They'd been given a room with a double bed...

She slipped past him wrapped in a sheet, eyes averted.

Stripping off in the steamy, fragrant bathroom, he luxuriated in the hot water, imagining her body as he soaped his groin. His pigeon was flaccid. He squeezed it, thought of all the chickens he'd stuffed, their wanton desires...

Nothing.

He'd rested his head against the tiles, he wanted to weep.

"Husband, come drink your *karkaday*," she called.

Sabr groaned. Five minutes ago, he'd been anticipating paradise between her legs. Now he feared his pigeon might never fly again; fretted how to hide his shame.

It was true what they said: the unlucky slip on dung, to fall into a cesspool.

26 SHREK 2

Locusts firm-fleshed and sweet as prawns, voraciously Nick tore off charred wings and legs, munching their crispy carapaces. They sizzled in the red-hot ash, Shrek turning them with a twig, muttering *Yajooj w Majooj, Yajooj w Majooj*, over and over. His litany had begun to sound familiar, almost comforting.

Stretching his legs, Nick scratched the sores on his ankles, warming his feet at the fire. They were filthy as Shrek's – his hands too. He no longer smelt their bodies, only sun-baked dust. Shrek was at home here, probing with his staff beside dunes for water to suck through a papyrus straw. Rodents and insects came like willing sacrifices, a fox snared in a trap of branches, a grasshopper plucked from a leaf.

All around, locusts were hatching on coelacanths and thorny shrubs. Nick had learnt the names of some plants and the terms for hot, wind and sandstorm – but beyond a few pieties the meaning of Shrek's rants was a mystery, though he understood God and Judgement Day from a miming of the deity and a cataclysm so awful that the earth would whirl into space.

Bab el-Hadid! Shrek cried, rending an invisible barrier before reeling back, as if from a tsunami. *Yajooj w Majooj!* Bending to ease an invisible weight from the sand, stepping aside to stamp his foot and smirk at the locusts.

Yajooj!

The Beast snorted, rolling over, swollen from the fresh vegetation it had gorged after days of tumbleweeds and thorns. A slimy green bubble erupted from its mouth in a spray of slobber. Nick flinched. He hated and feared it – it was Shrek's ally. Mounted on the Beast, Shrek had the supremacy of a knight over a serf, wielding his staff and a knotted whip that had come with the camel, together with a rope ending in a leg iron – a slave leash. Fettered, Nick could only plod five steps behind the Beast's rump, fearing showers of urine or a surge of speed that might drag him across the desert. And whenever Shrek dismounted, it hissed and snarled if Nick came too close to its master – like a guard dog.

It was hideous – red hair falling out in clumps, leathery pads with oozing sores, ochre teeth lunging from a shaggy neck that flexed like a serpent. Its sight and smell revolted him. He cringed from his own senses, tried to shut them down. Vision was scalding light or velvety darkness, hunger a knife twisted in the guts. His face blistered and cracked. Days ago, a tooth fell out; his gums were puffy and bled. Vitamin deficiency, Carina would have the remedy on her healthy shelf...

Carina, home; his eyes filled. She was *fading* in his memory. He struggled to recall his mother's name; other people were already nameless shadows. They were slipping away. Soon there would only be Shrek and the Beast...

As reality blurred into brutish purgatory his dreams grew more vivid: flashbacks to his childhood, a kaleidoscope of faces and sensations. They were his only escape from Shrek and the Beast, the endless desert. Once their meagre supper was eaten, Nick would lie down beside their campfire, stuff cotton scraps in his ears to muffle Shrek's babble and slip expectantly into dreamland.

She came to him swathed in violet silk, handed down from a litter by servants. Pearls and rubies sewn on her veils and pantaloons, a slender arm holding a golden chalice, barefoot, ankles encircled by silver chains with bells. She lifted the veil slowly, revealing her parted lips, flaring nostrils.

Yasmina – she'd finally come to him.

She cast off the veils, silk slipping from her shoulders, raven hair spilling to her waist. Her belly twitched, she stroked her thighs and exposed her shaven fanny, crooking a finger. His cock hardened, anticipating their ecstasy.

"Come." She breathed roses.

It was like sinking into a hot tub that massaged his gonads. All those weeks of pent-up desire between them – now it was happening! Her toes stroked his shins, her nails nipped his neck. At the moment of orgasm, her skin wrinkled and sagged, retreating from her teeth, her hair greying in his hand. She groaned, one hand on his buttocks, the other lifting the golden chalice to their lips, maggots writhing below its rim...

Recoiling, he heard a furious roar, felt an impact beside him and saw Shrek's staff planted in the sand where Yasmina had lain a moment before. She'd vanished like a phantom but Shrek was corporeal.

Raging in Arabic, he lifted his staff and brought it down on Nick's groin.

Devils – dust-devils. Sand and grit lashed his skin as they howled round his skull, dust penetrating his eyelids beneath the blindfold, tears wetting his cheeks – body-water, precious as blood. He shivered; his inner thermostat had broken; radiators at full blast on a hot day. *Heatstroke...*

Devils teasing with a respite before the next one charged in. His head sagged; he squirmed in search of relief for his thighs and shoulders. He'd been kneeling in the sand ever since Shrek kicked him awake at dawn. The sun was overhead now – had been for an eternity, would be forever, he despaired.

The leash hissed like a black mamba, jerking him sideways as the Beast shambled away. Shrek clucked his tongue – it halted. Nick struggled to resume the position imposed as penance for that vile dream. It was endurable – he'd rather suffer *anything* than Shrek urging the creature to lope into the waste, dragging his body till he was flayed to shreds...

Dying in agony, alone with the Beast...

God threw a dustsheet over the sky. A billion wings thrummed overheard, locusts falling as Shrek dashed about, a bulging sack in one hand, the other darting left and right, while Nick traipsed the circumference of his leash, an enfeebled assistant. The locusts had changed – no longer green but yellow and black, as long as his hand, their pinched faces enraged as he swatted them with a rag and stuffed their bodies into his sack.

They'd both eat well tonight ...

The desert had also changed. Ruddier than the gravel flats and sand hollows they'd wandered, and greener – till the locusts came. How far could a swarm travel in a day? If it kept moving, growing, crossing continents and seas, mightn't it pick the whole world bare? But for now – for them – the locusts were a movable feast.

Shrek belched, wiping grease from his chin. With a belly-full of locusts, he'd mellowed, crooning Arab ditties with a sly expression that suggested they were love songs. In the flickering firelight he seemed to gaze at Nick fondly.

"*Inta asil.*" A compliment, Nick sensed.

That morning – before the swarm came – he'd recited all the verses Shrek had made him learn, without error. Their meaning was as unfathomable as String Theory but he could rattle off the equations.

Shrek fumbled beneath his rags, extracting a silver bracelet with a turquoise Wadjet Eye – the sort of amulet once sold in tourist bazaars. He tossed it over the embers, to fall in the sand by Nick's feet. "*Tfuddel.*" Take it.

Nick slipped the amulet onto his wrist – shrunk to bone and tendon. Its Wadjet Eye encapsulated all the verses he'd learned. He need only touch it and the words would spill from his lips. It was a rosary, a string of prayer beads... *a gift*.

The Beast farted in the penumbra of the fire.

So what.

Many days later, they crossed a ridge and gazed down on the Gates of Hell.

"*Bab el-Hadid!*" Shrek exulted.

Below them the Valley smouldered, the river cutting a gorge through debris, ragged fires on precipitous slopes spewing boulders into the abyss.

"*Yajooj – huwwa hinna!*"

They were both ravenous – locusts had stripped the land. Even the Beast hung its head, exhausted. Shrek heaved the saddle off its back and sank against its flank with a sigh. Vultures wheeled overhead. Bones everywhere, picked clean, scraps of bristly hide emerging wherever Nick grubbed for roots.

He'd become a scavenger, muttering to himself, ribs exposed by rips in his shirt, his beard stiff with dirt. A stranger would see no difference between him and Shrek. Nick even found comfort in chanting verses while rubbing his amulets. Shrek had given him another for learning more verses, and hinted at a third to come...

"*Gohar,*" Shrek hissed. "*Taht – bil Bab el-Hadid.*"

Something down in the Gates of Hell, Nick understood.

"*Bijou, bijou,*" Shrek insisted. "*Taht – bil Bab el-Hadid.*"

Jewels, Shrek was talking about jewels. So what? Nick only wanted to *eat*. He wondered if there were fish in the river, glinting below them.

"*Samak?*" he asked hopefully.

Shrek chuckled conspiratorially. "*Insh'allah.*"

Nick's stomach growled; saliva flooded his gums. Steaming white flesh, the skin crisp outside, soft and oily within – grilled fish, he could taste it.

"*Yallah?*" Shrek was asking, not ordering him.

"*Yallah,*" he agreed, rising to his feet almost happily.

Shrek saddled the Beast and led it to the brink, murmuring in its ear. It shied away, tugging against the bridle till he struck its rump and dragged it down the slope.

Nick scurried behind, fearfully. The rocks were hot as radiators, shifting underfoot, the slave-leash rasping over jagged edges. He no longer prayed for it to fray and snap, only that it wouldn't jerk him off his feet. Shrek had picked the gentlest incline that the terrain allowed, but a fall would be fatal.

He coughed and blinked. The gorge was a giant slag heap combusting from within, stinking of rotten eggs and tar, twisted iron rods growing like stunted trees. Belatedly, he realised that it was rubble from an entire town, pulverised and rammed together; a tin can, a plastic lid, a human skull poking from the debris.

Midway down the Beast stumbled, shanks splaying. The leash catapulted Nick forwards, entangling his legs, dragging him over the rubble. A wave of pain and adrenalin – *no!* He clawed for a hold, but the Beast's momentum was irresistible, the leash taut as a hangman's rope. Suddenly he was free of its grasp, blood flowing over his palms and shins as the Beast rolled downhill in a shower of rocks, squealing.

Shrek's knife trembled from the slash that had severed the leash. A hundred feet below, the Beast came to a standstill in a cloud of dust, its cries ringing in Nick's ears. *Gotcha*, he exulted, despite his pain.

"*Yallah,*" barked Shrek, loping downhill as Nick staggered to his feet. The Beast was still thrashing feebly when Shrek wrenched its head down and slashed the nape of its neck. Blood spurted like a lawn-sprayer, drenching Shrek as he hacked deeper into muscles, dust stirred up by the Beast's death throes falling saturated by sprayed blood, as a gory porridge.

Abruptly, it subsided. Shrek stepped back, wiping his eyes, his beard dripping crimson. "*Shouf,*" he urged, smoothing aside a patch of clotted hair on the side of the creature's neck. Underneath was a symbol, branded on its skin – three interlocking Nike swooshes. As Nick stared witlessly, flies settled on the congealing blood.

"*Khalas,*" Shrek growled, throwing his tinderbox at Nick's feet. Without being told, Nick began to build a fire. Fuel was easy to find, but he took care to select a site away from smoke that vented from fissures on the slopes, potential infernos.

The Beast's head gazed impassively as Shrek incised its haunches, tearing cartilage and tissue, flensing muscle from bone. Its purple liver was as long as Nick's arm, shaped like a banana and sweating fat that flared in the embers, the aroma making him drool. With Shrek's blessing they gorged on fibrous flesh, cramming their stomachs, prising scraps from their teeth as flies swarmed over the Beast's carcass, even fouler in death than in life. But its flesh tasted delicious, half-raw or charred – meat!

Afterwards, Shrek honed his knife, muttering. *Yajooj, Yajooj,* his litany shrunk to a single word. What it meant Nick didn't care – bloated, somnombulant, the rocks were shaded and the buzzing of flies soothing as the hum of traffic. The severed leash trailed from his leg. He covered his face and drifted into sleep, to dream.

Yajooj... Whichever way he turned, the wall reached to the clouds. Gunmetal, riveted like a battleship, sweating molten copper that congealed at its base, it trembled and the earth shook with the noise of grit inside a steel drum. He was on all fours, beard brushing the earth, the skin on his palms and knees impervious as rhinoceros hide. Instinctively, his tongue flicked out to snatch flies; they tasted of blood.

His head rotated like a wheel on a rusty axle, his body immobile as cast iron. Nothing could harm him – not hunger, fire nor blows. His indestructibility and paralysis were one; he'd been trapped in this shell for as long as the wall had stood. Only recently had he learned to act by will alone...

He focused on a line of rivets, furrowing his brow, compressing his rage like a spring, to hurl a projectile. Rivets popped in a shower of sparks, to smoulder in the sand. A corner of the plate buckled – topaz-blue light seeping through a chink. He turned his head a fraction, focusing on the nearest intact rivets. Compressed his rage again and released another thunderbolt.

By dusk he had torn a single stamp from a perforated sheet the size of a city. His head hung with fatigue. Tomorrow, he would continue tomorrow...

When he awoke, the wall stretched unbroken from horizon to horizon.

27 YAJOOJ

Shrek shook him awake. The gorge was tar-black but for the stars overhead and the Nile glinting below. Nick's stomach turned at the stench of the Beast's carcass in the damp air. He shivered, hugging his rags to himself, touching his amulets for reassurance.

A roar reverberated down the gorge, geysers erupting as boulders plunged into the river. A predator prowling the sky, raining sparks on the heights as Nick cowered behind a slab. Luminescent eyes, wings beating thunderously, it spat a streak of fire, igniting an inferno upriver. *A dragon – a dragon, dragons existed...*

"Inta aref dilwati," Shrek muttered. *"Yajooj..."*

Gradually its roar faded and the flames choked on their own smoke. Trembling, Nick emerged from cover rubbing the magnesium glare from his eyes.

Dragons – here be dragons. He'd fallen off the edge of the world...

At first light, Shrek led him down into the mist – a clammy murk muffling the noise of the river foaming over cataracts. Nick trod warily in his footsteps, muddied to the waist. If it wasn't for Shrek, he'd have lain down and died of despair. Only Shrek had mastery over the wilderness, mastery over *him...*

Master – it no longer felt shameful, but comforting. Shrek had saved him, would do so again. Filled with joy at his epiphany, Nick began chanting, affirming that he followed *willingly*. When Shrek looked back, there was love in his eyes...

Rainbows hung over the mist as it burned away, sunlight reaching into the gorge to touch a spur of concrete rising like a cliff. Iron mesh entangled with creepers, blue-tailed birds probing violet flowers for nectar. Shrek swept them aside with his staff and beckoned Nick into a cave.

The echo of their footfalls betrayed its size. Nick trod in a puddle; it was icy cold, the air smelt fungal. A match flared; a glow illuminated Shrek's head, his stocky body swinging a paraffin lantern so Nick could see ahead.

He recoiled from a bovine face framed by a mossy headdress, its torso emerging from the mud at waist level, hands folded over its bosom. An idol, imbued with magic, hidden in a cave where only Shrek knew of it.

"Tallah." Shrek moved on, casting it back into darkness, lighting a fissure in the rock-face. Nick saw him grope inside and pull out a splintered plywood sign.

...WELLERY BAZAA...

He threw it aside, waving Nick closer. Delved into the fissure again to produce a tarnished silver clasp-bracelet, motioning: *Take it*. Gladly, Nick fastened it around his ankle, below his slave fetter. It was his third amulet – his third step towards salvation.

✳✳✳

Three days later they exited the Gates of Hell. Abruptly, the gorges receded to biscuit-dry hills, the river calmed to a sweep of royal blue. They both thanked the Almighty for their deliverance, and the carp that Shrek speared in the shallows. As it grilled, Shrek emptied his sack, spilling gold and silver torques and pendants upon the earth.

Shrek tried to explain, gesturing at the fish and the jewellery. Nick understood *samak* and *bijou*, but not the connection between them, not what it was about. He felt a wave of despair – he'd never understand; Shrek would abandon him in disgust; he'd die alone here... Tears spilt down his cheeks. He hadn't wept since atoning for Yasmina's visitation. He let them fall without shame.

Shrek leant forward to wipe Nick's cheeks.

"*Badi shwaya*," he crooned.

Not long.

Yajooj – they saw him from afar. Two vast truncated legs of stone, water surging between their paws over fragments strewn across the Valley: a colossus that once bestrode the Nile. A claw wedged betweeen cataracts, an ear lodged beyond the last waterfall.Nick looked for a monstrous torso or head, but they must have been atomized.

Nick had dreamt of Yajooj; inhabited Yajooj's mind, tasted blood on his tongue. He'd felt Yajooj's yearning, his fury, the power seething within. Confined behind armoured walls, struggling to escape and unleash his rage, to self-destruct. Thwarted for so long, till eventually –

This...

Here was Yajooj's footprint on Egypt. *From the tower of Syene unto the border with Ethiopia* went the prophecy – not Shrek's but another's. All the prophets were right, they'd foretold Yajooj's coming, the cataclysm of his making.

Shrek embraced him. They were both sobbing – from relief, despair, he didn't know which – but sure the end was nigh. *Badi shwaya.*

Clumsily they disengaged, wiping their eyes, calmed for the final stage.

Jacob's Ladder – a ladder to Heaven – it really existed, Nick marvelled. Shrek greeted it like an old friend, tugging its moorings, lashed to submerged rocks. Plaited fibres and creepers, cables thick as Nick's arm, the lower treads metal for ballast and tension – girders, car fenders – branches or timber slats as it ascended Yajooj's colossal leg, dangling above the falls. The ladder swayed as they climbed. Nick fixed his eyes on Shrek's calloused heels. He daren't look *down* – drenched in spray from the cataracts a hundred rungs below, dangling in the void below Yajooj's kneecap. The stony limb bristled with iron hairs, holds for intrepid climbers. Nick surmised that Shrek must have scaled its calf to suspend the ladder; his Master's fearlessness was awesome. Vortices assailed them, trying to hurl them into the maelstrom. Nick clung tighter, twisting the ropes round his forearms, weaving his body into the ladder.

At last he lay on the summit, rags drying as his pulse subsided. A scorching wind blew across their eyrie. With his cheek to the rock, its umber surface smelt of chocolate; licking it, he found it bitter as olives. Wearily he sat up and gazed around. Shrek handed him the goatskin, let him swig till it was empty. *And later?* His Master would find a solution…

Shrek began praying, prostrating himself towards the setting sun. Stiffly, Nick followed suit, chanting the litany, rubbing his amulets, trying to ignore a smear of fish bones and scales buzzing with flies. Gazing over the Valley, the river's limits lost in a golden haze, as dragons wheeled in the clouds.

"*Tamam.*" Shrek patted his shoulder. "*Tallah.*"

Fondly, Nick contemplated Shrek's wiry mane, his assured stride to the brink of a precipice. With the sun on their backs they gazed across the cataracts at Yajooj's other leg, canted so sharply Nick expected it to fall any moment. Severed mid-calf, it was lower than their vantage point. Then he saw the ropes, plunging from their limb to its neighbour. Not a ladder but a *bridge*: three cables cross-tied in a *V* like a rollercoaster track to oblivion.

Shrek clasped his shoulder. "*Ya habibi, inta asil!*"

With a jolt, Nick realised what he must do.

Shrek drew a pendant from his tunic. Ruddy gold from the dying sun, it swung from his paw like a censer. Nick smelt incense, heard a celestial choir urging him on. An act of faith: a test as old as religion. Martyrdom – Shrek wanted Nick to commit himself. To walk through fire, withstand torture. He'd come so far, endured such hardships, outlived the Beast and made its flesh his own...

He was ready.

Five amulets, he had *five* now: one for each limb and the pendant that Shrek had hung round his neck. Extra protection, a reward for Nick's courage paid in advance.

He wouldn't fail his Master...

Grasping the hand-ropes, he set foot on the cable. After weeks of roaming, his feet were calloused. The bridge sagged and oscillated but he felt its strength, trusted in Shrek's omnipotence. If his Master had created the bridge for Nick to cross, the only possibility of failure was his own weakness. *I am strong*, he assured himself.

He sang as he edged down the tightrope, louder as the roar of the cataracts increased. The raging falls were sublimely remote; he'd no sooner plummet to his death than the birds that swooped from ledges on Yajooj's shanks...

Near the end, he paused to savour his imminent grace. The air was elixir, the sun pure energy, charging each cell in his body. He felt god-like, immortal. His past life seemed a travesty mired in illusions. Only now, stripped to his core, tested to the limit, was he truly *living*, a spiritual entity, seeking its maker.

Knotted round boulders heaped with cairns, the ropes converged on a slab like burnt toast. He'd done it – he'd crossed the bridge, proved his faith. On solid ground, he turned to stare back across the gulf, lifting his arms in triumph, hailing his Master.

Shrek folded to his knees – thanking God for his disciple's survival. Kneeling to render his own homage, Nick chanted the entire litany. Finally he rose, frowning at the thought of re-crossing the bridge to enjoy his Master's embrace. It seemed a superfluous testimony of faith, unworthy of his valour.

Shrek stood upright, arms moving in unison – sawing.

Cutting the ropes –

No...

Nick leapt forward. As his foot touched the cable he felt it sag and flung himself backwards. Shrek's knife flashed – a handrail parted. The bridge twisted like a rag, its weight barely supported by the last cable. Turning, Shrek vanished from the skyline.

For a moment, Nick deluded himself that this was another test – to defy not only fear but gravity. Then he understood. *No.* Cut free, the bridge would dangle like a ladder from his eyrie. But *this* was an invitation to suicide – an alternative to simply jumping to his doom.

Shrek had betrayed him, marooned him on a pinnacle...

The sun sank behind the hills in waves of blood.

All night dragons prowled the sky, warring with thunderbolts and cascades of fire. He saw one die, ruptured by explosions, spiralling to earth as sulphur tainted the wind. Shivering in his rags, cursing Shrek in an alien tongue cut adrift from his mind.

I, I, I, my name is...

It stuck in his throat like a fishbone.

Hu amai?

Hu?

"*Yaaaa Magaddis!*" Shrek's call echoed from the rocks. The sun was up.

"Fuck off, I've had enough." Did he shout, or only think it?

I, I – my name is...

NICK, *Nick*, I'm...

Shrek semaphored his arms, demanding attention.

"FUCK OFF!" Nick's voice echoed across the abyss.

Cupping an ear, shaking his head, Shrek's reply was lost on the wind.

Turning his back, Nick paced his cell – a malformed stump fifteen steps long and six wide, tilted like a ramp. At the apex he lay on his belly, peering over the edge. Yajooj's shin plunged to an ankle veiled in spray. Unlike the other limb, there were no iron bristles on its pitted skin – no handholds in reach.

He prowled the edges in despair – till he found the rope.

Thick as a thumb, tied to an iron ring, it had worn a deep groove in the stump. Slimy with fish scales, *put there* for a purpose, used over time. He tugged, felt something drag; braced his feet and began hauling hand over hand. Easing as it rose, the burden swung into sight.

A plastic tub cut from a jerry-can, slopping water. By the time he pulled it in it was three-quarters empty. He quaffed it dry, tasting fish slime at the bottom. *Water* – he could draw water from the Nile, enough to drink. He wiped a finger round the tub, lifted a sludgy brown smear to his nostrils. *Sweet...*

Joyfully he wolfed rotten banana, rooting for another lick. Chewing fish scales – oily, salty: also nourishment. Starvation knew no taboos.

"*Yaaaa Magaddis! Yaaa asil...*" Shrek was calling again.

Waving a plastic tub on a rope, like Nick's.

Whirling it round his head to let it fly into the river foaming between Yajooj's legs. "*Shouf...*" His exhortation hung in the air.

Nick saw him playing the rope to haul his tub just clear of a channel where the water surged less turbulently. An angler fixing his rod before settling down to wait... The sun blazed down on them both. Nervously, Nick lowered his own bucket, fearing to lose it in the torrent. The rope would never support his weight – he acknowledged that – all that mattered was that the bucket stayed attached, so he could haul up water.

"*Shouf, shouf!*" Shrek waved, pointing upriver.

A boat raced towards them, sail furled, a helmsman fighting the tiller, passengers rigid with fear. The current swept them over a crest into a chute, screams audible above the falls. The boat spun wildly, nearly hitting a rock, before miraculously gliding into the calmer, deeper channel beneath Shrek's bucket.

Poised at the bow, a boy lunged at the tub, cramming something inside. Shrek hurled a shining object in a perfect parabola, striking the sail and rebounding into eager hands just before the boat plunged into another chute, hurtling away, its crew roaring "*Allahu akhbar!*"

Shrek hauled up his catch and brandished it above his head: a silver fish that writhed in his grip till he brained it on a rock. Nick's belly growled as he watched Shrek devour it, discarding the tail, head and bones. Now he knew how fish litter had reached their eyries.

Surveying the river above the cataracts, he saw no sail. Nick could only mimic Shrek's actions and hope. Muttering a prayer, he hauled up his tub, drank, and hurled it at the darkest water below. He saw it splashdown, jerked by the current, and dragged it from the water. *There* – maybe a boat could pull in to fill his bucket...

The sun was high overhead when it came. Not a sailing boat but a giant slug flexing with a throaty whine, saddled by figures hunched against the spray, domed and goggle-eyed, locusts with human mouths. *Yajooj's creatures* Shrek had warned when they saw them hatching in the desert. Nick held his breath as the slug manoeuvred alongside for a locust to slip something into his tub – something weighty.

He began to reel it in, halting just in time. *First, this...* Tearing off a bracelet, he pitched it into the abyss – yelping with joy as it fell among the locusts, a heartbeat before the slug was drawn into a torrent and swept downriver.

Hauling the tub aloft, he wept to find a fish wrapped in paper and a clump of bananas. *Now* he understood Shrek's creed, the revelation long obscured...

Yajooj was their Master.

28 JIHAD DOES IT

"Listen!" Tariq squinted at the sky. Birds erupted from the lemon trees as Talibs rushed into the garden, cocking Kalashnikovs. A dark mass clattered overhead.

"Get inside!" Sabr shoved them towards a cloister.

They heard ragged gunfire as the helicopter circled town, faltering as its drone receded. Cheering Talibs emerged from the bushes. Sabr exhaled; he'd been holding his breath – his legs were shaking. Boys ran outdoors waving wooden rifles, mothers hurrying behind, rumours flying. A Libyan helicopter had been shot down in the desert near the Scorpion. An emissary from Mecca had arrived to proclaim the rebirth of the Caliphate. It was a provocation by the Zionists...

Eventually, guards dispersed the chatterers and quiet returned to the Palace of Roses. Few noticed a curtained Toyota slip into the service entrance an hour later. As time passed, however, many remarked that Emir Yussef hadn't taken his usual afternoon stroll – may God preserve his strength.

Stonily, Emir Yussef regarded the Crusader envoy. Was his youth an affront to the Emirate or had they merely sent someone expendable? Certainly they must've feared their aircraft might be shot down while dropping a message. It was hardly a civilized way to announce an envoy. But ultimately that didn't matter – only his message did.

He motioned to the Crusader to refresh his lemon juice, so he might lie freely.

"Thanks. Like I said, Libya – the heretics – are mad with the Israelis – sorry, Zionist occupiers – who are blaming the, ah, pharaohs. Gaddafi's buying arms from Europe to extend the Protectorate. Whatever you call it, they could be bombing you in January and sending tanks into the oases a week later. However bravely you fight, the Emirate will be over – the heretics will have won."

"Maash'allah, God will decide. But why are you telling me this, how can your warning alter the outcome?"

"Plenty, if you'll hear me out. As to why we're warning you, it's simple. If the Libyans grab the oases it won't be long before they're staking claims on the Valley. All our plans would be in jeopardy. We can't let that happen."

"So one thief fears another, and seeks the Emirate's help."

"We'd also be helping you – to survive."

"So tell me how…"

Now they came to the crux, they both knew it.

"Fuel and spares for your Toyotas, RPGs for your martyrs. Satellite handsets and photos of Libyan troop movements. With all that, plus local knowledge, you could really chew them up – dozens of battle-wagons charging out of the dunes, that sort of stuff."

"So we shed our blood in your interests – is that your offer?"

"No, that's not all. We could provide other assistance…"

Emir Yussef hid a smile. This was going better than he'd expected.

***

There was an undercurrent of tension at supper – Sabr sensed it. The greybeards feigned small talk but looked strained, as Emir Yussef stared into space. A bespectacled Talib at Sabr's table whispered that the Emir was communing with the Prophet, that the veil hiding the future from the present had been lifted for him yet again. *Sure.*

Tariq grabbed a chicken leg. The boy gorged at every meal, lingering till the next lot of diners were tugging his *galabiyya*. People passed through the hall in order of status, age and sex. By some quirk of Taliban etiquette, Sabr and Tariq shared a table, ahead of men of lesser status. Across the hall, he could see his wife and Carina eating at the table for the Emir's womenfolk.

His wife! He couldn't get used to the idea. Years of eating any hay in his path, and suddenly he was locked in a manger! Not just that – his *zobra* was lifeless as a bar during Ramadan. Not a stirring, not an emission! Thank God, Yasmina had been tactful. She hadn't asked if her lord required anything, didn't query why he lay turned away from her, as far as the bed would permit.

In Koti, his village on Elephantine Island, Sabr's shame would've been exposed on their pigeon night, when his mother failed to hang a sheet from the balcony – not that this had ever happened in living memory. Chicken blood looked convincing if the bride proved to be sullied, or the husband impotent.

But Koti – Elephantine, Aswan – was gone forever. Sabr hadn't kin left in the world that he knew of. This woman – his wife – was all he had to preserve his honour, to let the world know he was a man – or a *khawal*. He watched her mouth wagging with the other women's – wondered what she was saying. He caught her eye – she winked, she was a whore, she loved him really... *Yani,* Sabr was fifty-fifty, he didn't know *where* he stood...

After supper, two Talibs herded them through dusty corridors to a conference suite with flickering strip-lighting and sound-proofed doors. At Carina's urging Sabr asked how long they'd be kept here, and received a gruff reply that he translated as "Wait a bit". Carina sensed he was distracted by Yasmina's presence; detected an unspoken dialogue between them. Was he was exerting his conjugal rights now they had a room to themselves? Had Sabr forced her to have sex, or had she consented like a meek Egyptian wife? There was a glint in her eye that might hint either way...

An hour passed before the doors parted and a familiar figure entered, bashful as a teenager on a blind date. It was Baines's evangelist, Morrison.

"Praise the Lord! We've been praying for you, Mrs Baring. And you too, Sabr – we'll talk about this later – and you, ah, *miss,* you'll be Yasmina."

"*Mrs* al-Adawi. We're married." Her hand closed on Sabr's.

"Right, great, so – good news all round, just like in the Bible!"

"How did you find us here?"

"All agency laptops have a transponder that kicks in if it goes live after two weeks' downtime. An anti-theft, anti-kidnapping device – that's how we knew." Morrison wiped his face. "Don't they have air-conditioning?" He sank into a couch and floundered there.

"*Haram,*" grunted Sabr.

"No!" sneered Morrison, hauling himself upright. "Thing is, Ma'am," – he leant towards Carina – "the Emirate has been *most* accommodating. Emir Yussef agreed to overlook your illegal entry, accusations of fornication and witchcraft, and a whole lot else. All they – we – want is to have you back safe in Hurghada."

"And Hosni Basha?" He was hunting us in the desert

"No problem, you're British, protected. As for the others, Hosni's got more important matters to concern him right now. If you slipped back into Hurghada or Suez, nobody would notice."

"And how do we get there, fly?"

"I love your English sense of humour. My helicopter's only a two-seater, no room for extra passengers. But Emir Yussef is a Good Samaritan, he's promised you a car and fuel to reach the Valley tomorrow – a chopper will collect you there. Simple."

"But what about Nick? Maybe this sheikh who had his laptop knows something".

"We'll get working on it at once. By the time you're back in Hurghada there'll be some solid leads."

"And the laptop, any clues on that?"

"As agency property, I'm taking it for examination. If there's anything, we'll find it. What's Nick's password, by the way?"

She wrote it down. "I'm counting on you, Luke."

"Scout's honour," he replied.

They watched him leave in a curtained Toyota, bound for the helicopter waiting at the Scorpion. A minute later, the final call to prayer echoed over the town. They were on the terrace so that Sabr could smoke a cigarette. Yasmina wouldn't allow it in their room.

"Imagine, back to civilization tomorrow, I can't wait."

Sabr shrugged. "Sure, when the Sphinx speaks."

"What do you mean?"

"Morrison – he's plastic. I don't trust him."

"But he came here in search of Nick, and rescued us."

"*Insh'allah*." He flicked the butt away.

"I don't get it. Our luck finally changes, and you smell a rat."

"Rat – what are you talking about?"

"Oh, never mind. What do you think, Yasmina?"

"It's in God's hands."

Carina sighed. "I'm going to pack."

Cotton bloomers, a nylon robe and the burqa; she looked forward to burning them all in Hurghada. Her T-shirt and cargo pants were so worn they might as well be junked. She felt something hard in a pocket and dug out Nick's tapes. She'd forgotten she had them, lucky they hadn't been found. What was the punishment for owning a cassette, having your ears cut off? But she was glad to have kept them, like a talisman – fate was smiling on them at last.

Jihad was bored of life in the Emirate. He hated the desert, and camels – stupid, smelly creatures that'd bite your nose off given a chance. Their snoring and farting, the wind moaning – that was all he heard. O for music – Ruby or

Samira – *Vin Diesel videos, ice-cream and ogling girls. His life was empty of joy. The Crusaders talked about bearing their cross – well, he had Dad.*

Imagine naming him Jihad – why not after a film star? But no, Dad chose Jihad – and that was just the start. All through childhood they'd been broke – Dad's Brothering meant no promotion at work. Then Dad was jailed and the family had to move to Kharga, away from Jihad's mates. He felt sorry for Dad's sufferings, but he brought them on himself. If he'd gone with the flow everyone's life would have been happier. Even now, when Dad was Emir of the Faithful, he hadn't lightened up.

He'd never learn. Instead of asking the Libyans or Crusaders to help restore the phones and power, the Emirate had shown its ass to Kufr and slunk back in time. Dad was always denouncing Jahalliyya – but what else was the Emirate but backwards and superstitious? No TVs, no mobiles, no YouTube – how were you meant to live like that?

The only cool technology in Jihad's life was a bazooka-sized anti-aircraft missile of Russian origin. He'd been told how it worked but never seen one fired. Like a flying shark, they said, drawn by heat or transmissions. That was sexy, but he'd never have cause to fire it at anything. As if Kufr could be bothered to invade – what was there to steal?

Three more days left till Kharga. Dad insisted Jihad should be active in the Emirate's defence, even if he'd rather be in a café or a disco with friends – if only! As it was, today's only excitement was to verify the passing of four outsiders on the road to Luxor. Not that Luxor existed now, but they were heading for the Realm of Unbelief, the lucky deviants.

Goats ahead, a herdsman with a hennaed beard – move, beardies! Sabr blasted the horn, slowed just enough for them to scurry off the highway. It felt great to be driving again, even a wheezy old taxi. Forty kilometres to Baghdad – he'd laughed at Carina's confusion, explained how villages in the oasis were named after Arab cities. There was even a settlement called Paris, at the ass end of nowhere.

They were all anticipating the end of Taliban restrictions. Carina had changed back into her trousers and T-shirt; both women lifted their burqas in the car. Amr Diab purring away; they were all swaying to the beat. The wall of cliffs on the eastern horizon had diminished to foothills. Soon they'd be leaving the oasis...

Zift – a checkpoint: three young beardies in a battle-wagon, a pickup with a heavy machine-gun mounted on the back. One of the Talibs slouched towards them, shoulder-length ringlets shining with oil. Sabr ejected the tape and threw it under the seat.

"*Salam aliekum*, where's your *firman*?"

Sabr showed him the document, ornately penned and sealed with wax. Permission to leave the Emirate, stamped with the Emir's own seal.

"Hey – what's that by your feet?"

Sabr's guts lurched. The cassette had slipped into view.

"Give me it..." *Allah!* "Amr Diab – cool!" The Talib glanced back at his comrades. "*Tamam,*" he called, secreting the tape in his jacket, winking at Sabr, as the others dragged a spiked chain off the road.

"*Ma'salama,*" they chorused, waving listlessly.

Sabr wiped his brow. It had nearly gone 180° at the last moment. Lucky that Talib liked Amr Diab – What a hairdo! With those ringlets, he had to be a *khawal*.

Al-hamdillilah, free at last! He stepped on the gas.

They'd hardly gone two kilometres when a tyre blew. He brought them to a standstill without injury and for once the women were grateful. Sabr would have reaped more praise by changing the tyre, but he couldn't find a jack in the boot. There was nothing else to do but traipse back to the Taliban and ask for help.

They greeted him like a cousin, their eyes bloodshot. "*Ya ragil,*" Ringlets drawled, "Come and smoke." *Why not?* It was a day for surprises. Guns laid aside, a hash-pipe circulating – bliss. It was some time before Sabr recalled what he'd come for. By then they were on first name terms – Ringlets was called Jihad.

"No problem," the guy laughed. "*Tayer*, you drive." They climbed into the back of the pickup, Sabr careful not to touch the machine-gun on a steel hoop welded to the chassis. "Walid's lawnsprayer," Ringlets joked, as the third Talib grinned like a shark.

They bounced onto the highway. Jihad hummed a tune, Walid joined in, they both winked at Sabr. If only they'd met earlier, he could've had some fun in the Emirate. Trust border guards to have dope when no-one else did....

Jihad almost fell off the battle-wagon as it slewed sideways – grabbing the gun-mount, gawping. From the taxi on the highway a boy dashed into the desert, then two unveiled women. The kid knew what he was doing and dived for cover, but the women kept going till they ran out of puff – sitting goats for the gunship hovering above the dunes. Jihad was transfixed by the Apache – straight out of Black Hawk Down, he'd seen the video. A Somali Brother boasted of downing one with a Kalashnikov in Mogadishu. The trick was to aim at the rotor transmission, firing down from tall buildings rather than wasting ammo on the armoured underbelly. If several gunmen fired simultaneously from different directions, it couldn't use its firepower against all of them.

Jihad's heart surged. No tall buildings in the desert, but he had something better than a Kalashnikov or a lawnsprayer – much better. Tayer stalled the battle-wagon; the others bailing out...

He swung the missile-launcher to his shoulder, sighted, pushed the lock-on button and held his breath through the heart-stopping pause before it was ready to fire.

The Apache poised to strike, quivering.

SHIT, he was toast –

A gust swept the valley, causing the Apache to dip into a dustcloud thrown up by its rotors. Allah blinds it, Jihad exulted, squeezing the trigger.

An invisible fist slammed him backwards as fire bloomed into darkness. Spinning, falling, he realized he was dying...

A martyr...

Darkness ruptured like a rotten hull. An ocean of light poured in.

He was entering paradise as God's Messenger had promised...

An Alpine garden with streams of alcopops and virgins where none would be denied endless pleasure – he was about to join them...

JIHAD

JIHAD

His name beseeched in time to slaps that rocked his head.

"Are you okay, man?"

Tayer's rat-face filled his vision.

"Man, you really fucked them."

Jihad smiled wanly. The helicopter was still burning, harmless as a campfire, its crew incinerated. "Right," he muttered, fighting the urge to spew.

29 THE LIAR'S TEETH

They'd talked it over as they changed the tyre. The hens were too shaken to think and Tariq only useful with a tyre-iron, but Jihad was smart, Sabr admitted to himself despite his envy of the guy's heroism. If El-Bahr was out – the Apache ambush confirmed that Hosni Basha was still on their trail – and they'd exhausted the Emir's hospitality, they could only run south. *Easy*, Jihad said. Return to the oasis and follow the road till you see a turn-off to Dush. Anyone there can show you the trail to Dunqul Oasis. Folk there were cool, the source of Jihad's hash. Stay the night at Dunqul and push on to Abu Simbel next day...

Into the arms of Nubia.

Coming from Aswan, Sabr could claim to be Nubian despite his cheekbones and copper skin, the gift of his Saiyidi mother. Almost everyone on the Elephantine Island had mixed bloodlines, from Bosnian troops stationed there in Mamluke times to Nubians from Wadi Halfa who settled three generations ago.

With the creation of the High Dam in the 1960s, Nubia was submerged by Lake Nasser – 800,000 Nubians displaced, their villages drowned. Some fifty years later, the High Dam was destroyed – the lake poured forth, obliterating everything downriver. In the chaos few noticed Nubia re-emerging, its terrain glistening black to the height of fifty metres above the Valley floor. Nile silt – the richest soil in the world, waiting to spring to life if seeded.

As the soil firmed the inhabitants of Wadi Halfa and Abu Simbel seized their chance, descending from towns left high and dry by the lake's disappearance to claim the land their great-grandfathers had farmed. By a momentous reversal of fate, the displaced had become the inheritors...

By the time the world noticed, Nubians were flocking from every corner of Sudan to forge a new homeland and defend it against others – Red Sea tribes and Janjaweed. As El-Bahr consolidated itself, the remnants of Egypt's armed forces were hurled against Nubia to crush its fledgling independence and restore El-Bahr's sovereignty over the far reaches of the Valley.

That much, everyone knew.

In El-Bahr, TV and radio reported the war like a one-sided football match that ran forever. The coastal road to the south was easily controlled, and the

Eastern Desert a natural barrier between El-Bahr and Nubia. In the Emirate, rumours of war in Nubia had the curiosity value of Moon landings. A *firman* was required to leave the Emirate, and anyway, farmers could live there, so why bother? But the backdoor to Nubia was unguarded – through Dunqul Oasis.

Three hours later they reached a football pitch-sized depression of tamarisk humps and palm clusters, with water if you dug a few metres into the sand, Jihad had said. They didn't bother, but plenty had; the surrounding rocks were covered in drawings of ostriches, gazelles and snakes, ancient hieroglyphs among them.

Another fifty kilometres to Dunqul – *insh'allah* they'd get there soon.

Vultures circled over fractured peaks; the route marked by bare camel ribs and discarded jerry-cans glazed black by decades of aridity.

Sabr saw a flash of light from a crag, answered further up the valley.

They were under observation.

Gradually the land sunk and became greener, acacia and tamarisk giving way to palms as they entered Dunqul Oasis. Rounding a corner they saw a roadblock and men emerging from the trees. Abbadah tribesmen, Sabr recognised them from bygone safaris. Cocoa skin offset by homespun tunics, bronze armbands and hair styled like Jihad's. Armed with Kalashnikovs, ancient rifles, swords – one had all three.

Marhaba, salam aleikum. They were friendly, thank God.

One mounted a camel and rode ahead to show the way. Everywhere, camels and goats foraged watched by half-naked boys or unveiled women. In Aswan, people said that the Abbadah didn't worry about their women's virtue because they'd defend themselves like men. Everyone knew the story of two rascals who tried to rape an Abbadah girl and got carved up by her grandmother. Tough bastards, heedless of borders or authority – that was the Abbadah. Roaming the Red Sea Hills longer than anyone could remember, masters of a few godforsaken oases no-one else wanted.

Dunqul was actually two oases: the depression where trails converged – where the Abbadah watered their herds – and another, halfway up an escarpment they called the Liar's Teeth. They had to leave the car in a palm grove and climb a steep path worn by generations of feet and hooves. At the top, a long row of caves, half-screened by palm fronds or ragged cloths – sanctuaries from the dazzling heat.

Children, women and elders emerged from the caves to greet them, tugging at their clothes, stroking Carina's skin. Some had never seen a European before, Sabr surmised. Fresh camel's milk, offered in a gourd, salted. Dates from the palm grove, a goat butchered and roasted – their hospitality matched the limits of their resources. Later, bitter coffee circulated as adults puffed on pipes of tobacco or hashish, until an elder broke the silence and asked for news of the world.

Where to begin, wondered Sabr.

✳✳✳

"Goodnight Luke, see you in church tomorrow."

"Sleep well, sir."

Morrison was a good staffer. Loyal, committed to the agency, he hadn't needed much persuasion to fly to Kharga and crawfish the Emir. As Baines had briefed him, the Emirate might be holding Nick Baring or merely his laptop, but either way could set impossible conditions for their release – like halting evangelism. Baines wouldn't quibble if it meant paying a ransom, but the Emirate anathematised money. So he'd resorted to the old Madison Avenue double whammy; nurture insecurity and promise palliatives – a Libyan invasion and arms that would never materialise.

Morrison had done his job well.

Nick Baring's laptop was on the desk, its battery dead; the Emir had wrung it dry poring over www.alazhar.org. Baines laughed when Morrison related Carina's account of events in the bank vault, and his own meeting with Emir Yussef. Sitting on Tut's gold when he hadn't two cents to rub together; worrying about fatwas in cyberspace – the Emir was in the grand tradition of Muslim whack-heads. But shrewd: in a theocracy such edicts were weapons, and he doubtless had enemies among the Brothers. Having seen the website, he'd probably been glad the laptop was leaving the Emirate – it saved him the trouble of destroying the infernal machine.

So let's see what's on it.

Excel files, inventories – he'd sift through them later. If there was anything on GM it would be in another folder, he wagered. Recalling their confrontation a month earlier, he couldn't remember Nick mentioning a *written* report – indeed he'd offered to omit GM's crime from the audit if Baines took action. But that didn't mean there wasn't *something* about it on the laptop.

He opened the Favourites menu and blinked at the familiar webpages. He knew that Nick had been sceptical of evangelism, hostile even. A private interest was curious, perhaps suspicious – had it been porn or gambling Baines wouldn't raise an eyebrow. He noticed a shortcut to a folder named *Weird* and clicked the link. The folder's document files were all named with initials. He opened one at random: *THS*.

Its contents hit him like a punch in the gut.

TransHumane Society

Established 1990, Little Rock, Arkansas, "To promote the restitution of peoples and lands according to the Holy Bible" [Meaning what?]. Inaugural conference at Fort Worth, Texas, 1991, was picketed by feminists protesting a delegate's remarks on TV that "rape has Biblical sanction." It claimed tax-deductions for organising conferences in Leipzig (1992), Belgrade (1995) and Sharm el-Sheikh (1999). Membership & subscription lists unknown. No known projects or publications, but a possible link with *What the Bible Says about Ethnic Cleansing – A Trans-humane Perspective* (Arkansas Overview Press 1994). A brief review in the UCLA Balkans Quarterly described this as "a farrago of deranged prejudices and cynical lies that a Holocaust denier might be proud of."
Why is a society like this sponsoring SF, and what else links them besides Kreutzer?

That was all but it was enough. A moment later he found Kreuzter's file, *NK*. He read it carefully, impressed by how far Nick had got using open sources. Of course there was a lot missing – Kreutzer had been wise to take down his homepage in the Nineties. And the TransHumane Society never flaunted itself online; a blog of stupefying boredom served as the portal for a members-only message-board, whose log-in identities changed daily. By contrast, Nick's file names were childishly simple. Baines guessed the subject of *CB* before he opened it.

Calvin Wesley Baines

Born 1952 in Fayetteville, North Carolina. Father an engineer & Baptist pastor. Graduated *summa cum laude* in civil engineering from Duke University, North Carolina. Played for NC Tar Heels at the Rose Bowl & served in Air National Guard. Joined Bechtel Corp 1978; managed infrastructure projects in Alaska, Philippines, Iran, Saudi Arabia, UAE, Thailand & China. Left Bechtel to found Sigma Solutions in 1994. Voted *Fortune* "Entrepreneur of the Year" in 1997.
A registered Republican & substantial contributor to congressional and presidential

campaigns over decades. Married Rosalyn De Witte 1979; one daughter, Shelley. After wife's death from cancer in 1997, gradually withdrew from business and public life (directorships, charities), and seems to have disappeared for six months in 2001/2002 – why? What happened?

In July 2002 sold majority interest in Sigma for $5.7 billion; announced retirement from business & appointment as CEO of Salvation First. Subsequently active in relief work in Zimbabwe, Tajikistan, Bangladesh & Syria, prior to being made director of relief & reconstruction in Egypt, four months after the Flood.

He detests the corruption at El-Gouna but seems well in with Hosni Basha. He seems to be a teetotaller but keeps whisky in his office. It could be for guests, but I've never seen him offer any. Also the framed photo on his desk, with a mourning band: his wife & daughter. He mentioned his wife's cancer but nothing about their daughter, yet his *Who's Who* entry states both are deceased. She wears an airline stewardess's uniform. Should look into this...

Baines forced his train of thought to halt, shunted it backwards to the year of Rosalyn's death. She'd watched him collect the Fortune award in a wheelchair; two months later she was gone. A marriage made in heaven, everyone agreed. It wasn't till later that people learnt about Lureen...

They'd met at an endowment party for his Alma Mater. Rosalyn was at home in a haze of morphine, a fortnight from death. He hadn't felt like flying down to Durham, but she insisted. *You'll see old friends.* In fact, none of his buddies were there, only guys he'd never liked or couldn't remember. But Lureen more than made up for that...

She was in PR, more than professionally warm and gorgeous. Creamy skin and a rippling mane the colour of the Titian in his boardroom – he felt as if he *already owned her.* Long fingers with carmine polish that matched her lipstick – she touched his hand, brushed his arm with her breasts. He was electrified, transported...

Lillith, Satan's harlot! Kreutzer snorted knowingly, four years later.

"Serpent of Seduction, Adam's twin sister, cast out of Eden for refusing to bear his child, for defying man's authority. An archetype in the Tarot – her number is eleven. The Satanist Crowley made her Lust in his Thoth pack." Kreutzer wet his lips. "'My name thou knowest not, and yet shall know, and know too late. But know thou this indeed: Joy is my sister. Sister I, to Death,'" he quoted.

Kreutzer was right.

At a motel on the Interstate, dripping with scarlet neon, she knelt and unzipped him, ripping her silk blouse to bare her pale breasts as she sucked him.

"You can do *anything* to me. Be rough."

He did, he was.

His heart bifurcated: he wept for Rosalyn's death and Shelley's sorrow, as he lusted for Lureen. Her submissiveness goaded him to go further. He'd tried cocaine before, but she made it integral to their lovemaking. She was a slut, a bitch-goddess – he couldn't resist her.

***

A tube train approaching the station: clatter and changing air pressure. People screaming – someone had jumped under the train, a bomb had exploded, jolting Carina awake.

Chips of rock leapt from the walls, the cave filled with dust. She saw Sabr hurl himself on top of Yasmina, heard a jackhammer tearing at concrete, a cry of pain from the corner. Shafts of light through the holed curtain across the cave mouth; the drilling receded – she felt the vibrations through the rock a few caves away.

Uhh-rr, uhh-rr: a terrible wheezing from an Abbadah boy. His mother wiped his mouth; blood ran down his chin. There was a deafening crump from some cavity in the Liar's Teeth, the curtain billowed inwards – a veil of acrid smoke.

Uhh-rr, uhh-rr, the boy died in his mother's arms.

Another boy, older, leapt to his feet.

Tariq! He darted into the smoke.

Carina stumbled after him.

A sunlit ledge strewn with bodies, Tariq crouched over a corpse, straightening up holding a Kalashnikov, staggering as it bucked in his arms, hosing fire across the sky, emptying the magazine in seconds.

His target had already disappeared behind the cliff's profile to drill its blind-side. There was firing from the palms below – Abbadah resisting. She heard rotors change pitch and the helicopter swept back into view, circling over the trees.

"*Hat rukaak!*"

Carina didn't understand him – and then she did.

She made herself look at the blood-soaked bodies, turn over men till she found what he needed. She tried to wriggle it loose; felt a catch depress. It slid free, heavy as a brick. She stumbled towards Tariq, treading on limbs.

Thrust it into his hand. He clipped it to the gun and knelt on one knee.

The helicopter was hovering just below the Liar's Teeth, so close she could see the crews' faces and the door-gunner firing at the treetops. Her hands were slick with blood; her heartbeat a drum. Time flowed like treacle, colours vivid as gems.

Tariq's shoulders shook as he directed a stream of fire at the cockpit. Plexiglas imploded, a head blew apart, smoke and fire bloomed. Rotors flailing, the helicopter plunged into the palm-grove, scything trees. A fireball erupted, wrapped in oily smoke stinking of kerosene, charred metal and flesh.

She felt Tariq trembling in her arms, hugged him as the world went dark.

The copter gunner survived the crash to regret he hadn't. Sabr heard screams from the palm-grove, remembered what was said about Abbadah women and their knives, thankful he didn't have to see it – the bodies on the ledge were bad enough. But he couldn't deny their right to vengeance. Over fifty Abbadah had been slaughtered while sleeping or trying to escape from the Liar's Teeth – mostly women, children or elders. Camels and goats had also been slain – the tribe's livelihood.

Yasmina told him the details when she returned. Her clothes were smeared with blood, her cheeks with tears, but her voice didn't quaver. She'd helped bandage wounded, heard the rumours circulating. Under torture, the gunner revealed that Dunqul had been targeted as a staging post for the Nubian guerrillas. El-Bahr's air force was looking for easy kills to please the generals in El-Gouna. Frontline commanders feared to attack Abu Simbel – the Nubians had all kinds of antiaircraft weapons that once guarded the High Dam. Now the Abbadah were burying their dead, preparing to leave for another sanctuary, known only to them, Yasmina concluded.

"May our Lord make it easy," Sabr grunted, shifting his weight, wincing. He'd been lying on his stomach for ages, crushing his pigeon, chaffing his elbows on the cave floor. He couldn't believe it – shot in the arse, a furrow across his left buttock. Thank God the bullet passed through his flesh, or somebody would've had to dig it out. It burned like chilli and he'd have an ugly scar, but *al-hamdillilah*, he'd saved Yasmina's life by covering her body with his own. A real Saiyidi man could do no more.

***

Baines had wanted to observe a decent interval before revealing his relationship with Lureen. Shelley was devastated by Rosalyn's death; she'd be enraged to learn he'd taken a lover only months after the funeral – let alone that the affair began when Rosalyn was on her deathbed. He only met Lureen in hotels – deluxe ones, after their first coupling in the motel – and asked her not to call any of his home numbers. A day at the New York Plaza, 36 hours in New Orleans, four in Dallas, they synchronized opportunities to meet as they criss-crossed America on business. Sigma Solutions was riding a bull market. Everyone was making millions. Baines was a billionaire. There seemed no limits.

He was drinking a lot, and doing coke even when he wasn't with Lureen. He junked Rosalyn's society crap, instructed his attorneys to tell the charities he had other priorities. Mergers and contracts – he had dozens of people at Sigma handling that; he cocked an ear at meetings, muttered an opinion, let them fight it out among themselves. Told his PA to decline interviews; let other execs step up to the plate.

Some shithead journalist raised a stink about Sigma's lobbying on Capitol Hill. Price-gouging over Camp Bondsteel in Kosovo, cost overruns supplying US troops in Saudi, and soaring phenyl levels in Arizona. He actually *sympathised* with Clinton – that dip-shit – when the Special Prosecutor was grilling him about where he'd put the cigar. Screw that.

"Not you, babe," Lureen crooned. "You're too smart to get caught."

But he wasn't – not when she engineered it. First she went worming stock market tips, insider knowledge of Sigma's mergers and acquisitions strategy. He hadn't minded nurturing her portfolio or bothered that it was a felony. Everyone was at it and only fools got caught.

Their affair remained secret till Shelley moved back to UCLA to resume her studies. As if on cue, Lureen began complaining. "I'm just a fuck to you, Calvin – and only when you schedule it." He couldn't blame her; just wished she'd wait a bit longer before pushing herself into his public life. They compromised on concerts, restaurants and corporate events, where Lureen posed as his PA. Baines drew the line at private parties with old friends, whose children knew Shelley and might gossip about her father's new girlfriend.

Aside from the haste with which he'd found a replacement for Rosalyn, there was the age difference between them. Lureen was only a decade older than Shelley – could be her sister. "Age isn't important, Calvin," she assured him – but he couldn't see Shelley feeling the same. He stalled for time; got Lureen's agreement to wait till the first anniversary of Rosalyn's death had passed. But finally he ran out of excuses.

Things came to a head at Shelley's graduation. Baines called to say he was coming with a friend, an alumna of UCLA visiting her old college. He hoped the feminine pronoun would smooth the way for Lureen's appearance, didn't say which year she'd graduated. There was a long pause before Shelley replied. "That's cool, Pops, you'll get to meet *my friends* too. See you then." She hung up.

It was a disaster. Shelley took one look at Lureen and bristled. Even Baines felt the dissonance between Lureen's hyper-sexuality and his daughter's tentative womanhood, between Lureen's ripeness and his own sagging flesh. Shelley took her scroll onstage without a glance at them; the moment her part in the ceremony was over she rushed to embrace another student. Bandana-wearing, saggy pants, a black from the ghetto, everything about him aroused Baines's hostility. Shelley dragged him towards them.

"Pops, meet Kwame. He's from Watts, majoring in Urban Street Art and Mythology. We're engaged to be married in the fall."

In the end he got her pregnant and left her, as Baines had known he would.

30 PIGEON NIGHT

I could have been a rally driver, thought Carina. With Sabr *hors de combat*, she'd nursed them across fifty kilometres of trackless desert to reach an asphalt road.

"Turn right," Sabr muttered from the back seats, his head on Yasmina's lap. His wound had gone septic, she whispered.

"*Louk!*" Tariq gripped Carina's knee.

Ahead, V-formations of prefab flats shimmered in the heat beside desiccated verges. A ram foraged in the streets. A ghost-town, abandoned intact.

Sabr raised himself to look. "Toshka. They built it when they were digging canals in the desert. After the Flood, no Lake Nasser, nothing to pump out – all that money wasted." Water was all, Carina realised. England's hose-pipe bans and water meters seemed benign beside this pitiless aridity.

"Take that road there, to Abu Simbel. It's the only town in Nubia."

The taxi responded to the smooth asphalt with alacrity. Having covered most of the track at under thirty miles per hour, it felt good to accelerate without fear of flying gravel. Celine Dion belted from the speakers; the Egyptians crooning to the theme tune from *Titanic*. Hearing one of Nick's tapes brought him closer. She'd endured so much for nothing, only to stumble on a fragile link to him.

Nick's laptop

Morrison had risked visiting the Emirate to recover it. Baines hadn't mentioned that went missing when Nick did. It held his audit on Salvation First, and a file on Baines which went way beyond Nick's remit. He'd been investigating GM and found himself confronting Hosni Basha. Whose gunship had been waiting for them, the day after Morrison had arranged their departure from the Emirate. Ergo, they were all in it together. She could trust no-one in El-Bahr except the British Embassy.

"Carina!"

She saw the tarmac vanish beneath sand. The wheels lost traction; she swerved, bumped down an embankment and regained control on a hard-packed surface. She braked; her hands shook. The Egyptians cursed their bruises. The sun would be over the hills in another hour, she reckoned. Driving in the dark would be impossible.

As if by telepathy, Sabr suggested that they spend the night here and continue on to Abu Simbel next morning. Everyone concurred and looked around.

They were in a vast kidney-shaped depression of sun-baked clay, evidently the bed of a lake that had dried out aeons ago; shoals of fist-sized rocks branched like creeks. Instinctively, they sought some feature to camp around; returned to the car and drove slowly over the flats towards a series of mounds. There were oval cavities surely made by humans, black megaliths like the fingers of a fallen colossus and a crude circle of leaning sarsens. She halted the car.

"I've heard of this, Nabta playa, they call it. The oldest place in Egypt," Sabr grunted as Yasmina extricated him from the taxi. "Before the pyramids; older than that place in England, what's it called, Stonebridge?"

Yasmina spread her burqa and helped him lie down. Without being told, Carina knew it was time to brew tea. Their Taliban taxi came with a blackened kettle and four dirty glasses. She scoured them with sand, rinsed with a trickle of water and wiped them with the hem of her T-shirt. She'd become water conscious, a desert dweller.

Unbidden, Tariq sloped off to hunt for fuel, returning dragging branches. He winked at her and smashed them with a rock, launching into a speech while keeping his head cocked towards Carina, anticipating Yasmina's translation.

"Tariq says he was very clever to have found wood in the desert. He poked in the ancient burial mounds, found a pit of cow bones roofed with branches. He ripped them out, the mound collapsed on the skeleton."

"He could've been hurt!" Evidence of prehistoric settlements at Nabta playa destroyed, Carina didn't give a toss providing Tariq was unharmed.

"He's one of God's fools – too stupid to die," Sabr snorted.

"You'd know about that," she retorted, on Tariq's behalf.

"Only God knows what's true," Yasmina soothed, touching Sabr's hand.

Scraping a hollow, Carina blackened her fingers on ashes and charred eggshells, traces of a prehistoric campfire. The oldest place in Egypt – how old was that? Tariq piled branches, packed kindling underneath. Sabr's lighter was nearly empty – if he hadn't been a smoker, they'd be fireless.

The Abbadah had given them some flaps of sorghum bread, a twist of tea and sugar to sustain them. In London, it would get thumbs down as a snack; at Nabta, it was supper for four. When tea was brewed, she clinked glasses with everyone.

Her shoulders were firm, supporting Sabr's weight, yet soft beneath her clothes.

"A little further, *ya albi*."

My heart, she'd never used such an endearment before. They were approaching the ring of standing stones. She'd led him from the campfire as naturally as a child to bed, but he knew what it meant. His heart thudded, his pigeon stirred. This place had cured him of the shameful malady, made him strong again.

She spread her burqa, covered it with a camel-hair blanket and helped him slide underneath. Next moment she was warm against him, her breath on his neck. A hand stroked his stomach; his muscles tightened. Her eyes shone in the starlight, her lips were moist, her tongue sweet. He slipped his hands beneath her shirt, stroked her nipples. She freed his pigeon and guided it towards her guava.

"*Tallah.*"

He felt her nails on his back, heard a whimper smothered by a sigh; her legs drew him tighter inside. Dear God, it was true, he was the first; her virtue was honey. He swelled with joy and pride, came rapturously; gasped his love for her.

Afterwards, as they lay entwined, she told him everything.

About Umm Salah's potion in his drink, causing narcolepsy, amnesia and impotence – which she'd ceased administering in Dunqul.

He should beat her blue but couldn't. He was blissfully tired; hadn't the strength to strike anyone – least of all a wildcat like her. More than that, he was awed by her cunning and determination. All that trickery to protect her virtue and then an impulsive surrender to love: she was a true Saiyidi woman, hot-blooded and virtuous. She'd never betray her husband, she'd defy the biggest Basha in the land if need be. She'd flown into his life like a rare bird; he'd caught her in his clap-net.

He covered her head protectively. Hours later, Sabr awoke to find his face wet, the blanket damp. A fine drizzle was falling on the desert.

Baines's office windows rattled from distant thunder. The horizon was solid with cloud, the air charged. Most staff had left hours ago; only the duty officer's floor was still lit. He'd been sitting in the dark, lost in memories.

Baines wasn't introspective by nature. "Move on" was his credo, but sometimes there wasn't an *on* – not for the dead, or those without reason to continue living. He'd been there once – till he met Kreutzer.

He'd been constantly drunk or coked, looking for trouble. Only pay-offs to aggrieved citizens kept him out of the courts, so his lawyers said. A few incidents made it to news desks, but who cared when the nation was suddenly at war? But that was hindsight talking – at the time he'd been heedless of his state, never mind his image.

Once he brawled with a bum and got taken to hospital. Another week, his chauffeur had to drag him from a casino in Vegas. Eventually he decided to end it all with a hunting accident. As a child he'd loved hunting in the woods. A gun would be instantaneous; his body might never be found. The idea of returning to leaf-mulch in solitude appealed to him.

The Ozarks: if the gofer had booked a cabin some place else, Baines would've got his wish, and surely gone to hell. But the Almighty had offered him a chance of redemption by guiding him to Kreutzer, who let him glimpse the divine plan foretold in the Bible. Martyrs and angels, the conflict with the Antichrist...

Rain sluiced down. The storm was nearly overhead, sheet lightning across the harbour. In the camps, drains would be backing up, tents and chalets flooding. Thousands of refugees faced a miserable night and a squalid tomorrow; only the farmers would be consoled, if their crops weren't destroyed by a flash-flood.

He watched the ramshackle townscape strobe black and silver; sensed fate poised to strike like a sniper, just as it had all those years ago – it seemed like only yesterday.

The sky over downtown Houston had been alive. Shockwaves echoed between skyscrapers, lightning lashed the seventy-fifth floor of the JP Morgan Chase Tower and the trifurcated ziggurat of the Bank of America Center. They had a ringside view from their penthouse in the Hilton Americas-Houston.

Lureen smiled wanly. "I'm pregnant, Calvin."

His jaw sagged. "You're sure?"

"Women know. I've done the test; seven weeks already."

"Shit – let's think about this. Honey, I hate to say this, but under the circumstances, the best thing would be to have an -"

"No way, how can you suggest it? This child's ours! If you tell me to get an

abortion you're no different from Shelley's husband, walking out on their baby. A total loser, you called him. Look at you – a billionaire coke-head who wants to flush our baby down the toilet."

"Don't drag that shithead into this!" He'd agreed to meet Shelley in Newark next day but recoiled at the last moment from forgiving her and accepting her child...

Lureen swigged her drink; he couldn't discern a bulge in her stomach.

"You're pregnant – drinking vodka and snorting coke. Some mom-to-be you are. I could report you for foetal abuse."

"Right, like I could snitch you to the SEC for insider trading. That's a felony, Calvin; that's ten years inside. Me, I'd plea-bargain down to six months' parole, never mind foetal abuse. They'd love me as state's witness."

"My attorneys would tear your testimony to shit in court."

"Maybe, but they can't argue against a DNA paternity suit. How much did that Russian hooker get for screwing a tennis star in a cupboard, Calvin? Do you want an SEC subpoena or a paternity suit?"

"Waddya want?" He heard himself slurring.

"Big bucks: enough for me to retire without worrying about my pension. C'mon, Calvin, you can afford it – your accountants won't notice the difference. Don't feel bad about it, think of the fun times we've had together..."

She sashayed closer, loosening her sarong; scooped up a handful of melon cubes and slipped them down her cleavage. "Cut us some more lines, I'm wet already."

As Baines wielded his Platinum card she gazed at the skyline. "Look at this city – all this wealth. What other country has so much?" She knelt beside him holding a silver straw. He matched her line for line, fucked her against a wall, on the floor, as the thunderstorm spent its fury. The coke pounded in his veins, kept him using her till the sun caught the JP Morgan Tower, turning it into a glittering control rod drawn from a nuclear reactor.

"Close the drapes, no calls." He'd taken a last gulp of vodka and plunged into oblivion as a catastrophe was unfolding on the Eastern Seaboard.

Baines swept the files from his desk, groped for Nick's laptop, clicked the folder he'd come to hate, the file he'd avoided opening, SB.

It felt like exhuming her grave.

New York Times personal tributes to the victims of 9/11: Shelley Gilroy

Shelley was a real friend in need. She loved to help people – that was one of the reasons she became a stewardess. To be honest, she was also looking for something she didn't get in childhood: love, validation. Her father was rich, always busy, never satisfied with her. Deep down, he never forgave her for being a girl rather than a boy. Later Shelley's mom had a hysterectomy and then she died. So Shelley was an only child. If you grow up surrounded by servants, with a mother who's always in hospital and a father who's hardly ever there, it scars you inside – so what if you've got millions in a trust fund?

Shelley tried to get closer to her pop after her mom died, but he started drinking and took up with a real gold digger. And he couldn't handle Shelley's relationship with a man of colour. When Shelley married Kwame and took his name, her father disinherited her. The marriage didn't last, but Shelley was blessed with a child, and managed to get by on her stewardess's paycheck. She really tried to reach out to her Pop, they even fixed a date to meet at Newark. But he didn't show up – made some excuse at the last minute – so she decided to fly back to San Francisco next day. On United Airlines 93.

I feel real, real bad about it. The way she died, for no reason, just because her father didn't care enough to meet her; because he was on a bender somewhere. He's not even around to write her obituary. And those terrorist fanatics! What did any of us do to deserve this? Every day I ask God why, but He hasn't answered yet.

Adele De Souza (co-worker)

Baines snapped on the desk-lamp; the bottle glowed amber. He'd kept a bottle of Jack Daniels in his office ever since he came to Egypt, to test his resolve against temptation and remind him of everything he'd left behind since his epiphany in Kreutzer's cabin. Now he lifted the bottle. Heavy as marble, its screw-cap resisted his fingers before yielding with a sigh. The Devil's breath stole into the room, every molecule tantalizing.

31 THE GOSPEL ACCORDING TO KREUTZER

Ten years ago, in the Ozarks. Wet branches slapping his jacket; hip-flask achingly light, his hunting rifle weighted with dread. He stopped for a breather, heard scurrying in the bracken, the air sweet with decay, his forehead slick with sweat. Sucked the last drops of bourbon from the bottle and flung it away, dizzily.

Shelley, Rosalyn, I'll be with you soon...

The rifle was too long for him to insert the muzzle in his mouth and reach the trigger. Its steel orifice rasped his scalp as he sought the best spot to blow out his brains. Bile rose in his throat, he vomited, his fingers fleeing the trigger guard. Looking up despairingly, he saw a wisp of smoke beyond the clearing and sniffed sour-mash on the wind.

A hillbilly cabin, logs stacked by size, and Old Glory twisted round a flagpole in the yard. A decal on the mailbox declared: *FREE CITIZEN: Armed to uphold the Constitution*. Baines listened for dogs, heard none, just flies buzzing the porch-door, invitingly ajar.

"Anyone home?"

He sensed emptiness, smelt moonshine, leant the rifle by the door and surveyed the lounge. A cast-iron range in the corner, stone walls hung with girly posters and a corroded Nazi eagle surrounded by framed diplomas, a stuffed racoon above the fireplace. A plasma TV wired to a video player sat across from a battered La-Z-Boy and easy table, where a remote control lay in a puddle by a half-empty quart of Jack Daniels. He could feel its burn, *needed it* – the householder would understand, Baines could pay, no problem. He heard a footfall, turned.

"*Gaw-on*, drink it." The hillbilly's eyes were as mesmerizing as the Smith & Wesson in his fist, mauvish and veined like jellyfish.

"I –" Words died. *I chickened out, I couldn't do it. I needed a drink, I saw your cabin. The door was open...* The rifle's butt by the hillbilly's leg: No chance...

"I said *drink*, Mister." His teeth were like a gopher's.

Fuck, Baines wanted to anyway. He plucked the JD from the table. "Thanks. Got any glasses?" Eerily calm, he blanked the gun as if it was a panhandler.

Doubt crept into Hillbilly's voice. "There, in the cabinet." His smile returning as Baines poured two glasses. "Not for me, jess you, Mister."

Baines shrugged, reaching for a glass.

"Wait!" His fingers froze.

Hillbilly's voice sank to a purr. "All these years putting out a welcome mat and someone finally obliges." He grunted with pleasure. "I won't waste a chance like this, no sir. I've a *notion* to test, jess from curiosity...."

"I'm listening." Baines felt sublimely detached.

"Ok..." Hillbilly wet his lips. "If there was cyanide in that bottle, would you rather drink it or have me shoot you? I'm serious – that's your choice, Mister." He waved the gun rhetorically.

Baines's lip curled. A fitting end: a truly zero-sum game. He knew he was expected to beg for his life, or make a futile attempt to flee, or attack his killer.

He wouldn't give him the satisfaction. This would be easier than he deserved, he'd go in seconds with the taste of bourbon in his mouth. Wordlessly he took the glass. It touched his lips as the man lunged forward to dash it from his hand.

"Jesus wept," Kreutzer panted, "I never met anyone stone-cold crazy as you. Let's have a real drink an' get acquainted."

So it began – the Lord threw Baines a lifeline. Kreutzer was no slick evangelist, but a trenchant apostle. *Time is short – we're at war with Satan.* Overnight, the American people had 3,000 martyrs – Baines's daughter among them. Murdered by the Antichrist in an assault on civilization, the first-responders, stewardesses and office-workers were now with Jesus. Those left behind must validate their sacrifice by vengeance. Christians weren't *obliged* to turn the other cheek – that was a fallacy. If you studied the Old Testament and Revelations, it was clear that war was *divinely ordained*.

Not *any* war – no. Its justification was the fulfilment of the scriptures. If the conflict met that criterion it was righteous. Seizing resources and displacing populations, likewise – that was how nations were forged. Look at Israel, Europe or the United States! Iran, Russia and China were the hosts of Tribulation – Persia, Magog and the Kings of the East – which would set the Euphrates ablaze. Billions of people would be scattered by catastrophes before the Second Coming. It was predestined, inevitable.

Kreutzer called it TransHumanism – said the Old Testament was full of it.

Exodus – God's chosen people flee Egypt and wander for forty years till they reach the Promised Land. To claim it, they must subjugate the Amorites and exterminate the Hittites, Girgashites, Canaanites, Hivites, Jebusites and

Amalekites 'man and woman, babe and suckling, ox and sheep, camel and donkey.' All *commanded by God* of His chosen people. *Look in the Bible*: Numbers 21:24, Deuteronomy 7: 1-2 and 1 Samuel 15:3 for starters.

The world was a mess because the peoples created by God had gotten mixed up. Niggers and spics in North America; Muslims in Europe; Chinks all over the globe – none in their rightful places. Immigration laws and border fences were umbrellas in a hurricane. You wouldn't find crap like that in the Old Testament. 'Make no treaty with them and show them no mercy,' it said in Deuteronomy, which also warned against miscegenation. If only Baines had told Shelley not to marry that nigger.

Kreutzer had no time for soft hearts – what was needed was *resolve*. For years he'd been networking, at home and overseas. German neo-Nazis talked big but only torched refugee hostels. In Belgrade he preached to the converted, already applying TransHumanism in their part of the world. Karadžić had presented him with a dagger, blooded at Srebrenica – it hung on the wall of Kreutzer's den even as the Serb languished in The Hague. The International Criminal Court was a hydra-head of Europe's Beast Government.

Ruefully, Kreutzer acknowledged that the staunchest exponents of his doctrine were the legions of the Antichrist: Muslims. Throughout its history, Islam had expanded and brooked no contraction of its territory. A land once claimed by Islam was Islamic forever, just as a Muslim was forbidden to renounce his religion, on pain of death. Saudi Arabia never tolerated a single church, however many Christians lived there – and the Saudis were considered *soft* by hardline Wahhabis.

Such intransigence could only be met in kind. God's champions against the Antichrist; each defined the other, the sharper the better. The Tribulations were at hand. The Beast Government – the European Union – tried to weaken the House of Israel with false assurances. When the Antichrist signed a seven-year Covenant guaranteeing Israel's security, it was a sure sign that the Tribulations had begun.

As Kreutzer raged at the legions of the Antichrist, Baines's guilt over Shelley's death was transmuted into dreams of vengeance and divine approval by the alchemy of Jack Daniels and moonshine.

Kreutzer let him drink for days, matching him glass for glass. Then, one morning, he dragged Baines from the La-Z-Boy and dunked him in a stream.

"Get sober, Calvin – the Lord's waiting."

It was his chance of redemption, as Coach Malloy had saved him to score at the Rose Bowl that semester at Duke University. He'd cashed in his glory and banked the cheque for his shattered knee to join Bechtel, and never looked back, till – when? When did hubris take hold? Starting an affair with Lureen when Rosalyn was dying? Rejecting Shelley for marrying that nigger and having his child? Or earlier, with Sigma and Bechtel? Whatever, he'd been punished – now he longed to atone somehow.

As Kreutzer expounded on rapture and Armageddon, Baines was soothed that it all had meaning, a *purpose* – that Jesus would triumph eventually. The Antichrist had many heads which must be fought in different ways. Capturing hearts and minds – yes – but scourging where necessary. Like blows to an anvil, the Tribulations would determine which faith was enduring and which was false. True believers like Kreutzer weren't complacent – the Lord demanded commitment, action, money, sacrifice...

Take Kreutzer's career as a government microbiologist. A year after he joined Fort Detrick, Nixon banned offensive bio-research. He'd hardly got used to the Anthrax Hall before it was sealed in concrete. When Kreutzer was asked to join a covert successor project he thought he'd finally get to push his research to the limits. The CIA had rumbled a Soviet bio-warfare program violating every clause of the treaty they'd signed – Uncle Sam had to catch up fast. Kreutzer's research into single nucleotide polymorphisms as the basis for ethnic weapons seemed certain of backing.

Instead, he'd been slandered and sabotaged by colleagues and nigger-lovers; his duplex bugged by the DIA. An agency capable of full-spectrum surveillance could fake evidence of *anything*, framing him for a misdemeanour that wouldn't stand up in court but which meant revoking his security clearance and the end of his career at Detrick.

Go quietly and take your pension, or else.

It was Kreutzer's tragedy to have been expelled from Eden before the Human Genome Diversity Project provided the template for ethnic weapons. He was Icarus, flying too high, too early...

He'd had offers of work from Arab states, which he reported to the FBI like a patriot – only to be treated as a crank. Disgusted, he quit Maryland and returned to the South, settling in Arkansas, his contempt for Federal Government, racial and cultural degeneracy shared by local Christian Identity groups, the Bible and *The Turner Diaries* always at his bedside. Like Earl Turner he'd been fired from a laboratory; the timeline of *The Turner Diaries* contemporaneous with his own struggle against ZOG.

Kreutzer wished he'd plugged Clinton when he was still Governor, before the Secret Service made it impossible. For a while he put his faith in the Constitution and tried to impeach the son-of-a-bitch, but Slick Willy wriggled off the hook. It made Kreutzer's blood boil that he'd been robbed of his vocation for a mail-order beaver video, while the President of the United States got blown in the Oval Office and kept his job!

Meanwhile, he realised that only the Bible had the answers, only Evangelical churches the influence, only corporations the means. *His* contribution was an idea, a catalyst, for others to refine and inject into the world.

Men like Baines, who'd found Jesus in time – before the Tribulations began.

Men with the wealth and connections to set the ball rolling...

It wouldn't take much – a few years' preparation and a billion dollars.

Rollback –

God's way forward in the new millennium.

Rollback!

32 ABU SIMBEL

Sabr came round from unconsciousness ears first. His eye-lids were gummed shut but he resisted the urge to rub them or even twitch – concentrating on the voices in his head.

"I know him, Basha – I was at school with his brother Mohammed."

And I know that voice from Koti, years ago.

"Born in Aswan, eh? But coming from Dunqul?" An older man: an officer.

"*Aiwa*, with an Englishwoman."

"English?" Hearing papers rustle, Sabr risked a squint at what was happening. Saw a cratered moon face with a nose like a turnip, that reminded him of –

"Driss – is that you, *w'allahi*? Where am I?"

"Abu Simbel – where else? Of course it's me, Sabr, have you forgotten all the times we played together?" Now he wore battledress and a red beret, with a flash identifying him as *Mukhabarat al-Harbyya* – Military Intelligence.

"Big deal," grunted the officer, a toad in rumpled khaki. "You came from Dunqul – from the direction of the Emirate. What's your mission, who sent you?"

"Nubia's my homeland," Sabr protested. "I was born in Aswan. We're refugees from El-Bahr; the coast was too dangerous, we had to travel by Dunqul. One of the Basha's helicopters attacked it yesterday – we made a run for it."

"A helicopter, eh? What kind?" So it continued till the toad got bored and told Driss to take him away. Outside, Driss rolled his eyes theatrically.

"Sorry about *him*. Imagine what *I* have to put up with! Major Masri has troubled bowels – you caught him on a bad day. *Ma'lesh*, it's over, welcome to Abu Simbel – welcome to Nubia!"

Awkwardly they embraced.

Driss had pull. A pickup to a military hospital to dress Sabr's wound and jab him with antibiotics, before lunch in an officers' mess. Sabr wolfed salad, chicken and rice, a banana and tea. His arse still hurt but his fever was ebbing. Now he wanted to sleep by Yasmina's side. The toad had said they were in a guesthouse near the temples, but he must see for himself. He hadn't come this far to lose her.

"No problem," Driss replied. "But let's see the temples first – I insist."

Why? Sabr had been to the pharaonic temples of Abu Simbel more often than he could remember, but he was loath to annoy Driss. Anyhow, the guesthouse was nearby, he'd see the others soon enough. So he feigned enthusiasm for Driss' suggestion – it was an order, really.

The town looked as he'd last seen it on the Black Day but denser, shacks wedged between houses festooned with satellite dishes and bougainvillea, the few wide streets thronged with vendors. Okra, aubergines and tomatoes, melons and dates, sacks of wheat and millet – no poorer than the food in Hurghada's bazaar but local, not imported. Smoked perch and carp too, if you could afford it, said Driss, smacking his lips. The *Mukhabarat* ate well, evidently.

On the road to the temples Sabr glimpsed the snout and tennis-racquet of a radar-guided antiaircraft battery nestled in a holiday village. Was *that* the guesthouse? Driss smiled blandly. *Imagine what you like, but remember the rockets in the garden.*

Goats browsed in the visitors' centre, chewing placards explaining how the sun-temples had been sawn into thousands of blocks and re-assembled on higher ground by UNESCO, back in the 1970s. He'd always found the idea of moving an entire rock-cut shrine idolatrous – surely God meant it to be submerged by Lake Nasser once the dam was built? But now it seemed to have been saved for a reason.

Cornering the false hill screening its landward side, Sabr anticipated the moment when he'd see the four colossi of pharaoh Ramses II, seated before his sun-temple. *There*, majestically intact – but not unchanged. The portal between the twin pairs of colossi was draped with netting, soldiers drifting in and out past entrenched cables. His eyes moved to the smaller sun-temple of Nefertari, where a missile jutted between the queen's statues. A military HQ occupying a World Heritage Monument – how was that for brazenness!

Driss read his thoughts. "We're smart – smarter than others realise. Our first and last defence is this." His arm swept from the colossi to a steel box in the earth. "A webcam – aimed at the temple. For El-Bahr to bomb it would be a disaster for its credibility at the UN." He waved at Nefertari's temple. "We don't show *that*, of course. Their air force knows we have missiles to spare, but neither side admits the fact: they to hide their weakness; us to remain *heroic underdogs*." He used the Western phrase ironically – Muslims would never attribute virtue to a dog.

"Now see what we're fighting for." He spun Sabr round to face Lake Nasser – but it was no longer there. The sandy terrain sunk abruptly, turning dark as tea, slopes alive with shoots, terraces of wheat and clover sinking to the bottom of the valley, the vegetation so green it hurt Sabr's eyes: fertility beyond the dreams of farmers rotting in Hurghada – a whole land bursting with life, straw-roofed villages sprouting on every hill above the Nile.

"Paradise," Driss sighed. "No wonder we fight over it."

I'm married – I've done it. We had sex last night. I could be pregnant. It's my fertile time. Yesterday she'd cared for Sabr, held his pigeon till it stiffened and guided it into her dove-cote – she must've been mad. If the Black Day had never been, her pigeon night would have meant crossing the threshold of married life, the prospect of pregnancy its joyous confirmation. But their marriage had been forced, and his fevered vows in the stone circle were only the cooing of his pigeon in her dove-cote. When her belly grew, he'd be off like a rat into a cane-brake.

So, whores are made. Before the Flood, getting pregnant out of wedlock meant plunging to the depths of society, selling your body to care for your baby, to keep a roof over your head. The older women at the Euro – who'd known Madam Hoda for years – were all in their *profession* for the same reason. A child, the blessed fruit of their womb, turned into a millstone round their neck by social prejudice. Yasmina had always pitied them in abstract, before the Black Day swelled their numbers a thousand-fold with women like her, without even the excuse of a child...

Bitterly, she wiped her eyes. Her life was a disaster, every tiny victory followed by another slide down the chute towards hell. Hosni Basha's parting words echoed in her mind. *You should've stayed in Suez, sucking Jews.* Was that the best her future could offer, that she should be resigned to, that she should strain to achieve? For the sake of a child – *her child* – left in a backroom at the Euro while Yasmina sucked for both their lives?

Bile choked her throat. She dashed to the window and spewed onto a flowerbed.

I'd sooner die – or kill it. Abortion was a sin but so was suicide. It was only last night Sabr impregnated her; his seed was just a smear in her womb, not yet a foetus. Pharmacology classes at Giza: Women's problems. HRT, birth control and fertility treatments dispensed on prescription. Abortifacients required a court order countersigned by an imam, but her teachers warned of other substances that could thwart conception at the outset. Abnormally high doses of Vitamin C, for instance...

They'd taken Sabr to hospital, there had to be a pharmacy in Abu Simbel. Surely they'd sell Vitamin C – or she could steal some. She hadn't any money... Did people even use money in Nubia? Perhaps it was like the Emirate?

As she slumped on the sill, she heard voices singing.

"Hear our joy, O God. Witness our joy, O neighbours!"

A dozen women rounded the corner ululating and clapping, robes rippling, hair braided with wheat. "Witness our joy, sister," they called. "Join us."

They carried a baby wrapped in a green shawl, passing it from one to another as the infant squalled. "Hear how lustily he cries," yelled a red-faced Saiyidi woman. "My son, Huss... " – checking herself before she uttered his name and drew the Evil Eye upon his head. "May Allah preserve him from harm," she added. "Join us, sister, come celebrate his circumcision."

A baby boy, his mother ecstatic, friends delighted, no shame or regret. *That's how it should be if the world was just.* The mother beckoned her as the procession vanished behind a hedge. In Nubia, it seemed they circumcised boys as infants, not waiting until they were seven or eight years' old, as Egyptians did.

Barefoot, wrapped in her *melaya*, Yasmina hurried after them. After two weeks in the Emirate the urge to cover herself had chiselled itself into her brain. She saw herself at the Euro through Taliban eyes – thighs sugared for the delight of infidels. *I hadn't any choice* – but that wouldn't placate the stone-throwers. Was this place like the Emirate?

They paused for her to catch up, on the cusp of the descent into fertility. Greeting her as the sand yielded to thick black mud that oozed between her toes, their laughter kindly – as if they knew that a seed of new life was germinating in her womb. Together, they shuffled down a steep path between terraces, past men hoeing with *galabiyyas* hitched to their knees, stealing furtive glances. This was women's business – everyone knew that. Below them, the Nile was cocoa-coloured with silt, seething like a milkshake in a blender.

"*Bismillah, er-Rahim, ad-Daim.*" The invocation echoed from the rocks above the pounding of water. Umm Hussein prostrated herself, beseeching God's mercy on her newborn. A ragged dervish rose from a boulder and moved among them, touching foreheads, muttering prayers beside the infant, un-wrapping its shawl. Yasmina turned away as sunlight flashed on a razor and baby Hussein's mew of agony was stifled by his mother's teat.

A hand fell on her shoulder. Turning, she saw Sabr grinning bashfully.

"I know what you're thinking," he said. "God willing, we'll be a family."

33 REVELATIONS

The Nubian flag was blue, green and black – for the river, the land and its people. One day their state would be recognised, its flag hang outside the United Nations. Nubia's declaration of independence was only a year old, but already cemented by their heroes' blood. So this Captain kept telling her, citing resolutions and victories. Captain Driss, he said, patting his chest self-importantly; responsible for her security and Nubia's.

Get to the point, Carina thought – but could hardly be discourteous since he'd promised to let her call the British Embassy. He even knew the number, it seemed.

Eventually he kept his word, producing a satellite phone. Wiggling its antenna till it connected, keying in numbers from a tiny notebook. Her call was routed to the heavens with a trill of beeps, romping home with a purring ring-tone.

"This is the British Embassy in Egypt. Press 1 for English, 2 for Urd –"
For godsake. *One...*

"Thank you. Now press 1 for Chancery, 2 for visa applications and appeals, 3 for commerce and trade, 4 for marriage and naturalisation, 5 for cultural activities, 6 for other." *Shit. Which option?*

Six. "Thank you for contacting the British Embassy. All our staff are busy right now, but you'll be placed in a queue. Please hold." Vivaldi's *Four Seasons* wafted from the speaker. "Thank you for holding. Our staff are still engaged but will be with you shortly. Please hold." *Greensleeves* on a mandolin till Carina was ready to scream. "Sorry to keep you waiting. We're very busy at the moment. Please try again later. To return to the menu, press 1."

"Bastards!" she growled – just as the acoustics changed.

"I *beg* your pardon?" A public-school voice, barely restrained.

"Err...sorry, forget that. I'm Carina Wilde from London, my husband went missing; it's been reported to the embassy. I'm at Abu Simbel, I need to be rescued." As if *that* made it clearer, she scolded herself...

"Ah, yes...*quite*. Now if I could put you on hold for a minute..." – the line went flat before she could protest.

The Captain rolled his eyes. "God willing, tomorrow, sorry – *Insh'allah, bukkra, ma'lesh* we say in Arabic – IBM, you get it?"

"Hello – am I speaking to Carina Wilde, to Mrs Baring?" His voice was orotund.

"About time! Yes, it's me, who're you?"

"Are you unharmed? Can you speak freely?"

She coughed. "I'm with a Captain from the Nubi –"

"Yes, yes. Put him on, please."

The Captain took the handset with a complacent smile.

They spoke at length in Arabic, arguing, cajoling. This is diplomacy, security – *men's business*, the Captain's face said. She'd happily strangle him and that embassy bastard, but her fate was in their hands. They were *trading* her, like a commodity.

At last the Captain relinquished the handset.

"Sorry," said the diplomat curtly. "Details, modalities – you can't have a handover without them. But don't worry – it's all fixed. You'll be travelling north tomorrow, the Nubians will escort you to a pick-up zone for our chaps to fly you out by helicopter. Just follow their instructions and you'll be fine."

The Egyptian splayed a podgy hand over his heart. "*Bukkra, insh'allah.*"

Back at the guesthouse she lay in her chalet with the fan spinning. The garden was scorched and unkempt. She felt lonely, billeted apart from the others. She hadn't the energy to go looking for them – only a deep slough of anticlimax. Her ordeal was nearly over yet Nick was still missing. Nothing had been resolved...

Challenge negativity, her Reiki teacher said. A bath with aromatic oils, a night at Covent Garden – whatever gets you going: sound advice in London but hardly appropriate to a faded hotel in Nubia. Hairy blankets, a plugless television and an antique music centre in the veneer panel between beds. A nicotine-hued bandwidth yielded Arabic chat shows and static; a slot for cassettes whirred when she pressed a button.

Nick's cassettes – they were still in a pocket of her cargo pants. Celine Dion – no thanks. The other one was something Egyptian, a palm tree logo on the front. Maybe that funky Hammer D-Ab that Sabr liked so much...

She clicked *play*, undressed and padded into the bathroom. Her disgust at the streaky tiles was allayed by hot water. Stepping under the shower, she heard a mournful skirling and a man droning. It was hardly proper music, more like a drunk singing to an untuned guitar. But she wasn't going interrupt her shower to silence it. Sand had invaded every crack of her body – she'd had enough of deserts for a lifetime.

Egypt was alien, off-putting – like this maudlin cacophony. She rested her forehead on the tiles, water massaging her neck. Superstition, intrigue, it wasn't *her* world. For all she'd learnt, her efforts to discover Nick's fate had been futile. GM, Hosni Basha, Morrison, Baines, their motives growing murkier with each layer of deceit.

The lament was lacerating – raw grief, sawing steel strings. She beat her fists against the tiles and wept...

Get a grip! She'd nearly fallen...Fracturing her skull in a shower after surviving helicopter gunships would be ridiculous. Tomorrow she'd be under the wing of the British Embassy. Even troops cracked after weeks of combat in Afghanistan, she needn't beat herself up with guilt. She'd simply reached the end of her tether – for now.

With shriek so attenuated she clenched her teeth, the singer struck two savage discords and fell silent. The tape hissed. Thank God, it was over.

She turned off the shower, wrapping a threadbare towel round ribs she hadn't seen for years. At least she'd lost weight, though her skin was leathery. It seemed unlikely the guesthouse ran to complementary moisturiser ...

"I swear by God..." – a man's voice from the bedroom.

An intruder – some Talib fanatic come to kill her!

She imagined a knife slashing through the shower curtain.

Desperately she looked around for an escape route. The only window was at head level, frosted glass, the size of an A4 folder. She'd never manage to squeeze through before he caught her like a fish flapping in a net, stabbing her from behind as he wished.

No – she'd learnt to fight, learnt courage. A *weapon* – there must be one! The chromed towel-rail fixed to the wall by brackets. She tore it loose, rejoicing in the dangling screws – the more jagged the better. Should she wait for him to enter or burst into the bedroom? The thought of her blood drenching the tiles decided her...

No – she'd take the offensive. Like Tariq, like Nick, like Saint George – now she understood – you had to believe you sat on the shoulders of giants or your insignificance would crush you.

For Nick, for Saint George, she lunged into the bedroom.

It was empty.

The voice came from the cassette player – an Egyptian, speaking English.

"My name is Shukri Abd el-Munim. I am sixty years old. Today I live in

Hurghada and work in a teashop, but before the Black Day I was an engineer at Saad al-Ali Station, by the High Dam."

She collapsed into a chair. It was a while before his words registered again.

"… watched it break and the lake pour into the Valley. I thank God for my survival, but what I saw will chase me to my death." His voice sank. "The Basha's spies were in the teashop yesterday."

She heard a cork prised from a bottle, a sigh. "But I have run ahead, I must start at the beginning – at the High Dam."

His tone grew elegiac. "There were twenty of us who were Sufis. Engineer or platform-sweeper, all equal in our love of God. We met during lunch or tea breaks to practice our *zikrs*, to chant God's praises. By the quay, when there weren't any tourists. We were there when the boat sank – it arrived earlier than usual, during our tea break."

She heard him gulp avidly, a furtive alcoholic. "My brother Abu Dawa divined the enigma … Forgive the rest of us for being blind!"

His voice broke. "We all had families in the Reservoir Colony or Aswan; we had to search for them though the Flood was like an ocean. Only the hills beside the dam were visible – perhaps our loved ones were there. We scattered like chickens chased by a dog. But there was nothing we could do. Only those behind the dam survived – and on the hills downriver. Scum from Sheba'ak, God curse them!"

He hawked and spat, resuming in a calmer voice.

"How I reached Hurghada is a story anyone here could tell." He sighed. "*Allah karim!* I won't speak of our sufferings. Only of what happened since God guided my Sufi brother Abu Dawa to my teashop six months ago.

"He shared my mattress that night – he had nowhere else to sleep. But he had come to Hurghada with a purpose." His voice grew portentous. "He had composed a *mawal*, a lament relating all that occurred in the last minutes before the Flood. He wished President Zaghloul to hear it yet feared to approach the Enclave. But he had heard of a silver box in Hurghada's bazaar, where anyone could deposit a message for the President. So he had recorded his *mawal* and would leave it there tomorrow."

A glass slammed on a table. "I tried to dissuade him. No good can come of swimming with sharks, I said. Zaghloul is just the tail of the Father of Lies. But Abu Dawa was stubborn as a donkey. Before he left he gave me a copy of the tape, lest the first go astray. I hid it behind the ice-cistern. Abu Dawa returned two days later. It had been proclaimed in the bazaar by the town crier that Hosni Basha wished to hear an explanation of the *mawal* from the singer's own lips."

There was a pregnant pause. "What else could I do but let him groom himself to meet his murderer?" Carina heard him snivel, tears wiped on a sleeve. "No, I have no proof that the Basha killed him – but he never returned from El-Gouna."

The cork popped again. "Four days later, fishermen found a body in their nets off Shadwan Island. They lifted it aboard and cut open the wrapping. It was a man of Abu Dawa's age and height, his body burned, his eyes and tongue torn out..."

A leaden pause. "When they returned to Hurghada the police took the body and gave it to a mosque that offered him a decent burial. There were a few mourners at his grave, but I wasn't among them. By then I'd listened to his *mawal* and knew that the Father of Lies meant to silence whoever knew its message.

Carina heard glass clink on glass, liquor flowing.

"Egyptians love spying. Everyone spies, if only to steal some bread," he confided. "When the dogs that rule us tell their spies to look for somebody, it's not a state secret for long – the whole town is wise before they get an answer!"

He was weary. "Hunting for those who knew Abu Dawa in Aswan... He never revealed my name under torture, but *something*. Now is the time to prepare for the end. I have spoken in English so Abu Dawa's words may reach the ears of those deaf to the Holy Qur'an. The world must hear and understand! There is an Englishman who comes to the teashop. He seems honest, not arrogant like other Christians. God willing, he'll deliver this message to a righteous imam who'll inform the world of its contents.

"Brothers, soon the dogs will come – I will fight them to the end.

"There is no God but God."

The tape ended with a squawk.

Yasmina found her sitting wrapped in the towel, hair in rats' tails.

"What's wrong? I'm here. I want to ask you somethi –"

"Listen to this – tell me what it means. About Nick..."

Carina pressed the button again. She'd replayed the postscript a dozen times, knowing that the Arabic dirge held some terrible secret. Was this tape found in Nick's belongings the reason why he'd vanished? Had Hosni Basha been trying to prevent another secret from emerging, and not merely his tomb-robbing? Was that only a side show, a red herring that diverted her away from... *what?*

She sensed Yasmina had a confession to make, a dilemma to share, but she couldn't wait. The singer was caterwauling over the atonal rasping of his instrument.

Yasmina sighed like a mother who's heard her child's favourite catchphrase too often, settling back on the sofa. Suddenly she flinched, putting a hand to her cheek.

"No," she gasped, "*Mish mumkin!*"

"What's he singing? Tell me!"

"*Ya kharabi!*" Yasmina shrieked, tearing her hair.

Don't go hysterical on me! Carina slapped her face. Yasmina had done it to her before; she had a right to reciprocate.

Yasmina glared, claws raised.

"*You,*" she spat. "*You* did it. *You* destroyed Egypt!"

34 GOD'S ZOMBIES

In the empty bottle refracting sunrise over the harbour, Baines anticipated the days till the second anniversary of the Flood – of Kreutzer's rapture.

Kreutzer knew how he'd die, the date was pencilled in.

He'd been recording himself for a long time; wanted his motives understood. Perversely, he compared himself to that gonzo dilettante, Hunter S. Thompson.

"American icons, both of us, like two kidneys, him left, me right. And boy, am I *right*. Goddam, I'll go out with more of a bang than a shotgun an' having my ashes fired off'n a rocket by Johnny Depp."

Baines smiled at the memory. Norm skulled on sour-mash, lucid as Socrates. "Roll-back", he'd drawled. "Clean out the rag-heads, scrub down the Middle East. Iraq, Afghanistan, we left too many people standing to screw up democracy. Saudi fell without a shot being fired, those yellow bastards. We won't make that mistake again. Clean them *all* out – leastways eighty-ninety percent, got to leave some to start over. But not enough to need policing; we've had too much shit from those scenarios. This one is pure humanitarianism, no Marines involved."

Implicating jihadis was integral to the plan – the death-toll would hang around their necks till the Second Coming. Kreutzer's aim was to discredit Islam with a monstrous atrocity that would open the way to create Goshen in Egypt. Not its Biblical namesake – the Delta slave-cities where the Israelites had toiled for Pharaoh – but a Christian land purged of Islam and allied to Israel, with Western culture in its DNA.

To recreate Goshen, *they* had to come as saviours: an aid agency, responding to the greatest disaster in history with a mandate from the UN – that was the vehicle Kreutzer wanted Baines to build. There were enough disasters in the world for any agency to establish its competence; with Baines's fortune and connections, finding the expertise wouldn't be a problem, only an effort.

The problem had been finding the nuke. The War on Terror frustrated them at every turn; sources that might once have served were under constant surveillance. They were on the point of returning to the alternative of using chemical explosives to destroy the High Dam, a prospect offering only a 30%

success rate rather than a predicted 89% for a one-kiloton nuke. Crashing an airplane into the dam had been ruled out. Ringed by antiaircraft missiles, it was so solidly built that even a direct hit by an Airbus wouldn't breach it.

Then – when Salvation First was setting up in Syria after the Hama earthquake – there was a tug on a line that ran from Jordan, back through the Caucasian diaspora to Ingushetia and Chechnya. A rich seam of influence and criminality; clans and blood-ties nourished by money. *We have what you want* was the message.

Dubai – the Burj al-Arab hotel swelled like a colossal sail over the sea. On a balcony two floors down, a servant exercised a falcon. Baines heard gulls shrieking over the clink of instruments, as their tech guy examined the nuke. It resembled a gas meter from Omsk, olive-green and plastered with scarlet labels. But then the Soviets had never gone in for fancy trimmings; brute utility was their forte.

As promised, it fit into a large Samsonite, but at 90 kilos needed a trolley or two strong men to shift it. Plutonium was *heavy*, the tech guy muttered. In the bathroom, taps gushing, he whispered that his main concern had been *maintenance* – components must be replaced on a six-month cycle or the bomb's yield would suffer. But the tritium booster and PAL trigger were fresh as daisies, good for five months at least. This bomb had been *cared for*, for many years.

Baines returned to the lounge. Talk about the clash of civilizations! Each sub-space individually styled, blue leather walls or Nineties minimalism merging into Chippendale repro or Saudi-Versailles, a plasma TV in a Baroque frame leaping from mullahs to porn as their host channel-surfed, the sound muted.

The guy called himself Hossein. Ivory-skinned, raisin-eyed, stubbled jowls over gold neck-chains, he claimed to be from Baku but could hail from anywhere on the shores of the Caspian.

"So?" Hossein demanded, tossing the remote onto a cushion.

Baines nodded, unlocked his attaché case and fanned the sheets across a table. "Take a look," he invited. "Eighty million bucks in bearer bonds."

Hossein took his time examining the watermarks and holograms. Abruptly, he laughed. "Bin Laden once offered us three million dollars for *twenty* bombs! *No way* could he find a seller – he was too cheap." He laughed again, slipping the bonds into a crocodile-skin document wallet.

Baines smiled thinly. Market forces had prevailed.

He was doing the world a favour by buying the bomb before extremists did.

Though Kreutzer recognised the security imperative, he lamented not *being there* when Baines scored. "Shit," he hissed on his cabin porch the last time they met. "It's like screwing a chick your buddy hit on while you were barfing in the john. It's unnatural." But he wouldn't miss the finale – his own rapture. "You know the ending in *Dr Strangelove* – where the pilot rides an H-bomb like a bucking bronco? I want it."

Why not? The whole plan called for deception from beginning to end. Why shouldn't Kreutzer get his rocks off?

Baines never experienced the endgame, only its aftermath. The Flood that laid waste from Aswan to Alexandria; sixty million dead by nightfall, as the jihadi video played on every TV in the world. Al-Jazeera led the story, as they'd intended; the Western media playing catch-up using excerpts from Al-Jazeera's footage.

Kreutzer was there – in the background. Hollering prayers and hugging himself with glee, only on the video it looked like despair. Twelve Middle Eastern Christians with personal reasons for hating Muslims and perfect Arabic, who played the jihadi speaking parts. And the mostly white 'hostages': an Evangelical tour group that behaved with dignified calm (spineless passivity, opined Ann Coulter on Fox TV). Naturally, the video omitted their actions hours earlier – rounding up the crew and other passengers, locking them in the lower-deck cabins and shooting a few – that would never be seen.

The last minute showed the boat nosing into the harbour beside the High Dam. Shortly before it sank, the digital footage was compressed and emailed via a chain of servers, to be re-recorded as a video and delivered by courier to Al-Jazaera. Only when Baines watched it in slo-mo did he catch Kreutzer's final gesture to the world.

Fuck you.

✳✳✳

Carina left at dawn with the soldiers in a battered Peugeot. Yasmina and Sabr weren't there to say goodbye, nor Tariq. Sad, yet also a relief... The tape had dug a frontline between them: the Egyptians entrenched, Carina scrabbling to fortify her own side. How easily they believed the worst on the basis of wild accusations. Some Sufi banjo player overhears hymns across a harbour and and instantly espies a *conspiracy of Crusaders and Zionists*. He tries to tell the world in a *ballad* – imagine CNN struggling to present the story using extracts. Each stanza savaged by experts till every shred of clarity was gone. No eyewitnesses to interview, nobody involved in its provenance…

Yet the lamentations of a witness to the dam's destruction had moved Yasmina and Sabr to fury. If other Egyptians were as easily convinced, the cassette was a time bomb. Whoever caused the Flood, it had laid waste indiscriminately. *This* bomb was different – a *psycho-weapon* that would shatter Salvation First's authority, Hosni's despotism and Israel's hold on the Canal. All those gas-field contracts and baptisms would be undone overnight. They'd surely do *anything* to stop the tape getting out – which might suggest a Crusader-Zionist conspiracy *post factum*, if not before the Flood.

Before the Flood or afterwards – did it really make any difference?

Muslims around the world had rioted over trivial or imagined slights. This was the mother of all conspiracy theories – how could they not believe in it? A psycho-bomb irradiated at any distance; no fallout shelter gave any protection. No wonder Yasmina refused to touch it, nor Sabr, after he'd listened. The cassette was a plague vial, infecting whoever owned it. Who would purposely crack the seal and pour it into the atmosphere?

The Seventh Seal opening, as in the Book of Revelation. The End Time, as Baines and Morrison had anticipated on the way to Saint Anthony's monastery.

She shivered, though the car was sweltering. Windows closed against the raging dust-storm, four perspiring soldiers and a driver who smoked – no wonder she felt ill. The sun was a silver glob in a milky pall; mirages squirmed like puddles of mercury between rotten teeth jutting from the desert. Everything seemed blasted by the hot sand-laden wind on their tail.

"Apaches can't fly in our *qibli*," said the soldier beside her, proudly. "Further north, who knows?" He shrugged. *Thanks*. She really needed to hear that. Returning to the land of gunships – would it never end?

Eventually the *qibli* ceased blowing and the soldiers judged it unwise to remain on the desert road. There might be landmines or Apaches, they confided. The Peugeot turned off on to a dirt track, followed it for half an hour, and suddenly Carina saw the Nile Valley. Spread out beneath sugarloaf hills, striped black, green and blue like the Nubian flag, the Valley was as wild as the Serengeti. Baboons hung from creepers as they left the car and hiked down to the river, where ibises waded in the reeds. The soldiers had obviously been there before. They began clearing dead reeds to uncover a sturdy rubber raft with an outboard motor.

Carina couldn't believe they meant her to travel like this: clad in camouflaged waterproofs harnessed to steel D-rings, helmeted and goggled. But they did. Weeks earlier, six hundred miles downriver, she'd sailed against the current in Tariq's felucca. But this would be running downstream at full throttle, with rapids ahead...

Laughing, the soldiers buckled her harness, then their own. Engaging the throttle, the helmsman swung the inflatable into the current as she braced her feet against the treads. Spray hammered her shoulders, hurled itself at her face. The engine roared over the surging torrent of caramel and cream. Gradually she relaxed and began to enjoy the thrill. The helmsman grinned beneath his goggles – she flashed him thumbs up in response.

This was the land that Yasmina and Sabr would inherit. Flung together, they'd make a new life here. Tariq, too, would find a niche. Relieved of her concern, Carina abandoned herself to the Valley's beauty. Sun-kissed fields and thatched huts; water buffalo, girls balancing pots on their heads. No pylons or telephone poles, no satellite dishes. Life would be idyllic, the world a bloody enigma beyond the horizon.

Who are you kidding? Girls drawing water from river that was their communal toilet; no schools or clinics; no future but subsistence farming... As for isolation from the world, the whole landscape was the result of a cataclysm unleashed by outsiders, Elysium littered with the debris of war. A skeletal missile battery, a helicopter strewn across a ridge – *independence cemented by our heroes' blood*, the Captain had said.

Far downriver, his fighters had raided Craven's agri-projects, killing and burning. It was in the script of any insurgency. Yet in their own land, Nubians lived in crushing poverty. Surely there was a way to help people instead of adding to their suffering?

Seen from Nubia, Egypt looked different. Refugee camps and fanaticism had shaped her view till now, but here was reason to hope. As the river's spate diminished, it meandered in shimmering arcs across a vast plain lost in haze. In Egyptian mythology, Creation emerged from watery chaos. In Nubia, the Flood had restored year zero. Civilization could start afresh ...

The helmsman cut the motor, let the inflatable drift. The others shucked off their harnesses and began sparring, whooping. *What the hell?* It seemed the victor had been chosen for an honour. Smirking, bowing to her, he delved into a pouch and extracted –

A grenade...

As she froze he lobbed it at the Nile. A geyser erupted, splashing them all; fish bobbing on the water as it subsided. They were laughing at her – a gobsmacked woman; soldiers – men – she was sick of their puerile violence. Whipping the motor, the pilot spurred the craft towards their kill.

"Fish like an Egyptian!" he chortled.

They had a fire blazing and the fish gutted in minutes; soon they were forking chunks onto tin plates. It tasted wonderful; she was ravenous. They'd brought pitta bread and salt, and a big clump of bananas for afters, with sweet tea to follow. Carina poured, leaving a frothy head on each glass, Bedouin style, as Sabr had taught her.

As the soldiers smoked and picked their teeth, she noticed one fish set aside. The helmsman saw her glance. "For Abu Shallalat." He placed the leftover bananas nearby. "The Father of the Falls. We bring him food – he gives us *baraka*."

Blessing – Sabr was always going on about it. She tried to imagine how a holy man would look. Like Saint Anthony as she'd seen him depicted at the monastery, wild-eyed and dressed in animal skins? "So we're stopping by to visit?" she asked.

The soldiers laughed. "Not stopping," they chorused.

Seeing her bemusement, the helmsman explained. "Abu Shallalat stands on a great pillar above the Falls. Nobody can reach him. He spends weeks up there, seeking God. Sometimes disciples follow him, to stand on pillars themselves – but never as long as the Father of the Falls. And only he keeps returning to the pillars."

Just like the early Christian Stylites, thought Carina. There was an icon of a saint standing on a pillar among the "Treasures of Gazprom".

"What for?" the grenade-thrower scoffed. "Looking for God – they won't find him there. Only sunstroke and fleas, nothing to give them *baraka*. Don't waste time on those zombies."

The helmsman flushed. "I steer, I know the rocks. If I need *baraka*, who're you to say! When Abu Shallalat left, many boats smashed. Pilots misjudged the falls and drowned." He wrapped his gifts in newspaper.

More Egyptian lunacy...

The Falls. Carina's heart raced, she nearly pissed her waterproofs. The river had split into myriad channels, pulsing sea-green and ivory between ebony rocks. As the thunder of the cataracts intensified, curtains of mist parted to reveal two solidified tornadoes, looming above the falls. Slowly, they resolved into two gargantuan legs. One taller, its calf bristling with stubble; the other tilted at an angle defying gravity. Dull grey skin, pockmarked and lumpy, as if concrete and rocks had been fused together.

Suddenly she understood what she was seeing –

The ruins of the High Dam.

A buttress and a shard from its curtain wall, seared by the blast which had ruptured the dam, unleashing the Flood: one devastating force begetting another. No wonder the soldiers were awed. 'Pillars' was hardly the word for these towering ruins.

Atop each tower a person was semaphoring.

"See," cried the helmsman. "Abu Shallalat has returned with a new disciple."

"So get *his* blessing," the grenade-thrower jibed. "Ask the Son of the Falls."

The helmsman swung the tiller, steering the craft crossways over rapids. Within seconds they were drawn into another torrent, racing towards the leaning tower.

"Ibn Shallalat," he yelled. The grenade-thrower lurched to the prow, straining to grab a dangling bucket and thrust his burden inside.

"Ibn Shallalat," the crew chorused, "*Hat baraka!*"

As their cry echoed off the rocks a streak of silver fell among the soldiers. When the grenade-thrower returned from the prow he handed a bracelet to the helmsman, who kissed it reverently. Carina expected him to put it on, but instead he took her hand and slipped it over her fingers. It was faintly warm, the silver tarnished.

"May Ibn Shallalat's *baraka* stay with you."

Looking back at the gargantuan tower, Carina saw a scarecrow, silhouetted against the sun, swaying like a zombie. The Son of the Falls. What blessings did he have to spare?

35 GOG

A chalet at the El-Gouna Mövenpick – a chalet deemed British territory. Charles and Camilla gazed owlishly from a gilt frame at the tea-cups and biscuits on the table. Carina's host was pink-tied and smelt of Body Shop for Men. She recognised his voice from the satphone.

Mowbray.

That was how he introduced himself; no forename. *First Secretary (Political)*, his card read, divulging his initials, *S.W.* To her knowledge, she'd never met a spy before – a spook from MI6. He looked like the cricket expert on the quiz team at the Slug & Lettuce; Nick had been the mainstay for general knowledge and geography...

Mowbray. She sensed the amorality of a Caligula beneath his Saville Row suit. He'd heard her story dispassionately, Nick's file on the table, the cassette halted in a player. He was willing to rehash Nick's disappearance but not the tape found among his possessions, attributing the destruction of the High Dam to Western 'Crusaders' – an eye-witness account of the worst atrocity in history?

"That's your interpretation, Mrs Baring – but there are others. The Internet is crawling with them. You can add yours to a million conspiracy theories." He sniffed.

"And what if it's true?" she snapped. "I'll talk to journalists, I'll convince them to investigate. Whatever the truth is, it'll come out in the end."

"An idealist, eh. It amazes me anyone still is, especially about this part of the world. Suppose I let you in on a secret – *another perspective* on what *really* happened. Let me pour you another cup of tea, it'll take a while to explain...

"Imagine you're the Iranian regime in 1997 – can you remember how it was then? Saddam Hussein still in power, boxed in by sanctions and no-fly zones, yet dreaming of WMD like he'd used against Iran in the past, with Western approval. The US would love to give you a bloody nose and the Israelis are equally hostile. The world looks dangerous, seen from Tehran. They badly need a *strategic deterrent*.

"Then, out of the blue – from Belarus – comes the once-in-a-lifetime offer of a suitcase nuke from the old Soviet arsenal. Mafia, ministers or ex-KGB –

whoever, it didn't matter, only the *item* did. Secret meetings in Belgrade and Alma Aty – fifty million dollars for a suitcase that can obliterate a city...

"But the Ayatollahs realized that their suitcase had some flaws as a deterrent. Patently a terrorist weapon, it had to be pre-positioned for blackmail. Its *existence* could only be proven by detonating their only nuclear weapon, whose *use* would incur overwhelming retaliation." Mowbray snorted contemptuously.

"In short it was a Sampson weapon, to bring the temple down on their heads. Without more warheads and missiles to deliver them, Iran would never attain the security of Mutual Assured Destruction. Oh, people decry MAD, but it was the bedrock of stability in the Cold War, so it's understandable the Iranians wanted some.

"And so they committed themselves to mastering missile technology and nuclear power. Their clandestine enrichment programme escaped detection for *eighteen* years. After they got caught out, they had to stonewall America, Europe, whatever diplomatic soup was thrown at them. It was reassuring to know they had the suitcase if a desperate threat was needed...

"Fast forward till three years ago. The Ayatollahs have survived sanctions and destabilization and are producing warheads for their Sejil IIs, targeting the Middle East, Europe and Russia. But there's a PR problem. Their campaign to defend their atomic energy programme rested on the assertion that Iran wasn't seeking nuclear weapons. To announce a nuclear test or reveal its warhead factories at Khak-e Sefid would undo all its propaganda gains – yet how else could their capability be demonstrated?

"Israel long denied its nuclear arsenal. Iran dissimulated with a different spin. While their negotiators danced the shuffle once performed by Saddam, the Ayatollahs were preparing to *use* their bomb – the suitcase they'd kept in the closet for so long."

Suddenly Carina saw where he was heading.

"You mean *here* – Egypt?"

"Why not? Is it *more* incredible than an obscure jihadi group wiping out an Arab nation for betraying the Palestinians? Oh yes – that's what we thought at the time – what the world still believes. Everyone has seen the jihadi video and heard them justify their actions. With no survivors to interrogate, nor any forensics, that scenario got taken at face value in many quarters. It was easier that way." Mowbray shrugged.

"But why should the Ayatollahs do such a thing? *Why*, for God's sake?"

"The Almighty was egging them on. All that Shi'a martyrdom cult, the Hidden Imam, Ayatollah Yazdi – you can't believe the time they spent debating apocrypha in the Expediency Council, it drove our Farsi analysts crazy! But that's by the way... where was I? Ah, yes, motivation." He paused for a swig of tea.

"Well, apart from martyrdom – and note, it was *others* that died by the million – there was realpolitik and religion. Establishing Iran as the new Caliphate: a beacon for Shi'a all over the Gulf – the first Muslim superpower since the Ottoman Empire – with the Shi'a on top of the Sunnis, as they *should* have triumphed, thirteen centuries ago. Theologically, it all ties in with the Haghani Circle from Qom and a sect called the Hojjatieh, who believe that chaos will hasten the return of the Mahdi, the Hidden Imam. In Shi'a terms, that's like the Second Coming of Christ. An intoxicating vision for an Ayatollah, you'll agree."

A thread of saliva shone in his mouth. "With one blow, they destroyed the largest Sunni Arab state in the Middle East – Persia's rival for supremacy since the days of Cyrus the Great – while shaming the Wahhabis of Arabia before the Muslim world. All those decades of preaching and funding jihad and *this* was the result, millions of Muslims thought. Oh yes, there were smug faces at Vauxhall and Langley when we saw Wahhabi extremism trying to hide under a rock. We thought the War on Terror had been won, near enough. We were so naïve – the intelligence community, the media, the bloody gormless public...

"Until six months ago, when VEVAK – Iran's Ministry of Intelligence and Security – sent its Israeli, American and Russian counterparts a clip of the suitcase-nuke seen in the jihadi video. Not aboard a hijacked boat on Lake Nasser, but in a suite at the Burj al-Arab hotel in Dubai. Naturally it didn't show who was buying or selling the bomb, but by having it on film and giving it to us, VEVAK was sending us a message. The Islamic Republic had a nuclear arsenal and would use it – *had used it* – aggressively or in retaliation, it wasn't a distinction that bothered them much. *Bring it on*, they said.

"Well – we hadn't the stomach for *that*. To admit we'd been outwitted and every statesman had got it wrong – that the public had been totally duped – was bad enough. But turning outrage into action was impossible. The Ayatollahs were snug beneath their nuclear umbrella, counting oil revenues and converts. By that time, the balance of power had shifted irrevocably in their favour." He tutted ruefully.

"As an intelligence officer, I take my hat off to them. It was the ultimate false-flag operation – a total war that never happened in the eyes of the world; a titanic victory undetected by the media. What else could we do but accept a *fait accompli*? As the Ayatollahs knew all along, French is the language of gracious surrender."

Mowbray ejected the cassette. "Take it," he sneered. "Play it on Newsnight."

***

One of Mowbray's underlings escorted her through the VIP channel. She had to wait while an official sought authorisation – purely from spite she sensed, a moment before the Egyptian confirmed it by hissing: "Deported. Not welcome in Egypt."

Bastards – she was about to tell him so when Mowbray's thug elbowed her into a lounge. "No point protesting. Do you want to be forced onto the plane?" She shook him off, trembling with rage. *Home*, when she was home she'd raise hell. MI6, Salvation First, the Egyptian government – they'd rue the day they'd done this. *Nick*, they'd buried him with their lies...

"Drink this." A large G&T fizzed under her nose. She weighed throwing it at his face but the aroma was so inviting – her need so overwhelming – that she downed it in two gulps. In seconds warmth was surging through her body, her head floating.

"Let's go." He seized her arm.

Glass doors hissed wide.

On the tarmac was an executive jet, three soldiers squatting in the shadow of a wing. Her knees went wobbly, her vision blurred, her tongue thickened...

Drugged...

The cassette dug into her heart as she folded at the knees.

When she came round they were airborne, a stewardess leaning over, make-up cracked with concern. "Thank goodness – we were so worried. Too much to drink at once," she clucked. "You live and learn." She smoothed the blanket over Carina's lap.

"What's happening," Carina whispered.

"You're flying home, to England."

"England?"

"Where else? You don't think you're being taken to – oh my, you *do*. Heavens no! This isn't a black flight."

"A what?"

"Never mind – it doesn't apply to you." She winked. "You look peaky. What you need is dinner – we've a great choice, beef sauvignon with *pomme frites* or lobster fricassee. I bet you haven't tasted either in weeks."

In a trice a tray was steaming under her nostrils. Pure ambrosia, the beef melting in her mouth, chips deliciously crisp. She wolfed it down, the sickly dessert, the crackers and cheese too. The glass of wine she left – she had to keep a grip.

Waiting for coffee, her eyes fell upon the magazine tucked into the pocket of the seat in front. THE END TIMES its title blazed in capitals, against the backdrop of a mushroom cloud. *Will YOU be saved?* She flipped the pages.

> GOG – how will we recognize him? In End-Time theology, Gog is a manifestation of the Antichrist, leader of Magog (Russia) and Persia (Iran); King of the Locusts, the Deceiver, the Destroyer.
> In Muslim theology he is Yajooj, imprisoned behind a giant wall of iron and molten copper.
> As the End Time begins he –

Carina thrust it back into the pocket, shuddering. Madness proliferating; lies and delusions cemented to make a wall dividing the globe. Where did they begin or end? Crusaders masquerading as jihadis, or an Iranian hidden hand: which seemed less implausible? You could even imagine a conspiracy manipulated by other conspirators; one deception inside another. No wonder spies called it a wilderness of mirrors. If Mowbray blamed Iran, was simply that to divert her from the real culprits?

What was the truth? Each assertion collapsed under scrutiny. Where was any evidence for Crusaders destroying the dam? Or proof that the bomb came from Iran? Had Nick stumbled upon the truth, or simply delusions? And even if the tape told the truth, would anyone listen? Such nebulous doubts would never prevail against *certainty*. Inertia, pride and laziness – the anchors of the Western world had sunk their hooks into one version of history. The jihadi video analysed, the cruise boat vaporized. No forensic evidence, only the tape to watch yet again.

History was what was televised...

Truth would emerge long after the dice had been thrown.

Through the porthole, the sun sank into a stew of tannin.

Darkness crept over the sea, waves turning to slate. No silver blaze of civilization but the coppery exhalations of oil-platforms as the upholstery exuded the rancid chill of an ice-box. *Hope dying, choked...*

Nylons rasped; the stewardess loomed in a cloud of Chlöe.

"Fantastic news," she blurted, thrusting a BlackBerry into Carina's hands.

NICK'S BEEN SAVED – BAINES.

"You're shivering," she cooed. "I'll turn up the thermostat."

NOTES & GLOSSARY

The quotations in Arabic script in the Prologue are from the Qur'an, from the chapters *The Moon* and *He Frowned*. In the order that they appear, these verses read:

Then we opened the gate of heaven with pouring water, and caused the earth to gush forth springs, so that the waters met for a predestined purpose. [54:11 – 12]

Lo! We let loose on them a raging wind on a day of constant calamity. Sweeping men away as though they were uprooted trunks of palm trees. [54:19 – 20]

But when the dread blast is sounded, on that day each man will forsake his brother, his father and his mother, his wife and his children; for each one of them will on that day have enough sorrow of his own. [80:33 – 37]

On that day there shall be many faces veiled with darkness, covered with dust. [80:40 – 41]

A

Abu Shallalat Father of the Falls. The honorific Abu is accorded to men once they become parents, but also used metaphorically to define a salient characteristic of a person or place.

Ahadith (sing. Hadith) Sayings or deeds attributed to the Prophet Mohammed, graded by Islamic scholars from 'sound' to 'unreliable'. The sounder the *hadith* the greater its importance as a guide to believers' behaviour since Mohammed is the 'perfect man', an exemplar for all Muslims.

Aib Shame; dishonour; rejection of religion.

Aiwa Yes (in colloquial Egyptian Arabic).

Alf zobr fi kussik A thousand cocks in your cunt.

Al-hamdillilah or hamdillilah Thanks be to God.

Allah karim God is generous. Said in response to a setback or calamity – after all, things could be worse had Allah decided so.

Anben A baptismal font or bath in a Coptic church.

Ann Coulter US columnist, who wrote after 9/11: "We know who the homicidal maniacs are. They are the ones cheering and dancing right now. We should invade their countries, kill their leaders and convert them to Christianity."

Apophis In Ancient Egyptian cosmology, the snake-god Apophis personified chaos and evil, threatening Re (see below) during his voyage through the underworld.

Antika An antique artefact, usually pharaonic (or fake).

Arak A fiery spirit distilled from grapes.

B

Bab el-Hadid Knowing only that *bab* means 'gate' and confronted by an infernal gorge, Nick takes Shrek's exclamation to mean the Gates of Hell when it actually refers to the Iron Gate that once separated Yajooj (see below) from the world.

Bab al-Wazir A quarter of Islamic Cairo named after a bygone Gate of the Vizier, whose main thoroughfare leads south towards the Citadel.

Baby Gaddafi The nickname may allude to Seif al-Islam, Colonel Gaddafi's second son, who dabbled in film producing, football management and motor racing before assuming an overtly political role as his father's heir apparent.

Baraka Blessing. Conferred by a holy man or woman, in person (if alive) or by visiting their tomb or shrine (if dead), this practice is condemned as idolatrous by the Wahhabis and other sects, but nonetheless widespread throughout the Islamic world.

Basha The Egyptian pronunciation of the Turkish honorific 'Pasha', a term of respect for anyone in authority dating from the era of Ottoman rule over Egypt.

Beast Government Evangelical Christians believe that one of the signs of the Messiah is the rise of a world government, foretold in Revelation as a Beast which is granted Satan's throne on earth. Many think that its 'ten horns and seven heads' refer to the European Union, the United Nations or ZOG; and the 'mark of the Beast' refers to barcodes. See also: ZOG.

Beit House.

Bismillah, er-Rahim, ad-Daim In the name of God, the Merciful, the Everlasting.

Black Berets Nickname for the Central Security Force, Egypt's riot police, drawn from the poorest, least-educated strata of society. Armed with Kalashnikovs and riot-staves, they wear black fatigues and berets.

Bechtel Corporation The largest engineering company in the US, its involvement in mega-infrastructure projects (often military) reflects its close ties to officials in Washington and the Kingdom of Saudi Arabia, culminating in the outsourcing of much of the reconstruction of Iraq to Bechtel since 2003.

Bukkra Tomorrow.

C

Catechumens Converts awaiting baptism into the Coptic Christian faith.

Citadel A spur of the Muqattam Hills fortified by Sultan Salah al-Din (Saladin) and enlarged by his successors; its great Mosque of Mohammed Ali is one of the landmarks of Cairo's skyline.

Commint Communications intelligence (Internet, telephone and radio intercepts).

Corniche A concrete embankment and esplanade beside a river or sea.

Cunning disease A euphemism for cancer.

D

Dahrik! Your back! A traditional warning-cry of Cairene street-vendors.

DIA US Defense Intelligence Agency. Besides gathering military intelligence overseas, the DIA is tasked with security at US military facilities such as Fort Detrick, investigating staff if they seem open to blackmail (as Kreutzer did).

Diwan A term of Persian origin, referring to high-ranking government officials or departments and, by extension, their audiences with petitioners, held while the official reclined on a couch (the derivation of the English word 'divan').

Djinn The Qur'an describes them as created by Allah from 'smokeless fire' and devotes an entire chapter to them – which confirms their existence, many Egyptians believe. Djinn are usually invisible, often harass humans and even possess them. Exorcists may try to harmonize relations between the djinn and its host rather than expelling it from the person's body, as this can be injurious, it's believed.

E

El-Arish City on Egypt's Mediterranean coast, 40 kilometres from the Gaza border.

El-Gouna A vast self-contained tourist resort built on a series of islands, 22 kilometres north of Hurghada, on the Red Sea coast. Since the Flood it has become the Presidential Enclave, housing the government and wealthy elite of El-Bahr.

El-Khalifa An old neighbourhood below Cairo's Citadel, named after the Abbassid Caliphs buried there.

Ezba Farm, settlement. In El-Bahr it refers to holiday villages that have become refugee camps.

F

Felucca A Nile sailing boat, used for fishing, ferrying, or tourist cruises. Rigged with a simple mainsail, a felucca can be sailed by a single boatman.

Fikh Commentary on the Qur'an and *ahadith* (see above); Islamic jurisprudence.

Fitna Strife, sedition or disorder within a Muslim community.

G

Galabiyya A loose, ankle-length robe worn by both men and women in Egypt.

General Intelligence Service (GIS) Though mainly focused on foreign intelligence, Egypt's GIS has also been responsible for the president's personal security since its chief, General Suleiman, impressed Mubarak with his cool-headedness during an ambush on their motorcade in 1995, and later crushed the Jihad Islami (see below).

Ghard Abu Muharrik Arguably the longest sand-dune in Africa, consisting of three stretches 100 – 125 kilometres long, it falls over an escarpment to reform as crescent-shaped dunes advancing up to 20 metres a year.

Gog In the Hebrew Bible, Gog is 'of the land of Magog' in 'the remotest parts of the earth', who leads a great host against Ancient Israel as 'prince of Rosh, Meshech and Tubal'. The prophecy of Ezekiel places Gog's attack in 'the final part of the years (or days)', implying that the name is cryptic or symbolic. Bible scholars relate the prophecy to the time of the Messianic Kingdom and identify Gog with Satan. In Revelation 20:8 Gog and Magog are shown to be 'those nations in the four corners of the earth' who allow themselves to be misled by Satan. See also: Yajooj.

H

Halal Permissible to Muslims, therefore lawful.

Haghani Circle An Islamic seminary in Iran founded by Ayatollah Yazdi, whose alumni hold positions throughout the government and security forces, working in tandem with the Hojjatieh (see below). The seminary teaches that believers must hasten the return of the Mahdi, or Messiah (otherwise known as the Twelfth, or Hidden, Imam).

Halliburton US contractors responsible for setting up and running Baghdad's Green Zone, plus other logistical support for the US occupation of Iraq. Dick Cheney and Donald Rumsfeld were both previously on Halliburton's board of directors.

Haram Forbidden to Muslims; sinful.

Hat baraka Give (us) blessing.

Hizb ut-Tahrir The Party of Liberation advocates the establishment of Sharia law throughout the world and a global Islamic Caliphate. Banned in Egypt since 1974, it has branches throughout Europe, North America and the Middle East.

Hojjatieh A secretive Shi'a organization founded to oppose the Baha'i religion in Iran, which supported the Shah but later switched sides to back the Islamic Revolution. Alleged to have later hijacked Iran's government and Revolutionary Guards, its highest-ranking member is said to be Ayatollah Yazdi, President Ahmedinejad's spiritual mentor. Western intelligence agencies claim that its doctrine of the imminence of the Mahdi (Messiah) includes the belief that this can be hastened by creating chaos. Some fear that this eschatology is behind Iran's pursuit of nuclear and missile technology and makes the regime's leadership oblivious to the 'rational' calculus of deterrence which guided the US and Soviet Union through the Cold War. See also: Sejil II.

Huwwa hinna He's here.

I

Ibn Shallalat Son of the Falls. Besides its literal meaning ('son of'), Ibn may denote someone or something arising from or emulating another person.

Inglizi Englishman; English; someone punctual (colloquial).

Insh'allah God willing. Constantly uttered in everyday speech, this phrase encapsulates Muslims' belief in divine predestination, whose corollary is that whatever happens is *maktoub* (see below).

Inta aref dilwati Now you understand.

K

Kafir An unbeliever. The Qur'an stipulates that they should be offered a choice. If they reject conversion to Islam, they may be tolerated within a Muslim society as 'People of the Book' (Jews and Christians) providing they pay a poll-tax and acknowledge their social inferiority, otherwise it is incumbent on Muslims to 'smite their necks' (cut their throats) or 'possess them with their right hands' (as slaves). The option of being People of the Book is not open to Hindus ('cow-worshippers') or any other religion, nor atheists. See also *Kufr* (below).

Karkaday An infusion of hibiscus flowers, drunk hot or cold in Egypt.

Khalas Enough; finished.

Khara alaik Shit on you.

Khawaga A foreigner; the word has mildly derogatory overtones in Arabic.

Khawal A deviant; a sodomite. The term is commonly applied to gays in Egypt.

Kodia A priestess at an exorcism, or *zar* (see below).

Kufr The Realm of Unbelief: anywhere in the world where Islam has yet to prevail. Anathematised in the Qur'an as the 'Abode of War', its nations are offered the choice of adopting Islam, submitting to it as 'People of the Book', or being conquered.

Kuss ummak Your mother's cunt; one of the commonest obscenities in Arabic.

J

Jahilliyya Era of ignorance and barbarism that supposedly preceded the coming of Islam. Twentieth-century Islamists such as Sayyid Qutb argued that Muslim countries had reverted to *Jahilliyya* by giving secular laws precedence over Sharia, so true Muslims were justified in waging jihad against these 'apostate' regimes.

Jihad Islami Egyptian Islamic Jihad, a militant group active since the 1970s, which assassinated Egypt's President Sadat and nearly killed his successor Mubarak. After its networks inside Egypt were eradicated by the GIS (see above) and the group was expelled from its sanctuary in Sudan, the remaining militants under Ayman al-Zawahiri merged with Al-Qaeda in 2001.

M

Maash'allah Whatever God wills.

Madrassa A religious school.

Magog First mentioned in Genesis 10, as one of the 'sons of Japhet' who founded seven tribes, Magog appears in Ezekiel as a land (*eretz*), whose name may mean 'the land of Gog', though some Biblical scholars relate it to a person or a host, similar to Gog. In the Qur'an, Magog is called Majooj.

Majooj In *The Cave* chapter of the Qur'an, he is a person or creature like Yajooj. Both names derive from the Arabic root word *Ajijj* (to burn, blaze or hasten), suggesting that fire is their means of war. Ahmadis (regarded as heretical sect by other Muslims) see Yajooj and Majooj as the ancestors of Western nations opposed to Islam that will ultimately be destroyed by a fire of their own making.

Mamlukes Foreign slave-warriors who founded their own dynasties which ruled Egypt for over 600 years. Originally from Central Asia, recruits were later drawn from all over the Near East and the Balkans. Notorious for their intrigues and profligacy, the Mamlukes remained powerful even after Egypt was absorbed into the Ottoman Empire, until finally crushed by Mohammed Ali in 1811.

Maktoub It is written (destined to happen). Muslims believe that everything is predetermined by God, from an individual's life to the future of humanity. When uttered, the word *maktoub* is often accompanied by the gesture of drawing an index finger across the forehead, where it is believed that one's fate is inscribed.

Ma'lesh Let it be forgiven; never mind; sorry.

Mashi OK; agreed.

Marhaba Welcome.

Mastaba A mud-brick bench or sleeping platform, in (or outside) traditional village houses. Also refers to the flat-roofed funerary complexes of Ancient Egypt.

Mawal A traditional lament: one of the basic forms of Arab music.

Melaya A flowing, ankle-length wrap worn by Egyptian women.

Minya City in the Nile Valley, 230 kilometres south of Cairo. Dubbed the 'Bride of Egypt' for the charm of its colonial architecture and the friendliness of its people, Minya became the epicentre of the conflict between Islamist insurgents and the security forces during the mid-1990s.

Mitnaka Slut.

Mo'amera Plot; conspiracy. Conspiracy theories flourish throughout the Arab world, where most media is censored by the state or has an overt agenda.

Mohammed Ali Albanian-born Pasha (1769—1849) who seized power in Egypt in 1805, modernizing the army and fostering industry, agriculture, education and administration by nationalizing all land and using forced labour. Famed for his ruthlessness and guile, he died a senile paranoiac, deposed by his own son.

Mohammed Tharwat Egyptian singer known for his pious observance of Islam and maintaining an orphanage in the Delta city of Tanta.

Mukhabarat Egyptians use the Arabic word for 'Intelligence' to refer to several spy agencies: Military Intelligence (under the Defence Ministry), State Security Investigations (under the Interior Ministry), and the General Intelligence Service, which comes directly under the Presidency (see above).

Munafiqeen Hypocrites: those who perform the outward signs of Islam but lack sincere faith.

Muqattam Hills A limestone massif that limits Cairo's urban sprawl in the direction of Suez, with an affluent suburb on its plateau, 180m above the city, and shantytowns and rubbish-dumps at its base, vulnerable to rock-falls from the plateau.

Mish mumkin It's not possible; you mustn't.

N

Na'am Yes (in formal Classical Arabic).

Nabta playa A desert depression that trapped water during the wet phase of Saharan prehistory (8000—6000 BC), when settlements flourished. A circle of megaliths weighing up to 1.5 tonnes each is thought to the world's earliest astronomical calendar. Tombs containing ritually sacrificed cattle may represent an early form of Ancient Egypt's cult of the cow-goddess Hathor.

Nuah Noah, as he is called in the Qur'an, where the Flood is related in chapter 27.

Nubians Indigenous people of the upper Nile Valley, whose ancient homeland was submerged by Lake Nasser as a consequence of the Aswan High Dam. With their own language and cultural identity, Nubians are Egypt's largest ethnic minority, with noticeably darker skins and more 'African' features than their compatriots.

O

Ofeq An Israeli reconnaissance satellite with cloud-penetrating radar-imaging capability.

Osiris In Ancient Egyptian mythology, Osiris was murdered by his jealous brother (see Sukkoth), who dismembered the body and fed its penis to a crocodile. His sister-wife Isis collected the bits and bandaged them together to create the first mummy, which she briefly resurrected to conceive a child. This Osirian myth fused with that of Re (see below) to form a dualistic narrative of resurrection and regeneration.

P

PAL Permissive Action Link: the US military acronym for the system of passwords and manual keys that safeguards a nuclear weapon from unauthorised detonation.

Pigeon night Traditional Egyptian nuptial celebrations, involving the consumption of pigeons (believed to increase sexual potency) prior to consummation of the marriage. 'Pigeon' is an Egyptian slang term for penis.

Ptah Ancient Egyptian creator-god; particularly associated with the Archaic and Pre-Dynastic eras. Portrayed swathed in bandages, as the first mummy.

Q

Qibli A hot, dry, sand-laden wind from the south.

R

RDX Cyclotrimethylenetrinitamine, or T4, a powerful military explosive.

Re A key figure in Ancient Egypt's creation myths, the sun-god had multiple avatars and was linked by marriage or paternity to other deities. Each night, he voyaged through the underworld, emerging at dawn to perpetuate the world for another day.

RPG Rocket-propelled grenade.

Rubb Hall A steel-framed, rapid-erect shelter used by aid agencies and the military, which can be configured as a warehouse or hanger.

Rubbish people A reference to the *zebaleen* who live on the outskirts of Egyptian cities, recycling scrap materials and raising pigs on household waste.

Raïs Boss; a term of respect for anyone in a junior position of authority.

Rollback Coined by the CIA to describe its (abortive) strategy for 'rolling back' the Iron Curtain in the 1950s, Rollback was applied with more success to nationalist/leftist Third World governments in the 1960s—70s. Later, neo-cons advocated overthrowing hostile Arab/Islamic regimes by force if embargoes or subversion didn't succeed – a doctrine epitomized in the invasion of Iraq in 2003. Kreutzer applies it to Egypt and takes it further, with genocide, environmental devastation and forced conversions, rather than mere Balkanization and shock and awe.

S

Sa'ad Zaghloul Nationalist politician (1859—1927) who achieved an end to Britain's 'Veiled Protectorate' over Egypt but not full independence, as leader of the Wafd party. Exiled to Malta by the British, he returned to Egypt in triumph in 1919.

Saint Anthony An early Christian hermit (c. 251—356) revered as the 'Father of Monasticism'. His fame in Europe owes to Athanasius of Alexandria's *Life of St Anthony*, whose descriptions of how Satan assailed Anthony with visions of women or monsters provided inspiration for artists from Hieronymos Bosch to

Salvador Dalí.

Saiyida Zeinab The Prophet Mohammed's granddaughter, said to have settled in Egypt after her brother Hussein was killed at the battle of Karbala (680) which finalized the schism between the Sunni and Shi'a sects of Islam. In Egypt, Saiyida Zeinab is regarded as the patron saint of Cairo and of women, though some scholars doubt that she is buried in the mosque that bears her name; another in Damascus also claims to be her burial place.

Saiyidis Inhabitants of Upper Egypt: defined as the length of the Nile Valley upriver (south) of Cairo, or more narrowly as beyond the bend in the river at Qena. Saiyidis like to think of themselves as generous, honourable and salt-of-the-earth. Other Egyptians stereotype them as impulsive, stubborn and stupid.

Sejil II An Iranian-manufactured ballistic missile, first test-fired in 2009; being solid-fuelled, it can be launched without the 45-minute fuelling time (observable by spy satellites) required by earlier missiles with liquid propellant. With a range of 2000—2500 kilometres but a relatively limited payload, military analysts reckon the Sejil II makes little strategic sense unless it will ultimately carry a nuclear warhead.

Sekhmet In Ancient Egyptian cosmology, the lioness-goddess Sekhmet personified the destructive power of the sun, in the form of the fiery Eye of Re.

Sha'ban Abd al-Rahim Controversial Egyptian pop singer famous for his earthy persona and risqué, or politically outspoken, lyrics; his *I Hate Israel* was cited in the Knesset as proof of anti-Semitism in the Egyptian media.

Shahadah The Muslim profession of faith: "There is no god but Allah and Mohammed is his prophet". By uttering it three times, one becomes a Muslim.

Sheba'ak A shantytown on the hills above Aswan, notorious for its criminality.

Sheesha A waterpipe for smoking tobacco, flavoured with molasses, apple, etc.

Shirk Polytheism, blasphemy, or apostasy from Islam. The four main schools of Islamic jurisprudence stipulate that offenders should be offered a chance to repent but should be killed if they refuse (the basis for the fatwa against author Salman Rushdie and many other 'apostates').

Shouf Look.

Shukran Thank you.

Sukkoth One of the earliest gods in the Ancient Egyptian pantheon; sometimes identified as an ally of Re but more often as his enemy. Better known as 'Seth' (the Greek rendering of his name), for murdering his brother Osiris (see above).

T

Tabla A drum with a clay hourglass-shaped body.

Tallah Come.

Tamam OK; well done.

Tet-Alef A rank in the Israeli Defense Forces, roughly equivalent to Colonel.

The Turner Diaries A novel published in 1978 by the American neo-Nazi William Luther Pierce, describing a future race-war in the US which leads to the extermination of all Jews and 'Mud People' (non-whites); the title refers its 'hero', Earl Turner.

U

Umma The community of Muslims (worldwide, or local).

U5MR, CMR, Asset Management, Commodity Tracking Aid agency metrics and monitoring systems for keeping track of refugees' health and logistical programmes.

Usqut Be silent!

W

Wahhabi Arabia It can be inferred that the Saudi monarchy no longer rules Arabia, having been overthrown by local Wahhabis some years before the Flood. 'Wahhabi' refers to the Islamic reform movement founded by Mohammed Ibn Abd al-Wahhab in eighteenth-century Arabia, whose pact with the House of Saud led to the Wahhabi form of Islam becoming the state religion. The decadence and corruption of Saudi royalty has long been at odds with Wahhabi Puritanism.

W'Allah azim I swear by God.

W'Allah or W'Allahi By God!

Y

Ya gazala O Gazelle: a traditional compliment to a woman's beauty.

Yahudi Jewish: in the Canal Zone after the Flood, it refers to Israeli shekels.

Yallah Let's go.

Yajooj Gog and Magog appear in *The Cave* chapter of the Qur'an as Yajooj and Majooj. The verse describes how 'the Two-Horned One' (variously identified as Alexander, Darius or Cyrus the Great) finds a tribe threatened by Yajooj and Majooj, who are 'evil and destructive' and 'caused great corruption on earth'. He builds an iron wall to confine them until doomsday, when their escape will be a sign of the end: "But when Gog and Magog are let loose and they rush headlong down every height. Then will the True Promise draw near (21:96—97). See also: Gog.

Ya kharabi O downfall: an exclamation of horror or dismay.

Ya Magaddis O Pilgrim; traditionally said to a Christian.

Yani I mean/you know.

Ya ragil O man.

Yardang A freestanding wind-eroded rock formation, typical of the Western Desert.

Ya wahled O boy.

Z

Zar An exorcism ritual practised from pre-Islamic times to the present day, used to cure all kinds of psychological and physical afflictions ascribed to possession by Djinn. Such rituals are usually restricted to women and held in secret, unlike the Coptic Christian exorcisms held at certain monasteries, where men are involved.

Zift Dirt; a euphemism for shit.

Zikr A Sufi ritual to induce unity with God, achieved by hours of swaying, chanting, praying and prostrations. Some Islamic sects regard the custom as heretical.

Zinah Fornication or adultery, punishable by death by stoning under Sharia law if four male witnesses testify that it occurred.

Zobra Penis (colloquial).

ZOG The anti-Semitic myth of a secret Jewish conspiracy to control the world, first advanced in the forged Protocols of the Elders of Zion, has been re-branded since the 1970s as the 'Zionist Occupation Government', meaning a cabal controlling a country through a puppet regime. Some believers in ZOG regard it as one of the heads of the Beast Government (see above) and a sign of the End Time.

Lightning Source UK Ltd.
Milton Keynes UK
171028UK00001B/22/P